BITTER SIXTEEN

Stefan Mohamed

SALT

CROMER

PUBLISHED BY SALT

12 Norwich Road, Cromer, Norfolk NR27 0AX United Kingdom

Printed in Great Britain by Clays Ltd, St Ives plc

Typeset in Sabon 10/13

ISBN 978 1 78463 013 3 paperback

1 3 5 7 9 8 6 4 2

for Mum and Dad

CHAPTER ONE

THE WORLD'S A weird place.

Sorry to state the obvious, but it really is. And it's a lot to take in when you stop to think about it. Luckily, life is generally constructed in such a way that your world starts small and sensible and gradually gets larger and weirder. There's a gradient, a logical, incremental process that expands your horizons and your perception bit by bit, so that it doesn't overload your poor little CPU and leave you jibbering in a white room being fed thrice daily through a letterbox. This tends to be the way of things.

Except for when it's not.

Exhibit A – my life. Up until I turned sixteen, my notion of 'trouble' was, while a relatively broad church, still a church preaching the gospel of 'this is a small world getting very gradually larger'. You had your common or garden varieties of trouble, which might lead to harsh words from your parents or teacher, or maybe to detention, suspension or even expulsion, God forbid. You had your more hardcore varieties, which could lead to embarrassment, fury, heartbreak or serious injury, although I'd still count these as pretty common. Then you had stuff you heard or read about – old ladies being mugged, cars being jacked, animals being injected with stolen plutonium, or whatever – that you were fairly unlikely to experience first-hand.

But there's also the other stuff. Stuff like:

Cowering behind a table while the room fills with bullets.

Brutal and chaotic battles to the death.

Superpowers. Although, having said that, they're pretty cool.

Six or so months after I'd turned sixteen, I had cornered the market in trouble. In fact, I pretty much needed a whole new scale for measuring it, and my world had gone from small and – mostly – mundane to proper 'save me Jebus' *weird*.

But I'm getting ahead of myself.

Friday, September the twenty-third, the night before my sixteenth birthday. I had recently begun my last year of compulsory education and everything was leading up to exams. I was supposed to have mapped out my future, to know exactly where I was going and how I was going to get there. I needed colour-coded timetables and ring binders. I needed a plan. I needed dedication and I needed to be cohesive, and I needed careful structure and guidelines. I needed to be focused. Serious and organised. This would be The Most Important Year Of My Life, if you believed what my teachers were saying, and everyone's parents were encouraging them to do well. To revise and get the best results so they could do exactly what they wanted when they left.

Well, almost everyone's parents. My parents just wanted me to make some friends. They said that after four years in secondary school I should have friends. I think one friend would probably have done. Maybe they weren't entirely wrong, but it's not as though *I* minded, which should have been the important thing. Anyway, I had my dog.

I digress. It's the night before my sixteenth birthday and I'm lying spread-eagled on my bed with a splitting migraine, heat prickling beneath my skin, and although I know my English teacher would mark me down for mucking around with tenses, it's necessary, 'cos my perception is all a-wonk. My eyes flit around my room, the torn sketchbook sheets I've covered with charcoal trees and crumbling cityscapes during too many sleepless nights giving the whole thing an arthouse-animated-horror-film feel, de-caying zombies shuffling across the foreground of my brain and the headache pulsating in my eye sockets. I'm trying to distract myself from the pain, thinking about what's going to change, if anything. Thinking about the conversation I had with my parents this evening.

Mum: So, are you having a party?

Me: No.

Dad: Why not? You're sixteen! You should be having a piss-up!

Mum: Frank . . .

Dad: What?

Me: I'm not having a party.

Mum: You can invite some—

Dad (*anger rising*): Friends? For Christ's sake, Mary, he doesn't *have* any friends!

Mum: Frank!

Me (*sorry to have caused an argument but not really in the mood to listen to it*): I'm going to bed.

Dad slams his fist down on the table. Mum goes to the cupboard, presumably to get a bottle of wine and pour herself a glass. Or three.

I go upstairs.

A party. I'd barely been to enough parties to know how you acted at someone else's, let alone how you went about organising your own, especially with no real friends to invite. Don't get me wrong, I wasn't feared and loathed at school, at least not by everyone. I'm pretty sure some people liked me, and there were certain people who I liked as well. I just kept them at arm's length. I didn't let them in, they respected my very cool and fascinatingly enigmatic need for solitude. Or my social ineptitude, whatever you want to call it. They laughed when they needed to, I answered their questions, they left me alone. Well, most of them. A few refused to and that was why I had enemies. They don't appear until later, though. So let's look forward to that, eh?

The seconds are tick-tick-ticking. My clock counting down – *up?* – towards the sixteenth of sixteen fairly uneventful years.

Being a teenager is like this: an inspirational Hollywood-style montage interspersed with little bits of idealised sadness to give it some spice, scored to some sort of Taylor Swiftian ballad thing. Teenagers studying and laughing together, falling asleep on their beautifully-written essays. Attractive boys and girls kissing. Less attractive boys and girls kissing but in silhouette behind curtains because there's a reason there is no such genre as 'ugly-people love story'. Some kids crying and cradling each other in the rain because rain is always good for atmosphere, and crying in the rain looks good in trailers, and even though something awful has happened, their camaraderie ties them together, plus tragedy is character-building. Jumping for joy when their exam results come in, exactly the ones they needed to get into Wherever. Bullies making up with their victims at the end. Everyone getting a piece of cake. The world welcoming them with open arms: 'Well done guys, you are now free to do literally whatever you want!'

Being a teenager is not really like that. Well, maybe somewhere in America? But I go to a small secondary school in Wales, so America might as well be a fictional country. So who cares.

Maybe it's more like this: a moodier, stylishly-lit montage, with images melting into each other like frames from a Frank Miller-era *Daredevil* comic, scored to something like 'Heart-Shaped Box' by Nirvana if you want to take it seriously, or some kind of scuzzy emo anthem if you want to go the whole black-eyelinered hog. Subscribing to the Disaffected Outcast cliché where we all sit around in the dark and listen to Loud Music That's Not Music, It's Just Noise, and write really bad poetry about the dark pit where hope and love used to live before they were evicted by PAIN. Some of the shadowy space cadets smoke like they recently invented smoking, and in the gaps between re-watching *Requiem For A Dream* and not really understanding Sartre they read out that idiosyncratic alienated poetry in *South Park* Goth voices: 'Love was a rabid cat, with pus where a kiss should have been. And my soul was its scratching post.'

Is being a teenager like that? Hopefully not. If anything, it's probably somewhere between the two. Except with more texting, and the self-esteem issues turned up to eleven. Either way, visualising montages is not distracting me from my headache.

And for the record, I don't understand Sartre either.

I was born at exactly one minute past midnight on September the twenty-fourth, and one time my mum got extremely drunk on extremely expensive whisky and told me that the pain of labour was nothing compared to the pain of watching your only child grow up without friends, which wasn't a mega-nice thing to say, although I didn't really react. I just took the whisky away from her and went to bed, and when my dad got home there was a lot of shouting. I sometimes wonder why they've never divorced. Maybe they couldn't decide which one would get me. Not that they don't love me, I'm sure they do. It just sometimes seems like neither of them really knows what to do with me, which makes them anxious. It shouldn't, though. I'm perfectly happy to be left alone in my bubble. Old people today, eh?

Thirty seconds until I turn sixteen. I'm not expecting it to be dramatically different from being fifteen. I'll be able to get married, which is unlikely to happen. I'll be able to ride a moped – I think – which is also unlikely to happen because teenagers who ride mopeds look like pizza delivery boys. I'll be able to have sex legally. Also fairly unlikely, unfortunately.

I might have missed something, but if I can't remember it then it's probably not that important.

Ten seconds. The agony is nearly splitting me open. The two sides of my head straddle the San Andreas Fault and any minute now the back of my head is going to go full *Scanners* and spray my mattress with bits of skull and brain, and blood will pour, bubbling and steaming, from my mouth and ears and nose and eye sockets, and then my eyeballs will burst with a sound like someone biting into a grape and streams of gore will hit the ceiling, and if by some miracle I'm not dead I'll drown in my own goop.

Or not.

One second.

Happy birthday. Or *penblwydd hapus* in the original Welsh. I—

BOOM!

The migraine reaches a crescendo and the white-hot, bullet-kissing pain is more intense than anything that I've ever felt before. It eats me alive and spits me into a volcano and I moan, my vision going white. My whole body tingles like I've been charged with electricity, my skin fizzes like sherbet and my internal organs are immolated. I throw my head back . . . and hit nothing.

I open my eyes. The pain is gone, leaving a delicious coolness in my head, and I'm levitating a foot above my bed.

This is . . . not standard procedure.

Did I pass out? Am I dreaming? No . . . I know what dreaming feels like . . . don't I?

Did I die?

Probably not. My migraines are bad, but they're not *that* bad, my own hyperbole notwithstanding.

So . . . process of elimination . . .

I'm floating in the air.

What.

What.

WHAT.

I'm not sure how to react. A hysterical giggle slips out, far too loud, and I slap a hand over my mouth . . . and immediately drop back down onto my bed. Bed feels real.

This *feels real.*

Happy birthday, Stanly. We hope you like your present.

6

CHAPTER TWO

I DIDN'T SLEEP FOR the rest of the night. Too busy flying. Well, maybe floating is more accurate. Once I had ascertained that I was definitely not dreaming and that what had happened had – pretty much – definitely happened, and decided that even if I had completely lost my marbles I might as well see how deep the rabbit hole went, I set about trying to do it again. With a *lot* of concentrating I eventually managed to levitate above the ground for a maximum of five seconds, although each successful effort left me so drained that I had to wait about fifteen minutes before I could try again. Starry black blurred into the silver blue glow of dawn, and before I knew it half past nine had rolled around and someone was knocking on my door. I was dishevelled and wired, and still dressed in yesterday's clothes, but it didn't seem to matter hugely when compared with my discovery. I made a noncommittal grunting sound. 'Grunt to you, too,' said my mother's voice. 'Happy birthday.'

I got up and opened the door and she hugged me, wearing her black dressing gown that she'd had since I was a child. The smell used to be a comfort. I actually hugged her back and found myself smiling, and she said sorry about last night and asked when I wanted to come down. I said I'd shower then I'd be there. She didn't say anything about my clothes, and for almost a second I considered mentioning what had happened.

Maybe not, eh?

I shaved and showered, and wondered about this power. My

birthday present. The energy that had flooded my body, like fire rushing through my arteries, enabling me to float. I wondered if I had any other new abilities. At this point it didn't really occur to me to wonder how or why I had this thing. I just accepted it. I'm pretty good at accepting things.

I called upon my vast reservoir of willpower and decided to stay in for the day with my parents. There'd be plenty of time for experimentation tomorrow. In the meantime I went downstairs and my mother had cooked fried eggs on toast and my father was outside smoking a cigarette, and there were a number of small wrapped packages on the table by my breakfast.

'So,' said my mother as I ate. 'Doing anything special today?'

I shook my head. 'Staying in, I think.'

'Ah.'

My father came in and smiled formally. 'Morning, Stan. Happy birthday.'

I smiled. 'Thanks.' I don't like being called Stan. They named me Stanly, which I like. I also like the fact that they left out the *e*, luckily. I'm sure there are lots of kids who would be quite put out if their parents deliberately spelled their names wrong on a whim. But it was a rare instance of my parents doing something different just for the hell of it, just because they thought it would be interesting, and also one of the even rarer instances where our respective ideas of what was interesting intersected. Stanly. Makes you look twice, doesn't it? I like that. Or maybe I've made myself like it, because the alternative is having a deliberate mistake instead of a name.

But I definitely *don't* like Stan.

'Um . . . Mary?' said my father. They exchanged one of those conspiratorial looks that parents think children don't notice and went into the next room. I finished my eggs and toast and stared down at my plate, at my knife and fork, at the crumbs and hardening stains of yolk. Normal plate, one of about twenty identical plates we'd had forever. Normal cutlery, same old faded red handles. Normal breakfast, same old eggs that come from chickens

8

that come from eggs and so on. Normal day, same old being a bit older than I had been before.

EXCEPT I CAN FLOAT IN THE AIR I CAN FLOAT IN THE AIR I CAN FLOAT IN THE AIR WHAT THE HELL WHAT THE SHIT I CAN FLOAT IN THE AIR.

I had to stop myself from leaping up and running around the room, or smashing my plate over my head, or making myself hover in the air, just to see my parents' faces when they came back in.

What the hell is going on?

I closed my eyes and breathed deeply. *Calm down. It's happening. It's mental, but it's happening. It* is *what is going on. Have a normal, quiet birthday, and completely and totally lose your shit tomorrow.*

I'm pretty good at accepting things.

Within reason.

My parents returned moments later, which gave me a good reason to look as normal and nonplussed by reality as possible. 'Do you want the small things first?' said my father.

'Or the big one?' my mother smiled.

I smiled back and shrugged. 'The little ones?'

'OK.' They sat down. 'Go on.'

I opened the cards first. As I went through them (twenty pounds from my cousins in America, a cheque for fifty from my grandparents, book tokens from some more cousins, a Happy 14th Birthday from an absent-minded uncle in New Zealand, nothing from my cousin in London), my mind kept wandering. Visions of myself speeding across the wood behind my house, dancing from tree to tree, tugging me away from material things. I shrugged them off. *Plenty of time for experimentation tomorrow, remember?*

Tomorrow.

And the day after, and the day after.

I was getting ahead of myself again, sort of. There was no guarantee that this power would ever extend further than allowing me to levitate a few inches off the ground. Maybe that would be it. Maybe I'd call myself Floating Boy, and form a League of

9

Thoroughly Mediocre Gentlemen alongside Captain Lampshade, blessed with complete mastery over all the lampshades in the world, The Sometimes A Bit Invisible Girl, able to make her feet invisible every other Wednesday, and The Metaboliser, endowed with the ability to digest things really fast.

'Stanly?' said my mother. 'Are you all right?'

I realised that I'd completely zoned out. 'Sorry. Not enough sleep.' They exchanged bemused looks and I hurriedly set about opening the packages they'd handed over. A few DVDs, a CD and a couple of books. They were good ones and I thanked and hugged my parents with more affection than it was usual for me to show them. My father grinned now. I appreciated his enthusiasm – I think it was actually genuine – but the grin was a bit much, it made him look a bit deranged. 'Do you want to see the big one?' he said.

I nodded and they left the room again, returning with a large wrapped box and an electric guitar in a case. My eyes widened. A month ago they'd asked me what I wanted for my birthday, and I'd said an electric guitar. I could see my mother perking up when I said that. I could almost read her mind. Yet another montage, but a very short one that mainly consisted of me forming a band, doing big gigs and making lots of friends, possibly even getting a girl of some kind. I hadn't expected to actually get the thing. I momentarily entertained a mental image of my own, windmilling the shit out of 'Johnny B. Goode' at a high school dance in 1955, but was quickly shaken out of it by my father asking if I wanted lessons. I said that I'd just fiddle about for now, that'd be fine.

I spent the rest of the day fiddling about. A few of my parents' friends came by and wished me a happy birthday, some bearing chocolate and cards, and I thanked them politely before going back to my guitar. I knew bugger all about guitars, all I knew was that this one was blue and it looked cool, and when I plugged it into the amplifier and turned it up it made everything shake. And woke Daryl up.

Ah yes.

Daryl was my dog. About a year ago I had been at a sort of

free-for-all, no-invitation-required party because I was bored. I was sitting with a group of stoners, trying to keep up with their up-and-down, side-to-side conversation, when a very laid-back skateboarder called Mikey handed me a spliff. I'd never tried it before and almost respectfully declined – but they all seemed to be having so much fun. I wanted to have fun. I very rarely had fun, at least not with people. So I accepted it. I just wanted to try something new and have fun like they were having.

I spent the rest of the night having fun. The memory is sort of filtered through a kaleidoscope: I can see trees and dancing and a bonfire and a band, and I can see myself staggering home at about four in the morning, and I can see a hedge, and I can see a dog. This is where Daryl comes into the story.

He was a small, mostly white beagle who looked more like Snoopy than most beagles, although that might just be my perception of him, and he was ambling along quite happily, sniffing at the bushes by the side of the road, enjoying the country air. I knelt down and patted him and murmured some nonsense to him.

And he answered me.

Now, I've seen stoners in films. They're always talking to dogs and the dogs are always talking back. I didn't think anything of it. The conversation went sort of like this.

Me: Slurred gibberish.

Dog: Yeah? It's like that, is it?

Me: More gibberish, then: Yep.

Dog: What's your name, kid?

Me: Stanly.

Dog: I'm Daryl.

Me: Hi.

We shake hands.

Me: So like . . . you um . . . (More gibberish).

Daryl (*laughing*): Yep.

Me: Want to come to my house?

Daryl: Yeah, sure.

Me: V'lost my keys. Probably be locked.

Daryl: That's fine.

Me: There's a bench.

Daryl: Cool.

So we walked home and my parents found me in the morning, sleeping on the wooden bench on the patio overlooking the railway line, a beagle curled up next to me. I opened my eyes and, strangely, didn't feel weird at all. I looked down at the dog. 'Um . . . Daryl?'

My parents also looked at the dog. 'Whose dog is that?' said my father.

'Mine,' I said. 'I found him and he came along with me.'

'Stanly,' said my mother, 'you can't just bring any old stray home!'

'And I thought you didn't like dogs,' said my father.

'I didn't before,' I said. 'But I do now. Can I keep him?'

'He might have a previous owner,' said my father.

'He won't mind,' said Daryl, whose eyes were still shut.

There was a very long pause, finally broken by my father laughing. 'Very good, Stanly,' he said. 'Ventriloquism. Very nice —'

'No, that was me,' said Daryl, opening his eyes and stretching. 'I do have a previous owner, but not one I want to go back to.'

I was as surprised as my parents. I thought it had been the weed talking.

'What the fuck is this?' said Daryl. 'The Piano? Why aren't you saying anything?'

I glanced at my parents, half expecting them to admonish Daryl for his language. They didn't, though. Probably distracted by the fact that it's a beagle talking. For my part, I was trying to work out what was stranger – the fact that he was referencing The Piano or the fact that his reference to The Piano was actually a reference to The Piano from an entirely different film altogether. 'Um . . .' I said. 'What film is that from? I know I recognise it.'

'Is that really the issue?' my mother said.

'What's the issue?' asked Daryl, perfectly innocently.

'The issue is that dogs don't talk!' she shrieked.

'Oh,' said Daryl. He turned back to me. '*Dogma*.'

I smiled. 'I *knew* it!'

My mother spluttered. 'It's not . . . it's not *dogma*, it's . . . it's common sense! It's—'

'No,' I said. 'The film that he was quoting. It's called *Dogma*.'

At which point my mother temporarily lost the power of speech, which was kind of ironic I suppose.

Once everybody had calmed down, Daryl explained that his previous owner was a really boring old man who ignored him ninety per cent of the time. Daryl felt that he was wasted on this singularly un-talkative guy so had decided to leave, and he'd been walking for about an hour when he met me. I immediately said that he could stay, and my parents didn't seem to have the will to rescind my invitation. I think they were too freaked out to protest.

To be fair to them, they adjusted to the idea of a talking dog fairly quickly. It was amazing really. They had always seemed so grounded in a very specific interpretation of reality, and here they were holding a conversation with a beagle. There were a couple of occasions – mostly instigated by my father – where putting him on the Internet or contacting the national news came up, but I put the kibosh on them by threatening to go on hunger strike, which deeply distressed my mother and baffled my father, who wasn't used to me showing that kind of enthusiasm about anything. My dad's last attempt at turning Daryl my new pet dog into Daryl the Amazing Talking Dog, Eighth Wonder of the World, went like this:

Dad (*holding video camera and using a 'talking to unique individuals' voice*): Hi there, Daryl!

Daryl: (*stares blankly back at him*)

Dad: I said, hi there, Daryl! How are you today?

Daryl: . . .

Dad (*getting irritated*): Come on, don't do this. You know you can talk, I know you can talk. Think how much money we could make if we got this on TV or the Internet. Come on. Talk to me.

Daryl (*wagging his tail dumbly*): Woof!

Dad (*really irritated*): You're taking the piss now.

Me (*looking up from my fish fingers and chips*): He's not going to do it, Dad.

Dad: But we could make so much—

Mum: Frank. Come on, now. I know it's been hard adjusting to Daryl. And strange. And . . . hard. But he doesn't want to go on TV, and Stanly doesn't want him to go on TV. Let's just leave it now.

Dad: This is bloody ridiculous! We have the most unique animal *in the world* living in our house, and you won't even let me—

Me: I don't have to eat these fish fingers you know, Dad. I could just as easily not eat them.

Dad (*not wanting a repeat of my hunger strike and huffily switching off the video camera*): Fine! Fine! Have it your way! (*Angrily leaving the room*) Bloody dog . . .

And that was how Daryl became part of the family.

He never explained how it was that he could talk. He said he'd never met another dog who spoke any human language, and asked us if it was a problem, and we all said no. Well. I said no. 'Are there any other things you want to tell us about yourself?' asked my mother. My father – when he wasn't trying to trick him into becoming a viral sensation – rarely spoke to Daryl directly. I think he found it too weird.

'I don't eat dog food,' said Daryl. 'I hate that processed convey-or-belt shit.'

My mother raised one eyebrow.

'Sorry,' said Daryl. 'That processed conveyor-belt *crap*. I like to eat at the table, but if that'll freak out your visitors I'll eat somewhere else, just so long as it's not from a bowl on the floor. I'll go for walks on my own if you don't want to take me. I have a superb sense of direction so I'll find my way back easily. I like cats. I can use a human toilet.'

'Really?' said my mother.

'Do I look retarded or incontinent to you?' asked Daryl, frostily.

'Sorry.' *My mother is apologising to a dog*, I remember thinking. *In genuinely humble tones. This is the best thing that has ever happened to anyone.*

'That's OK,' said Daryl. 'Um . . . I think that's about it.'

So that's Daryl.

Daryl appraised my guitar. 'That is a piece of work,' he said. 'That is . . . the mutt's nuts. So to speak.'

'I know,' I said. 'Want to try it?'

He put his large head on one side. 'Do I look that dextrous? Use yer loaf.'

I played with the guitar until about ten o'clock, when my mother said we should really consider the neighbours – subtext: *your father's patience will only stretch so far, even on your birthday* – so I reluctantly packed the instrument away and went upstairs with Daryl.

My room was small, with a dark grey carpet and walls just blue enough to not be white, but too pale to be completely blue. There were film posters all over them, as well as a few of my own drawings – some on paper, some drawn straight onto the wall, to my parents' chagrin – and a painting of a green lady that my uncle Nathan had done a few months before he died. It had a strange hypnotic quality to it, and I never spent too long looking at it because the last time I stared for more than a minute I went catatonic and my mother thought that I'd OD'd on something. Where there weren't posters there were shelves stuffed with books, DVDs, CDs and notebooks. My desk was so cluttered I could hardly write on it, and it was impossible to find anything that wasn't on a shelf because it would either be under my bed (The Dead Zone, as my father once referred to it) or buried on my desk under a pile of old coursework drafts, notebooks, drawings, books that I couldn't fit on my shelves, or coasters made from scratched CDs. I also had a few curios scattered around the room – a wooden Japanese kokeshi doll named Miko, for example. She was beautifully crafted, very smooth and shiny, with delicate flower patterns on her dress. I found her in a small shop the first (and only) time I'd been to

London, and the elderly shopkeeper had told me that a long time ago some families in Japan were so poor that they had to sell their daughters into slavery or prostitution, so they made dolls to remember them by. I'd been so moved that I bought the doll immediately. Might have been a complete lie, but I didn't really care, a story's a story.

We watched *Casablanca* and, as always, Daryl cried at the end. 'How many times have we watched this now?' I asked, as the credits ran.

'Not enough,' sniffed Daryl.

I switched off the player and the TV and stretched, and Daryl regarded me with his big dog eyes. 'So. What was your best birthday present?'

I waited a long minute before I answered. I knew he was the only one I could possibly tell. The only one who wouldn't freak out. 'My powers.'

Daryl put his head on one side. 'Um . . . what?' He had a sort of Rowan Atkinson-esque way of saying *what* that always tickled me.

'The moment I turned sixteen I got powers,' I said.

'What powers?'

'Levitation,' I said. 'I can float. About a foot off the ground.'

Daryl didn't say anything for a minute. Then he said, 'You're messing with me.'

'I'm not,' I said. 'You know I'm not. Look at my face. This is a truth face.'

He looked, and I knew he knew. 'Jesus.'

'I know. It's . . . I don't know. This kind of stuff doesn't happen. It shouldn't . . . should it?'

Daryl was momentarily lost for words, which was the second supremely weird thing that had happened that day. Then he laughed. 'Stanly, I'm a dog who talks. QED.'

I shrugged. 'I suppose.'

Daryl's tail was wagging. 'Show me?'

'Tomorrow,' I said, yawning. 'I'm . . . I'm too tired now. I've been awake for like thirty-six hours. I'm . . .' The rest of the sentence drowned in yawns.

Daryl nodded and settled down. 'Fine.' I switched off the light and stroked him, and in the dark he whispered, 'Are you scared?'

I shrugged. 'No.'

'Why?'

'Don't know.'

'Oh.'

CHAPTER THREE

THE NEXT DAY was cloudy, and the air was moist. Daryl and I were up in the woods behind my house, and I was standing by a very tall tree, feeling energised. 'OK,' I said. 'Watch and learn, doglet.' I closed my eyes and concentrated hard, trying to find the sweet spot, the right mental angle. Hearing a sharp intake of breath from Daryl I opened my eyes again, and sure enough I was floating about a foot off the ground. I slowed my breathing and tried to stay completely focused and calm, managing to stay there for about ten seconds before I dropped. The dog's tongue was hanging out. 'What do you think?' I said.

'Wow,' said Daryl. 'I mean . . . wow. That's . . . that's all right, that is.'

I tried again. And again. And again. So many attempts, but I couldn't beat ten seconds. 'Have you thought about springboards?' said Daryl, after a while.

I looked at him, frowning. 'What?'

'Springboards,' he said. 'Using things to propel yourself. Walls, trees, rocks. That kind of thing.'

The penny dropped with a loud power chord and I smiled and took several strides back so that I had a decent run up. 'Free your mind,' said Daryl. 'You're faster than this. Don't think you are. *Know you are.*'

'Yeah, whatevz, Morpheus.' I breathed in and ran straight at the tree. I ran with music pounding in my head, sweat on my skin and a bubble filled with butterflies expanding in my stomach, and at the last minute I jumped, planted one foot on the tree, spun . . .

. . . and floated, almost majestically, through the air. The bubble exploded and the butterflies took flight and I yelled in triumph. Daryl was laughing delightedly. I flew towards another tree, stuck my foot out and kicked myself off it, bouncing across to another one. I danced between trees for nearly a minute before suddenly dropping out of the air and hitting the ground hard, flat on my back, the wind rushing painfully out of me. The thump sounded exactly like a human body hitting the ground, funnily enough.

When I had recovered sufficient breath I got to my feet. 'Bollocks,' I said, stamping a foot in frustration.

A rock flew through the air, hit the cliff face and exploded into tiny dusty fragments.

There was a long silence.

I looked at Daryl. 'Did—'

'Yeah.'

'I—'

'Uh-huh.'

'It—'

'Mm.'

I nodded. 'OK.' I looked at a pile of twigs and raised my hand. Nothing. I concentrated *really* hard. Nothing. I concentrated so hard that my temples fused and my eyes hurt and electricity danced in my skull, and a solitary twig rose up off the ground and hung wobbly in mid-air, looking like an extremely dodgy special effect. I moved my hand very slowly, tracing the movement that I wanted the twig to make, and it followed. Trying to avoid letting exultation overthrow concentration, I kept going, managing to keep the twig in the air for thirty seconds before it dropped.

Daryl was shaking his head. 'Fair play, boyo.'

I grinned, and tried it on him. Nothing. I tried for several minutes, ignoring his profane indignation, but there was nothing. I stamped my foot again, but still nothing happened.

'Maybe you just need to develop it,' said Daryl. 'You're just starting, you know. It's not like you can just pick up a tennis racket and become . . . I dunno, some famous tennis player, I don't know tennis. You need practise.'

'I have to go back to school tomorrow,' I said.

Daryl grinned. 'That's *perfect*! The perfect training ground! That rock was way heavier than that twig, but it took more effort to lift the twig, didn't it?'

'But I was pissed off when I moved the rock.'

'*Exactly*.' Daryl was doing a funny little dance. 'Maybe concentration isn't the key! Maybe *emotion* is the key! Strong negative emotion might help. And what better place to strongly, negatively emote?'

'School.'

'School! It's possibly the best breeding ground for resentment, anger and misery you could find. Within a week you'll be like . . . like Gandalf, Willow and Dumbledore got caught in a horrific teleportation accident.'

'What would that look like?' I said. 'I'm picturing . . . like . . . Willow's head, wearing Willow's hat – you know the one – on Gandalf's body, but with the voice of Dumbledore? And one of Dumbledore's arms sticking unconvincingly out of the shoulder, Eighties BBC Zaphod Beeblebrox style?'

'Something like that.'

'Wouldn't it be confusing, though? They've each got powers derived from a completely different set of magical laws . . . would it be a combination of all of them? Or could they pick and choose? They could probably pick and choose, right?'

'Yeah.'

'And do you think the whole entity would be gay? Seeing as how two of the component people were?'

'Probably.'

'So in a week's time I'll be an old lesbian dead gay guy? With three arms?'

'Nothing wrong with being old, a lesbian or a dead gay guy,' said Daryl, reproachfully. 'Or having three arms.'

'Sorry. Just spitballing. It's not all going to be fried gold.'

'Fair enough.' The dog put his head on one side. 'Seriously, though, you know I'm talking sense.'

I nodded. 'You're quite insightful, for a small dog.'

Daryl shrugged, which is an especially funny movement for a dog to do. 'Judge me by my size, do you?'

By the time we returned to the house I was no better at levitating objects, but I could fly between trees like the best of them. I hadn't managed to lift anything more substantial than a twig, but my canine master said it would take time. He seemed to be enjoying it almost as much as I was.

'Do you have any homework?' asked my mother, bringing me back to Earth with a thud that shook my entire being.

'No,' I said.

'Did you have a good day out?'

'Yeah.'

'Did you have a nice day yesterday?'

'Yeah.'

She nodded. 'OK. Well . . . are you hungry?'

'Not really, thanks.'

My father looked up from his newspaper. 'What were you doing out there?'

'Nothing,' I said.

'You were doing nothing for a pretty long time.'

'It's tiring,' I said.

'Doing nothing?'

'Yeah.'

My father shrugged and went back to his paper, and as I headed upstairs I distinctly heard him mutter, 'There's something wrong with him.'

'There is nothing wrong with him. He's just different.'

'He's *weird*. And it's nothing to do with me.'

'Oh just wash your bloody hands of him then, why don't you?'

'Don't swear at me!'

21

'I'll swear at you if I bloody want to, you can be such a *bastard* sometimes!'

'*What?*'

'You heard me!'

I stomped up to my room and closed the door without touching it. I switched on the lights without raising my hand, and hurled the one and only photograph of my parents that I had against the wall and the glass broke. I stood there, boiling over like too much magma, and flexed my mind, feeling energy crackle in the room.

Daryl, who was sitting on the bed, nodded sagely. 'Looks like I was right.'

I raised my middle finger and a magazine rack fell over.

In the morning the atmosphere was flammable. My mother was tetchy and my father was still in bed, and I ate my toast in silence while not really watching the news. The headline was something about more missing children in London.

The buses that took most of the kids to the local secondary school left from a garage at the end of my road, so I was always the first on and had my pick of the seats. I tended to sit in the corner at the back because then there was no-one to sit behind you and kick your seat and stick stuff in your hair and generally be a pain, and you could zone out and pretend that nobody else existed. This morning I waited on the bus for about five minutes before it set off, staring out of the window, listening to some random download on my MP3 player. A band with one singer, two guitar players and about fifteen drummers, playing the music of teenage rebellion. The music you get in the elevators in Hell. I made a mental note to delete it from the player and put the Red Hot Chili Peppers' *One Hot Minute* on, and imagined myself wearing a long black coat and fighting zombie versions of people from school.

Kids got on and as I watched them take their seats I felt something. It was like I was seeing them differently. On Friday they'd been . . . I don't know. Equals, I suppose. Ish. I was on the same

22

level as them, anyway. We were all human. I was still human, obviously, but now I was . . . different. Genuinely different; more than just feeling that way. It was strange. And then something scary occurred to me: if one of them attacked me, I could theoretically kill them without moving a muscle.

Why was I thinking like that? I didn't want to kill anyone.

Good job, really. A psychic person would be like the best murderer ever. Thoughts don't leave fingerprints, after all.

When we got to school I was last off the bus as usual, and wandered to my form room, looking at people, enjoying having a secret. Our form gathered in an English classroom and I always sat at the desk at the back and read or wrote or drew or whatever, but today I just sat and watched everybody coming in, talking, laughing, arguing. A few of them acknowledged me with nods and waves, but nobody spoke. I nodded back at them.

Then Zach and George came in. Zach looked like a furless rat that had been stuck in a hydraulic press. Pinched, pale face, bleached blonde hair in gelled spikes, nasty thin blue eyes, mouth stuck in a constant grin. And his ears stuck out. He was always shooting witless barbs my way, or shoving me as I passed him in the corridor, or throwing things just to get a reaction, and while I'd never give him the satisfaction of showing it, I hated his stupid twattish guts. He'd never pick a proper fight because he was a wimp, but he had friends who were taller, and that was how things worked in school. George was a good example of this. He was tall and built like a brick shithouse and always looked slightly confused, and he had a pierced eyebrow and liked rugby and tractors. That was the extent of him as a person. In some ways, he was almost an existential tragedy.

Zach was walking with his usual swagger. His John Wayne walk, although he probably wouldn't have a clue who that was. He tried to intimidate people, and almost everybody thought he was a wanker but they would never say so because of his tall mates. People were friends with him even though he was a wanker. *Because* he was, in a way. Everybody was grey. I definitely didn't

23

believe the world was black and white but I had very definite morals when it came to school, and if I didn't like someone I didn't smile at them. I didn't laugh at their stupid jokes. I didn't give them the benefit of the doubt.

I was finding Zach's swagger particularly annoying today, and clenched my fists in my lap. My eyes darted upwards so I wouldn't have to look at him and my fists dropped down by the sides of my chair, and a pile of books on a shelf above Zach's head over-balanced and landed on him in an avalanche of infinitely satis-fying thumps. He fell down and his face hit the cold uncarpeted floor with a noise like a pig's corpse being smacked with a paddle. People laughed. Even George laughed. Outwardly I was dispas-sionate but inside I was hysterical. Perhaps school wasn't going to be so bad from now on.

I quickly realised that I hadn't been transplanted to a comic book or a superhero movie. The world didn't stop for me because I had some new abilities, no mysterious bearded mentors came out of the woodwork, no supervillains came knocking at my door. I still had to do essays and prepare for my exams, and the ability to levi-tate and move things with my mind wasn't going to help with that. I was still bound by the laws of my world, and my world was one of coursework and structure.

That night, having studiously ignored my parents (who were studiously ignoring each other) I told Daryl everything I did that day. The books on Zach's head. Opening and closing windows to annoy teachers I didn't like. Tripping people I didn't like when they seemed about to hassle me, or when they seemed about to hassle someone else, or just generally whenever I saw them. It was all petty. It was childish. It didn't befit someone as mature as I liked to think I was. But it was *fun*.

'So,' said Daryl. 'This is it from now on? You use your powers to irritate people you don't like?'

'No!' I protested. 'Well . . . a bit, maybe. What do you suggest I do?'

'You could try using them for good,' said Daryl. 'Help the help-less. That kind of thing. With great power comes great –'

'Please don't finish that sentence,' I said.

'Sorry.'

'And helping the helpless?' I lay down on my bed and stared at the zombies on the ceiling. 'Easier said than done. I live in a small Welsh town where sod all to the power of *nothing* happens. There are no murders. No robberies. No muggings. No cars get jacked. No houses get broken into. Last week's headline in the *County Times*? "Strimmer Stolen". There's not much scope for superhero-ics and the situation doesn't exactly scream "higher purpose".'

'You could leave,' said Daryl.

I didn't say anything. The thought had occurred to me but I'd buried it. It was a page I hadn't coloured in, which I'd shoved to the back of my ring binder so I could forget about it. 'And go where?'

'Dunno. Cardiff?'

I raised an eyebrow. 'Cardiff. The Welsh equivalent of Gotham City, as literally no-one said ever.'

'Maybe not,' said Daryl. 'London?'

'How would I get there?'

'Get a train, you plank,' said Daryl. 'Or drive.'

'I can only drive in first gear.'

'Get some lessons off your dad,' said Daryl. 'Two birds? One stone? Bond with your distant father *and* get an escape route.'

The phone rang and I picked it up to avoid the subject. 'Hello?'

'Hello? Stanly?'

'Yes. Who's that?'

'It's Eddie.'

Eddie. My cousin in London. So much for avoiding the subject. 'Oh!' I sat up. 'Hi.'

'Hi. Happy birthday.'

'Oh, thanks.'

'Having a good day?'

'Sorry?'

'Today?'

25

'It was Saturday.'

'Sorry. Shit. *Did* you have a good day?'

'Yeah, thanks.'

'Sorry I didn't send you anything.'

'That's all right. It's nice of you to call.'

'Get some . . . good presents?'

I inhaled sharply. For a second I thought . . . no, I didn't. 'Um . . . yeah. Got an electric guitar.'

'Ah,' said Eddie, after a pause that suggested he'd been expecting me to say something else. 'Cool.' *Does he know?*

'What did you get for your sixteenth birthday?' I asked.

'Mine? Man. That's a long time ago.' There was something in his voice. A definite something.

'You can remember though, surely?'

'Well . . .' And now I could hear in *his* voice that he could hear something in *my* voice and I was itching to say something, but I didn't want to, just in case. 'Well?' I prompted.

'Can't really remember. And I asked you first.'

'And I told you.'

'Did you?'

My heart stopped. My brain turned to pure electricity and jagged forks of it wrapped up my room and mailed it to a black hole in deep space. After a pause that lasted centuries I said, 'You know.'

'So you do have them.'

Daryl was watching me. 'He knows?'

I nodded. Nobody spoke for lots of seconds. Eddie broke the silence. 'How are you dealing with it?'

'How do you *know*?'

'I . . . just . . . long story. Probably not for a phone conversation.' I could hear him moving uncomfortably. 'I . . . I just called to make you an offer.'

'An offer?'

'If you need a place to go . . . someone who knows what you can do. Someone to help . . . you know where I live. Any time.'

26

He was inviting me to London. I looked at Daryl. His expression was doglike. 'Are you psychically linked to my dog?' I said.

'What?'

'Nothing.' I looked out of the window. A line of red burned across the horizon like a strip of Christmas paper soaked in petrol.

'Any time?'

'Any time.'

'Thanks. Cool. I appreciate that.'

'Keep me posted on any developments.'

'I will.' I closed the blinds. 'Thanks for calling.'

'That's OK. Take it easy.' He hung up and I looked at Daryl again. The confused silence lasted until supper time.

The next day I had two lessons of Drama, and our teacher Miss Stevenson asked us all to sit in a circle because she wanted to talk to us.

I liked Miss Stevenson. She was thirtyish and had blonde hair with purple streaks in it. I didn't imagine that the headmaster liked her having her hair like that, but she still kept it, and she wore trendy glasses, long skirts and T-shirts, and was very pretty. Today she was wearing a long denim skirt and a *Dawn of the Dead* T-shirt. I didn't have a crush on her at all.

'OK, everyone,' she said. 'I know you're all anxious to get on with your devising.'

Devising was a part of the drama course where we got into groups and wrote and performed our own script. I was in a group with two girls called Tamsin and Dani, who were OK. As I sat in the circle my eyes kept drifting to a boy called Ben King. I'll elaborate on him later.

'But,' said Miss Stevenson, 'I wanted you all to be the first to know that the school play this year will be *Romeo and Juliet.*'

There was a general silence.

'Don't all cheer at once,' said Miss Stevenson. 'I'm planning to do a slightly abbreviated version in modern dress, with modern props. Kind of like the Baz Luhrmann one. Has anyone seen that?'

Everyone looked at each other. Then Andrea put up her hand and said, 'Baz who?'

This was the kind of media-unconscious world that I lived in. God bless teachers like Miss Stevenson.

'The one with Leonardo diCaprio,' said Miss Stevenson. I could hear the weariness creeping into her voice.

There was a general chorus of 'oh' and 'he's so fit' and 'nah, he's gone well fat now'. There were twenty girls and four boys in our Drama group.

'Anyway,' said Miss Stevenson, 'that's what I'm planning to do. There'll be auditions at lunchtime on Wednesday, so anybody who's interested *please* turn up. There'll be a notice about it in assembly tomorrow. Now. Everyone has work to do? Go do it.'

Everyone moved off into their groups. I was about to go and join Tamsin and Dani when Miss Stevenson said, 'Stanly? Could I have a quick word with you, please?'

I walked over to her desk. We had Drama in a big hall that was also used for parents' evenings and exams, and there was an adjoining room where Miss Stevenson kept all her things, and a big desk covered in props and scripts and stuff. She was looking at something in a red binder. 'You weren't in the last school play, were you?' she said, without looking up.

I shook my head. 'No.'

'Why not?'

'I . . . I forgot to audition.'

'That's a shame.' She closed the binder and looked at me. 'Because, let's be brutally honest, it sank without trace.'

'Wasn't Ben the lead?' I said, entirely innocently. *Oh yeah, entirely.*

'Yes.' I could hear the unspoken 'unfortunately'.

'So . . . what did you –'

She looked at me. 'Would you like to try out for Romeo?'

I blinked. 'Um . . . I . . . why me?'

'Your work over the last year has been fantastic,' she said. 'You're a natural performer. The fact that you're so quiet is what

28

makes it great. You're very shy and insular, but when you're out there you pull a rabbit out of a hat, for want of a better cliché. I really think you'd be good.'

'I thought . . . you said there'd be auditions . . .'

'I know, but I just wanted . . . were you thinking about coming?'

I looked at the floor. 'Um . . . well . . .'

'You don't put yourself forward,' said Miss Stevenson. 'That's both a strength and a weakness. Also . . . I must admit I did maybe see you as a darker character like Tybalt. You're familiar with the play?'

'Yes. I've seen the Baz Luhrmann one.'

'You know who Baz Luhrmann is?'

'*Strictly Ballroom. Romeo + Juliet. Moulin Rouge. Australia.* That terrible Chanel advert.' *Stop showing off.*

She smiled and breathed a sigh of relief. 'Thank God. All you teenagers treat us teachers with barely-disguised contempt, like you're the bleeding edge of cool, but when a roomful of sixteen-year-olds in the twenty-first century can't tell me who Baz Luhrmann is, it's worrying to say the least.'

I smiled. 'I . . . I'm a bit of a geek, I suppose.'

'Well,' said Miss Stevenson. 'The geeks will inherit the earth. In fact, they already kind of have. So you're on the right track.' She put her binder down. 'What was I saying?'

'About Tybalt . . .'

'Oh yes. I'm not trying to make any statements about the aura you project, but I did think maybe you'd be better suited to a darker character. But that's just me and besides I can't think of many others who could do it. Not from the top years, anyway. So you'll audition?'

'Sure.'

'Great. You'd better get back to your group.'

I nodded and went over to Tamsin and Dani. They were both really nice, I didn't give them enough credit when I said that they were merely OK.

As I sat on a bench in the playground half-watching the football and eating my Toffee Crisp, I thought about how strange it was. I'd adapted so quickly to the idea of having powers. One minute I was normal, the next I could float and move things with my mind. Who knew what else? And here I was. Just taking it in my stride. Going with the flow. Like a little Fonzie. And what's Fonzie like?

Oh, back to the subject of Ben King. Well, actually Benedict. He insisted on calling himself that. I suppose there's nothing really wrong with that seeing as it was his name, but it added an extra dimension of pretentiousness that he really didn't need because he was stuck-up enough without it. Plus it's a name you can only really pull off if your surname is Cumberbatch. He was about my height (five feet eight inches, if you're interested) with a spotless complexion and blonde hair that was always shiny, and he was always overly nice to everybody, especially girls, but there was always an ulterior motive. It was a sort of 'oh look at how nice I'm being' niceness rather than a 'it's nice to be nice' niceness. He was fake. A phony. And if sitting reading *The Catcher In the Rye* and feeling incredibly, unjustifiably superior to everyone else had taught me anything, it was that phonies were the enemy.

He also thought that he was a really intense actor, which he most definitely wasn't. He'd starred in *Bugsy Malone*, the last school play, and he'd obviously convinced himself that he was in *Goodfellas*, and it had been terrible. His American accent had alternated between Bronx, Deep South and somewhere in rural Australia, for a start. But still, he was popular. They loved him. *He's a sinner, candy-coated*, etceteras. He'd never liked me either, not since primary school, but he pretended to, which was another thing about him that got up my nose. He used to go out with a girl named Angelina, who everybody thought I fancied, and I sort of did, not that that made a difference, and he'd once said to me, 'You hate me because I'm with Angelina, don't you?'

My surprise was genuine. 'No! Of course not!'

'Really?'

'Really. I don't hate you because of Angelina.'

'You don't?'

'No. I hate you because you're a massive bell-end.' I remember thinking *that was really childish* and then replying *who cares?*

I do, I'd insisted. And although I was ashamed, the look on his face made it worth it.

And now I'd nabbed the role of Romeo from under his nose. *How's that for a slice of the fried stuff?*

Was I a vindictive person? Was I the worst kind of petty? Possibly. Probably. But I couldn't deny that it was satisfying.

That evening I got home to find my parents sitting at the kitchen table having a Serious Discussion about Their Relationship and The Future. It was one of those talks that I found simultaneously depressing and irritating because they were so insipidly nice to each other, and the fact that the conversations usually came after a blazing row just reinforced my annoyance. One minute they'd be screaming curses at one another, the next minute they'd be drinking tea and eating chocolate Hobnobs and talking about their Feelings. I grabbed an apple from the fruit bowl and headed upstairs, followed by Daryl.

'So,' I said, lying on my bed and trying to decide which DVD to watch. 'What did you do today?'

'I read the new *SFX* that came in the post,' said Daryl.

'Ah, give it here?'

'It's downstairs. I'll get it when the Aged Parents have stopped emoting.'

'Cool. Anything else?'

'I watched some *Buffy*.'

'Any good?'

'Always good.'

'Naturally.'

Daryl flopped down at the end of the bed. 'What about you?'

'I got offered the role of Romeo on a plate.'

'I didn't mean that! I meant . . . you know. Power-related?'

I sat up. 'Um . . . important news? I was basically given the lead role in the school play?'

'I'm happy for you,' said Daryl. 'Applause, applause. But it has nothing to do with your powers.'

'Sod off.' I grabbed a DVD and put it in the player.

'What is wrong with you?' asked Daryl. 'For God's sake, Stanly! You were blessed with supernatural powers when you turned sixteen and now you're watching . . . you're watching frigging *Finding Nemo*! Why aren't you out honing your skills? The least you can do is operate the DVD player psychically!'

'I stopped a girl from dropping her lunch tray,' I said. 'And did a couple of backflips to impress some first years.'

'You can do backflips now?'

'I kind of . . . channel the floating into it,' I said. 'Nearly broke my neck the first time I tried it. Getting pretty good now, though.'

'That's awesome.' Daryl turned his head away.

'Oh don't sulk,' I said.

'I'm not sulking,' he sulked, sulkily.

'Whatever.' I patted him too hard and turned on the TV and the DVD player without moving my hands. 'There!'

'Great.'

For a few moments I contained myself, but the urge to rib the stroppy beagle overcame me and I started singing, in my best Eric Cartman voice. 'Na-na-na-na-*na*-na, I've got super *powers*, na-na-na-na-*na*-na.'

'Shut up!' he retorted, but he was already laughing and I clipped him gently round the ear and we watched the film in companionable silence.

'That was good,' said Daryl, afterwards. 'Not *powers* good, but—'

'Fermez la bouche, silver plate,' I said. 'And go and fetch me my *SFX*, will you? I can't be arsed to do coursework and I want a good read.'

'You got a 700-page horror masterwork for your birthday,' said Daryl. 'That's probably a good read.'

'Just go and fetch it, will you?' I said. 'There's geek news this geek needs to be a-knowin'.'

Daryl reluctantly got off the bed and padded over to the door. 'What did your last slave die of?' he muttered, as he left the room.

'Insubordination,' I said.

'LOL.'

'LOL it up, fuzzball.'

He'd got me thinking, though.

There was definitely more to be done with these powers.

33

CHAPTER FOUR

I KNOCKED ON MR Jones The Careers Adviser's door and waited. He was one of three Mr Joneses we had at school, so whenever anybody referred to him it was usually as Mr Jones The Careers Adviser, or sometimes Mr Jones Careers. 'Come in,' he said.

The office was a tiny musty box, its walls covered with inspirational 'you can do anything if you set your mind to it'-type posters, and Mr Jones was sitting behind a comically small desk, reading the paper. His brow scrunched. 'Hello,' he said. 'Do we have an appointment?'

'No,' I said. 'Sorry. I actually . . . I've only just started Year 11, I don't think we can book appointments with you yet.'

'No, I don't think you can,' he said. 'So . . .'

'I just wanted . . .' I knew I remembered seeing him reading *SFX* at one point, and a quick scan of the room confirmed it – the new issue was poking out from under a pile of papers. 'I'm writing a story. And I'm doing a bit of research. For the story. And I thought maybe if you had five minutes . . .'

'I do, but –'

'Basically, it's about a boy my age,' I said, 'who finds he can fly and move things with his mind. And I was wondering what sort of jobs that might qualify him for.'

Mr Jones The Careers Adviser still looked confused, but he was also intrigued now, I could see it. He smiled slightly. 'All right, five minutes. Sit down.'

I sat. 'So,' said Mr Jones. 'I think my first question would be . . . why doesn't he become a superhero?'

'Bit too obvious,' I said. 'Plus, I'm going for a real-world kind of thing with the story. No supervillains, and he's not always going to be in the right place at the right time when a train is about to crash or a building falls down.'

Mr Jones laughed. 'OK. I like that. Well. Let's say, for the sake of argument, that revealing these powers to the public wasn't a problem. And that he wasn't going to be dragged away to some lab to be experimented on. What sort of thing might flight be useful for . . . deliveries, perhaps? He'd put most bike messengers, pizza delivery boys and the like out of business. Could use his telekinesis to carry a huge sack of post. Completely bypass traffic. Things like that.'

Delivery boy or superpostman. Great. I laughed. 'Yeah, I suppose. And he could psychically hold angry dogs out of the way while delivering letters.'

'Yes. And assuming that he wasn't limited to lifting a certain weight, telekinesis could come in useful for construction. Carrying bricks, girders and the like. Or equally, demolition. He could take a building apart one brick at a time.'

Cool. 'Scope for supervillainy there as well,' I said. 'Taking buildings apart.'

'True, true, if that's the way you wanted to go.' Mr Jones thought for a moment. 'If he did want to go the superhero route, however, there's always the emergency services. Telekinesis would come in extremely handy when putting out fires, extricating people from crashed cars or rubble. Maybe even surgery.'

'Chasing down criminals.'

'Yes. Slightly more practical than hanging around dark alleys waiting for damsels in distress to come tottering down them. Is there any kind of upper limit on these powers?'

I shrugged. 'Haven't decided yet.'

'Because if there isn't, then there's really nowhere you couldn't go with them,' said Mr Jones. He seemed to be warming to the subject. 'Say, for example, a building was on fire. Your character could remove people from inside, put out the fire, stop the building from falling down *and* perform surgery on anybody who was wounded. Stem bleeding, repair arteries. And then if somebody called in a crashing plane, he could quickly nip up and bring it in for a safe landing.' He laughed. 'Sorry. Keep coming back to superheroics.'

'Yeah,' I said. 'That's not a problem . . . I was just trying to think of alternatives.'

'I think that stories condition us to think like this, in a way,' said Mr Jones. 'Any time you read about a character suddenly bestowed with supernatural powers, naturally it seems that they should turn those powers to keeping the peace, helping the less fortunate. Doing things that other people simply can't do, rather than being better at things that other people can do already. If that makes sense.'

'Hmm,' I said. 'Yeah. That makes sense.'

'In a way, I think it's easier for people to deal with, the idea that this super person is flying around tackling the big things, disasters and the like. It means that normal people can just get on with their lives, do their jobs. If the super person was interfering with the general status quo, that could really shake things up.'

I nodded.

'It depends on your character as well,' said Mr Jones. 'Would he even *want* to live a quiet life, using his powers for mundane, day-to-day things? There's nothing inherently wrong with that, of course. But characters in stories tend to want to go where the action is. Wherever that may be.'

I nodded again.

'I'm sorry,' said Mr Jones, 'I'm going to have to cut this short. I have an appointment. But thank you, it's been very interesting – a nice change of pace from my usual meetings! I'd like to read the story when it's finished, if that would be all right.'

'Yeah,' I said, suddenly feeling bad that I'd probably never have a story to show him. 'Hopefully it'll get finished. Feels like one that's going to run and run. Thanks for your help, anyway.'

Pizza delivery boy.

Construction worker.

Fireman.

Superhero.

Hmm.

I snoozed through a Welsh lesson and headed to the Drama Hall when lunchtime came around. I waited for about five minutes while everyone else filed in, and eventually Miss Stevenson said, 'OK. Everyone here? Good. Now, I want to assign the two leads first, naturally. Romeo?'

I put my hand up half-heartedly. Not because I didn't want the part, but because I didn't want to look like Ben King, who was straining his arm, seemingly in an attempt to pop it clean out of its socket. We seemed to be the only two applicants. If Miss Stevenson was feeling less than favourable towards Ben, she didn't show it. 'OK,' she said. 'Ben first?'

Ben walked out into the centre of the hall, looking smug. Miss Stevenson handed him a piece of paper. 'You've seen the film?'

'Yes,' he said. 'The modern version and an old version.'

'Have you read the play?'

'We're studying it in English at the moment,' he said. 'We're reading it as a class. I'm playing Romeo.'

'That's good,' said Miss Stevenson. 'You have a head start.'

Ben shrugged and looked at the ground. 'Not really.' His false modesty act. My fingers twitched and I fought the urge to throw him out of the hall using the powers of my mind. *Irrationality is such an ugly trait.*

Yeah, especially when it's a trait you hate to see in other people.

Oh leave me alone. Aren't I allowed to be a hypocrite every once in a while?

Of course. After all, it's not like hypocrisy is also a trait you hate to see in other people, is it?

37

Oh piss off.

'OK, Ben,' said Miss Stevenson, sitting at her desk. 'Can you read this to the assembled, please? As much feeling as you can get.'

Ben cleared his throat. 'The measure done,' he said, falteringly, 'I'll watch her place of . . . place of stand, and touching hers, make blessed my rude hand. *Did* my heart love till now? Forswear it, *sight*! For I never . . . ner . . . ne'er saw true beauty till tonight. This night.'

I could sense laughter hiding behind the dispassionate masks of the other hopeful junior thespians. Even Miss Stevenson was having trouble. Me? I'm saying nothing for fear of sounding childish.

'Thank you Ben,' said Miss Stevenson. 'Um . . . that was good. Now Stanly? Would you mind?'

The look that Ben cast me was one of molten hate, but it was only momentary, practically subliminal, switching smoothly to a smile as he handed over the piece of paper. 'Good luck,' he said.

I smiled back. 'Cheers.'

'Got the part,' I said to Daryl that night. 'Piece of piss.' He was watching *The Simpsons* while I didn't do my Chemistry homework. I stared at it for a long time but it might as well have been in Klingon for all the sense I could make of it.

'That's great,' said Daryl, absently. 'Which part?'

'Romeo.'

'Oh! That's great!' He sounded as though he meant it. 'What about Eggs Benedict?'

'He . . . didn't do so well. It was quite funny, actually. Miss Stevenson offered him Tybalt and he basically snatched the book off her, saw that Tybalt has about seventeen paragraphs of dialogue, none of which are particularly long, and said it was a waste of time. I could see her getting really pissed off and she said that it was quality rather than quantity. She reminded him of Judi Dench in *Shakespeare in Love*.'

'Why?'

'Well, she's only in it for about eight minutes and she won an

38

Oscar. Anyway, the point of the story is that Ben said he didn't want to be in the play *anyway* – it was the *anyway* that I really liked – and stormed out. He was in a mood all the way through afternoon lessons.' I laughed and Daryl laughed with me.

'So,' said Daryl, after feigning interest in my day for a few more seconds. 'Eddie.'

'What about him?'

Daryl sighed his 'you're not taking things seriously enough' sigh. 'He called you up to ask about your powers! How could he possibly have known about them? It doesn't make sense!'

'Who cares?' I said. 'Maybe he has The Sight. Maybe the signs are aligning. Maybe he read it in a bloody fortune cookie, what's the difference? He knows and that's nice. He offered me a place to stay if I need it, and that's a relief. Why are you trying to read so much into it?'

'He sounded like there was more he wanted to say,' said Daryl, 'you said so yourself.'

'He *told* me there was more he wanted to say,' I said. 'He just didn't want to say it over the phone is all. Look, I may not have spoken to him in years, but I remember quite clearly how he was always worried about something. There was always something on his mind, there was always a subtext and there was always something he wasn't telling you. That's just the way he is.'

Daryl didn't answer for a minute. Then he looked at me. 'Sixteen?'

I nodded. 'What about . . . oh. Sixteen . . . you don't think—'

'I think,' said Daryl.

It seemed so obvious now I thought about it. 'But . . . why wouldn't he have said anything?'

'You know him better than I do,' said Daryl. 'I'm just saying, that's all. It's not like I've written the definitive article.'

'I should call him,' I said.

'Did you get his number?'

'Nope. I'll ask Mum.'

My father was out, and my mother was sitting at the table doing a crossword. She looked up. 'Hi.'

'Hi,' I said. 'Um . . . do you have Eddie's phone number?'

'Eddie?'

'My cousin. Your nephew.'

Her expression changed completely. Only a few muscles moved, but where a moment ago there had been mild interest there was now deep concern. 'What do you want his number for?'

'To ring him with.'

'I . . . we don't have it.'

'We *must* have it.' I grabbed one of the six dozen or so phone books from the shelf and started to flick through it. 'Is it in here?'

'Why do you want to talk to him?'

'Well . . . I wanted to talk to him about my guitar. I think he used to play . . .'

'The clarinet,' she said. 'He used to play the clarinet . . . maybe he still does, I don't know. But you'll have to do a lot better than that.'

'I just want to talk to him!' I said. 'He's my cousin! What's wrong with me wanting to talk to my cousin?'

'Because I don't want you associating with him!' she yelled.

I was taken aback. My mum rarely shouted at me. We both looked away and there was a fairly awkward silence. 'I'm sorry,' she said. 'It's just . . . he's a bad influence. He's not . . . he's a troubled boy.'

'He's not a *boy*. And when did you last speak to him anyway?'

'What does that have to do with anything?'

'When?'

She sighed angrily. 'Oh . . . not long after he left.'

'He left when he was sixteen! That's eight fu . . .' I thought better of it. 'Eight years ago!'

'He really hurt your father,' she said.

'And?'

'Stanly!'

40

'He doesn't give two shits about me, why should I care about him?'

She was getting really angry now. 'Stanly! Watch your language and don't you dare speak about your father like that—'

'How come you're allowed to? I'm sixteen years old and I don't have freedom of speech?' *Yeesh. Way to* not *sound sixteen.*

'Of course you do! You just . . . of course your father cares about you! Your birthday, he . . .'

'Letting me have the guitar was your idea. I'll bet it was.'

She looked mutinously at the floor and spoke in a low voice. 'Edward grew up with a father and no mother. He was always a troubled child. When your uncle died, Frank tried to help Edward but he wouldn't hear of it. He left after an argument and set up home in a city that his father hated, hundreds of miles away. He cut himself off and for all we knew he could have been dead!'

'But he's not!' I said, my own anger rising like the mercury in a thermometer. 'He's not dead! He called me last night!'

'He what?'

'He phoned last night and I spoke to him. He wished me happy birthday. We didn't talk for very long and I didn't get his number so I wanted to call him. There! He's fine!'

My mother sat down. There was another very long pause. My house was a house of pauses. Finally she said, 'It's in the address book with the marmalade cat on the front.'

I took the book. 'If you had his number why didn't you just call him?'

She didn't look at me, she just said, 'You know how stubborn your father can be.'

I called Eddie and he picked up after nearly twenty rings. 'Yeah?'

'Eddie? It's Stanly.'

'Oh! Hi, Stanly. You OK?'

'Yeah, I'm fine. I just . . . your call was a bit confusing.'

'Yeah . . . I'm sorry about that. I just . . . you know. You never know who's listening!' He said it like a joke, but I knew it wasn't.

'Hmm. So when can we have this conversation you can't seem to bring yourself to have?'

'We can have as many conversations as you like if you come to London.'

'Why are you so desperate to have me there?' I asked.

I could hear him moving about as he talked. 'Do you really think that someone with your abilities belongs in a little town like Tref-y-Celwyn? I know I got sick of it pretty fast.'

Another power chord of realisation. 'You have powers too, don't you?'

'C'est possible.'

'You're taking the piss.'

'Something you're also pretty good at, if I remember correctly. You really should come down. You'd be good company.'

He sounded like he was pouring himself a drink. His voice changed slightly, as though he was holding the phone between ear and shoulder. 'Look, Stanly. I know I haven't spoken to you for years. I call up out of the blue inviting you to London. It's got to mess with your head, I'm sorry. And maybe you wouldn't be safe if you came down here, maybe it's better for you up there, but also maybe safe isn't what you need, maybe you need to be tested and . . . listen to me rambling. Sorry.'

'You keep apologising. You don't need to.'

He laughed. 'Yeah. I'm sorr . . . I mean, yeah.'

'How did you *know*?'

'I just knew,' he said.

Silence.

'You still there?' he said.

'Mm.'

'Don't come immediately. Come when you're ready, if you decide you want to. I know your parents don't like me all that much . . .'

'Maybe if you spoke to them—'

'No.' He was insistent. 'No, I couldn't. Not after all the . . . I couldn't. Just . . . remember my offer, OK?'

42

'Can I have your address?'

'Yeah. Got a pen and paper?'

'Uh-huh.'

I wrote down his address. 'Great. Thanks. You may be seeing me . . . but not soon. I have commitments.'

'Commitments?'

'Yeah, I'm Romeo.'

'Eh?'

'In the school play.'

'Ah, I see. Nice one.'

'Cheers.'

'Well, good luck. Take it easy.'

He hung up and I looked at Daryl, who put his head on one side. 'Curious?' he asked.

'As a fox,' I said.

CHAPTER FIVE

I WALKED ALONG AN uneven stone path suspended between two cliffs. The sky was dark purple and laced with spiders' legs of lightning, the air heavy, sulphuric. Somewhere, someone was singing.

I reached the end of the path. A door was set into the rock, marked with some arcane inscription. *Speak friend and enter.* I looked up, kicked off and flew up to the peak of the cliff, where Ben King was juggling fruit and singing to a smiling girl in a lace coffin. I roared at him and we fought with our brains, drawing blood without touching, striking with false memories and concentrated anger. I quickly gained the upper hand, picked him up and hurled him over the edge, and as I watched him plummet into nothingness I realised that I was standing on a massive pile of bones: skulls, legs, arms, ribs, a tower of skeletons. I raised my hands to the reddening sky and suddenly there was blood pouring out from under my feet and cascading down the tower of bones and—

I sat up, shaking, and looked at the clock. Three in the morning. I was wide awake and knew I wouldn't sleep again. Daryl was sleeping peacefully at the end of the bed, and I got up as quietly as I could and got dressed. As I was lacing up my shoes I heard the dog murmur groggily. 'What are you doing?'

'Going out,' I said. 'I need air. And I'm going to practise.'

He nodded.

'Do you want to come?'

He shook his head. 'Too sleepy. A proper training session and I'm too tired to enjoy it. You're a dick.'

'Love you too.' I opened the window. 'Sleep well.'

He grunted.

My house was three storeys tall, and my bedroom was on the top floor. I stood on the outside sill, shut the window as far as I could and looked across to the huge tree that faced my window. I took a deep breath . . . *can't balls this up, can't* . . . and kicked off from the sill, spun, planted both feet on the trunk of the tree and ran vertically downwards. I used the tree as a springboard, flew across, spun and continued the run on the wall of the house. Just as I was congratulating myself on a perfect, graceful exit I lost balance and hit the pavement. *Thud*. I swore and wondered whether my parents might have heard . . . but no. They wouldn't have. They both snored like buffalo.

I ran along the road, bouncing from one side to the other, glad that I was pretty much definitely not going to bump into anyone in this sleepy-ass town at this time of night. It wasn't all graceful, and occasionally I slipped and almost impaled myself on fences and gates, but I was rapidly becoming much more comfortable with my powers. I could feel it inside, deep down. Gravity was only there in an advisory capacity now. I ran along walls and flew as much as I could – definitely flying now, not floating, ha *ha* – and when I reached the end of the road I touched down slowly and perfectly. I ran across the bridge and sprang over to the pub by the train station, running along the wall, resisting the urge to whoop and laugh, and channelling the energy I had suddenly gained I performed a huge leap, flew about forty feet – *shiiiiiiiiiiiit*! – and landed on the roof of Tref-y-Celwyn Tyre Supplies.

Crouched like a gargoyle, silhouetted against the moon, I could see the whole town sleeping under dull orange and spectral silver. My playground. I laughed and began my dance again, with the wind as my partner. I reached the primary school where two cats were facing off, their backs arched and their tails fluffed up like toilet brushes. I lifted them both up just by looking and deposited them on opposite sides of a fence where they continued hissing at each other for about ten seconds. Then they left, as if bored.

45

Whether they even noticed what I'd done was academic. I'd *done* it. Lifted the creatures with my mind. This was the stuff.

I flew up the high street, leaping ten feet at a time, and ran straight to the clock tower. I ran and I ran and then I leapt, and my feet hit the tower and I ran up as far as I could physically propel myself and then backflipped. Everything was in slow motion, an invisible camera panning around me, three hundred and sixty degrees. It was ecstasy, total control, total freedom, and Mr Jones The Careers Adviser's words came back to me. *Is there any upper limit to these powers?* Right now, it didn't seem like there could be . . . but even if there was, this would be enough for me. I landed perfectly and blew a kiss to the moon.

It was starting to get light when I got home. I ran up the wall, opening the window with my mind as I went, and slid silently in. Daryl didn't stir as I undressed and got back into bed. I could grab about three hours of sleep . . . that is if I could . . . could . . . (*yawns*) . . .

Time for another montage. You can choose the music. Days shifted imperceptibly into weeks, and then months, and for the remainder of September, the whole of October and about half of November I spent my nights flying and my days working. Every Monday night the cast of *Romeo and Juliet* stayed after school for an hour and a half, and by the end of October I had learnt all of my words. It was impossible, I was doing everything, surviving on about four hours of sleep a night, but Daryl said that the more I did the more I'd be able to do, which was easy for him to say 'cos he did bugger all, but turned out to be true. The play was a dream. I'd actually started some of my coursework (none of it was close to being finished, but whatchyagonnado?). My powers were developing at a rate that both thrilled and scared me, although it was good fear.

And it wasn't just the flying. The telekinesis, or whatever it was, was getting better. I stopped people from falling over, I stopped balls from breaking windows, I did minor-league good deeds that were nonetheless extremely fulfilling, considering the fact that before Saturday the twenty-fourth of September I hadn't given much of a shit about anybody except myself. I did also indulge my dickish side, but I justified it to myself, saying that constantly messing with the blinds in Mr Jones Chemistry's class (as opposed to Mr Jones Careers or Mr Jones PE) was basically a victimless crime, as was slowly de-tuning our happy-clappy RE teacher Mr Nelson's guitar as he tried to teach us Christian values through the medium of appalling songs. Plus, it helped with precision. As did messing with the headmaster's hymn book during assembly so that he kept losing his place. And re-directing balls during PE so that they hit people I didn't like. And so on.

My helping-the-helpless act didn't go quite so well, stretching only to seeing off some kids who were bullying some smaller kids, and I didn't even use my powers for that, just the badass feeling that came with them. It worked surprisingly well, and I actually became semi-popular for a while. People called me Romeo in the corridor, which was kind of annoying but kind of not, and less popular kids in the lower years said hi to me when they saw me, because I'd helped them. That bit was pretty good. In fact, I was starting to find that acting like a normal person and being a more-cynical-than-thou loner weren't mutually exclusive, as I'd always thought they were.

One Monday in mid-November, I stayed after school to rehearse. The girl playing Juliet was called Kloe, and she wasn't in my Drama group, although we were in the same year. She was slightly taller than me and very pretty, with long chestnut hair that shone like hair from a shampoo advert (really), and her brown eyes were always full of humour. She was really nice, which made working with her easy, and made the romantic bits much less embarrassing and awkward than they might have been.

Tonight we stayed an extra half an hour to do the balcony scene, which wasn't actually going to involve the traditional balcony. Instead the two of us were going to stand on either side of a wall facing away from one another and talking, not actually

47

seeing each other for the whole scene. Mrs Bush, who was one of the English teachers, had been assigned to prompt and after watching this scene for the first time asked whether the wall was representative of the psychological barrier of the feud. Miss Stevenson said yes, but I think it was mainly because it would have been too arduous to build a balcony.

Kloe's mum picked her up at six o'clock. I knew that my dad would be late – I could time it pretty much to the minute – so I went to the high street to get a drink. As I walked back down the alley towards the school, drinking my can of Shloer (or the speech impediment drink as my mother called it), four people stepped out of the darkness, two in front of me and two behind.

Zach and George were in front, with two Sams flanking me. I was trapped, and my stomach lurched because I'd not actually been in a situation like this before, but I made sure it didn't show. *No sweat, yeah?* I finished my drink, threw the can into a conveniently-placed skip and wiped my mouth, smiling pleasantly. 'Hiya, fellas.'

Zach walked forwards and looked me in the eyes. 'I don't like you,' he said.

'Really?' I said. 'Why's that, then?'

One of the Sams clipped me around the ear. 'Fucking shut up, gay boy.'

Gay. The best insult any of them can come up with. Gay boy, bender, poofter, faggot, blah blah to the power of blah squared. I don't need to use the word pathetic, it automatically lends itself. I could feel myself getting angry. These people thought they had the right to make other people's lives miserable. They thought they mattered more, that their pathetic primitive tribal need to assert dominance superseded their victims' right to not be screwed with on a daily basis. They couldn't comprehend the sometimes irreparable damage that they caused to some kids, even after all of the stories about kids hanging themselves and overdosing, they still persisted. I can almost sympathise with kids who just cut out the middleman and take out all the bullies with a semiautomatic. I'm

48

at pains to say that I don't condone it, but I can appreciate the cumulative affect of daily torment, for those with thinner skins than mine.

'You're a freak,' said Zach. 'Are you Jewish?'

I swear I'm not making this up. I shook my head. 'Nope. Are you?'

A slap around the head from one of the Sams.

'Course I'm *fucking* not,' said Zach. He looked around conspiratorially. 'Hey, *Romeo*. Want to hear a joke?'

'Not really.'

Zach shrugged. 'Suit yourself.' He was still smiling, but I could sense his rather small mind working furiously, trying to think of something witty or original. Finally he asked how my mum was. Yeah, really.

'Fine,' I said.

'Yeah,' said Zach, looking around at his cohorts and grinning proudly. 'She was pretty fine last night.' They all laughed.

Wow, I thought. *This is . . . really embarrassing*. 'Did you rehearse this whole thing?' I said. ''Cos I think your script could have done with a couple more drafts.'

'Shut up, you drama poof,' said one of Zach's minions. *Ooh, good one.*

I imagined meeting Zach for a battle in a Gothic temple. *Me with my guitar, him carrying a broadsword. Zach wearing black, me wearing red. He looks at my guitar and snorts: 'What are you going to do? Power chord me to death?'*

I shake my head and pull a Samurai sword out of my guitar. 'No,' I say. 'Bisecting you from your nuts to your noggin ought to do.' And I smile as Zach gulps.

But this wasn't a titanic battle of mortal foes. It was five lads in the dark in a small Welsh town eight miles away from another small Welsh town. Violence was inevitable, but not balletic kung-fu violence with liberal doses of slow motion. Dirty punches. Part of me – more than part of me, actually, most of me – wanted to just say *sod it* and rise into the air, psychically yanking their feet from

49

under them and spinning them around, daring them to ever so much as *look* at me funny again . . .

Can't.

Shouldn't.

But I wanna . . .

'Yeah, drama *poof*,' said Zach, bringing me crashing back to reality.

'Word of advice, guys,' I said. 'Improv? Not your game.'

Witty banter exhausted, Zach threw the opening punch. Right into my chin. It hurt, and his minions all laughed, but then I head-butted him in the face extremely hard and heard a crack, and the laughter stopped. I wasn't sure if his nose had broken or not, but a gratifying quantity of blood came out and he stumbled backwards, making a noise that sounded like *bwah*. Now George hit me in the face and it knocked me off balance for a second, giving both the Sams the chance to hold me still as Zach came for me, blood streaming from his nose, screaming curses. He punched me in the stomach and I brought both feet off the ground, planted them on his chest and kicked off. The two Sams and I hurtled backwards and they fell to the ground, losing control of me. I turned a perfect backflip and landed on my feet and took a second to think how unbelievably *freaking* cool that must have looked before Zach ran towards me. This time I hit him really hard and he spun sideways, smacked into a wall and fell to the ground. George was running at me too. He threw a punch and I dodged it, grabbed his arm and swung him. I had very little actual physical strength so I channelled some brain energy into the swing to give it some *oomph,* causing George to hit the wall rather harder than I had intended. *Oh well. Rather him than me.*

At this point the two Sams exchanged panicked glances and ran away, which was a relief, and I steadied my breathing, dusted myself off and walked past Zach, back towards school. No puns occurred to me, unfortunately.

～

He threw the first punch, I thought as I lay in bed that night, mulling over what had happened. They'd deserved what they'd got. I'd even go as far as to say that it has been satisfying. And I hadn't cheated . . . not exactly.

I hadn't even told Daryl yet. I was waiting for the dream. The bones. The blood. The dream I'd been having on and off for a while. It felt like a message. A prologue. Maybe the fight had been chapter one. I didn't know how keen I was for chapter two.

There were no repercussions from the fight with the Fantastic Four, but word got around. Everyone always found out about stuff like that. I was treated with extra disdain by the people who liked Zach, and I got extra smiles and pats on the back from people who didn't like him. The other three, George and the two Sams, were superfluous, background noise. Cardboard cutouts. No-one paid them much attention because they weren't really there. People paid attention to Zach because despite being a grade-A arsehole he had a level of Neanderthal charisma that appealed to fellow Neanderthals and gave him power. I'd taken it away briefly and that was good, but I was happy for that to be the end of it.

December arrived without further incident, but as the nights got colder and sporadic snow showers began, my night-time training sessions became more difficult. Eventually, after a frost-bitten encounter with a rather large dog who didn't take kindly to being attacked with psychically-propelled snowballs, I gave up on them altogether, and settled for digging out my old Lego and building models with my mind. Daryl didn't like the cold and spent most of his time indoors watching DVDs.

Romeo and Juliet kept getting better. Mark Topp, who was playing Tybalt, was doing his evil part very well and Kloe was way ahead of me in terms of character nuances. In fact, apart from a few of the year nines, who were still horsing around far too much during the opening fight, everybody was pulling their weight. We had remodelled Friar Lawrence as a sort of comedy pimp and he always had everybody laughing, and Paris was a practically invisible beige-wearing man who spent more time texting than looking at people. Miss Stevenson's experiments were all interesting and, so far, successful.

The final lesson of term was English. Our teacher had been kept away by the snow because he lived in the hills, and we had a supply teacher who hadn't been given anything to work with, so everyone was just sitting around doing whatever, exchanging Christmas cards and chatting away. I was sitting by myself, absently doodling some kung-fu snowmen, and half-listening to two boys discussing some creepy Internet thing they were surreptitiously viewing under the table on a phone. 'It's blatantly bollocks,' said Reuben. 'Smiling Joe's fake. Like Slender Man, or something.'

'Who cares?' said Jack. 'It's *wicked*. Read this bit, the way he *eats* them—'

'Stanly?'

I looked up. Kloe was smiling down at me, holding a handful of Christmas cards in red envelopes. 'Hi,' she said. 'Sorry to interrupt.'

'It's fine,' I said.

'You seemed deep in thought.'

'Deep. Yeah. Thoroughly submerged.' We laughed only a little bit awkwardly – considering how close our characters were in the play, we hadn't exchanged much in the way of real-world dialogue.

Kloe shuffled through her cards and handed one to me. I noticed that she'd spelled my name right, which was impressive. 'Wow,' I said. 'Thanks! I um . . . sorry, I don't really do Christmas cards . . .'

'That's fine,' she smiled. 'Don't worry. I know it's pretty naff. I just, you know, I quite like it, as it's our last year and everything.'

'Cool,' I said. *What's a funny thing to say? What's a Christmas pun? Do girls like puns? Are puns a good thing?*

'Well, merry Christmas,' she said. 'See you in January!'

'Yeah, you too,' I smiled. *WHAT'S A FUNNY THING TO SAY?!* 'I mean, merry Christmas too.' *TOO LATE, YOU KNOB.*

Kloe smiled and walked away and I opened my card. It was

very tasteful: a silhouette of a Bethlehem-esque scene beneath bright starlight. Inside, the message read MERRY CHRISTMAS ROMEO. LOVE KLOE. XX

Two kisses. What did that mean?

Probably nothing.

Probably definitely nothing.

All the same, I managed to sneak a glance at a few other boys' cards, and none of them had more than one kiss. Some had none.

Probably definitely nothing.

Nothing or not, I felt a warm maple-syrup bubble in my stomach. And as I sat on the bus home, watching the freezing confetti fall, I thought about Kloe and smiled to myself.

'Two kisses,' said Daryl. 'Wow. I mean . . . Jesus. That's amazing.'

'Oh, cheers,' I said sarcastically, sprawled on my bed and breathing in the smell of holidays.

'Not what I meant,' said Daryl. 'It's just . . . have you ever had a girlfriend before?'

'Not really. I mean . . . no.'

'And suddenly some hottie comes onto you out of nowhere?'

'Not really out of nowhere. We're in the play together. And, y'know. She's nice.'

'Aha! So you're sweet on this slice of woman!'

I didn't make eye contact, just lazily played with my guitar, fiddling with the strings without touching them, trying to play a complex riff without much effort or success. Finally I said, 'Look, it's obviously nothing. It's all just because of the play. It's a weird situation, she's a pretty girl and we're both having to act out these romantic scenes, and obviously people bond in those situations. And . . . and it's not like she'd have given me a card if we *weren't* in the play together.' I was right. She wouldn't have. 'We'd never exchanged a word before we were cast.'

'I thought you said she gave cards to everyone?'

'Well, I don't know. Most of the people in our class seemed to have them.'

53

'But you're the only one who got two kisses.'

'Only based on the small sample I took. And it might just be an extra kiss for being a good actor. Or something.' *Or was it?* I asked myself. *Shut up*, I replied.

Daryl sniggered. 'Hmm. Yeah. OK.'

'Do you think I should have got her number?' I said.

'Why? Would you have called her?'

'Probably . . . maybe . . . not.'

'Maybe you could get her a Christmas present. Girls like presents, or so I'm told.'

'She lives one town away. How would I get it to her?'

Daryl shook his head. 'You can be dense on an epic scale when the mood takes you. Can you fly or not?'

'Oh, yeah.'

'Going to get her a present?'

I grabbed a pillow with my mind and hit him with it. 'Maybe. I don't know. Should I get her something if I'm not sure if I like her?'

'Imagine if you don't,' said Daryl, 'and then you realise that you *do* like her when the opportunity's passed you by. You'll be royally hacked off to say the least.'

I shrugged. 'I'll think about it.'

'You do that.'

'How come you're so insightful? Have you ever had a meaningful relationship?'

Daryl shrugged. 'Only with Buffy. And Faith. Also Scarlett Johansson. *Rrruff.*'

I laughed and later we ate fish and chips and went out for a walk. I showed him some flying and we talked about girls and films and magic. If that night was an indicator of how my life was going to proceed, I was in for a fairly sweet ride.

I was standing on top of the London Eye, looking across the city, and I could see people moving like zombies on the gridded streets. Smoke rose in vicious colours from the manhole covers and I had a headache. I gritted my teeth, and far below somebody exploded like a piñata. Multi-coloured viscera soaked the other passers-by but they ignored it, carrying on with their mundane business. I felt another stab of pain and screamed and some more people burst like sacks of fat. I fell to my knees and a building split in two, crumbling into nothing. All around me the city was falling apart and people were becoming piles of gore.

I opened my eyes, salt water cooling on my face. I wiped it away and my room swam into focus. The sky was clear and moonlight hung from cobwebs like liquid nitrogen dew. I sat up and switched on my lamp. Daryl didn't stir. I looked up at the trees that I had drawn on the walls. They were moving, swaying in a breeze that couldn't be. I blinked and rubbed my damp eyes and still the trees moved, and things were moving between them, zipping like bees, leaping from branch to branch so fast that I couldn't see them. I shook my head and thought *no*, and the trees all caught fire. The flames spread across my ceiling, engulfing my room. My skin burned, became ash and I dissolved into—

I woke up. It was ten o'clock in the morning and Daryl was watching *Trainspotting*. I sat up, brushing sleep from my eyes, and looked at the trees. Still. No fire. I shook my head and psychically lobbed some balled-up socks at Daryl. 'Bit early for heroin, isn't it?'

'Choose life,' said Daryl, in an impeccable Scottish accent. 'Choose a job. Choose a career. Choose a family. Choose—'

'—Breakfast,' I said, sliding out of bed.

Daryl shrugged. 'That works too.'

I pulled on a T-shirt and some trousers and went downstairs. Mum was out and my dad was having a smoke on the patio. I made some fried eggs on toast and took them upstairs and while I ate them I drew pictures on my sketch pad, colouring them in with a mixture of pencil crayon and felt tip. Decaying zombies and yellow rabbits. Ghosts. A monkey juggling stars. Mushroom people with swords. Trees.

'So, what are we going to do today?' asked Daryl.

I shrugged. 'Dunno. Eat chocolate and watch DVDs, probably.'

Daryl tutted.

'What?' I asked.

He shrugged. 'Nothing. I just thought maybe you'd be doing something a bit more . . . power-related?'

'What is it with you and vicarious fun?' I asked.

'I just like watching you fly! That's all. Jesus.'

'Well, what if I don't fancy it?'

'That's fine. Fine, I don't mind.'

I dabbed the last crust in a bit of spilled yolk and finished it, then took my plate downstairs and washed my hands. When I got back to my room Daryl was reading a magazine, and I unpacked my guitar, hooked it up to the amplifier and started to play.

I had been twiddling for about half an hour when Daryl said, 'Have you thought any more about London?'

'Haven't asked Dad about the driving lessons yet.'

'How come?'

'Dunno.' I tried a series of chords and the amplifier projected a horrible discordant mess, so I switched it off, bored. 'He doesn't seem to like me much lately.'

'All the more reason for you to ask for the lessons,' said Daryl. 'Male bonding and so on.'

'I'll ask him on Christmas day,' I said. 'It's the one day of the year he's guaranteed to be in a good mood otherwise Mum'll divorce him.'

'Fair enough.' Daryl shifted on the bed, looking uncomfortable.

'What?' I asked.

'Nothing. I just . . . thinking about it, I'm not sure it's actually that good an idea.'

'What?'

'Going to London.'

'Why? You were advocating it something fierce before. I thought maybe you'd got a job with the Tourist Board without telling me.'

'Yeah.' He shrugged. 'Dunno. It's just a long way away. And ever so slightly different from this little rural timewarp.'

'I'm not going to go without a good reason,' I said.

56

'You don't feel the call of epic superhero destiny?'

'I don't know,' I said. 'Kind of. Seems a waste not to try to use the powers for good, rather than delivering post or building extensions. I just don't know how the hell it would work. And plus . . .' I thought about Kloe. 'I might be developing a potential reason to stay. So we'll see.'

At about five o'clock the phone rang. I picked it up. 'Hello?'

Silence.

'Hello?'

Click. They'd hung up, whoever they were. I tried to re-dial, but the number was withheld. 'Hmm.'

'What?' asked Daryl.

'Mystery caller,' I said. 'Didn't leave a number.'

'Ooooh. I bet it was Kloe.'

'I doubt it. She hasn't got the number.'

'Could have looked it up in the phone book,' said Daryl, as if I were a dunce.

'Hmm.'

'Who else could it have been?'

'Eddie, maybe?'

'Maybe.'

I put the phone back in its cradle and picked up my guitar again. Daryl watched me for a few minutes, then went over to the DVDs and scrutinised them. 'So,' I said. 'What are we going to do tonight?'

'The same thing we do every night,' said Daryl. 'Try to take over the world.'

I laughed just south of hysterically for about eight seconds, then shook my head. 'That's not funny.'

'I agree,' said Daryl. 'I'm sorry. Narf.'

CHAPTER SIX

Christmas Eve arrived and I sat and stared at the phone, debating whether or not to call Kloe. I didn't have her mobile number, but I'd decided to follow the advice of Daryl the Great Dog Detective and look in the phone book, and had found her house number. I picked up then immediately replaced the receiver about six times before an angel finally appeared on my left shoulder and said, in a weary voice, 'For God's sake. This is ridiculous. Just call, see if she's there, ask if maybe she fancies meeting up at some point over Christmas. You can always dress it up as a private rehearsal for the play.'

The devil on my right shoulder, who seemed more neurotic than Satanic, scrunched up its face. 'What if she's not there? What if you have to talk to her *parents*?'

'So what?' asked the angel, belligerently. 'Say you'll call back!'

'But it'll be embarrassing.'

'Screw "embarrassing" you wimp! Two kisses! Are you a Hulk or a Hobbit?'

'They're taking Stanly to Isengard—'

'Shut up and phone her. And stop manifesting your internal conflicts.'

They vanished and I dialled, and nobody answered, and I bottled it and didn't try again.

'Did you ask her if she called on Saturday?' asked Daryl, when I returned to my room.

'No.'

'Are you going to meet up?'

'No.'

'Did you actually speak to her?'

'No.'

Daryl shrugged. 'Oh well.'

'Oh well? It was your idea. Ish.'

'Yeah, emphasis on the "ish". Obviously I don't want you to throw away this potentially golden opportunity, but y'know. Your destiny is in *your* hands, farm boy.'

'Sod this,' I said. 'We aren't having this conversation.'

'Cool. Whatever, kiddo. Your density will bring you to her.' Daryl began to dance in a lopsided, dog-like way. '"I'm not Peter Pan, I don't BEEP with fairies, but I bust more rhymes than virgin cherries" . . .'

I threw a cushion at him with my mind. 'Numpty.'

'Is what it is, yo.'

'Meaning what?'

'Errrmdunno.'

I emerged from beneath the duvet at about eleven the next morning. I hadn't had a stocking since I was twelve, so the old excitement wasn't really there, but when I went downstairs everyone was in a good mood and my dad had made pancakes, and Mum had put a Christmas CD on, and Daryl was doing a pretty passable Nat King Cole impression, crooning along to 'Chestnuts Roasting On an Open Fire'. 'Well,' I said. 'This is festive.'

'You almost sound as though you mean that,' my mum said, smiling.

'I almost do.' I gave her a hug. I hadn't felt this Christmassy in years.

We ate pancakes, and presents came and went. I'd bought my mum some candles, a plate, a stuffed cat and a Rolling Stones CD, and I'd got my dad some tedious-looking book about economics that he'd been going on about, and *The Towering Inferno* on DVD, as I knew he was a big fan of both Steve McQueen and Paul

Newman. Neither of them asked when I'd had time to go shopping or how I'd travelled and I didn't tell them. They gave me two CDs, two books, some guitar music and a special edition two-disc *Casablanca* DVD, and I gave Daryl a Humphrey Bogart poster, quite a lot of chocolate and *Fargo* on DVD. My parents had got him a basket. It was really nice, as baskets go, and Daryl seemed to genuinely like it. I put it by my bed and stuck the Bogie poster on the wall next to it.

Dinner was chicken, as my mum had a strange irrational issue with animals that gobbled, and there were roast potatoes (a household speciality) and too many dishes of vegetables and chipolatas, and extra stuffing because Mum knew how much Daryl and I liked it. 'Dad?' I asked, after ten minutes of contented, silent eating. 'Do you think that maybe you could give me some driving lessons sometime?'

My dad stopped eating mid-chew. He exchanged a bemused glance with my mother, swallowed his food and nodded. 'Of course. Er . . . yes. Fine. How about tomorrow? Most people will probably be inside sleeping off their hangovers so town should be pretty empty. We could do it in the community centre car park.'

'Great,' I said. 'Thanks.'

Nobody else spoke for the duration of the meal except to say 'mmm' and 'that's lovely', and afterwards I helped with the washing up, enjoying my parents' obvious confusion.

That evening I sat and tried to work out some of the music that my parents had given me, and Daryl ate his own body weight in Doritos and read magazines. Suddenly a thought struck me. 'Do you believe in God?' I asked.

Daryl didn't look up. 'I am a dog.'

'Which is relevant because . . .'

'Because . . . because I'm a dog. I don't think about stuff like that. I'm not human. I don't subscribe to your newsletter.'

'Your favourite film is *Casablanca,* you love The Beatles and you can recite *Trainspotting* backwards. You're human enough to tell me whether or not you believe in God. It's even an anagram of you, you're closer to it than I am.'

'That's *well ffff*rigging funny,' Daryl deadpanned. He paused for a moment then said, 'Which God do you mean, anyway?'

I raised both eyebrows and made a noise that sounded like "nguh?".

'Do you mean the Christian God? The beautiful merciful divine presence? The guiding light behind their self-defeating, hypocritical dogma?'

'That's *well ffff*rigging funny.'

'No pun intended. Or do you mean Allah, or one of the many heads of Hinduism, or Odin, or the Egyptian sun deity Ra, or perhaps—'

'Are you saying "no" then?'

Daryl shrugged. 'I think the notion of God is flawed and the way most religions put it into practise is a load of divisive, puritanical sex-fixated bollocks. As a way of life I suppose Buddhism isn't so bad. It's basically a lot of sitting about under trees being nice to one another and eating lots of rice, and doesn't involve lashings of bigotry and irrationality.'

I shrugged and affected a country accent. 'Fair dos, like. Fair dos.'

'What's brought on this bout of theologising?'

'Well . . . it's Christmas.'

'Are you joking?'

'Yeah. I . . . dunno. I was just thinking about my powers.' I strummed ineffectually as I spoke. 'Wondering whether they were . . . I don't know. Divine or something.'

'Do you believe in God, then?'

'No . . . once upon a time I did, though. Well. Sort of. I basically thought that God was like a sort of Super Santa Claus. I'd be really good and then pray for a bike or a Playstation or whatever. As far as I could see if you were really good and then prayed to God then it didn't matter whether it was Christmas, May Day bank holiday or the fourteenth Wednesday after Pentecost, you'd get what you wanted. It never happened, of course. Then one day a vicar came into school and told us all this stuff about being nice to one another and I told him about my plan and he was a bit shocked. He told me off.' I sighed, and stared pensively into the middle distance. 'That was the day I . . . lost my faith. So to speak.' I tried to keep a straight face, but cracked almost immediately.

Daryl laughed. 'Priceless.'

'To be fair, I can kind of understand people believing in bullshit to make the world make sense,' I said. 'I quite like my world unexplained though.'

'Hey,' said Daryl. 'Don't you try to corrupt me with your Atheist propaganda. I'm happy with my dog delusion.'

I laughed. 'You've changed your tune since about thirty seconds ago.'

'I pride myself on being both irrational and bewilderingly changeable.' Daryl sneezed. ''Scuse me. So did you ever *really* believe in God?'

I shrugged. 'Don't think so. It was more wishful thinking than anything.' I played a riff and it sounded pretty good. 'Finally!'

'Shiny,' said Daryl. 'Hey. Appropos of absolutely nothing . . . if you go to ye olde London town, which I'm still not sure is a one hundred per cent kosher plan, will you take me with you?'

I looked at him. 'What kind of a question is that?'

'A perfectly legitimate one,' said Daryl. 'Are you going to take me with you?'

'Of course!' I said. 'How could I leave you behind? You're like my good right arm or whatever. Plus my parents would just drive you insane and you'd blow your brains out all over your Bogie poster.'

'Thanks.' Daryl sounded relieved.

'Why do you ask? Something on your mind?'

'No. I just . . . your talk about God made me wonder if there's really a place for me. You know . . . anywhere. I'm a talking dog. I'm not something that was ever meant to be. So that begs the question – what would I be if there was no-one who needed me?'

'Oh Jesus,' I said. 'Is it really time to get metaphysical?'

'Sorry.' Daryl shrugged his dog-like shrug. 'I don't know. I was just wondering what I'd do if you left.'

'Can't you think of anything? Besides waste away?'

'I don't know. Walk the Earth like Caine in *Kung Fu*.'

We both laughed. 'We could do that together. I mean, if I was going to try being a globe-trotting superhero, what better companion than a talking dog?'

'True.' He didn't seem convinced, though, so I said, quite seriously, 'I'll never leave you.' Inwardly I cringed at the inspirational teen movie corniness of the statement – not to mention the homoerotic subtext, which would have felt a wee bit odd even if I hadn't been saying it to a beagle – but Daryl seemed grateful. 'Thanks,' he said. And he meant it. I carried on trying to play but I could sense that Daryl still wanted to talk. 'What's up?' I asked.

'What *would* I be if there was no-one who needed me?' he asked.

'Um . . . I don't know,' I said, setting down my guitar. 'Are you sure that's how it works? I would think that anything – dog, fairy cake, pillar box, whatever – is the same whether it's needed or not.'

'Not necessarily. A pillar box, if you're not using it to post letters, it's just a red shape, isn't it?'

'Maybe?'

'Makes you think, doesn't it? Like . . . when you're not playing the guitar, is it still yours? And where does the music go once you've played it? And—'

'You are currently having an excess of thoughts,' I said, picking up my guitar again. 'And I am not qualified to address any of them. Watch a film.'

Daryl did his funny shrug. 'OK.'

My dad gave me my driving lesson the next day, and another the following weekend. He said I had a knack for it, which was nice, although I felt horrible considering why I was doing it. But I squashed the low-level self-loathing under a heap of 'necessary evils' and got on with it. If I had to do it, I had to do it. There was nothing more to say.

The holiday shuffled on with little incident, and suddenly New Year's Eve arrived, bringing a party kicking and screaming along with it. My parents told me about it a few days before.

Mum: Stanly? We're going to have a party for New Year.

Me (*impassive*): We are?

Mum: Yes! Won't that be fun? Do you have anyone you want to invite?

Me: Not really.

Mum: Oh.

The party ship landed and party people debarked, none of them younger than forty and none of them particularly interested in me. I wasn't especially interested in them either, and was planning to go out and spend the night training with Daryl. However . . .

'No,' said my mother, closing the front door a second after I opened it.

'What?' I asked.

'You're going to stay and be sociable,' she said.

'Oh *what* . . .'

'You heard me,' she said. Her tone was resolute. 'We hardly ever have parties and whenever we do you never even show your face. I want you to stay and talk to people.'

'I want to go out.'

'It's freezing cold! Why do you want to go out?'

'I want to try out the new abilities that I got for my birthday. I want to dance across the rooftops of Tref-y-Celwyn and I want to mess with chavs by throwing snowballs at them with the power of my mind. Daryl was going to come. We were going to toast marsh-mallows.'

What I actually said was, 'I just want to go for a walk.'

'No,' she said. 'It's too late anyway.'

'I'm sixteen years old!' I protested. 'It's ten o'clock! I can't just go out for a walk?'

'No.'

An hour later I was up in my room, lying on my bed, listening to early Eminem and sketching pictures of dinner parties set on fire, their horrendously over-dressed attendees running around in flames and exploding like overripe melons full of viscera. 'That's disgusting,' said Daryl.

I didn't answer. Daryl sighed and switched off the music. 'Hey,' I said. 'I was listening to that.'

'How old are you?' my dog demanded.

'What?'

'How old are you?'

'Sixteen.' I had to fight the urge to add *duh*.

'And you're sulking in your room. Why don't you just make the best of the situation? Go downstairs, socialise with the boring grown-ups, see in the new year, maybe get a little kiss off the younger and more attractive ones . . .'

'Nope,' I said, snapping my fingers to bring back the music. 'Not in the mood.'

Ten to twelve. A knock at my door. I made a flippant gesture to lock the door, and twirled my finger so that the volume on my hi-fi went up.

'Stanly!' yelled my mother. 'Open the door!'

I didn't answer.

'Open this door immediately!'

Zero.

'If you don't open this door I'm going to donate your guitar to the Air Ambulance.'

She wouldn't.

'*Stanly open the door this instant!*'

Daryl leapt off the bed, nosed the hi-fi off and jumped up on his hind legs against the door, sliding the lock back with one paw. My mother opened it and stood there, dressed in a red sari, her face tinged crimson with anger and booze, a hefty glass of wine in one hand. 'Stanly,' she said, trying to keep her voice level. 'Come downstairs.'

'I don't want to,' I said. Every second I felt more like a horrible sulky teenager, the type that usually pisses me off so much that I have to lie down in a darkened room after more than fifteen seconds' contact with them, but equally, calming down and being rational didn't feel like an option.

'Stanly, everybody wants to see you.'

'No they don't. You just want to cover up the fact that your marriage is failing by presenting a well-behaved child as a symbol of harmony.'

What? Where the hell did that come from? She hadn't deserved that and I was an evil, nasty little shit and I instantly hated myself. Daryl went and hid under the bed. My mother looked deflated. She stared at the ground. The colour had left her face. She didn't say anything, just turned and went downstairs. Several minutes later I heard people cheering. Party poppers. My stomach was full of battery acid. I switched off my light but I didn't sleep for a long time.

The next few days bled unbearably into one another. My mother wouldn't talk to me and my father, who wasn't a fantastic communicator at the best of times, didn't try to act as a neutral party. He was as curt to me and as distant with Mum as he usually was, and the atmosphere was so thick with awkwardness and misery that I had to go outside. I went for long walks in the snow with Daryl, the cold doing its best to numb my body although its work had already been done. Daryl was quiet. We had talked about the incident and I told him I wished I hadn't said anything, and to my surprise he said that what I'd said wasn't necessarily wrong. He just thought I could have been more tactful, and maybe brought it up at a more appropriate moment, and in a less confrontational way. I laughed at that. The idea of my dog, the acid-tongued guided missile of tactlessness, lecturing me on being diplomatic was ridiculous, especially seeing as how he was completely right. I knew I should apologise, but I couldn't. It was too hard. Too much time had gone by.

I'd never felt less like someone with superpowers.

Luckily, though, I did have superpowers, and they were an excellent distraction from feeling like a twat. I went up to the woods alone the next day and tried to see how high I could go. I couldn't just take off and fly Superman-style, not yet. I had to concentrate, and rise, and keep concentrating in order to rise further, but it was definitely getting easier. I managed to get to the top of a pretty tall tree today, aware that this was extremely dangerous.

Oh well. Serves me right if I break my legs.

I grabbed the top branch and sat down to catch my breath, and realised that there was someone walking through the woods towards me. My heart nearly stopped. Had they seen me? Probably not. They were walking normally, not looking up. I squinted. It was a man in a grey suit, looking fairly out of place. He had his hands in his pockets, as nonchalant as anything, and as he walked past the tree he glanced up and nodded. 'Afternoon.'

What did that mean? He *had* seen me fly up the tree? Or was he just aware that I was there? I nodded back. 'Hi.'

He kept walking, never breaking stride, and within half a minute he'd disappeared. I made absolutely sure that I was completely alone before descending, trying to make it look like I was climbing.

Must be more careful.

Can't be seen yet.

When I got home, I found my mother crying at the kitchen table. My dad wasn't around. Mum was smoking a cigarette. I had never seen her smoke before – and inside the house, no less – and it was quite unsettling. I put my arm around her and didn't say anything, and she cried and cried.

The following morning relations between us were fine, but my dad was in a towering bad mood. Everything he did was accompanied by a bang. He slammed doors. He slammed the toilet seat. He slammed down mugs and chairs and books. He threw newspapers at nothing. He took great satisfaction in being as noisy as possible when putting coal on the Rayburn. He kicked things. He swore and shouted at the slightest provocation. It was unutterably tedious, and my mother evacuated to see her friend Perdita and I went up to the woods with Daryl to practise flying again. I also tried using telekinesis at the same time, but it was a huge strain. I could just about manage to throw a couple of pebbles while running vertically up a tree trunk and then I had to lie down. The dog suggested that I make this my next target, so I made sure to get as much practice in as possible before school started again.

Finally, on the last night of the holiday, Daryl came into my room to find me sitting cross-legged in the air about two feet off the ground, with a cushion levitating next to me. He nodded approvingly. 'Nice one.'

'Thanks,' I said, through gritted teeth.

'Feeling the burn?'

'Kinda.'

'Want to lie down?'

'Yeah.' Thump.

CHAPTER SEVEN

ROMEO AND JULIET was scheduled for the fourth, fifth and sixth of March. We had just under three months and I knew it was going to be fine. It was going to be *special*. Miss Stevenson gave me her phone number in case I wanted to discuss anything and I put it on the first page of a new notebook. I didn't think I would actually use it because I was in such a good mood about the play, but it was nice to have the option. It was also nice to be congratulated by students from the lower years for my performance at the previous night's rehearsal, and it was *great* when Ben King witnessed it, to see the look of robbed triumph on his face. I was being petty again, but it was worth it. Sometimes being petty is therapeutic. Kloe-wise, there were no new developments, although I felt slightly more confident about engaging her in conversation outside of rehearsals, and I started to think that any attraction had all been in my head. It was disappointing, but OK – at least I got to act with her.

On the first Friday back after Christmas I was in the playground, sitting on my bench and reading *The Rules of Attraction*. There was a small crowd a few metres away made up of boys and girls from various years, all standing in a circle around two sixth formers who were freestyling. I listened with half an ear. They were quite good. One (Wayne, possibly?) was dissing the other because of his lacklustre performance as Dandy Dan in *Bugsy Malone*, which was pretty tame when you consider how heated and personal the battles get in real places. When Wayne had finished, his opponent – Doug? – stepped forward and launched into a tirade of rhymes that insulted Wayne's clothes, his haircut, his poor standard of homework, his bad luck when it came to women, his house, his possessions, his parents, his taste in music and the spot on his nose. When he'd finished the crowd erupted in cheers and the two boys shook hands and started to wrestle. I switched off at that point and lost myself in my book.

The next lesson was Chemistry, and as usual I sat on my own at a desk at the back paying no attention, drawing zombies in my exercise book. Mr Jones Chemistry had always affected the disposition of someone who knows an awful lot about their chosen subject but isn't particularly interested in communicating his knowledge to younger generations, and as spokesperson for the younger generation this suited me fine, as I had no plans to ever need the secrets of molecular bonding for anything. I quickly drifted away, lacking even the energy to mess with the blinds or snap chalk, the atmosphere was that oppressively dull.

I don't know what kind of music you'd have for Mr Jones Chemistry. Some comedic but slightly pathetic tuba, possibly? Or maybe not even music at all, just some insistent white noise with a slight irritating whine around the upper frequencies.

Anyway. Mr Jones Chemistry stands at the front of the class and reads to us from a textbook published in 1983. The kind of book that has cute little pictures and jokes and rhymes to appeal to 'the kids' and be self-referential and tap into the zeitgeist. The kind of book whose supposedly kid-friendly schtick fell embarrassingly flat when it was first published and now functions better as a historical curio than as an actual educational aid. Mr Jones reads. And he reads. And he reads. And he puts one of the annoying diagrams on the overhead projector and tells us to copy them down. He's a very tall thin man with tweed skin, and listening to him is like being in a car travelling at the same speed down a barren motorway with no variation for hours. And hours.

Finally I pop up at the back of the class and raise the pump-action shotgun that has spontaneously appeared in my hands. It's always a pump-action shotgun. I offer a suitable B-movie quip as I cock the weapon – hey deadhead, ker-chack, etc – and fire. My teacher has conveniently become a member of the living dead and his head explodes in a shower of—

'Stanly!' said Mr Jones, sounding as though he was repeating himself.

I snapped out of my daydream. Everybody was staring at me. Some were laughing because they thought I was deliberately pissing the teacher off, some of them were mocking me and doing zombie impressions, which was kind of fitting. I blinked stupidly. 'Mm? Sir?'

'Would you like to answer the question, for the benefit of the room?' His face was blank. It was a lot like my mind in that respect.

I blinked again. 'Um . . . fifty . . . newtons?'

Mr Jones nodded. 'When potassium is exposed to water the result is . . . fifty newtons?'

'No?'

My teacher took off his glasses and cleaned them. 'Stanly. Your habit of disappearing for long stretches of time in my lessons is becoming more and more annoying and in the end it's only hurting *you*. It makes no difference to me what mark you get in your exam. I'll still . . .'

He kept talking but his words were drowned out by comedy organ music in my head. I nodded and apologised in time to his droning, but I heard nothing that he said.

I was rehearsing my duel with Tybalt that lunchtime and I went to the Drama hall five minutes early. The only items of costume I had so far were a black trenchcoat (there was a sort of gangster motif when it came to the feud) and a pair of black fingerless gloves, but I did have the prop gun I would be using in the real thing. There was a screen at the back of the stage onto which various things such as cityscapes and building interiors would be projected, and Mr Hooper the IT teacher was doing something complicated with flashing lights and sound effects for the guns. Technically the whole thing was quite complex, and that was before you even got to the dialogue.

I practised the choreography that Miss Stevenson had meticulously prepared, spinning around and firing, ducking behind chairs. It was great fun. I was tempted to try doing it while flying, maybe lift up some desks and bits of scenery as impromptu shields, but if somebody saw me then I would have a lot of explaining – and possibly fleeing – to do. Daryl and I had agreed that it was imperative for me to keep my powers a secret, and I had no problem with that. It was quite cool. Plus, nearly being seen by that random guy in the woods had spooked me a bit.

Mark came in. His Tybalt costume consisted of a smart white suit and two guns. The way he moved was amazing, like Chow Yun-Fat or something, and he delivered his lines with a cold malevolence that some of the younger players actually found quite intimidating. It's funny because when he wasn't in character he was the nicest guy you could ever meet. He was a year older than me and one of the few cast members that I considered a friend. 'Aiit killer,' he said. 'Ready?'

I nodded. He shook his head and laughed. 'Why so serious?'

I shrugged, but allowed myself a small smile.

Now Miss Stevenson came in, juggling a folder, a bag, a clipboard and a cup of coffee. 'OK guys . . . oh good, glad you're ready. Nice to see a bit of initiative. Let's get going, shall we?'

That evening I got home and found my dad sweeping up broken china. I ignored him and went upstairs where Daryl was lying on my bed watching *The Usual Suspects*. 'What's going on?' I asked.

'I just heard them arguing,' said Daryl. 'Then something smashed and the door slammed. I think your mum's gone out.'

I threw my rucksack down and punched the wall, ripping out a cloud of dust and leaving a fist-shaped dent. The walls in our house were crap. 'This is so . . .' I couldn't finish. I hit the wall again, then threw myself into my computer chair and began to move random things with my mind, twirling stuffed animals and sharpening pencils, removing CDs from their cases and putting them back in again. Daryl switched off the DVD and watched me. Finally I lost control and yelled 'Shit!' and everything fell out of the air.

My mother didn't come back until after dinner. I'd made myself some rice and shoved some chicken nuggets under the grill. My father didn't talk much, just sat outside on the bench and smoked. I asked Mum if she was OK and she shook her head and went to bed.

Then, strangely enough, I went outside and sat by my dad. He looked at me and continued to smoke. 'That's bad for you,' I said.

He chuckled ruefully. 'So I've heard.' He took several more drags before flicking away the butt and chuckling again. 'That's my last one.' He didn't look at me.

I cocked my head. 'Really?'

He nodded. 'No more.'

'How many times have you said that before?'

'Never. Bit scary.'

We sat in silence for a few minutes. Then he said, 'Things aren't good right now.'

I didn't answer.

'It's my fault.'

An unusual moment of self-awareness. I shook my head. 'I don't know. It's everyone's fault, probably. It's mine. It's yours. It's Mum's. The only innocent person is probably Daryl.'

My dad looked up at the moon, which was slinking out from behind a cloud. The stars, dead thousands of years ago, flashed and winked like sequins in oil. 'That dog. Bloody talking dog. I can't believe I've never mentioned him to anyone.'

'No-one's ever asked?'

'Why would they? No-one ever comes round any more. Except for New Year.'

'I . . .'

'Don't worry. We're not angry.'

73

I was not equipped to be having this conversation. 'Can I have another driving lesson soon?'

'You don't need many more,' he said. 'I only gave you two over Christmas and you can do just about everything you need to do. You'll need to have official lessons of course, when you're seventeen, but . . .'

'You said I had a knack.'

'You've got more than a knack. Took me twice as long to get used to it.' He stood up and his tone changed from thoughtful to decisive. 'I'm going to apologise to your mother.'

At that moment I wanted to tell him. I wanted to tell both of them. I wanted to levitate a china cup or a slice of bread or a chair or a table or Daryl. I wanted to run up the side of the house and dance from our chimney to the neighbour's chimney. I wanted to show them the amazing things I could do.

But I didn't.

Later on, I was sitting on my bed. Daryl was watching the end of *The Usual Suspects*. 'So,' he said, as the credits rolled. 'I have a question.'

'Yeah, Kobayashi is a mug,' I said. 'We've had this conversation before . . .'

'Not about the film, jackass,' said Daryl. He switched off the TV and the player and turned to me. 'Your folks,' he said, sounding conspiratorial. 'They're . . . making up.'

I raised an eyebrow. 'Please don't suggest what I think you're—'

'I'm just sayin'.'

'Bleargh,' I said, recoiling at the idea that Daryl had forced into my head and fighting the accompanying visualisation with every ounce of mental strength. *Think pink elephants. Think pink elephants. Think pink elephants.* A herd of pink elephants trotted through my mind, shielding me from someone else's hideous and highly personal montage, and I threw Daryl a look that, had it been accompanied by a similarly dirty telekinetic attack, might well have killed him. '*Bleargh,*' I repeated.

74

Daryl shrugged. 'Just. Sayin'.'

'You are filthy and evil and depraved and disgusting.'

'You say that like it's a bad thing.' Daryl jumped off the bed and padded over to the shelf. 'Now . . . let's see. Ah! *Hard-Boiled*. Looks like fun.'

Black frame. Superimposed white titles: FRIDAY. Fade up on me sitting in the playground minding my own business.

Ben King walked over to me and stood in front of my bench with his arms folded. 'We should talk,' he said. He sounded fairly diplomatic but it was obviously an act. The concerned eyes, the friendly smile, the level tone. It was all cancelled out by his body language. He was itching to punch me.

'Fine,' I said.

'Can I sit down?'

'Dunno. Can you?'

He shrugged and sat down next to me. 'I know we don't get on very well.'

'Don't we?'

He laughed. 'You're really defensive, aren't you?'

'Only when attacked.'

'I'm not attacking. I just want to . . . clear the air. You know. Make peace, call a truce, whatever you want to call it.'

'I don't really want to call it anything.'

He raised his eyebrows. 'What is your problem?'

'I don't have a problem.'

'Is it because of Angelina still? That was ages ago, I'm not even with her any more. We're just good friends.'

I nodded. 'That's nice.'

He stood up. 'God! What *is* your problem? What is it that you have against me? What are you jealous of? Is it because—'

'I'm not jealous of anything,' I said, mildly, keeping my poker face on. 'I am not having a psychodrama about you. OK, I'll admit it, I don't like you very much. I think you're egotistical and two-faced. And it's not because I'm *jealous* of you. I couldn't give a piss

75

that you're in the top set for Maths and play the violin. Whoop-de-frigging-do. I'm doing great, feelin' fine, and the only reason that our little differences have escalated into *this* is because you wanted to be Romeo and I got the part. And that's a pretty lame grudge to break to new mutiny.' *Wow. That almost sounded like you never rehearsed it.*

Ben was obviously seething. His face was red and his fists were clenched. I felt an eruption of triumph that was almost immediately buried by shame. *Cut yourself some slack. He's a tool.*

'OK,' said Ben. 'Fine. I tried to be reasonable but you're obviously not into that.'

'Nope,' I said, with a happy-go-lucky grin. 'I'm an enemy of reason.'

'If I see you outside of school I'm going to beat the shit into you,' he said. His entire façade slipped away, his protective layer of self-righteousness became ashes and the ashes crumbled around his ankles.

'*Out* of me, surely?' I said.

'What?'

'Don't people beat the shit *out* of people, rather than into them?'

'Whatever! I don't give a shit!'

I shrugged, and grinned widely.

'What are you grinning at?' he said. 'I mean it. I'll break you in half.'

'OK!' I said, extending my smile to manic proportions.

He left, fuming, and I reached into my bag and took out my book and didn't think about him again. Probably.

Fade out.

I was still awake at one o'clock that night, unable to sleep but unable to properly concentrate on anything either. I'd remembered Smiling Joe, the creepy thing that Reuben and Jack had been discussing at Christmas, and spent a fairly diverting twenty minutes looking it up on the Internet. It was quite cool, at first.

Most people online seemed to call it Smiley Joe rather than Smiling Joe, and inially it looked sort of like online folklore, a creature that wandered the UK's cities doing evil deeds, accompanied by dodgy Photoshopped images and exclamation-mark-strewn blogs discussing its origins. I liked the weirdness, the conflicting stories people came up with, and the entertainingly gruesome artists' illustrations of the creature, which ranged from grinning spider creatures to a tall, spindly-limbed witch covered in mouths (Smiley Jo, naturally), but after a while it started to look as though the stories had sprung from real events, a series of kidnappings and murders in the Eighties and Nineties, and I lost my appetite for research. Once you knew that there was real tragedy and horror there it was a lot harder to enjoy the creepy stories, or laugh at unconvincing videos of 'sightings' that made Loch Ness Monster recordings look like Oscar-winning documentaries.

Stupid Internet.

Time to go out.

Leaving Daryl to sleep, I slipped out of the window and floated unsteadily along the road, past trees and houses outlined by orange and tinged with the sensual silver of the full moon. Somewhere, something howled. I reached the end of the road and crossed the bridge, my breath lingering in the chilled steel air. I needed to warm up so I began to run and fly, using low walls and fences and trees as springboards and leaping as far as I could, pushing my limits, trying to combine the movement with the rising technique that I'd almost perfected. At one point I reached an alley between two houses and bounced upwards from wall to wall, ending up on the roof of the bank. I ran along, ran, ran, and – *no, no, maybe not, maybe not, ah sod it* – leapt. My hair went *whoosh* and gravity gave up as I sailed through the air, landing on the roof of the off-license at the top of the high street. I sat there for five minutes until my breathing was back to normal and was about to descend when I noticed something.

Tref-y-Celwyn was built on hills, the steepest of which was also the main street. At the very top was a pub called the Horton Arms, and at that moment a girl of about nineteen was walking down from it, dressed in improbably little clothing considering how cold it was. She was walking pretty fast and a guy was chasing her, yelling her name. 'Julie! Julie! Come back here! Julie!'

She got to the clock tower, the guy still following her. He looked quite a bit older than her. I kept out of sight, watching, hoping it wasn't as bad as it looked, sneaking along the parapet. I chanced a glance back towards the Horton but nobody was coming.

The guy grabbed Julie and pushed her quite roughly against the phone box by the clock tower. She started to cry. 'Richard, just leave me alone . . .'

'What are you playing at?' he said, his voice low but quite terrifying. 'Carrying on with that prick from the Lion like some tart!'

'Let me *go* . . .'

He raised his hand. I couldn't believe there was nobody. Nobody could hear, or worse they *could* hear but couldn't be bothered to come and check. I was filled with fury at how uncaring this town was, and it mixed with the different strain of rage that I was feeling against this Richard bastard like two volatile chemicals, and I acted. I lashed out with a tentacle of mental energy, stopped his hand with my mind and threw him, and he slammed into the front of the antiques shop, hard. Julie screamed. The guy quickly regained his composure and rounded on her, spluttering. 'How the hell did you do that?'

Still nobody came. This was unbelievable. I kept my hood up, and as he advanced on the girl I took his feet out from under him, made a grabbing motion with my fist and psychically dragged him away from her. Julie wasted no time and bolted. I pulled my hood down over my face, darted along the roof, leapt across to the clock tower and ran down. Richard was still on the floor, looking shellshocked. 'If I see you try to hurt her or anyone again,' I said, adopting a deep, gravelly Welsh accent and trying not to think about how stupid it sounded, 'I will *end* you, boyo.'

'Who the bloody hell are you?' he snapped, sounding more Welsh – and more intimidating – than I did.

'Y Ddraig Ddu,' I said.

Richard stared blankly at me. 'A drag what?'

'It's Welsh for The Black Dragon,' I said.

He continued to stare at me.

'Forget it,' I said. 'Just . . . be nicer. From now on. OK?' And with that I ran off dramatically into the darkness.

Note to self: think of a better superhero name.

I didn't tell Daryl. I didn't tell anybody. Julie or Richard must have said something because for the next few days there were whisperings about peculiar goings-on in Tref-y-Celwyn, but there was no paper trail. Nothing led back to me. I was safe.

And I felt amazing. I hadn't thought at the time about how it might have turned out – he might have beaten her to a pulp or he might have calmed down and let her go. He might have caused me some serious damage. Julie might have turned out not to be a damsel in distress and lamped *him* one – generally, that was how girls rolled in Tref-y-Celwyn. They didn't take no shit from no-one. But whatever. I had intervened and I had helped and it was a good feeling. In my own minor way I felt like a hero, and that was enough. I didn't need to tell anyone and I didn't really want to because it seemed like it would cheapen it.

I was in a good mood all the way through Monday, despite it containing the most zombiefying series of lessons on my timetable, and I attacked *Romeo and Juliet* with renewed passion. One small act and I felt as though my life had been transformed. Maybe there was room for superheroics in my little Middle-of-Nowhere home after all.

CHAPTER EIGHT

There was a party at Mark Topp's house the following Friday. He lived outside Tref-y-Celwyn in a massive house with a huge garden and his parents were away, so he did what any self-respecting irresponsible teenager would do and threw a party. He invited me and initially I wasn't hugely enthusiastic, but in the end I decided to go.

The night was strangely warm considering how cold it had been for the last week, and the tikki torches and bonfires that Mark had lit helped things along nicely. People were dancing and laughing and talking everywhere, and although I recognised a lot of them, there were a great many unfamiliar faces, most of them older, most of them under various influences. Kloe was there, dancing wildly with a tall dreadlocked guy I didn't know, and I sat a little way off on a bench by the bonfire, drinking a beer and feeling odd green stomach flops every time I caught a glimpse of them. *That's new*, I thought. *No it's not*, I replied. *No it's not*, I agreed. *Hmm*, I added. I watched for a little while longer, curious about this new-but-not-new feeling, trying not to look as though I was watching, but I quickly realised that this behaviour was bordering on creepy. In fact, it had hopped over the border and was messing around on creepy's lawn. I turned away hurriedly, just as an older guy I didn't know stumbled onto the dancefloor. He was definitely the most wasted person at the party, which was quite an achievement, and he had a jug of something in his hand. In a flash, I saw what was giong to happen. He was going to stumble and spill his jug all over Kloe.

Or not.

I concentrated, and exerted just the right amount of force for him to fall sideways rather than forwards. The jug's contents splattered harmlessly into a bush rather than over Kloe's head, and the wasted guy tumbled onto the lawn. There was a chorus of laughter and clapping, and I smiled to myself. *Sick move.*

''Sup blud,' said Mark, making me jump. He fell down next to me with two beers in his hands and grinned widely. 'You're the life and soul of the party.'

'I try my best.'

'You're like Van Wilder right now.'

'Who?'

'Why aren't you dancing?' Mark took a generous gulp from one of his cans. 'There's plenty of girls here and I'm sure we could find one who appreciates enigmatic edginess, or whatever look it is you're going for.' He was obviously enjoying ribbing me, and although I felt like I should have been annoyed, I liked it. It felt like a normal friend-y thing; something I wasn't used to having with anyone other than Daryl. I summoned the blankest expression in my arsenal. 'Do you mean this look?'

Mark put his head on one side. 'Hmm. Was thinking more brooding-in-the shadows than post-lobotomy hangover.'

'Speaking of lobotomies,' I said, staying as blank as possible, 'your eyes seem to be having issues with focusing.'

Mark nodded, matching my serious face with a pretty serious one of his own. 'I have been drinking for quite a long time.'

I gave in and laughed. 'What time is it now?'

'Um . . . late.' He stood up and said, 'Come *on*!' The DJ had just dropped 'Play That Funky Music White Boy', and the dancefloor was buzzing. Mark crossed his eyes and flapped some jazz hands. '*Play* that funky music.' He paused, then added 'White boy.'

A gorgeous purple-haired girl about Mark's age came prancing over and kissed him. 'Nice moves, Mark. S'like *My Left Foot*.' She was American.

'Thanks,' said Mark. 'Bethany, this is Stanly.'

Bethany smiled and waved. 'Hey!'

'Hi,' I said, feeling shy and awkward.

'Why are you sitting on your own?'

'He's brooding,' said Mark. 'He does it really well. I'm sure if we left him to it he could do it for the rest of the night.'

'Well, that's awesome and all,' said Bethany, 'but no substitute for dancing like an idiot. Come on, come dance!'

I was struck with a mental image of me falling over everybody, spilling beer over all the girls, especially Kloe, then stumbling into the bonfire and igniting like dry grass. 'Um . . . not a good idea,' I said.

'What are you?' asked Bethany. 'Some kinda klutz?'

'He's no klutz,' said Mark. 'You should see this cat move! We have a duel in *Romeo and Juliet* and he does all this twirling stuff, he moves like a . . . um . . . thing that moves! Like really well!'

'How much have you had to drink?' asked Bethany, rubbing noses with Mark.

'Not enough!' he declared, in a Shakespearean baritone, before draining his beer, throwing it away and beating his chest like King Kong.

'Great,' said Bethany. 'And to think I came over here to *escape* from ridiculous drunken frat boys.'

'No such luck.' Mark switched to an over-exaggerated American college bro accent. 'Come *on*, dude! Let's, like, initiate this poor freshman.' He leaned forwards and grabbed one of my hands and Bethany grabbed the other, and they dragged me out onto the makeshift dancefloor (actually a huge patio with lots of empty plant pots). A guy called Rob was in charge of the decks, and he abruptly switched from Wild Cherry to drum and bass, which I'd only recently come across. I hadn't quite made up my mind about it yet, but as everyone went from funky dancing to full-on raving – which was funny to see – and Bethany and Mark, who were still holding my hands, began to dance, I felt something akin to a *whoooooosh* . . .

Hmm. I think I like it.

An hour – or maybe many hours – later, we went inside. There were two people from my year necking on the pool table. 'Hey!' said Mark. 'We have sofas, bathrooms and spare rooms for that. Get off, game time.'

We had a few games and Bethany destroyed both of us. Then we went back outside and danced some more, and spliffs were passed around. This time I declined because I didn't think I could handle coming across another talking pet on the way home, and as I watched various people smoking I wondered for a second where Mark's parents were. *Who cares*, I thought. *Yeah*, I agreed.

I didn't actually go to bed, in the end. At eight o'clock the next morning the three of us were still talking, and I was wondering when Kloe had left and wishing we'd exchanged more than the two shy smiles we'd managed, when suddenly Bethany looked at her watch and exclaimed, '*Shit*. My train's in like an hour.'

'Train?' I asked.

'I'm going back to New Orleans,' she said.

'To wear that ball and chain,' sang Mark, far too loudly.

'*Shhhh*,' someone mumbled from the corner. 'Sleeping.'

Bethany ran upstairs and I turned to Mark. 'What's going on with you and her?'

'She's my pen friend,' said Mark. 'Or my pencil friend. And sometime email friend. Depends on what mood we're in. She's been staying for a fortnight and she goes home today.'

'Shame.'

'Ain't it just.' Mark stood up and clutched at his head. '*Oooh* . . . headrush. Coffee?'

'I hope that'll be enough,' I said, suddenly realising how rough I felt. 'Can caffeine be injected intravenously?'

'I couldn't tell you,' said Mark. 'Milk and sugar?'

'Both. Lots. You know, I didn't even realise there was a direct train line from Tref-y-Celwyn to New Orleans.'

'Not quite direct. I think you have to, like, change at King's Cross or something.'

Mark, Bethany and I walked into town and waited on the platform for the train, which ended up being fifteen minutes late. Bethany gave me a hug. 'Really nice to meet you!' she said.

'You too,' I said.

'I'm sorry we couldn't hang more.'

'Me too.'

She turned to Mark and they embraced, kissing a lot, while I tried to look everywhere but at them. Finally they had to break apart and she got on the train, and waved at us as it pulled away, Mark waving back so hard I thought he might bust his wrist. Bethany disappeared quickly, and I patted Mark on the shoulder. 'Come on,' I said. 'I'll buy you breakfast.'

We had bacon sandwiches and more coffee at the bakery, and then I said, 'Do you want to come to my house?'

Mark nodded. 'Sure. Don't think I'm ready to face the pit of filth that mine has become.'

My parents weren't awake yet and we sneaked upstairs, and I hovered (not literally) awkwardly while Mark inspected the place. 'I like your room,' he said. 'Nice posters.'

'Thanks,' I said. Daryl was lying on the bed and I could tell he was itching to talk to me, and a voice in my head said *screw it*. I nodded at Daryl. He shook his head. I nodded again. Mark noticed, and raised an eyebrow. 'Are you communicating with your dog?'

I nodded harder. Daryl shrugged and rolled his eyes. 'Fine. Hi Mark. I'm Daryl, Stanly's dog. I can talk.'

Mark raised his eyebrows. 'Oh. Um. That's . . . um.'

'Yeah,' I said. 'Well. I thought you'd like to know.'

Mark looked at me. 'That's pretty good. I didn't know you could . . . ventriloquise. Is that the right word?'

'No,' my dog and I said in unison.

That clinched it. Mark's eyes widened, and he walked over to

Daryl and sat down next to him, fascination, amazement and disbelief fighting for possession of his face. He patted him gingerly on the head. 'You are . . . the luckiest person I know.'

'I am?' asked Daryl.

'Not you,' said Mark. He looked at me. '*You.*'

'Why?' I asked.

'You have a talking dog. A dog. That *talks*. That's the coolest thing that there has ever been, in the history of ever. I would *kill* to have a talking dog.'

'You would?'

Mark frowned. 'Um . . . depends who I had to kill, I suppose.'

Daryl made a strange canine *hurrumph* sound. 'I'm obviously not that special then.'

Mark looked apologetic. 'Oh . . . that's not what I meant! Um . . . I'm sorry—'

'Ignore him,' I said. 'He's messing with you.'

Daryl laughed. 'He speaks the truth.'

Mark laughed as well. 'This is amazing!'

'You're taking it better than I thought you might,' I said.

'Did you think I was going to cry "heretic"? It's amazing! Your dog talks! It's . . . it's amazing!'

'You said that already,' said Daryl. 'But thanks, feel free to say it more. I'm going to watch *Reservoir Dogs,* if that's cool with y'all.'

'He likes *Reservoir Dogs*?' asked Mark.

'He *loves Reservoir Dogs*,' I said. 'And *Dog Day Afternoon,* and *Man Bites Dog.* And *Lady and the Tramp.* He goes all soppy over the spaghetti bit.'

'Unbelievable,' said Mark, as Daryl put the DVD on. 'Amazing.'

At some point I figured I'd have to introduce Mark to my parents. They were having breakfast downstairs, eating eggs and bacon over what sounded like a civilised discussion, and they both looked surprised when we came in. 'You're back!' said my mother. 'I wasn't expecting you back this early.'

'Have a good time?' asked my father.

'Yeah,' I said. 'Great.'

'What time did you go to bed?' asked my mother, managing to look both crafty and innocent at the same time.

Mark and I exchanged guilty glances. 'Um . . . we didn't,' I said.

My parents looked amused, even my dad. 'Misspent youth,' said my mother. 'So, are you going to introduce us?'

'Mark,' I said.

'Hi,' said Mark. 'The party was at my house.'

They shook hands. 'Hi Mark,' said Dad. 'Are you—'

Don't say 'are you Stanly's friend?', I thought, *because if you do I am going to—*

'— in Stanly's year?' my dad finished.

'Sixth form,' said Mark. 'I'm Tybalt in the play.'

'Oh, lovely,' said my mother. 'Yes, Stanly told us about the play.'

Oh bollocks.

'He's really good,' said Mark.

Oh shit.

'Well I'm glad,' said my dad. 'He's always been quite artistic, but he's never really shown it off like this.'

Mark frowned in confusion. 'Um . . . well it's more performance really, but I get what you mean, I suppose you do have to be artistic.'

Now my parents were confused. 'Is he on stage?' asked my mother. 'I was . . . he told us . . . Stanly, you told us you were just helping out backstage.'

Mark looked at me and raised both eyebrows, and I tried to tell him with my eyes that I'd rather they didn't know, but if he understood he certainly didn't pay any attention. 'He's Romeo,' he said.

'Wow,' said Mark, later. 'I can't believe you didn't tell them.'

'I told them I was involved with the play,' I said, searching through a box for one of my many sketch pads. 'They asked what I was doing, I said I was helping with scenery design and stuff. They were pleased but didn't say much.'

'I still don't get it.'

I fished the pad out of the box and flicked through it before answering. More zombies. A rainbow. A rain of fire. Animals. Characters from *Trainspotting*. A turtle. I looked at Mark. 'I knew that if I told them then they'd just go "Oh my God, now you can make some real friends" and I'm sick to the back teeth of that.'

'Sick of what?' asked Mark.

I sat down on my bed. Did I want to open up? It didn't matter. Daryl did it for me. 'He's never really had proper friends,' he said. 'He's always been a loner and that really worries and/or pisses his parents off, delete as applicable. They're always nagging him to make friends. When they gave him that guitar—'

'Oh yeah,' said Mark, taking the guitar. 'I was going to ask if I could have a go.'

'Knock yourself out,' I said.

'As I was saying,' said Daryl, as Mark fiddled with the guitar, 'when they gave him the guitar they figured he'd start a band and make friends. He didn't. Then when he got the part of Romeo *he* figured that if he told them they'd say it was a wonderful opportunity to – guess what? – make friends. And it has been, kind of. You're probably the first person he's actually invited over since . . . well, before I knew him.'

I reached out and tried to smother Daryl with a pillow, but he wriggled away and laughed. 'He gets a bit touchy sometimes.'

Mark pulled off a complicated riff and shrugged. 'I don't know why you've developed this whole loner thing. It's not like you're genuinely antisocial and apathetic and all that.'

'I like my space,' I said, uncomfortable with being analysed. 'Part of being an only child, I suppose.' I took a few more sketch pads out of the box and started to look through them.

Mark shrugged. 'Fair enough.' He tried another riff and it came out jagged. 'Whoops. It's up to you, mate, I ain't here to change anyone's ideology. But I definitely think it's more fun to be fun.'

I didn't say anything, and we sat and he played guitar and I drew and Daryl made us laugh.

That night I went out into town, hoping for some trouble. I kept to the rooftops, and I was in my black ensemble with the hood up, so there was no danger of being noticed. After about an hour, I was disappointed to conclude that everything was peaceful, and that nobody was in trouble.

'Come on then! Come on! Let's bloody go!'

Me and my big mouth.

I followed the shouting to the car park behind the Saint George, one of the pubs that Tref-y-Celwyn has in abundance. Two guys were squaring off, spitting beer-soaked obscenities at one another. They were both in their early twenties and were swaying heroically, and I watched for a minute, trying to work out what to do. There were people coming out of the pub and I thought for a second that maybe they'd try and split them up, but no. We got 'Come on, smash his face in' and 'Don't let that prick talk to you like that' and 'Break his neck' and 'Punch his teeth down his throat' and many more highly constructive suggestions, and suddenly the two guys leapt at each other, and I heard the impacts of fists against faces. I wanted to dive in. I wanted to psychically throw them to opposite ends of the car park and then maybe fly among the on-lookers, knocking them down with my mind and my fists. I wanted to stand there at the end, silent and still at the centre of a circle of collapsed, moaning drunks.

But I didn't. I couldn't. Instead I jumped off the roof, landed by the phone box next to the clock tower and phoned the police to tell them what was going on. Their response time was legendarily useless, but it was worth a shot.

For once they were prompt, and the high street was suddenly lit by the blue lights of their car. It roared into the Saint George's car park and two large officers got out and headed for the fray. I had lost my appetite for crime-fighting (not that you could really call it that) and went home, slid into bed and dreamed about smashing glass and broken teeth.

The next morning I switched on the TV and saw a news report: a house in east London had been broken into. A family of four had been living there and the parents had been murdered, the children were missing and there was speculation that no forensic evidence had been found. Just a lot of smashed glass (déjà vu), a man and a woman with broken necks and two missing eight-year-olds. I switched the TV off and sat boiling, thinking about how wasted I was in sodding Tref-y-bloody-Celwyn while stuff like that was going on elsewhere. I was deluding myself, though. Even if I did become London's Dark Avenger, I couldn't hope to battle every criminal and psychopath operating there. As much as I'd enjoyed entertaining the possibility, in truth it was a dumb and probably unhealthy fantasy, so I had scrambled eggs and did some Drama coursework badly, and brooded.

CHAPTER NINE

THE PERFORMANCE DATE was closing in. Rehearsals were becoming more intense and we were being nagged mercilessly about revision by every teacher. I kept up with the lessons I enjoyed, but my attitude to the others didn't change – I sat, practically catatonic, through every science, maths, RE and German lesson, feeling information drift into one ear and immediately exit from the other, without even considering leaving anything behind. Teachers had mostly given up telling me off for zoning out. By now I think they were relieved I turned up at all.

On the last Thursday in February I was sitting on my bench at school, reading, when I heard raised voices. This was nothing new – quiet voices would be more unusual on the playground at break time – but something made me look up. The two Sams, and a third kid called Dan, had cornered a boy from the year below who had had the temerity to wear a Slipknot hoody over his school jumper. They were giving him the usual treatment – the stream of homophobic insults, elegantly counterpointed by questions about what vile sexual perversions he got up to with the 'Goth sluts' in his year who liked 'all that shit music', the comments about his mum, the threats – and the boy was just taking it, resigned, just wanting it over with, and as I watched I felt that anger rising again, the rage I'd felt when they'd ambushed me after rehearsal, that feeling of *how dare they*, fury at what kinds of people got their kicks by degrading and terrifying those who were weaker, but it was mixed with the frustration I'd been feeling lately, the feeling of power-lessness, of *uselessness,* an unholy chemical reaction, and God at that moment I wanted more than anything to reveal my powers to the school, I wanted it so much that I almost ripped my book in half from gripping it so hard. I wanted to soar into the air and rush towards them, tear my bench from the ground and hurl it at them, take their legs out from under them, and then I wanted to pick them up, psychically wedgie them and parade them through the corridors, smashing windows as I flew, picking up any other bullies I happened to come across, the rest of the abusive *scum* that crawled around in this school, I wanted to drag them all kicking and screaming to the canteen, rub their faces in the bins, overturn the tables to make a dock and hover over them, eyes glowing, judge and jury and—

I snapped out of the fantasy so abruptly that I jerked where I sat. I couldn't. Couldn't do any of that. *No. Not happening.*

Calm the hell *down, Stanly.*

Of course I couldn't do any of that. What I could do, however, was get up and stride towards them with my best mean face on. I'd heard some of their Neanderthal crew talking about me since that first fight, they'd used words like *psycho* and *nutter.* Sitting on his own in the playground, not talking to people. Fighting. They thought there was something wrong with me. *Good.*

'Oi,' I said.

They turned, and there was actual fear there. They really were scared of me.

If only they knew.

'Fuck off,' I said. Part of me kind of wanted them to take offence, to try and fight me – *I could tell Daryl I was defending myself, that'd be OK surely* – but they didn't. They just looked at one another and sloped off, sneering. If I hadn't been so angry, I might even have laughed at how easily, how abruptly I'd taken away their power. The kid in the Slipknot hoody muttered a thank you and scampered away, and I went and got my stuff from my bench, headed inside and found an empty music practise room, where I psychically battered the shit into a drumkit with a pair of ragged sticks.

That evening, Eddie called again. I was upstairs fiddling with my guitar and Daryl – who I hadn't told about my little episode earlier in the day – was watching *Fight Club* and reciting the entire script at the same time. The companionable silence was so noisy that I didn't even notice the phone until my mum called up the stairs. 'It's Eddie for you,' she said, neutrally. I was surprised, partly because I hadn't heard it ring, but mostly because Eddie's call was actually being passed on, and not fielded away. 'Oh,' I called. 'Thanks.' I picked it up and waited for the click as Mum hung up the down-stairs receiver. Didn't particularly want her listening in. 'Hello?'

'Hey, Stanly. How's it going?'

'Yeah, fine. How are you?'

'OK, thanks. Just . . . checking you're all right.'

'Why? What's the matter? Why wouldn't I be all right?'

'Nothing. Just checking.'

I gestured at Daryl to switch off the volume on the DVD. 'Are *you* all right?' I asked.

'Yeah, fine, fine. Just got a feeling.'

'And why did you get this feeling?'

'I just . . . I just did.'

'What do you *mean*?' I was starting to lose patience. 'Why do you have to be so bloody cryptic? Why can't you just tell me what's going on?'

'Sorry, Stanly. I just . . . you've got your abilities now. And as far as I know I'm the only other person you know who knows.'

'You are.'

'So I feel a bit responsible. That's all.'

'That's all?'

'That's all.'

'There's not some mysterious danger you're trying to keep from me?'

'Not as far as I know.'

'Are you sure?'

'Yes!'

'OK then.'

'Great.' Eddie paused. 'Well . . . I'd better go.'

'No wait! Eddie—'

'Sorry mate, I need to get to work. I'll call again. Take care of yourself.'

Click.

Saturday. I was walking on my own in the woods, absently picking up twigs and pebbles and tossing them about. The sky was a watery shade of blue and soft sunbeams highlighted the skeletal trees, and every now and then I heard birds disagreeing in sweet voices.

CRACK.

I stopped and looked around. There was nobody there, but I could definitely hear rustling and footsteps a little way away, and low humming. I had a feeling that I recognised the voice.

I looked up at the tree next to me. It was over thirty feet tall, not as high as some of them could get, but it would serve my purpose. I ran up the trunk and hid in the topmost branches, wishing for spring and the cover of leaves. It wasn't until I was settled in what seemed like a great hiding place that I remembered how well this had worked out last time.

Too late now though, as somebody had just appeared over a hill of dead leaves and bracken. It was Ben King. I rolled my eyes. He didn't live in Tref-y-Celwyn. What was he doing here? These were my woods. They had been since I was a child. I silently descended from the tree and dropped the last few feet without the aid of my powers, and Ben spun around. He scowled. 'Oh. It's you.'

'Yeah,' I said, casually. 'How's it going? What are you up to?'

'Walking,' he said.

'Mmm,' I nodded. 'I thought you lived outside Llangoroth?'

'I do,' he said. 'I walked a long way.' He said it as if I would be impressed.

I nodded again. 'OK. Fair enough. Carry on.' I turned to leave but Ben said, 'Hey. Wait.'

I turned back. 'What?'

His face was complicated. Part resentment, part . . . respect? And also part something else . . . something I couldn't read. 'Yes?' I prompted.

'I really do think that we should sort this out,' he said.

'I don't,' I said. 'I think we should just stay away from each other.'

'It's going to be tricky,' he said. 'I'll be at the play every night.'

'Well, that's up to you,' I said. 'I'm not going to quit just because one member of the audience doesn't like me.'

'I think lots of members of the audience don't like you,' said Ben, 'but that's not what I mean. I'm going to be there for Kloe.'

'OK,' I said, frowning with confusion, and then understanding. 'So . . . are you two . . . having a thing?' It was the first I'd heard of it.

'Well,' he said, smiling smugly. 'We're . . . she's . . . yeah, we are.'

'That's nice,' I said, forcing a jovial smile. 'But nothing to do with me. Be there for Kloe, that's great of you, really. I commend you for your exquisite manliness. But there's nothing to sort out. Like I said, let's just stay away from each other.'

'She's mine,' he said.

'Cool,' I said. 'Good for you. I'm not interested in her.' It came out sounding more offensive towards Kloe than I'd intended. And I wasn't convincing myself at all. I could feel that jealousy coming back, stirring in my mind like a sleeping dragon. I could feel its heat, and I knew Ben could too. 'Just make sure you're not,' he said.

Aha, I thought. *Now I see what it's all about.* I allowed myself a small smile.

'What does that mean?' Ben snapped.

'Nothing,' I said. 'I just . . . I think I've got you figured out. That's all.'

'Really?' he said, shifting, looking like he was ready for a fight. 'What have you "figured out", then?'

'Do you really want to know?' I was dying to tell him, I'm sorry to say.

'Absolutely.'

'You're worried that I'm going to try and steal Kloe from under your nose,' I said. 'Like I nabbed the part.'

Ben's scowl was pure volcanic hatred; his voice dripped with it. 'You'd better not even be fucking *contemplating* it.' To be perfectly honest, I wasn't even fucking contemplating it, but all I did was shrug. 'Whatever,' I said. 'Ciao.' I turned and walked away, and as I walked I heard him pick something up, heard him throw it. *Felt* him throw it. Yeah. There was definitely something sixth sense-y going on. Without looking I psychically moved whatever it was, altering the trajectory by about a quarter of an inch, and the rock missed my head by millimetres and sailed past, arcing down the bank and bouncing off piles of stones and fallen tree trunks. I considered turning around and seeing just how much damage my superpowered mind could do to someone Ben's size, but common sense prevailed, and I kept walking without breaking stride or even glancing back. He couldn't possibly have realised that I'd done it. I tried to make my back look nonchalant, but I certainly didn't feel that way.

So he's throwing rocks now.

This might be bad.

Freeze-frame on school canteen. Caption: Monday. Un-freeze. I'd forgotten to make sandwiches today, so grabbed a burger and some rice – the only genuinely edible-looking items on the menu – and sat on my own. I was halfway through eating when Kloe appeared and sat down opposite me. 'Hi,' she said, brightly. She had pasta.

'Hi,' I said. *Don't be awkward. Don't be awkward.*

'Are you ready?' she asked. 'Three days to go!'

'I think we're all ready, pretty much,' I said. *Don't be awkward.*

95

'Do you . . . reckon it's going to go well?' *Don't be awkward.*

'Yeah!' she grinned. 'I mean . . . up until last week it was looking a bit bad, but then we had the dress rehearsal and it all just came together. It's amazing. I think it's going to be amazing. Well, when I'm not panicking and nearly hyperventilating I think it's going to be amazing.'

I smiled. 'Me too. To . . . both. Of those things.' *Don't be awkward!*

Kloe swallowed a mouthful of pasta and shook her head. 'God. I've been getting *so* stressed lately.'

'Really?'

'Yeah! Haven't you? Just thinking about performing the play makes me nervous. And all the coursework as well. You've not been getting stressed?'

Really and truthfully, I hadn't been, but now I realised that I'd agreed with her about panicking, and I hurriedly nodded. 'Yeah,' I said. 'I mean . . . a bit. Mostly it's OK. But yeah, the odd panic, definitely.' *DON'T. BE AWK—*

OH. GOD. JUST. SHUT. UP. PLEASE. BRAIN.

'You're so lucky,' said Kloe. 'It's even been affecting my dreams.'

'Yeah?'

'Yeah! I had one last night, it was *so* weird, I was performing to an empty room . . . at least I thought it was empty. Then I realised there was actually someone there, in the front row, this little girl in red pyjamas just . . . watching. Really freaked me out.' She ate some more pasta.

I was at a loss. *This is why you don't talk to girls.* I offered a sort of non-committal 'Dreams are weird' response and tried to avoid eye contact. *You absolute berk.* Now I noticed that Ben was sitting a few tables away with a group of his friends, most of whom I actually quite liked. He was glowering at me. 'I think your boyfriend's getting jealous,' I said. *Finally, something to say. Not ideal, but something.*

'You what?' asked Kloe.

'Boyfriend,' I said. 'Ben. I don't think he likes you sitting with me.'

96

Her face was a mask of bewilderment. 'Ben?'

'Ben King?' I asked. 'Aren't you two, like . . . going out?'

'No!' she said. 'Who told you that?'

'He did,' I said. 'At the weekend. I met him and he basically said you two were . . . going out.'

'He didn't!' *Hmm. Interesting.*

'He said . . . he said "Kloe's mine". And got pretty arsey, to be honest.' I couldn't help feeling a lot better, even though Kloe did not look happy.

'That lying bastard,' she said, anger trickling into her voice like oil in a spring. 'He tried it on with me at Katy's party and I basically told him to shove it up his arse and now he's . . . prick!'

'Kloe—' *Have I gone too far?*

Nope.

She stood up and turned around, scanning for the Prince of Lies. The two of them locked eyes, and Ben's face switched from simmering resentment to 'oh shit' in about half a second. *To be fair, it wasn't the best-laid plan, was it pal?*

'You lying little *shit*!' yelled Kloe.

Silence. No more knives and forks, no more indefinable hubbub of chatter, no more chewing and swallowing. If there'd been someone playing bar room piano in the corner, now would have been their cue to stop. Everyone was looking over in our direction, and I could see a number of teachers standing up, some of them looking like they were about to come over. Ben stood up, raising his hands in a placatory gesture. 'Kloe—'

'How many more people have you told?' asked Kloe, volume rising, her face getting quickly redder. 'Have you been saying it to everyone? Does everyone think that I'm your *girlfriend*? Did you tell them how you tried to stick your hands down my pants at Katy's party, you nasty little pervert?'

'I was just—'

'Fuck. *You*!' She slapped Ben around the face so hard that he staggered backwards a few paces. It made a stunningly loud noise, and left a blossoming crimson rose on his cheek. Teachers were shouting but Kloe ignored them and stormed out of the hall. Ben looked stunned . . . and then his eyes landed on me, and the mercury burst free of the thermometer.

We have just lost cabin pressure.

Please put your tray and seat backs in their upright positions.

Place your head between your legs and kiss your—

'*Asshole!*' he bellowed, running towards me.

'Me?' I said. 'What did I do? You're the one who did the lying, you dick—'

Oddly, Ben wasn't keen to debate this line of enquiry. He seemed rather more keen on yanking my table aside, dragging me to my feet by the collar of my polo shirt, driving his knee into my stomach and hitting me in the face. I fell to the ground, tasting copper in my throat and on my tongue, struggling to breathe. My jaw hurt. People were cheering, some were yelling 'Pwn him, Stanly' and others were yelling 'Kick his ass, Ben' and the teachers were just generally shouting. Mr Jones PE was coming towards us and Ben was ignoring him, too busy aiming a kick at my face.

Right. So this is what's happening, then.

I grabbed his foot and pushed him backwards hard, and he lost his balance and fell onto a table, scattering plates of food. I got to my feet, suddenly feeling quite righteously pissed-off, clenching and unclenching my fists and making a major effort not to psychically blast all the tables aside and bounce Ben around the room. *Should really lob him out of the window or something.*

No. Can't. Remember?

Couldn't do it to Dan and the Sams, can't do it now.

Typical. I'd never been in a fight before I'd got my powers, and since they'd materialised I'd been in *two*, and had barely even been able to use them.

S'not fair.

Ben jumped off the table and ran at me again, and I compromised by grabbing him by both shoulders and slamming my head forwards, cracking him right on the bridge of his nose. *This seems to be becoming my signature move.* No blood came out this time, but he covered his face with his hands and sprawled on the floor, rolling around, moaning in pain.

FINISH HIM!

No. Don't.

I stood there, hands shaking, breathing deeply, trying to calm myself down, the voices of teachers and students a muffled blur at the very edge of my perception. Zen. Enlightenment. The philosophy of calm.

I am a detached, dispassionate observer.

I am Stanly's sense of self-satisfaction.

It's funny how things that seem major at the time can end up being pretty small. As I walked towards the headmaster's office, flanked by two silent teachers, my thoughts were clear. I was going to be suspended, my parents would be called, it would go on my permanent record, Ben's parents would come, maybe the police. The usual suspects, and all the trouble they'd bring. But I didn't care about that. For one thing, it was all heavily diluted by the memory of Kloe slapping Ben around the face, an image I knew I would treasure forever.

No, the only thing I was worried about was being taken off the play three days before opening night and leaving Miss Stevenson in an impossible position. *Well. That and ruining all of Kloe's hard work.*

And not getting to act with her.

And . . . hmm.

No, I couldn't possibly do that to them, and it was the first thing I said to Mr Dylan (the headmaster) when I got in there. 'Will I be taken off the play?'

The answer was no. Mr Dylan had talked to Ben and Ben had done his noble thing. It was his fault, he had started it, I'd been defending myself, he didn't want to involve anyone, he didn't want me to be punished, he shouldn't have done what he did, he was sorry, blah, blah, blah. I was almost angry with him for being so selfless, because I knew that he didn't regret attacking me. OK, I'm being a hypocrite because I didn't regret attacking him either, but it's the principle of the thing. Possibly.

I got away with a lunchtime detention, probably on the grounds of it being a first offence. I can't describe the relief. I spoke to Kloe, who was still seething, and told her about the fight. 'Good,' she said, and I was delighted inside, and before I walked away I was pretty sure we held eye contact slightly longer than normal. I was also pretty sure I saw something in her eyes. Some sort of . . . something. It made funny things happen in my stomach so I decided to make a sharp exit. 'Stanly?' she said.

I spun around a little too enthusiastically. 'Yeah?'

'I . . . why would you think I'd want to be with Ben?'

'Um. I . . . dunno. He's nice, I suppose? And . . . I mean . . .'

'No, he's not nice,' said Kloe, as if I were challenged in some way.

'No . . . I suppose he's not.' I shrugged. 'I dunno. I guess . . . I don't know why he'd make it up? And I mean, you and me don't know each other *that* well, and . . .' *Aaaaargh please say something before my out of control bibbling kills us both, and please can it be what I want to hear, please, thanks!*

'Well, I don't like him,' said Kloe. 'Not at all.' And she smiled, and I knew – or at least I was pretty sure that I knew – what the smile meant, and I smiled back, probably far wider than could be considered cool under the circumstances.

'Brilliant,' I said. 'I . . . I don't like him either.'

When I got home I gave Daryl a blow-by-blow account of the fight, which didn't take long. 'It's about bloody time,' he said. I was tempted to tell him about my little moment with Kloe, but I doubted that he would consider 'I don't like him either' to be as much of a deal-sealer as I thought it was.

It definitely was, though.

Probably.

CHAPTER TEN

THURSDAY ARRIVED, ALONG with a cocktail of trepidation, excitement and a strange kind of weightlessness. I coasted through lessons, my eyes lingering on the clocks and on my watch longer than they did on questions regarding alkanes and interquartile ranges and what the character of Candy brings to *Of Mice and Men*. The final lesson of the day was Drama, and as Tamsin and Dani were both away I helped Miss Stevenson set things up while the rest of the class practised their devising. We didn't say much to each other and I could sense that she was angry about something. Finally, when we were behind the curtain and no-one could see or hear, I asked her what was wrong.

She stopped in the middle of lifting a stool, put it down and turned to me. 'I was so angry when I found out about you and Ben.'

'Why?' I asked, even though I knew.

'Imagine if Mr Dylan hadn't been so lenient,' said Miss Stevenson, her face red. 'Imagine if he'd taken you off the play. What would I have done then? You're essential. Without you, there would be no play. There almost wasn't.'

'Mr Dylan wouldn't have done that,' I said, although that wasn't the point and I knew it.

'That's not the point,' said Miss Stevenson, 'and you know it.'

'I'm sorry,' I said. 'It's complicated how it happened . . . and that's the first thing I asked him, anyway.'

'What?'

Ah, I thought. *Our dear headmaster neglected to mention this.*
'That was the first thing I said when I went into his office,' I said.
'I asked him if I was going to be taken off the play. Do you think
I'd have left you in the lurch like that if there was anything I could
have done? I would have taken any punishment, just so long as . . .
it was the only thing I was worried about. This play is currently the
most important thing in my life.' I wasn't exaggerating. Right now,
flight and telekinesis were firmly in second and third place.

What about Kloe?

Shut up, brain.

Miss Stevenson didn't say anything for a minute, but the redness
was draining slowly from her cheeks. Finally she said, 'I should
hope so,' and smiled.

I smiled too. 'And if I'd let Ben beat me up, we would have had
a Romeo with a black eye and possibly some teeth missing. I doubt
Juliet would have given him a second glance if he'd looked like
that.'

'Don't push your luck,' said Miss Stevenson.

'Sorry,' I said, but now we were both almost laughing. 'He did
kind of start the fight as well, to be fair, I only finished it—'

'I *said,* don't push your luck!'

'Yes, Miss.' I saluted. 'It's going to go *off.*'

'It had better.'

I hung around the Drama Hall reading until half past five, then
donned my costume (black cargo trousers, a white long-sleeved T-
shirt, black trenchcoat, black shoes and fingerless gloves), put my
prop gun into the shoulder holster that somebody had found for
me and sat waiting to be called for make-up. After about twenty
minutes Mark came over to me, along with another Sixth Former
named Becky, who was playing Juliet's mother. 'Have you seen
this?' she asked, handing me a newspaper clipping. It was a very
short piece about the play and Kloe and I were the only ones mentioned by name. I nodded. She looked at Mark with an amused
expression. 'You were right.'

'I told you,' said Mark. 'Nothing phases him.'

'There was one thing I noticed,' said Becky. 'I think they spelled your name wrong.'

I looked. S-T-A-N-L-Y. No, that was right. 'That's how my name is spelled,' I said.

'Really?' asked Becky. 'Oh. Why?'

'My parents thought it would be interesting,' I said. 'Or at least, my mum did. I think my dad wanted me to be called Ron.'

'You're not a Ron,' said Mark.

'I know,' I said.

My parents were coming tonight and Saturday night, and somehow I had managed to persuade the school to let them bring Daryl on the Saturday. I didn't know whether Ben would be there tonight. A great many people were going for the opening, people who I had just recently started to call friends. It was as though my life was suddenly developing several years too late. I was happy.

I got made up and thought about my first lines. They were there, crystal clear. No problem. Satisfied, I went backstage and found Kloe fiddling with some props. She saw me and smiled, and my stomach did more funny things. 'I'm really nervous,' she said. 'Are you?'

I wasn't, but I nodded anyway because I felt like that would look better, which was all kinds of pathetic. Kloe smiled a tense smile, then checked her watch and gasped. 'Oh my God! We're starting in fifteen minutes!' She hugged me. 'Good luck.'

'You too,' I said, hugging her back. By my calculations, the hug lasted about two seconds longer than it would have if there weren't something between us, and I could still feel it long after she'd broken away and headed for the changing rooms.

Everyone assembled backstage, and Miss Stevenson gave us a very short pep talk before heading out to the front. I chanced a quick glance around the side of the curtain and saw that the place was absolutely full, although I deliberately didn't focus on specific faces, not wanting to recognise anyone. Then Lauren, the Social

Inclusion teacher, who was doubling as prop mistress, said, 'Go out into the hall, we can't afford to clutter up back here.'

I nodded and went and sat by Harry Taylor, who was playing Paris. Neither of us said anything. Time passed. People talked non-stop around us but I just sat calmly and thought about everything. I was perfectly at peace. It was an amazing feeling. I suddenly felt like—

The door opened and Lauren poked her head through and said that I was due on stage.

I got up. Various people whispered good luck and I thanked them tonelessly, then went and stood behind the curtains, stage right, ready, listening.

'Many a morning hath he there been seen,' said Lord Montague, a sixth former named Adrian, 'with tears augmenting the fresh morning's dew.'

And now the fear blossomed. In fact, erupted would probably be a better word. My stomach had been lined with Sambuca and now somebody took a lit match to it, and butterflies emerged from the inferno, and my brain and my stomach were alive with beating, flaming wings, and I didn't know my first line.

'My noble uncle, do you know the cause?' asked Benvolio. Charlotte. One of the few male characters played by a girl. Maybe the only one. At that moment I couldn't remember.

I tried to calm myself again, to achieve enlightenment. Zen. Cool. I thought of people in films being cool. I thought of the Fonz and I thought of William the Bloody. I thought of Chow-Yun-Fat. I thought of Brad Pitt in *Fight Club*. I thought of Humphrey Bogart. I thought of his little nod to the band playing the Marseillaise in *Casablanca*.

'Could we but learn from whence his sorrows grow,' said Adrian, 'we would as willingly give cure as know.'

I slouched onstage just as Lord and Lady Montague left, and Charlotte looked at me and waved. 'Good-morrow, cousin.'

I pretended to sip from the empty can of beer in my hand. 'Is the day so young?'

'But new struck nine,' said Charlotte.

'Ay me,' I said, crunching the can in my fist and tossing it away. 'Sad hours seem long.' I looked towards the other end of the stage. 'Was that my father that went hence so fast?'

Charlotte nodded. 'It was.' She sat down on a low prop wall and started to clean her gun. *Nice bit of business, that.* 'What sadness lengthens Romeo's hours?'

'Not having that, which having, makes them short,' I said, staring into the middle distance, trying not to let my real emotions show.

It was a revelation. There was nothing. No bullies out there in the world, no wars, no missing children. There were no looming exams, no parents, no girl trouble, no London. No powers. No audience, even. Just me and my fellow actors, and for the two hours traffic of our stage we were the world. A bubble, microcosmic. I truly felt I belonged somewhere and revelled in it, and when Kloe and I kissed in the party scene . . . something definitely happened. Something that was definitely different from every rehearsal we'd had.

That's definitely something.

It definitely was.

Shit, I hope nobody in the audience can tell.

We reached the interval without making any major mistakes, which was fairly amazing, and as I headed backstage I was showered with congratulations, people shaking my hand and clapping me on the back. Kloe hugged me and I hugged her back, and for a second I wondered if we were going to kiss again . . . but we didn't. Whether it was because she felt nothing of what I felt or simply because there were too many people I didn't know, but there were no lips.

Must be the second thing.

Hopefully.

All of the words were kind, the faces were masks of happiness, contentment, companionship. It was a headrush. Miss Stevenson ran backstage and she hugged me too. I didn't shy away, hugging her back. She had tears in her eyes and smiled through them. 'It was OK?' I asked.

'Yes,' she laughed. 'It was OK.'

The interval lasted for fifteen minutes, and I stood outside and stared up at the sky, a blackboard scattered with chalk dust, with clouds gathering at the edges. I could smell rain in the air, moisture on concrete, but it didn't matter.

I wondered what my parents thought. Were they proud? I hoped so. Suddenly, more than anything, I hoped that they were proud of me and that they appreciated my achievement. I decided not to go and see them now, I would wait until the end. Maintain the illusion of the theatre. I wondered whether my elation showed, whether it was obvious, or whether I just channelled it into my performance. I wished that Daryl was there.

'Stanly!'

I turned. A girl in my year named Emma, who was playing the Nurse, was standing in the doorway looking worried. 'Ben came backstage,' she said. 'He's hassling Kloe.'

I started to walk, determined, striding. Purpose. I nodded at Emma as I passed her and headed backstage, where I saw Kloe staring defiantly at Ben, her arms folded. 'You're so amazing,' he said, his melodramatic sincerity turning my stomach. 'You really are! Amazing! I love you!'

'Thanks,' said Kloe, 'that's nice, but . . . how can I say this? I don't like you at all. In fact lately I absolutely *despise* you.' There was real satisfaction in the word.

'Please,' he said, 'just give me a chance . . .'

'Just. Piss. *Off*!' she said, raising her voice.

'Ben,' I said. 'Just go, man.'

He turned around and the simpering plea for adoration left his face. The hatred came back and it was a scary thing. The gloves were off. 'Oh,' he said, walking torwards me. 'I've been waiting for this.'

'What?' I asked. 'Oh, you've got to be f—'

He punched me in the face and I staggered backwards and hit

the wall. He'd got me on the cheek, and the punch stung like a bastard. 'Ow!' I yelled.

'Ben, you prick, just get lost!' cried Kloe. I heard the distant hubbub behind the curtain evaporate, and now Ben grabbed me and threw me through the curtain. I lost my balance, hit the floor and rolled out past the stage, and people jumped. Several cried out. My dad, who had been talking to my English teacher, said, 'Stan? What—'

Ben came out after me and Miss Stevenson yelled, 'Ben! What the *hell* do you think you're doing?'

Ben ignored her. He aimed a kick at my ribs, but I rolled sideways and got wobbly to my feet. 'You *bastard*!' he yelled, throwing a punch. I dodged. 'It's your fault!'

'What is?' I asked. Everyone was watching. My parents, Miss Stevenson, Mr Dylan, kids from school, Kloe, everyone was staring in amazement, some were even shouting, but no-one came near us. Even my parents seemed too shocked to intervene.

'Everything!' he yelled. 'You ruined *everything*!'

'You ruined it yourself!' I shot back. 'I just happened to be there!' *I'm Yoko.*

'*I hate you*!' screamed Ben. '*I fucking hate you*!' He threw another punch. I grabbed his arm and threw him away from me, and he sprawled on the front of the stage, right next to the big wooden stick that had been used during Mercutio's fight with Tybalt. He saw it, picked it up and got to his feet. I saw what was going to happen. Mr Dylan yelled his name furiously.

Ben swung. I ducked but I lost my balance and fell on my back, and Ben leapt towards me, his face a terrifying, snarling mess. He was going to bring the stick down on my head. It arced down towards my face.

I didn't even think. I just raised my hand and he stopped in mid-air.

And it was as though I'd stopped everyone else as well, because everything halted, freezing like a spell. Nobody spoke. I could feel eyes and I could see Ben's face as he tried to comprehend what was happening. Then I heard a glass smash on the ground. I shook my head and realised that for the first time I didn't hate Ben. I pitied him. This might be the ruin of my fledgling life and it was his fault, but I didn't hate him. I spoke and the deadness of my tone actually scared me. 'You couldn't even let me have one night,' I said.

'What?' asked Ben. It was peculiar, him responding to me so normally, considering that I was keeping him suspended above the ground.

'You couldn't have come tomorrow?' I asked. 'You couldn't have ruined everything *tomorrow*? You couldn't have given me *one night*?' I shouted the last two words and flung Ben with my mind.

OK. Maybe I do hate him.

A lot.

He flew, smashing into the doors that led out of the Drama Hall and breaking them open. Wood splintered and glass shattered, and Ben landed on his back in the hallway and lay there, shifting subtly in pain. I got to my feet and took a few steps towards him. *Now* my *gloves are off.* I was going to do what I should have done yesterday. I was going to bounce him off the walls and the ceiling with my brain, dribble him all around the school like a bleeding, screaming human basketball. Break him and fix him and break him again. I felt drunk.

Then I looked to my left and saw the audience, my parents, teachers, fellow pupils, and it was as though I suddenly realised what was happening, what had just occurred, and the rushing blur of fury subsided, overriden by a feeling I can only describe as *oh shiiiiit*. People were staring at me. Some were quizzical. Some were aghast. Most were looking at me like I was a freak.

They're not wrong.

I turned to my parents. Our eyes met and it seemed as though they finally understood me. They knew what had been happening for the last few months. They knew everything. In a weird way, it was almost nice.

And still, nobody spoke. I unhooked the shoulder holster and let it fall to the floor, then left the hall sharpish, people parting hurriedly to make way. Outside, the chalk had vanished from the sky and it was raining lightly, and I started to run down the street, strangely calm, set, focused. I had to go home, I had to get Daryl and I had to leave. Probably for a long time. Maybe . . .

'Stanly!'

I turned, slowing down slightly. Kloe was running after me. I stopped and she reached me quickly, grabbing both of my hands. There were tears in her eyes. 'Where are you going?' she asked.

'Away,' I said. 'I . . . I don't know.'

'Please don't,' she said.

'I have to,' I said. 'I can't . . . I have to.'

Words seemed to fail her. She stared into my eyes for a second that went on and on, and it told me everything I needed to know, and I pulled her to me and kissed her hard. She kissed me back, and I wrapped her up in my arms, and we embraced, and it was so intense I felt as though I might collapse. It was amazing that nobody came out after us. Momentary luck in a luckless void. This was our time together. I had no idea if we would see each other again.

We broke apart and I touched her cheek. 'I'm sorry.' Then I turned and ran, leaving her crying in the rain.

I got home about half an hour later using a mixture of sprinting and flying, and opened a window with my mind when I realised I didn't have my keys. As I dropped on to the kitchen floor I heard Daryl gallop downstairs, much faster than I'd ever known him move before. He skidded in, growling, but immediately saw that it was me and relaxed. 'Jesus,' he said. 'You gave me a heart attack . . . you're soaking! What's going on?'

I took a minute to tell him everything and he accepted it as calmly as I had. 'You'll have to take your dad's car,' he said.

My parents had two cars. They had gone to school in Mum's, and I thanked no-one in particular that I had learned to drive in Dad's. It wouldn't be long before they got back, so I ran upstairs to get stuff. I grabbed my guitar and filled my rucksack with clothes, a couple of books, my MP3 player and a notebook. I took the ninety pounds from my savings tin and threw that in as well, followed by my bank card, and I was about to put in the tiny stuffed elephant my dad had given me on the day I was born, but I couldn't bring myself to pick it up. I turned away, chucking in the *Casablanca* DVD for luck, and ran back downstairs. 'Find the car keys,' I said to Daryl. I wrote a very quick note explaining as much as I could as succinctly as possible, grabbed a spare key, unlocked the door, went outside, re-locked. It was pouring with rain now. I put my stuff on the back seat of the car and got into the driver's seat, and Daryl got into the passenger seat, and I fastened his seat belt and started the engine. The petrol tank was pretty much full. 'Thank Christ for that,' I said. I locked the doors, took a last look at my house, reversed out into the road and began to drive.

Fifteen minutes after we left Tref-y-Celwyn, Daryl finally said something. 'Can we have a CD on?'

'Sure,' I said. I grabbed a random compilation CD and put it into the player.

'Thanks,' he said, and fell silent.

The rain had stopped and the road was shiny, and I cast unnecessary things to the back of my mind and thought about getting to London. There was a map in the glove compartment, I knew that. Eddie had said day or night. I had the scrap of paper with his address. I had all bases covered, apart from a sizeable lack of knowledge about the rules of motorways, although I hoped that void could be filled with common sense. One tank of petrol would hopefully be enough to get me there. The night was new and the Beach Boys' 'Wouldn't It Be Nice' was deliriously incongruous in my ears as I drove towards a new and uncertain world.

Two hours into the drive, Daryl said that he was hungry. 'Sorry,' I said. 'I forgot to pack food.'

'Can't we stop?'

'Oh yes,' I said. 'I'll just pull into a motorway service station as the underage driver of a stolen car and get a Twix and a packet of Sensations for my talking dog. Use your loaf.'

'Sorry.'

I shook my head. 'No. I'm sorry. I'm sorry for all this. It's . . .'

'It's all right. It's not your fault.'

'I'm still sorry.'

I'd put *Abbey Road* into the CD player without thinking, and as the smoky purr of 'Come Together' faded, 'Something' began. Of all the songs. Immediately all I could think about was Kloe, wet-eyed and pleading with me in the middle of the road, and I turned the music off and pulled into a lay-by, and for the next ten minutes I cried harder than I had ever cried in my entire life, and my dog was helpless beside me.

CHAPTER ELEVEN

A<small>T ABOUT HALF</small> past one in the morning we passed over Westminster Bridge, deep in London's massive looming unreality, and I was keeping my breathing as regular as possible, trying not to be completely overwhelmed by the lights and the sheer scale of the place. It felt as though the buildings were looking at me accusingly, or hungrily, preparing to swallow me up.

Kind of already been swallowed, though.

We'd been luckier than I'd have thought possible so far, having avoided the attention of the police and other drivers, and even though I'd had a few minor panic attacks coming into the city, Daryl had been surprisingly helpful with negotiating roundabouts and multiple lanes and stuff. He'd definitely been here before, but I didn't ask him about it. It wasn't exactly the most mysterious thing about him. I kept switching the radio on and off, but there was no mention of me. There was no reason that there should have been; I very much doubted that my parents would put out a missing persons report. But just in case . . .

'Are we there yet?' I asked, as we exited the bridge to a fresh spit of rain.

'Not quite,' he said. 'Don't worry. Follow those signs.' He indicated with his nose.

Eddie lived near Brixton, and Daryl managed to get us there almost without incident, although I did drive the wrong way up a one-way street at one point, resulting in another minor panic attack. 'It's fine,' said Daryl, 'it's fine, it's fine, just go there . . . go there! Go there! *There!*'

'OK, I'm going there!' I yelled.

'No need to shout.'

Finally we pulled up outside Eddie's house and got out of the car. The place didn't look like much of a sanctuary; like most of the houses along the street it was mouldy and forlorn, its minis-cule front garden a sorry heap of bindweed. I could see distant, shadowy buildings standing stern against a dull, drizzle-flecked orange grey sky, and hear faraway sirens. And more nearby sirens. I felt strangely light, physically at least, as though my body was in a dream but my mind was still awake. Part of me, a fairly major part, felt as though my body was still in Tref-y-Celwyn . . . no, not even there. It was still standing in the rain outside my school, wrapped up in Kloe, in her . . .

Shut up.

Feels like a dream? Then it's a dream. Ride it.

And stop thinking about her. That is an order.

Daryl was enjoying an expansive stretch, and I unloaded my stuff, locked the car and walked up to Eddie's door, which was dull red and had 23 printed on it in peeling white paint. It was after two now, but there was still a light on, and I rang the bell and waited. Nothing. I rang it again. Finally I heard someone moving, and a peephole opened. 'Stanly?' asked an incredulous voice.

'Yeah,' I said. 'Um . . . hi. Sorry. Can I come in?'

'Of course!' A bolt was drawn back, and I gave Daryl a mean-ingful look. He knew what it meant. Don't speak yet.

Eddie looked very different. He was much taller, and sported some serious five o'clock shadow, and had dyed his hair white blonde. He was wearing a vest and jeans and no shoes, and his arms were all muscle, and he had an unlit cigarette behind his ear. 'Come in.' He smiled and stood back to let me in. He took my bag, but I held onto my guitar. *Like a Linus blanket.* Daryl followed, and Eddie glanced down at him. 'Who's this, then?'

'My dog,' I said. *Well duh.* 'Daryl.'

'Hiya, Daryl,' said Eddie, in a talking-to-dogs voice. 'Um . . . I can make up the sofa for you, Stanly, if that's all right? Sorry, if I'd known you were coming—'

'It was a sudden decision,' I said.

Eddie frowned. 'Did something happen?'

'You could say that,' I said. 'I'll tell you all about it . . . but have you got anything to eat first? We're starving. Didn't want to risk stopping on the way down. Being an illegal underage driver and all.'

'Of course,' nodded Eddie. 'Yeah, go through to the living room, I'll fix you something.'

'I can do it . . .'

'Don't be silly. What does Daryl eat?'

'What do you have?'

'Bacon,' said Eddie. 'Does he eat bacon?'

'He'll eat bacon,' I said. 'We'll . . . we'll both eat bacon.'

Eddie nodded. 'OK. You two go and sit down, I'll put some bacon on.'

The living room was small and equal parts tatty and cosy, and we sat awkwardly on a sofa covered with an Indian throw. There was a small portable TV, a rickety shelf unit full of CDs and books, and a hi-fi system that looked as though it had seen better decades. The curtains drawn across the window were ragged and a bit stained. Daryl shifted around on the sofa for a minute, then jumped off and padded over to a slightly squashed pouffe in the corner. He curled up on it, and I stretched out on the sofa and relaxed for the first time in hours. Neither of us spoke. We were safe, although I still wasn't sure whether I was awake or not.

Eddie came in a minute later with two mugs of tea and a bowl of water. 'Bacon's on,' he said. He handed me some tea and placed the bowl of water down next to the pouffe. I shook my head at Daryl, hoping he wouldn't protest because he hated eating and drinking off the floor. He didn't, he just leaned down and had a drink.

'OK,' said Eddie. 'So what's the story?'

I told him, and he said 'ooh' and 'aah' and 'shit' in all the right places. When I reached the part about throwing Ben he stiffened, and his tone took on a worrying urgency. 'Everyone saw you?'

'Yeah,' I said.

'Shit,' he said. 'Carry on.'

I did, omitting Kloe entirely because I didn't want to think about her, and when I was done I said, 'It's bad, isn't it?'

'Bad, but not terrible, necessarily,' said Eddie. *Wow. That might be the least comforting comforting thing he could have said.* 'I mean . . . people will try and rationalise it for themselves. I doubt you'll have newspapers and police after you or anything . . . but still best to keep a low profile. Probably not a good idea for you to stay here any longer than necessary – your parents will guess immediately, for one thing.'

I wondered if that was for my benefit or for his. 'Where can I go?' I asked.

'I have friends,' said Eddie. 'It's OK, we'll find a place for you.' He smiled, and headed back to the kitchen to sort out the food. I glanced at Daryl. 'What do you think?' I whispered.

He shrugged. 'I have absolutely no idea.'

'Innit.'

Eddie returned with bacon sandwiches, and we ate them. I had plenty of questions, and I was sure he did as well, but I was too tired to ask any, and Eddie didn't pressure me. He said I could sleep on the sofa, and offered to make it up for me while I used the bathroom. I felt like I should have offered to do it myself, but sometimes you've just got to accept someone's hospitality.

I brushed my teeth, washed my face and stared at myself in the bathroom mirror. I was a fugitive, of sorts. Odd indeed. I looked down and watched the water swirling into the plughole, thinking it looked suspiciously like my life, then back at the mirror, half-expecting to see Kloe's despairing face staring back at me. But it was just me, pale and anxious, alone. I felt the tears threatening to return so I slapped myself, roughly washed my eyes again and went back downstairs. Eddie had made up the sofa with a duvet, a sleeping bag and several pillows, and it looked so inviting that I felt weights vanish from inside me. 'I might have gone overboard with the bedding,' he said. 'I don't really ever have people over.'

'It's fine,' I said. 'It's amazing, actually. Thanks.'

'*Dim problem*,' said Eddie.

'You still remember your Welsh.'

'Bits and pieces,' he said. 'Great language. Completely barmy. But good fun.' He stood leaning against the doorway, managing a passable impression of a reassuring smile, and I almost felt slightly OK. 'Don't worry, we'll sort everything out.' He didn't sound as convincing as I thought he probably wanted to, but it was nice of him to say it, and I was about to say thanks and goodnight when the phone rang. Eddie's brow furrowed and he picked it up. 'Hello? Mary . . . yes, he is. I . . . yes, he's fine. I . . . just . . . hold on.' He looked over at me. 'It's your mum. Do you want—'

'I'll speak to her.' I took the phone from him and he turned and left the room. 'Hi,' I said, feeling like that was possibly the most inadequate word I could have selected.

I heard her sigh, and when she spoke it sounded as though her throat was sore. 'Stanly,' she whispered. 'Thank God. I . . . we couldn't think where you'd gone. Everybody at the school was going mad, we just had to leave . . . we drove around half the county looking for you, then I suddenly remembered you asking for Edward's number . . .'

'I'm all right,' I said. 'I just . . . I had to leave.'

'Stanly, what *happened*?'

'You know what happened.'

A pause. Then, 'Yes. I suppose I did . . . I mean, we did. Frank kept on saying "I knew there was something", over and over again, I was almost begging him to go outside and have a fag.' We both managed a laugh.

'I . . . can't come back,' I said. 'Not for a while anyway.'

She didn't ask why, or beg me to come back. She just said, 'I understand. Promise me you'll be careful.'

'I promise.'

She was crying again. 'I love you so much.'

'I know. I love you too.' I meant it, even if it might not have sounded like it. 'I'll call sometime. Not sure when.'

'OK. Bye.'

'Bye.'

'Oh, Stanly?'

'Yeah?'

'You were really good. I wish we could have seen the second half.'

'Thanks. Me too.'

I put the phone down, and Eddie came back in. 'You OK?' he asked.

I nodded. 'Yeah. Think I'll go to sleep.'

'All right. Goodnight.' He smiled awkwardly and headed upstairs.

''Night.' I switched off the light and snuggled down into the pile of bedding in my makeshift pyjamas (boxer shorts and a T-shirt with the same *Dawn of the Dead* design that Miss Stevenson had been wearing so long ago), and Daryl came and joined me but didn't say anything. I wrapped myself up, hiding from the world, and tried to bury the fear, tried to bury Kloe's face. I spent a long time wondering if I'd wake up in Tref-y-Celwyn, ready for the first night of the play, and very nearly convinced myself that it was going to happen. When I did manage to sleep I dreamt all night, and the dreams weren't nice.

I woke up at ten o'clock the next morning, lying on my front with a patch of dribble on the sofa by my mouth. Daryl was curled up by my feet, still snoring away. I managed to extricate myself from the tangle of bedding and sit up, and for a moment I felt a stab of almost overwhelming disappointment that I'd woken up here, but I pummelled it fiercely into the very basement of my gut. It served no purpose. I was here and that was what was happening. I ran my fingers through my matted, sleep-greased hair and rubbed crunchy dust from my eyes. Dim light was coming in through the window, and I could hear rain being blown against bricks and tiles. The living room had no actual door, just a doorway that led into the hall and across to the kitchen, and I wandered through and found Eddie sitting on the counter reading the paper. He looked up and smiled tiredly. I wondered if he'd slept since I arrived. 'Morning,' he said. 'Breakfast?'

I nodded.

'Coffee?'

'Yes please.' My voice was slurred and husky.

'Bagels?'

'Definitely.' I stretched and felt all my bones crack. 'I'm going to go and get washed. Can I use the shower?'

'Sure. There's a towel on the radiator.'

I went upstairs to the bathroom, stripped off and got into the shower, which was noticeably posher-looking than the rest of the house. As I rubbed shampoo into my hair I wondered what Eddie did for a living, and as I rinsed it out I caught sight of my reflection in the glass, wet and unshaven.

Shit. I'd forgotten my razor.

Oh well. Fugitives have facial hair, don't they?

Yeah. Anti-hero stubble, innit.

Don't you want to be an actual hero, though?

Maybe I'm re-defining the concept.

Or maybe I just have some facial hair.

It definitely seemed as though I had less control over my thought processes these days.

When I returned to the kitchen there was a full caffetière waiting next to some untoasted bagels, a tub of butter and a jar of jam. Eddie had taken the paper through to the living room and was sitting cross-legged on the floor, as Daryl was still asleep on the sofa. I toasted, buttered and jammed some bagels, took them through and patted the dog gently awake. He yawned and licked his lips, and looked as if he were about to speak. I shook my head slightly and said, 'Hungry?' in a voice that I hoped sounded like I was talking to a regular dumb dog.

Daryl shook his head, which would have been something of a giveaway had Eddie been watching, and settled back down. I shrugged and started to eat. 'Any good news?'

'Not particularly. Kids still missing. Did you hear about that?'

'Bits and pieces,' I said. 'Kids gone, parents murdered, no forensic stuff?'

'Yeah. Police got in trouble for letting that info slip.'

'Any theories?'

'A few,' said Eddie. 'None of them nice.' He folded the paper and looked at me. 'Do you have any idea what you're going to do?'

'No. I will. Soon . . . I have to figure out some stuff. You said I could come here if I needed somewhere and I do . . . but . . .' I broke off and sipped my coffee. 'Honestly? I don't know what I'm doing. I don't know how long I'm staying, what I'm going to . . .'

'It's OK,' said Eddie, 'you can stick around for as long as you need to.'

'What do *you* think I should do?' All of my confidence was slipping away. I had been running on pure adrenaline last night, but right now I didn't feel in a fit state to go around the corner for a pint of milk, let alone drive a stolen car several hundred miles across an unfamiliar country to an even more unfamiliar city. I felt plaintive and very young, and also pissed-off with myself for feeling like that – after all, I had some pretty special advantages, which was more than most teen runaways had.

Yeah. 'Cos they've been a great help.

Ooh, the burden of specialness. Better shave off that anti-hero stubble.

Shut up, brain.

'Like I said,' said Eddie, 'I'm not sure it's a great idea for you to stay here, but I have some friends who live nearby. Well . . . nearby by London standards, I suppose. Connor and Sharon. They're . . . like you. They have abilities.'

'Do you?' I asked.

'Yes.' He didn't sound like he wanted to talk about it, but I did. 'What kind?' I asked.

'Physical stuff,' said Eddie. 'Speed, strength, endurance. Stuff that should have left me years ago.'

'Did it appear when you turned sixteen?'

He nodded slowly. 'Yeah, around then. I almost managed to convince myself it was normal at the time . . . but it's not.'

'Do you mean, like, *super* strength?'

'Let's just say I can take quite a beating.' Eddie smiled grimly. 'And dish one out, if needs be.'

'Super strength, then.'

'If you want. Definitely abormal. You could even say other-worldly. Plus, if it was just regular fitness I'd have lost it by now, without a doubt.'

'Why's that?' I realised I was bombarding him with questions, but the dude had been Mr Cryptic every time we'd spoken on the phone, so I felt pretty justified in digging for a few specifics now that we were speaking face to face.

Eddie sighed. 'OK. Guess it's all coming out now . . . look, when I first came to London I spent years in various dives and shitholes with various unsavoury people, doing far too many bad drugs, pretending I'd never had parents and fighting my way in and out of as many stupid situations as possible. Then I met Connor and Sharon, and now I have a pretty good job and a decent life, and I only do good drugs. You know. Paracetamol. Various strong anti-depressants. All the essential ingredients of twenty-first century life.' He winked. 'But yeah. Connor, Sharon and I are . . . freaks to-gether, I suppose. You'll be among friends, I can promise you that.'

'I *was* among friends,' I said. 'Finally. I finally had friends and I finally had a life and I almost had a girl, and then that twat came along and screwed it all up. *I* screwed it all up.' My empty plate flew into the air and smashed against the wall. Eddie looked from it to me and back again, one eyebrow raised. 'Sorry,' I said, moving to clean the mess up.

'No worries. Rubbish plate anyway.'

There was another long silence. My life was violence, weird-ness, elation and misery interspersed with long silences. Finally

I thought of something. 'Eddie. You're . . . pretty open-minded when it comes to weird shit, right?'

'I like to think so,' said Eddie. 'Why?'

I looked meaningfully at Daryl. He blinked sleepily and said, 'Hi.'

'Uh,' said Eddie. 'Hello.'

'I can talk,' said Daryl. 'I'm a talking dog. A dog who talks.'

Eddie nodded slowly. 'OK. Nice to meet you. How's it going?'

'Not bad. Been better. Been worse.'

'Cool.' Eddie smiled and turned to me. 'I'm going to go and see Sharon and Connor. I'll explain about you and I'll be back ASAP. Are you OK here alone?'

'I'll be fine,' I said. 'I'm not alone, anyway. Thanks.'

My cousin nodded and went out into the hall, returning a minute later wearing a dark jacket over his vest and jeans. 'There are spare keys hanging in the kitchen,' he said. 'Just in case. I'll be back soon.'

'OK,' I said. 'Bye.' He disappeared, the door opened and shut, and I was alone with my dog. After yet another long silence, Daryl said, 'Well, I am *starving*. Where's the food then, *butt*?'

I spent nearly an hour sitting by the phone debating whether I should phone someone or not. I wanted to call Mark and tell him I was all right. I wanted to call Miss Stevenson and say how beyond sorry I was that her show had been ruined. I wanted to call Ben King and tell him what a world-class bell-end he was and that if I ever saw him again I would eviscerate him with my brain. I wanted to call Kloe and spout melodramatic sentimental drivel. I wanted to tell her to come down, that we could start a new life here with Eddie and his friends. I didn't actually have her number with me but I was sure—

'What the hell are we doing here?' asked Daryl.

'What?'

'Why are we here?' he asked. 'What's going to happen? What are we doing?'

'I don't know,' I said. 'Eddie's gone to talk to his friends—'

'How do we know we can trust Eddie and his friends?' asked Daryl. 'What if Connor and Sharon are made up? What if Eddie has gone to some secret branch of the government who round up people with powers and brainwash them and turn them into sleeper agents? What if you go to see Connor and Sharon and end up in a laboratory? And me? What if they dissect me to see what makes me talk? And then they'll give you a trigger and they'll make you do their evil deeds for them. One minute you'll be walking down the street, the next minute you'll hear 'Where Is the Love' by the Black Eyed Peas and you'll turn into a single-minded monster of doom, annihilating people left, right and centre with your mind powers! What if—'

'You're babbling,' I said. 'We talked about this conspiracy stuff. Stop it.'

'Sorry,' said Daryl. 'But you still have to be careful. Always be on your guard.'

'Don't you trust Eddie?'

Daryl looked puzzled. 'Actually – my soliloquy notwithstanding – yes. I do. Although it does seem odd that he's gone to talk to his friends in person rather than just phone them up.'

'He said they live nearby,' I said. 'And . . . I dunno. Sometimes it's better to talk about things face to face. Things like, "please can my runaway superpowered misfit cousin please come and live at your house, possibly indefinitely".'

'Fair point,' said Daryl. 'At any rate, you still have to be careful.'

'I will,' I said. 'I'll be careful. We'll be fine.'

Daryl nodded. 'Are you going to call her?' he asked, after a pause.

'Who?'

'You know *who*.'

I didn't say anything. Daryl came and sat next to me and I stroked him, and time passed. One o'clock came, followed by half past one, and I picked up a copy of *Time Out,* trying to take my mind off Kloe's face, the salt of her tears burning in my brain.

There were plenty of films on. An independent cinema in the city was having a Golden Oldies season. They were showing *The Maltese Falcon*. Bogie goodness.

The front door opened and closed, and Eddie walked through to the kitchen with two bags of shopping. I followed him. 'News?'

He nodded, and began to unload groceries.

'Good news?'

He nodded again. 'We're going to see them. Grab your stuff and I'll finish putting this away.'

'Dog's coming too?'

'Dog's coming too.'

'*Dog* has a name, human,' said Daryl.

'Daryl,' said Eddie. 'Sorry. Shall we go?'

CHAPTER TWELVE

I F COMING INTO London had felt like being swallowed, heading down into its hot, stale-smelling bowels, a maze of clanking echoes and indistinct announcements over crackly tannoys, was like the final stage of digestion. I'd been on the Underground once when I was little, but I'd forgotten how strange it was, and how many people there were. How many people there were *everywhere*. Daryl and I stuck close together, and I distracted myself by thinking about zombies and wondering if I looked cool wandering around with an electric guitar. Eddie had tried to insist on carrying some of my stuff, but this time I'd refused. It made me feel a smidge more independent in this vortex of unfamiliar sounds and smells.

Get used to it, kid.

It's home now.

Off the train, up a hundred steps, and down more streets. The pavements were shiny with the rain and the sky was unsettled, and I could smell a particular scent of wet concrete that I always associated with cities. Endless cars, sirens, people talking and shouting, trains rattling, and the faraway thundering rumble that signalled a storm. An unfinished skyscraper stabbed its way to the sky, looking like a spaceship midway through construction. For some reason, that thought made me feel a bit better. *Good old spaceships.* 'Are we nearly there?' I asked. If Connor and Sharon lived 'nearby', it certainly wasn't by any definition of the word that I'd ever encountered.

'Yep,' said Eddie. We had reached a cul-de-sac. It was substantially more upmarket-looking than Eddie's road, and he led us to a small house about halfway down the street and up a path lined with tidy flowers. Eddie rang the bell, and we were met by a smiling young man about his age. 'Hi,' he said. 'You must be Stanly.' Using my legendary powers of observation, I decided that this was Connor. He was just over six feet tall by my estimate, with short black hair and cobalt eyes, and his natural expression seemed to be humorous and welcoming. He was wearing faded jeans and a black T-shirt with a cartoon zombie on it, which made me warm to him even more, and his feet were buried inside big furry werewolf slippers. I nodded and smiled. 'Yeah. I'm Stanly.'

'Connor.' He held out his hand and we shook. He had an Irish accent, smooth and reassuring, and I liked him immediately. 'And this is . . .?' he asked, looking down at Daryl.

'Daryl,' said Daryl.

Connor laughed. 'Eddie told me about you, but part of me thought maybe he was spinning yarns. Obviously not. You really do talk.'

'Yep,' said Daryl.

Connor shrugged. 'OK, then. One more special exhibition for our weird little museum. Come on in. And then Eddie can explain again why he trekked all the way here, then trekked all the way back to get you, so you could then trek all the way back here together.'

'I prefer to do things face-to-face,' said Eddie, defensively.

'You prefer to take the long way round,' said Connor.

'And I had shopping to do.'

'Sure you did.' I sensed that this kind of exhange was fairly typical. Connor winked at me and we followed him inside, down an uncarpeted hall and into a big kitchen. Everything in there looked old but sturdy: the oven, the cupboards, the furniture, the lights, the walls. And I got a definite Seventies vibe from the décor. Seated at the table reading a magazine was a girl. Or a woman. I'm never sure how old a female has to be before she graduates from girl to woman, or if it's up to the girl (or woman) herself. She was Connor and Eddie's age, at any rate, and she wore blue and had bright blonde hair with darker streaks in it, and laughing blue eyes, and was just this side of stunning. She smiled. 'Ah. You'd be Stanly.'

I nodded, slightly embarrassed now. 'Mm.'

Connor laughed. 'He doesn't say much.'

The woman – *young woman? Woman girl? Oh God, whatever* – stood up and gave me a hug, which was nice. 'I'm Sharon.' She knelt down and patted Daryl. 'He's cute.'

'She's not wrong,' said Daryl. Sharon didn't stop patting him.

'Eddie wasn't bullshitting,' said Connor. 'The dog really does talk.'

'So he does,' said Sharon, as though it were the best thing she'd heard all day. She finished petting Daryl, then stood up and looked me up and down for a minute. 'Would you like to see where you'll be sleeping?'

'Yes, please.'

Connor had poured himself a cup of coffee and was leaning against the counter. Eddie was hovering, and the Irishman laughed. 'Ed? Take a chill pill, yeah? There's nothing wrong. You're making me nervous.'

'Just . . . making sure Stanly's all right,' said Eddie, in the voice of someone hurriedly making up an excuse. It was interesting how he suddenly seemed a lot less cool now we were with his friends.

'He'll be fine,' said Connor. 'I scoured the wardrobes for ninja assassins before you arrived.'

'Very funny.'

Connor laughed. 'Seriously, old man, chill. Don't have a cow, or whatever animal stressed-out people had in the Fifties.'

Sharon put a hand on my shoulder. 'Come on, let's leave the boys to their banter. Sometimes it goes on for hours. Your room's upstairs.'

There were pictures all the way along the wall leading up to the landing, framed photographs of the same rain-swept lighthouse from different angles. The landing had three doors and light blue walls, and Sharon nodded to the only unpainted door. It swung open. I frowned. 'Did you do that?'

She smiled. 'Just to prove you're among like-minded people.'

It was a small room, but very cosy. There was a sofa bed against the wall, a desk underneath the window and lots of shelves stuffed with books. I liked that Eddie and his friends had so many books. The window offered a view of wet streets and some tall, nondescript buildings, mostly obscured by the gathering mist. I put my stuff on the bed and turned back to Sharon. 'Will it do?' she asked.

'Yeah,' I said. 'It's great. Thanks.' I was still feeling slightly awkward.

'Good. Are you hungry?'

'I had breakfast a little while ago . . . but I could probably eat again, to be honest.'

'OK. Well, do you want to come back downstairs or stay up here?'

'I'll come down.'

As she was about to go down the stairs she turned around and pointed at the white door. 'Bathroom.' Then she pointed to the red door. 'Mine and Connor's room.' She carried on down the stairs and I followed, Daryl at my heels.

Eddie and Connor were talking in the kitchen. Eddie still seemed agitated, but Connor seemed to have managed to become even more laid-back, nodding and answering calmly, his tone soft and placatory.

'What's the matter?' asked Sharon.

'Ed's a bit rattled,' said Connor. 'Worried about his little cousin.'

I'm not little.

You're kind of little.

OK, fair point.

'I'm just . . . concerned,' said Eddie, trying to keep his voice level. 'Are you two going to be all right looking after him? I mean you both have to work . . .'

127

'I've been doing double shifts at the hospital lately,' said Sharon. 'I can do some swaps.'

'To be honest, he can probably come to work with me,' said Connor. 'It's no bother. I'll bet Skank would even give him a job.'

'Skank?' I asked, trying to keep my incredulity at a polite level.

'Sylvester,' said Connor. 'Everyone calls him Skank. I . . . really don't know why. He's my boss.'

'Where do you work?' I asked.

'It's called 110th Street,' said Connor. 'Sort of comic book and general geek shop tucked away in a back street in Camden. Pretty well respected, does a lot of business. I'm sure Skank would give you a job, if you wanted one.'

This felt like a bandwagon I'd be keen to jump on. 'That'd be great!'

'I'm not sure about that,' began Eddie. 'It—'

Sharon interrupted him. 'Eddie, he'll be fine. What are you worried about?'

'The police?' asked Eddie. 'Truant officers or something? Or your run-of-the-mill criminals? I don't know why I even said he should come here. On a scale of one to ten, this city is not the safest place to be—"

'I'll be fine,' I said. I was starting to get a little irritated. 'And I don't need to be . . . coddled.'

'I'm just trying to look out for you,' said Eddie. 'If anything . . .'

'Nothing will happen,' said Sharon, soothingly. 'The police aren't going to notice him, they've got plenty of other things to worry about.'

'That doesn't usually stop them when they want to make life difficult,' muttered Eddie.

'On a scale of boy-who-won't-attract-any-attention to murderous drug dealer, where does Stanly come?' asked Sharon. I had to bite my lip not to laugh. 'And anyway, he looks about seventeen, maybe eighteen, we'll just say he's left school already and he's working at 110th Street. If it comes up. Which it won't. And as for criminals: number one, how often do we get accosted by criminals,

128

and number two, have you ever met anyone Connor or yourself couldn't take care of?'

I saw Connor's eyes flash with pride when she said that, and Eddie nodded reluctantly. 'I suppose.'

'Stanly's not bad at taking people either,' piped up Daryl. 'He flung Eggs Benedict, what was it? Twenty feet?'

Everyone looked at Daryl. Sharon and Connor looked amused, but Eddie seemed more worried than ever. 'Um,' I said. 'Something like that. But it's not . . .'

Daryl was in no mood to back down. 'He's amazing,' he said. 'He threw someone his own size using just his mind. And he can almost fly!'

'Flight, eh?' said Connor, impressed. 'That's something I've not seen before. We're going to have to check out your powers, I'm very interested to see what you can do.'

'Mutual,' I said.

'All in good time,' said Sharon. 'But first, I think we should eat something. Connor isn't working until tomorrow, so he can take Stanly to see Skank. Until then, we can concentrate on getting to know one another. Does that sound all right?'

'Fine,' I said. 'Great.'

Eddie nodded. 'OK.'

Sharon smiled her calming smile. 'Good. Now what does everybody fancy?'

After a large lunch of chilli and rice, Eddie got up and said, 'OK, I'd better go. I've got a couple of things to do. I'll pop back later.' He looked at me. 'You're cool?'

'I'm cool,' I said, trying to reassure him. 'Thanks.'

'Good.' He left.

Connor shook his head. 'Wow. I haven't seen him this agitated for at least a week.'

'Leave him alone,' said Sharon.

Connor raised his hands. 'I was just saying. You know I love him, but he can be a bit . . . neurotic. Woody Allen dressing up as Dante.'

'Dante?' I asked.

'Do you not get a wicked *Devil May Cry* vibe from his hair?'

I laughed. 'Ah. That Dante. Yeah, I see what you mean.'

'He's just worried,' said Sharon, starting to clear away the plates. 'And he's actually got a reason to be worried, for a change. Pudding?'

I shook my head. 'No thanks. Full.'

'Daryl?'

Daryl shook his big head. 'No, thank you. I'm also of the full.'

We cleared up, then Connor said, 'OK, Stanly. Do you want five bars rest or are you up for showing us what you can do?'

'No, I'm fine,' I said, eager to be doing something. 'I'll show you.'

'Great.' He opened a cupboard. 'Go and stand at the other end of the kitchen.'

I obeyed, and waited. Sharon was sitting on the counter, watching with interest. Connor rummaged around in the cupboard, and withdrew three juggling balls. 'We'll start small,' he said. 'So you're . . . telekinetic, would you put it like that?'

'Yeah, I suppose.'

'OK, let's start there. Not really the right room for flying. I want you to stop the balls using just your mind. Try not to raise your hand or anything. If you ever had to use your powers out in the real world, you'd want to do it inconspicuously.'

I nodded. Connor raised one of the balls. 'Ready?'

I nodded again, and Connor threw the ball. I flexed my mind, but the ball kept coming. I flexed harder. It was still coming. I closed my eyes and tried to make a net with my brain. Nothing hit me. Cautiously I opened my eyes and saw that the ball was hanging motionless about an inch from my nose. I breathed deeply and it dropped to the floor. Connor was grinning. 'That was good,' he said. 'Now we'll try to increase the range.'

He threw another ball. This time it hit me in the forehead. 'Shit,' I said.

Sharon looked amused and concerned at the same time. 'You all right?'

'I'm fine,' I said.

'Sorry,' said Connor. 'Let's try again.' He threw the last ball. I did the net thing, and it stopped a full two feet from my face. I kept it there, completely still in the air.

'That's good,' said Connor. 'Now can you send it back at me?'

I tried to visualise the force coming from my brain. I could almost see it, a fist made of transparency closing around the ball, and I pulled the fist back as far as it would go, snapped taut, a coiled spring . . . and let rip. The ball flew towards Connor with more velocity than I'd intended, but his expression didn't waver, and he caught it a few centimetres from his face. Sharon clapped. 'Very nice!'

Daryl was looking appreciative. 'That's the way to do it.'

Connor tossed the ball from one hand to the other. 'You want to go again?'

'Yep,' I said.

For the next ten minutes he threw the ball at me and I caught it without moving my hands. Half an hour later I was stopping it when it had barely left Connor's hands, and I was feeling more confident and started to show off, dribbling the ball between his legs as he tried to catch it and bouncing it off the ceiling. Finally the effort started to hurt. Sweat was appearing on my forehead and dripping into my eyes, and I felt weak and lightheaded. The ball dropped and I leaned against the fridge. 'You OK?' asked Connor, looking concerned.

'*Bendigedig*,' I said, but my voice was heavy. 'Just . . . need to sit down.' Connor led me over to the table and pulled out a chair, and I fell gratefully into it. My vision was slightly dim and had to catch up with my eyes as I moved my head around. It was like being stoned, but in a bad way. Sharon poured me a glass of water and I gulped it down, and within a few minutes I felt fine again.

'Are you all right?' asked Connor. 'I'm sorry. I shouldn't have pushed you like that . . .'

'You didn't make him show off,' said Daryl. 'He did that all by himself.'

'It was pretty impressive, though,' said Connor.

'Yes,' said Sharon. 'Very. Are you sure you're all right?'

'I'm OK,' I said. 'I'm fine. Thanks.' I stood up. 'What's next?'

'Next?' asked Connor. 'Well . . . first of all, what does "bendi-gedig" mean?'

'It's Welsh for "brilliant", innit *butt*,' said Daryl.

'Ah. OK, thanks. Second, "butt"?'

'Welsh slang term of endearment. Like "mate".'

Connor nodded. 'Great. Instructive. OK, thirdly . . . I think a proper break is in order. Cup of tea?'

'*Bendigedig, butt*,' said Sharon. She looked at Daryl. 'Did I do it right?'

'A-plus,' said the dog. 'Now say "Llanfair-pwllgwyn-gyllgo-gery-chwyrn-drobwll-llanty-silio-gogo-goch".'

Sharon blinked. 'OK. So . . . tea?'

That evening we all sat in the living room, chatting. Eddie had re-turned from his errands and was sitting cross-legged on the carpet. I was in a leather armchair, Sharon and Connor were on the couch and Daryl was curled up in front of the open fire. It was a really nice room, with a big TV and hi-fi system, and various paintings and framed photographs on the walls. Connor and Eddie were sip-ping beers, and Sharon was drinking Shloer (the speech impedi-ment drink, I thought, feeling a pang of homesickness). I wasn't thirsty.

'So I'll take you to work with me tomorrow,' said Connor. 'You can meet Skank. You'll definitely like him. He's a wee bit eccentric but a really decent guy. He doesn't care about the law and stuff like that, he wants people to do what they want so he won't worry about your age or your . . . backstory.'

'Does he know about . . . you know?' I asked.

'Yes,' said Sharon. 'He knows.'

'He's safe,' said Eddie.

I nodded, feeling a little overwhelmed by everything. 'Thank you,' I said. 'For all of this. I wasn't expecting so much . . . I mean . . . I wasn't expecting you to be dicks or anything, but I certainly wasn't expecting this much . . . kindness. You didn't need to . . .'

'We've all had to find our feet in this city under difficult circumstances,' said Sharon, 'and we've all had to rely on other people's kindness. So there's no need to worry.'

I smiled. 'OK. No more worrying.' *Yeah, that's the likeliest of all the likelihoods.* I turned to Eddie. 'So where do you work, then?'

'Bouncer,' said Eddie. 'You're lucky you arrived last night, that was the only night this week that I was off-duty.'

'How late do you usually work?'

'Five is usually the limit,' said Eddie. 'The club I work at shuts then.'

'Where do you work?'

'It's called Twilight,' said Eddie.

'Really?' asked Daryl. 'Is it all sparkly? And full of pale pussy-whipped vampires and lunkheaded werewolves and girls who should know better?'

Eddie fought a smirk. 'I did ask my boss if he wanted to change the name, actually, but he was adamant. It's been Twilight for fifteen years, and it's staying that way.'

'Brave man,' said Daryl.

'No-one's going to call him on it,' said Eddie. 'He's a powerful guy, very well-connected. Slightly shady but . . . good. I got the job after I saved him from a mugger. Lucky coincidence.'

'You beat a lot of people up?' I asked, casually.

'Mostly I try to avoid it,' said Eddie, 'but you know how it is. You're behind some old dear in the post office, you're in a hurry . . .' He finished the last of his beer. 'Pay's pretty good, though.' He looked at his watch. 'I should probably get going.' He got up and Connor put out his hand. Eddie grasped it and they embraced briefly, and Sharon hugged him gently. Eddie looked at me and frowned. 'Do we hug yet?'

I shrugged. 'I don't know.'

Eddie looked awkward. 'Well . . . neither do I.'

Connor laughed. 'I can see this going on for a long time, so on behalf of both parties, *yes*. You do hug. Now get on with it.'

We did the handshake-hug thing, which made me feel like one of the boys despite myself, and Eddie said, 'You'll be —'

'— absolutely fine,' said Sharon. 'Stop worrying or I'll get offended.'

Eddie smiled ruefully. 'Sorry.' He went out into the hall and opened the door, turning back for a second to say 'Thanks'. Then he headed down the path into the darkening evening.

'Bye!' I called. Sharon and Connor waved, and shut the door.

Connor turned to me, a mischievous look in his eye. 'OK,' he said. 'Here's the plan. There's an old playground near here, rarely used by anyone. Very occasionally there are people there, teenagers mostly, but they won't be a problem.' There was no pride in his voice, just a quiet confidence that was reassuring. 'If we go there some time after ten we can have a little demonstration. To be honest, we wouldn't normally use our powers out and about if we can help it . . . but it's a special occasion. And I'm pretty keen to see what you can do.'

'Can I see what you two can do as well?' I asked.

Connor nodded. 'Quid pro quo.' He yawned. 'OK. In the meantime, I suggest that we watch some TV and load up on caffeine. You and Daryl like films?'

I smiled.

CHAPTER THIRTEEN

WE ENDED UP watching *Spirited Away*, which felt quite fitting, and when the film had finished Connor stood up and stretched. 'Ready?'

I nodded. We went out into the hall, and Connor pulled on his boots and grabbed a brown leather jacket from a peg in the hall. 'Do you have a coat?' he asked, slinging a sports bag over his shoulder.

'Yeah.' I still had my Romeo trenchcoat.

'You going to wear it? Chilly out.'

I nodded, ran upstairs and retrieved the coat from the pile of things by my bed. I put it on, and as I left I caught sight of myself in the mirror. The mish-mash of baggy jeans, trainers, hoody and trenchcoat looked pretty cool. I liked it. My new dark avenger look. *Don't count your chickens*, I thought. *You're not a Jedi yet.*

Downstairs, Sharon had put on a very long blue coat with grey toggles. I looked down at Daryl. 'Game?'

'Game,' said Daryl. There was something in his voice that I couldn't work out, but I left it.

The night was brisk and the moon was large, and I put my hands in the cavernous pockets of my coat and wrapped it around my body, glad that Connor had suggested it. 'So where's this playground?' I asked.

'A bus and a walk away,' said Sharon. 'It's near the site of one of the Smiley Joe kidnappings, that's why no-one tends to go there.'

'Smiley Joe?' I asked. 'That online horror story thing?'

Connor gave Sharon a swift look that jarred with his laid-back persona. Sharon looked away. 'The child kidnappings,' she said, quietly.

'Oh,' I said. *What?* We walked, and the silence was awkward, and I could feel that Daryl's curiosity was as bright and sharp as mine, so I ignored it and pressed on, in as nonchalant a voice as possible. 'So, what, Smiley Joe's real?'

'Smiley Joe's nothing,' said Connor. 'A name they gave this phantom kidnapper.'

'The one with no fingerprints,' said Sharon, 'and no DNA evidence.'

'For God's sake,' said Connor. Humour was creeping back into his voice, but there was an acidic edge to it. 'There is no such thing as Smiley Joe. It's just reality and stories getting mashed together.'

'I'm getting mixed signals here,' I said.

'Yes,' said Sharon. 'This is one of the rare occasions where Connor and I disagree. I believe in Smiley Joe.'

'Who *is* Smiley Joe, then?' I persisted. 'A real person? I read a bit about it. I thought it was just stories at first, but then there was something about some kidnappings. Did someone take the name from the stories, or did the story —'

'I told you,' said Connor, 'it's bullshit.'

'I don't know how you can be so sure,' said Sharon, mildly. 'You, me, Eddie and now Stanly can all do things that regular human beings can only dream about. Earlier on Stanly was dribbling a ball with the power of his mind. Daryl is a *talking beagle*. How can you not be open to the possibility? After everything we've seen . . .'

'Exactly,' said Connor. 'Everything we've *seen*. I accept that there's some bizarre stuff out there, Sharon, but until someone actually finds and shows me some monstrous man with a giant head, I'm staying skeptical.'

'Or until someone makes us fight it,' said Sharon.

Something changed when she said that. Connor had been irritated before, unwilling to have a discussion, but now he looked genuinely angry. 'I'm not having this conversation,' he said. 'OK? It's just some psycho, a messed-up human being, who needs to be put behind bars before he ruins any more lives. Nothing more.'

Sharon said nothing and we carried on towards the bus stop. Daryl and I exchanged silent *what the hell*s, but neither of us was brave enough to broach the subject again.

Monstrous man? Giant head?

Things were definitely getting weirder.

Although we got off the bus in a busy, friendly-seeming area, the comparatively short walk felt like it took us a long way. One minute there were people and car noises and general hubbub, the next just empty streets and shadows, and finally the playground, which looked less than inviting. I could feel Daryl's agitation. This wasn't Tref-y-Celwyn any more. I wasn't sure it was London. Maybe it wasn't even a real place.

There is something inherently creepy about empty playgrounds at the best of times, especially at night, and this one was maintaining the tradition admirably. The slides and monkey bars and climbing frames all looked slightly crooked, silhouetted against the orange murk, and one solitary swing creaked and moved minutely as though it had recently been used, although the others were perfectly still. Everywhere I looked I saw little children with red eyes giggling, or the outlines of big giant heads. I looked to my companions for reassurance, and found it in Connor's easy, unruffled stride as he casually went and sat down on a bench by the swings, and in Sharon's smile, which was luminous, even in the dark, as she sat on a swing and watched. Even Daryl was putting on a brave face.

Jesus, Stanly. It's a playground. *Engage wimp factor 9.9, why don't you? Oh yeah, you're already there. Pull it together. Immediately.*

I must have looked as worried as I felt because Connor laughed. 'Don't worry,' he said. 'Nobody really comes here. Kids are too scared, and I doubt that the toughest gun-toting heroin dealers in

London would do their business in this playground. Even the teenagers who come here don't tend to hang around late.'

I felt slightly better. Slightly.

'OK,' said Connor. 'Let's try some flying, shall we?'

'I can't really fly,' I said.

'You can almost,' said Daryl.

'I can't.'

'Show us what you *can* do,' said Sharon, gently.

I nodded, and tried to push all of my negative vibes, performance anxiety and other general worries into a locked chest at the back of my skull. Then I forced the lid shut and wrapped it in chains, and dropped it to the very bottom of a deep, dark cerebral ocean. Calm. I was Rick Blaine again. Cool. Kool and the Gang.

I opened my eyes without realising that I'd closed them and ran straight at the swings, planted my foot halfway up one of the metal support struts and made as many upward steps as I could before gravity started to get pissed off. When that happened I pushed away and pretended that physics was rubbish, that everything my teachers had told me was fantasy and wild theories, hogwash and balderdash . . . and it worked. I was in the air and I wasn't coming down. I stayed there, suspended, and let myself down slowly when I felt like it, and not a second before. I landed with perfect grace and grinned. I was definitely getting closer to mastering it. Sharon and Connor were clapping, and Daryl was wagging his tail. 'Skills,' he said.

'That was amazing,' said Connor. 'Really impressive, I've never seen anything like it. Can you do it from a standing start?'

I shrugged. It had worked once, but I'd had trouble recapturing it. 'I'll try.' I shook myself, letting my elation seep away, and concentrated on leaving the ground behind, on swimming through the air. The air was water, the air was a pool. Bending rules, breaking laws, just because I could. Again I opened my eyes and I was floating again, about fifteen feet above the ground, and Daryl was jumping up and down yelling, 'Yes! Yes! That's my human!' and Connor and Sharon were staring, open-mouthed. I felt pretty astounded as well. Excitement flared in my head and for a split second I was afraid. My perfect calm was going to evaporate, I was going to fall and break something . . .

But I didn't. I stayed there. And I started to realise that it was nothing do with calm, or anything like that. What had Daryl said, so long ago? That negative emotions helped? That wasn't it. That was just overthinking. There *was* no ideal state of mind, it was just something I could do. It was a fact. Running isn't dependent on your mental state, is it? Obviously it helps, but ultimately running is just a thing you can do. This was no different. It all dawned on me at once, a revelation that I could do this any time, regardless of how I felt, and I knew, just *knew,* that I'd broken a barrier. I could feel it. Just like that. *Snap.*

So I did it. I propelled myself through the air, and now I was finding that I could move with complete ease, Superman-like. I just spread my arms – and I flew. I stayed up for several minutes, swimming in the sky, and as the wind slipped loving fingers between every hair on my head, as though I were a child returning home, I felt an overwhelming, perfect joy envelop my entire being. This was where I belonged. This was the gift. This was freedom, pure and simple. And although I didn't venture *too* high, I knew that one day I'd be surfing clouds like it weren't no thang.

It felt absolutely incredible.

When I touched down Connor and Sharon were speechless, and Daryl was laughing hysterically. 'That was *the coolest goddamn thing I've ever seen,*' he managed to say, before collapsing from the sheer intensity of his laughter. Connor stood up and held out his hand, and we shook. 'Well,' he said. 'I seem to be fresh out of superlatives.'

I grinned, feeling lightheaded and hot and slightly unsteady. I needed to get some strength back so I sat on the bench, and Daryl trotted over and sat next to me. 'OK,' I said. 'Your turn, Connor.'

Connor smiled. 'I thought you might say that.' He shook himself, focusing, laser-like, and ran straight towards a lamppost. He planted his feet on it and for a second I thought he was going to backflip off, but he didn't. He ran all the way up, then put his feet on the underside of the glowing orange light and walked along it, upside-down. When he reached the end he walked around it, righted himself and walked along the top of the lamp, put his feet on the top of the post and walked vertically downwards. At the end he somersaulted and landed on his feet. He did a little bow as I clapped. 'How did you do that?' I asked. 'It's not flying, is it?'

'Not exactly,' said Sharon. 'It's like . . . like he can shift his centre of gravity. All he has to do is plant his feet on a surface – vertical, horizontal, upside-down, it doesn't matter – and he can walk along it just as easily as he'd walk along the street.'

'I've tried flying,' said Connor as he walked back over to us. 'Didn't work. Must say, I'm a wee bit jealous of your skills . . . but I'm pretty happy with mine, all the same.' He looked pleased with himself without being smug, and I found myself liking him more and more.

'That's not everything,' said Sharon. 'He's also incredibly strong and fast.'

'Like Eddie?' I asked.

'No,' said Connor. 'Not quite as good as Eddie. He's ridiculous. Blistering.' I wondered what might have happened, what scrape or misadventure they'd been involved in that had required Eddie to be 'blistering'. It felt as though there were stories to be told. 'What about you?' I asked Sharon. 'Your powers?'

'She makes a kick-ass Sunday roast,' said Connor.

Sharon shot him a withering look. 'Thanks, because I definitely don't get enough sexist banter at the hospital.'

'Sorry, darlin'.'

Sharon shook her head, although she did look amused. 'Well, you've seen that I can move things with my mind,' she said. 'Like you. But I also have a sort of awareness of people's thoughts. Sorry, that sounds stupid. Everyone can be aware of people's thoughts. It's . . . I can sense emotions on a deeper level than people normally might. I . . . it's quite hard to explain.'

'Can you read minds?'

She shook her head. 'It's not that. I suppose it's . . . empathy?' She laughed. 'Super empathy. That sounds silly, but it's the best way I can think of to describe it. Put it this way, even someone who was a good enough liar to fool a lie detector wouldn't be able to fool me.' She looked slyly at Connor. 'As he's found in the past.'

'So,' said Daryl. 'We've got two telekinetic types. I think that calls for a bit of a demonstration?'

Connor laughed. 'I thought it would come to this. So I devised a little game.' He reached into the sports bag and pulled out a tennis ball and a pair of rackets. 'You any good at tennis?' he asked me.

'I have no idea,' I said.

'Nor do I,' said Sharon. She eyed Connor suspiciously. 'What is this, Connor? Brain tennis?'

'Got it in one,' said Connor. 'You hold a racket each – with your minds, of course – and I throw the ball, and you bat it to each other.'

Sharon shook her head and laughed. 'Trust you. This is because I wouldn't let you watch Wimbledon, isn't it?'

I liked the sound of this, and immediately levitated one of the rackets and practised swinging it for a minute. It was easier than I'd been expecting. I'd definitely broken a pretty major wall; things were already coming much easier and faster. I stood about fifteen feet from Sharon, who lifted up her bat without even looking at it, and we faced one another, grinning.

'Ready?' asked Connor.

'Sharon!' cried Daryl, in a Scottish accent. 'You will go on my first whistle! Stanly —'

'Shut it, Muttley,' I said, sticking my tongue out.

'*You* shut it.'

'I'll take that as a "ready",' said Connor. He tossed the ball to me and I swung the racket, and now I was grateful for the hours I'd spent on Eddie's handed-down Sega Mega Drive all those years ago, because my hand-eye co-ordination was pretty damn good and this was basically the same thing, except it was more brain-eye co-ordination. *And brain and eye are much closer together.* I hit the ball and it flew towards Sharon, and she thwacked it straight back to me. The rally lasted about sixteen hits, and then I swung and missed and the ball hit me in the head. 'Ooh!' cried Daryl. 'Wipeout!'

'Do you want to go on?' called Sharon cheekily, her tone full of humour and . . . affection? Already? It was funny, I had known her and Connor less than a day, and we felt like old friends. I grinned cockily. 'Just warming up,' I said, and served.

We got home at quarter past twelve. The house was pleasantly warm after the cold world, and I hung up my coat and leaned against the wall, breathing deeply, feeling the psychic exertion. 'So,' said Connor. 'How d'you think that went?'

'Great,' I said. 'Fantastic.'

Connor laughed. 'Enthusiasm. A rare and beautiful thing.' He yawned. 'Well, I'm going to turn in. I have to go to 110th Street for about half ten tomorrow. Does that suit you?'

'Fine,' I nodded.

'Excellent. Goodnight.' He mounted the stairs and headed up.

''Night,' I said. 'And again, thanks a lot.'

'Don't mention it.'

Sharon was leaning against the door, looking as worn out as I felt. 'You OK?' I asked.

She nodded. 'I'm fine. Just tired.' She took off her coat and hung it up. 'Are you?'

'You're the empath, you tell me.' It was supposed to sound humorous, but it came out sounding almost pleading, and I looked at the floor. I didn't know how to answer her question. I'd been so engrossed in playing superpowers that I'd forgotten everything . . . but now it was coming back. Peace and quiet had opened the floodgates, and all I could see were those horrified faces, hear Miss Stevenson yelling Ben's name, feel Kloe's lips and tears . . .

Sharon's eyes were full of concern, and I felt embarrassed for being so obvious. 'I don't need to be empathic to tell you're not all right,' she said. 'Do you want to talk?'

I managed a weak smile. 'I'm fine,' I said. 'Just . . . need to go to bed.' I took off my shoes. 'Thanks for everything.'

She smiled. 'It's fine. Sleep well.'

'Thanks. You too. Come along, Gromit.' Daryl followed me upstairs and I shut the bedroom door behind us, got changed and lay down on the bed, flicking the lights off with my mind. Daryl curled up at the foot of the bed and whispered something that I couldn't hear. 'What?' I asked.

'Sure you don't want to talk about anything?' he asked in a louder whisper.

I shook my head. 'No. I just want to sleep.'

'OK. 'Night.'

''Night.'

'Hey, Stanly?'

'What?'

'You were *sick* out there.'

I laughed. 'Yeah, I know.'

'Great, kid. Don't get cocky.'

As I lay there in the dark, a thought struck me. *Shit, forgot to ask Sharon about Smiley Joe.*

Ah, I'll do it tomorrow.

Best to wait until Connor wasn't around, probably. What had Sharon meant, 'until someone makes us fight it'?

What was going on here?

I re-lit Connor's spliff for him and watched as he inhaled, then exhaled, the smoke rising up his nostrils in a spectacular multi-coloured Irish waterfall. He inhaled again, and blew the smoke out of his ears, and it rose up towards the ceiling, and I watched it mingle with the patterns there. Connor stared into me and laughed. 'Taken by a big giant head?' He shook his head, and the patterns shifted, and I shrugged and left the room, walking into a dimly-lit kitchen with a sink full of dirty dishes. Kloe was there, sitting on the counter, jamming with Eddie on a ukulele. Eddie had a clarinet. They were playing 'Life Is a Minestrone' by 10cc. Daryl was eating chilli out of a bowl on the floor, grumbling the whole time. A spider scuttled past him, the sharp, scuttling movement making me jump.

Suddenly the song stopped, as if sucked back into the instruments, and Kloe grabbed Eddie and started to kiss him violently. I felt myself getting angry. 'And you don't want to see him angry,' said Daryl, over his bowl. Kloe kept on kissing Eddie and he was kissing her back. Really hard. They were groping each other. They were using their tongues. I was so far beyond furious that I couldn't help myself. I eviscerated Eddie with my thoughts and was about to decide what to do to Kloe when the kitchen started to collapse around my ears. Kloe was standing in front of me, sobbing, and Sharon was watching, shaking her head, her arm around a little girl in red pyjamas. Kloe looked at me. Deep into me. Deeper than anyone was allowed to look. 'Don't go,' she said. Then everything was fire, and—

I sat up in bed, my face wet with tears and sweat. It was still dark, and I could hear the city groaning outside. I fell back against the pillow and made myself calm down, and pictured comforting things until I slept again. A rainbow. A lizard on a leaf. A plate of spaghetti and meatballs. A wide, lush meadow. Ben King inside a giant flaming wicker man. Usual happy place stuff.

CHAPTER FOURTEEN

W HEN I WOKE up again it was just before nine, and I didn't
have a clue where I was. Panic rose in my stomach and I sat up,
looking around the room for something familiar. Daryl was there.
That was good. That made me feel better. Where the—

Come on.

Calm down.

I took several deep breaths, and willed myself to remember.
London. Connor and Sharon's.

Safe.

No need for panickings.

I rubbed my eyes, and now the dream came drifting back into
view, blown on an uneasy mental wind. Kisses and fire and evisceration. It sounded like the title of an awful concept album.

'You all right?' asked Daryl. I jumped, not having realised that
he was awake, and didn't answer for a moment. He repeated the
question, and I shrugged. 'Going slightly mad.'

'Knitting with only one needle?'

'You got it.' I got out of bed and opened the curtains. The city
was festering under a thin mist, and the sky threatened rain. I
looked at myself in the mirror and ran my hands over my cheeks
and chin and the skin under my nose. I badly needed a shave. *I'll
go out and buy a razor today.*

I showered, brushed my teeth and headed downstairs. Daryl
was down there already, sitting at the table eating bacon. Connor
was reading the paper. 'Morning,' he said. 'You all right?'

'Yeah,' I said.

'Hungry?'

'Mm.'

'Scrambled eggs OK? That's about all I can do, Sharon's the master chef. Plus, *someone* ate the last of the bacon.' He shot Daryl a sardonic look.

'Hey, you offered!' said the dog.

'Yeah, I know. Make the most of it. It's Pedigree Chum for you from now on.'

'This truly is the darkest timeline.'

'Scrambled eggs is fine,' I said. 'I mean . . . are fine. Do you want me to—'

'You can make the coffee,' said Connor, crossing to the cupboard and rummaging around for eggs.

I made coffee and drank two cups before the eggs were done. Connor looked fairly professional as he beat and stirred, serving up a perfect plate of scrambled eggs and toast which I ate with another cup of coffee while Connor and Daryl discussed music. It turned out they were united in their affections for The Beatles, The Clash, Pink Floyd, Nirvana and Queen. Daryl, however, did not share Connor's love for 10cc. 'They're all right,' he said. '"I'm Not in Love" is OK, in a soft-rock, smudge-eyed, drive-time-radio sort of way. But "Dreadlock Holiday" is overrated. And some of their songs just piss me off. Like "Life Is a Minestrone". What a truly horrendous novelty piece of shit.'

I stopped mid-chew. 'Life Is a Minestrone'. A clarinet and a ukulele. Kisses and fire and evisceration.

Connor must have noticed my expression. 'You OK?'

I nodded slowly. 'Yeah . . . um . . . just a bit of déjà vu.'

'Uh-oh,' said Daryl. 'It's a gl—'

'Not one word about glitches in the Matrix,' I warned.

'I was *going* to say it's a glitch in . . . your face.'

'Good one.'

'Your face is glitchy.'

'Yeah, good one.'

'Glitchy face.'

'Great.'

Connor still looked concerned. 'Are you sure you're OK? You're a bit pale.'

'I'm fine,' I said. 'Tired.' I tucked into my breakfast and tried to clear my mind. When I'd finished, I shoved my plate in the dishwasher and stretched. The grogginess was finally lifting. 'So when are we going to the shop?' I asked, trying to sound decisive.

'What's the time?' Connor looked at his watch. 'Um . . . need to be there for half ten . . . we should probably leave in a minute. Take the Tube.'

'Cool,' I said, looking at Daryl, who was taking his turn with the paper. 'Will you be all right here alone?'

'Great,' he said, not looking up. 'Can I use the DVD player?'

'I don't know,' said Connor. 'Can you?'

'He opens his mouth and hilarity ensues,' said Daryl. 'I'll take that as a "yes, Daryl, make yourself at home".'

'Sure,' said Connor. 'Knock yourself out.'

I suddenly remembered my chin. 'Um . . . d'you think it'll count against me if I look like this? I forgot my razor.'

Connor laughed. 'Don't worry. Skank won't mind.'

'Really?'

'Trust me.'

As soon as we stepped into 110th Street, I saw what Connor meant. I assumed the guy in his late twenties standing there was Skank, and he didn't look like he cared what he looked like, let alone other people. He had an epic, tangled black beard and messy hair, and he was wearing an oversized Boba Fett T-shirt, beige shorts and sandals. He nodded at Connor. 'Morning, slugger.'

'Hi, Skank.' Connor nodded in my direction. 'This is Stanly. Eddie's cousin.'

'Ah.' Skank walked over and looked me up and down. 'Good build. Ever worked in a shop before?'

I shook my head. 'No.'

147

'Ever worked?'

'A bit. Kind of.'

Skank nodded shrewdly. 'Cool. Coolcoolcool.' He returned to the counter and spoke without looking back. 'Take a gander at the premises. If you like what you see, come over and I'll give you the test.'

I looked at Connor. 'The test?'

Connor smiled. 'Don't worry. It's not as bad as it sounds.' He made to walk away but I stopped him. 'Yeah?' he asked.

'Um . . . I'm a bit confused,' I said. 'This place looks too small to need more than two people looking after it.'

Connor nodded. 'Ah. Thought you'd notice that.' He gestured at Skank, who was reading a *Daredevil* comic. 'Skank is the owner. He oversees stuff. He only talks to customers who he believes are on his level.'

'His level?'

'Knowledge-wise,' said Connor. 'The guy is a fountain of trivia. Knows everything about science fiction, horror and fantasy. *Everything*. He answers people's questions, but only if they're either really obscure or really clever. The rest of the time he sits around and reads comics and things.'

'What do you do?'

'General dogsbodying,' Connor grinned. 'I tell people where to look for stuff, I take orders, I manage the phones, I offer helpful advice when Skank's too up himself to make eye contact. There's online stuff to be done as well, and at the moment I man the till, but I'm guessing that's something I might pass to you.'

I nodded. 'OK.'

'You want to take a look around?'

'Uh-huh.'

Connor left through a door behind the counter. It had a massive banner hanging above it with something written in another language. I think it was Elvish, but I couldn't be sure.

I did as Skank said and took a gander. It was a fairly hardcore dungeon of geekery. Where the walls weren't covered with shelves full of stuff they bore posters of films and TV shows, many of which I'd never heard of, along with collectors' editions of comics in sealed plastic sleeves, new toys, much older toys (in their original packaging, naturally) and a few glass display cases that contained rarer items. There was a staircase in the corner leading to the second floor, with a sign reading BOOKS AND MORE COMICS UPSTAIRS hanging next to it. I wondered how much money this place took, how much Connor was paid, how much I'd get, how Connor and Sharon could afford their house on their income.

Stop thinking about other people's finances, said a voice in my head. *It's rude.*

I shrugged. If they could afford it, they could afford it. None of my business. Satisfied that I liked the premises, I walked over to the counter. 'Um . . . Skank?'

Skank looked up. 'You approve?'

'I approve,' I said. 'Um . . . this test . . . what—'

Skank raised his hand. 'Worry not, young Padawan. Just a few questions, nothing too strenuous.'

He just called you a Padawan. It's not too late to run away.

I don't think I have the right to run away.

Why?

Because I know what a Padawan is.

'You'll have to excuse the prequel reference,' sad Skank, sitting back in his chair. 'I didn't get much sleep last night. Pull up a chair.'

I grabbed a stool and sat down, resting my elbows on the counter. Skank nodded. 'Right. Question one of eight. Your favourite episode of *Buffy the Vampire Slayer*?'

I liked that he assumed I had one. 'Um . . . that's really difficult.'

'Good answer. That gets you a pass, but just out of interest? Could you suggest one?'

'Um . . . I like the musical . . . and *Conversations with Dead People* . . . um . . . *Becoming*. Definitely.'

'Part One or Part Two?'

'Do I have to choose?'

'Yes.'

'Part Two.'

Skank nodded. 'A wise choice. Personally I would go with *Hush* but that's just me.' He stroked his beard. 'Question two. Your favourite genre film?'

I couldn't answer that. 'I can't answer that.'

He nodded again. 'Good. I couldn't either.' He cleared his throat. 'Question three. Best James Bond?'

'Connery.'

'Excellent. Daniel Craig would have got you a pass, but Connery scores higher. Roger Moore would have meant a premature end to this edition of Genre Mastermind. Question four . . . this one's just off the top of my head . . . best film featuring John Cusack?'

'*Grosse Pointe Blank.*'

'Intriguing. I like *Being John Malkovich*, but there you go. Question five. Favourite Doctor?'

'Excuse me?'

'Doctor.'

'As in . . .'

'*Doctor Who.*'

'I've not really watched *Doctor Who.*'

Skank shrugged. 'Well at least you didn't say Sylvester McCoy.' He was twiddling his thumbs. 'Question six. This is a two-part question. Have you seen *Akira*?'

'Yes.'

'In English or subtitled?'

'Japanese, with subtitles.'

Skank seemed impressed. 'This is going very well. Question seven. Children of the night . . .'

It took a minute for me to catch on, but I did. 'What music they make?' I offered, finishing the quote.

Skank nodded. 'By the skin of your teeth, whatever that means. And the final question – this is a three part question, or possibly three separate ones. Can you operate a cash register?'

'No.'

'Are you willing to learn?'

'Yes.'

'How soon can you start?'

'Nowish?'

'Consider yourself hired.' He held out a hand, and I noticed he had the Red Hot Chili Peppers' logo tattooed on his inner wrist. I liked this guy. We shook, and he said, 'Welcome to 110th Street. OK. Now. This is how the till works.'

Connor and I finished for lunch at two o'clock and spent our break in a Chinese eatery around the corner from the shop. I had barbecue spare rib and egg-fried rice and Connor had chicken chow mein. 'Connor?' I asked.

'Yes?'

'You know Skank?'

'I'm familiar with his work.'

'Is he . . . a real person?'

Connor chuckled. 'Oh, he's real.'

'Does he have any powers?' *Have I asked this question before?*

'To be honest,' said Connor, 'I'm not sure. He does have a . . . persuasive aspect that I've often thought might be a bit extracurricular. But it's never really come up. He's very private. What I can tell you is that he's extremely generous, very loyal and totally incorruptible.'

Totally incorruptible, repeated one of the worryingly varied voices in my head. *What does that mean?*

It means he can't be corrupted, said a voice that I had now designated 'talking to morons'.

I know what it means, said the first voice. *But what does* Connor *mean by it?*

By now I was realising that Connor's laid-back exterior hid a rather mysterious interior, and I didn't press the matter further. We chatted amiably while we ate and then went back to the shop to find Skank arguing heatedly with a couple of teenagers about the Silver Surfer. Connor and I broke it up and the teenagers left without buying anything. 'Pricks,' muttered Skank.

The rest of the afternoon passed quickly, and I successfully rang up several sales. At five thirty Skank cleared his throat and said, 'OK, travellers. Hop it. See you tomorrow.'

'What time do you want us?' asked Connor.

Skank thought for a moment. 'Um . . . eleven. Give or take.'

'OK,' said Connor. 'See you tomorrow.'

'Yes.'

I held out my hand. 'Thanks for the job.' Skank shook absently and nodded, and as Connor and I opened the door, I heard the mysterious proprietor say, 'Be seeing you'.

I definitely liked Skank.

CHAPTER FIFTEEN

W E RODE HOME on the Tube and I amused myself observing people. I was particularly delighted by a huge black guy in an expensive-looking leather ensemble sitting across from us; he'd barely moved since we'd got on, but now he reached into his bag, withdrew a copy of the first Harry Potter and started to read, a contented smile spreading across his previously stony face. I shot Connor a sly grin. He was smiling serenely. 'So,' I said. 'What's Skank's deal?'

Connor raised an eyebrow. '"Deal"?'

'Yeah. There's got to be something you haven't told me.'

'Such as?'

I hesitated, but he seemed in a good mood so I chanced it. I told him about my . . . what were they? Suspicions? No, they weren't really suspicious enough to be suspicions. I simply voiced my curiosity about the shop, and about his and Sharon's financial situation. Far from being angry, he looked relieved. 'Is that it?' he asked. 'I thought you were going to drop some sort of bomb.' He chuckled softly. 'Well . . . you're right. There is something about Skank I'm not telling you. He's a millionaire.'

I hadn't been expecting that. I don't know why. Now it seemed obvious. 'Really?' was all I could come up with.

'His dad was big in advertising,' said Connor. 'Did you ever see that advert . . . what was it for . . . it was a beer advert. The one with the panther and the waterfall?'

'Rings a vague bell.'

'Well, his dad came up with that. Then there were loads of others. Mostly cars. He made himself a hell of a lot of cash out of them, and then his wife divorced him, some ridiculous argument about decorating or interior design, wallpaper or something. She went to live with some reggae artist. Didn't want any money, so he left it all to Skank. When Skank first told me I thought he had to be taking the piss. You've seen how deadpan he is; half the time I don't know if he's being deadly serious or taking me for a ride, but he swore it was true. Anyway, the upshot was that his dad left him all that money and now he's loaded. But he's a bit eccentric, as you might have gleaned, so he spent as much money as he needed on a really nice flat and then decided he wanted to own a comics shop, just on a whim. He bought the shop a few years ago, back when it was a delicatessen owned by some old Jewish couple, converted it and *voilà*. I'm pretty sure he's got a few other business ventures going on the side as well, although he keeps them to himself – the shop does well, but not *that* well. But at any rate, he likes having people around, even if he doesn't always show it, so he pays me far too much for what I do just because he's a nice guy, and I'm sure he'll be equally decent to you. So, there you are.'

A few people had been listening in, with varying degrees of amusement and disapproval on their faces. A woman in her mid-twenties was smiling broadly, an old man had been looking scandalised since Connor had said 'piss', and the guy opposite me was peering interestedly over the top of his book. I couldn't think of anything to say. The story was so weird it had to be true. It was like finding a little private sitcom in the middle of all the uncertainty and foreboding, and it made me feel a lot better about everything. 'Thanks,' I said.

'For what?'

'Just . . . thanks.'

We got home to find Sharon and Daryl side-by-side on the couch. Daryl was watching an old black and white film I didn't recognise, and Sharon was reading. 'Hi,' she said. 'You guys hungry?'

'Not right now, thanks babe,' said Connor. 'Stanly?'

'Not really.' I patted Daryl. 'Had a good day?'

'Top notch,' he said, sounding like he was in as good a mood as me. 'Did you get the job?'

'Yeah.'

'What did you think of Skank?' asked Sharon.

'Odd bird,' I said.

Sharon nodded. 'Yes. That fits.'

'But I do like him,' I added, hastily. 'A lot.'

She smiled. 'Thought you would.'

I sat in the armchair and Daryl came and sat on the arm next to me. 'Eddie called,' said Sharon.

'Is he OK?' I asked.

'Yeah,' said Sharon. 'Fine. Worried, though.'

'Seriously? Him?'

'I know. By the time I'd regained consciousness he'd put the phone down.'

Connor came in, bent down and kissed Sharon. 'Quiet shift?'

'Quietest. I was just telling Stanly that Eddie called.'

'Let me guess. He was worried.'

'Go figure.'

'Go fish. Is he coming over?'

'No, I think he just wanted Stanly to call him when he got in.' Sharon looked at me. 'Do you mind?'

'No,' I said. 'That's fine. Where's the phone?'

'In the hall.'

The phone rang about three times before Eddie picked it up. 'Yeah?' He sounded a little on edge, amazingly enough.

'Hey, it's Stanly.'

'Oh! Hi. Are you OK?'

'I'm fine, thanks. You?'

'What?'

'Are you OK? You sound . . . wired.'

'Oh . . . no, I'm fine. So you got the job?'

'Yeah.'

'Great. What did you think of Skank?'

'I liked him.'

'Yeah, he's a good guy. Listen, um . . . I can't get over there tonight. Can you put me on to Connor? I need to have a word with him.'

'Sure. So I'll see you tomorrow?'

'Probably, yeah. Take care.'

'You too. Bye.'

I held the phone away from my ear and called, 'Connor! Eddie wants a word!'

'Thanks,' said Connor. He took the phone. 'All right, man? What's up?'

I returned to the living room and sat back down. Daryl and Sharon were talking about politics and I watched for a minute, bemused and heartened by this exchange between woman and dog. Whenever I used to watch the news Daryl would watch with me and he ate up anything to do with politics just so he could sound off about it. He was very opinionated, for a dog. Politics has always been an area where I switch off, so I drifted into standby mode. After about five minutes Connor poked his head around the door. 'Something's come up. I'm going to meet Eddie.'

Sharon looked straight at Connor and I could tell she was trying to read him. He shook his head. 'Nothing wrong, babe. Eddie stuff. I'll be back soon.' He blew her a kiss, threw on his coat and left the house. I gave Sharon a questioning look. She seemed troubled. 'I couldn't read him,' she said. 'I try not to anyway, it's not fair . . . but sometimes . . .' She shook her head. 'I don't know.'

'I thought you said you couldn't read minds?'

'I can't. But I can still sense things. Anxiety. Anger. That sort of thing . . . and there was nothing.' She looked briefly at the floor, then back at me. 'Anyway.' She smiled. 'I seem to remember you wanted to have a chat?'

I put on my best baffled expression.

'About Smiley Joe?' she prompted.

156

Oh yeah. Him. I nodded. 'Oh yeah. Him. That. What's . . . what's all that about?'

'Well . . . it's not a nice story,' said Sharon.

'I don't mind,' I said. 'I'll stop you if it gets too scary.'

'OK.' Sharon shifted on the sofa. 'How much do you know about him?'

'Not a lot, to be honest. Bits and pieces, but most of it is pretty contradictory. Some kind of evil creature that does bad things in various cities, that was about the only through-line.'

Sharon nodded. 'There are lots of theories. All the usual craziness – demon escaped from Hell, scientific experiment gone wrong, God's punishment for our permissive, gay-friendly society. Some people think he's a . . . physical manifestation of the darkness in London. Or in the world. I'm not entirely sure what I believe about his origin, but I believe in *him*.'

I nodded. 'Go on.'

'The first case was back in the Eighties,' said Sharon. 'Long before I lived here, but I've heard the story from people who were there. Two children went out to a play park near a derelict block of flats in North London. Lots of people thought they were haunted. I don't know about that. They've been demolished now, anyway. The two children were a brother and a sister. They were last seen buying sweets from a newsagent around the corner from the park. The newsagent knew their family well and they told him where they were going. He was the last person to see them.'

'Alive?'

'At all. They disappeared completely. No witnesses, no evidence, nothing. Not a lot was made of it that first time, but over the course of the next year ten more children disappeared under identical circumstances. Vanished without a trace. There was a panic, a curfew was imposed, children were rarely allowed outside unless it was absolutely necessary, and when they did they were always with their parents. Then, suddenly, the disappearances stopped. For the next two years, nothing happened.'

'Then?'

'Nineteen eighty-nine,' said Sharon. 'A family called Harris. Their neighbours heard smashing and screaming and called the police, but when the police got there they found the parents dead, the front door smashed and the children gone. As before, there were no witnesses and no evidence of any kind. The children were another brother and a sister. Their names were Carl and Louise, eight and eleven. The panic came back and the police combed the city for two days, and after three the children turned up. Carl didn't speak and he hasn't since, but Louise told their story. She described their kidnapper, she described them fighting for their lives, she described them pushing the thing into the incinerator in the basement where he had taken them and running away. They became brief celebrities, talk shows and magazines and newspapers all wanted them, but their remaining family refused to let them speak.'

'Are they still alive?' I asked. My skin was very cold, and I was developing goosebumps. The MO was the same. A house in London. *No fingerprints, no skin samples. Just a lot of broken glass, a man and a woman with broken necks and two missing eight-year-olds.* An incinerator? What the hell was this?

'Yes,' said Sharon. 'As far as I know.'

'There's more, isn't there?'

'Yes,' she said again. 'The reason it was so huge was the way Louise described the kidnapper. I remember reading the description. I read it again and again – you know the way something is horrifying but you can't not read or watch? I used to be quite a fan of horror films and stuff . . . anyway. Louise's exact words were *like a man, but not.*'

'"A man, but not",' I said. A shiver was making its way slowly over my whole body, taking its time.

Sharon nodded. 'She said that his head was too big. And that he didn't move like a man – and that he tried to eat them.'

I sat, letting the story sink in. I couldn't think of anything to say. I had been feeling good about London, and now my own curiosity had spoiled it. I half wished that Sharon had followed Connor's advice and not said anything. That there might be something in that stupid story . . .

'Nobody really believed that part,' said Sharon, 'as I'm sure you can imagine. Carl never said anything and Louise was badly traumatised anyway. People put it down to that. There were no more kidnappings, so the incinerator story was at least assumed to be true. After that, people kind of forgot about it. Went on to the next thing, the way they do. Once it had stopped there was no reason to care. Louise and Carl went to live with an aunt and uncle and everything seemed to be all right, more or less.'

'But it's not,' I said. 'Because he's back.'

'I think so,' said Sharon. 'I don't think it's a copycat, and I don't think it's some sick human like Connor does. I think it's a monster.'

Daryl nodded solemnly. 'Right. Well. Thanks for that, Sharon. Now I'll never sleep again.'

'You and me both,' I said.

Sharon smiled sadly. 'There's more going on in this city than you might think. Connor would rather pretend it's nonsense than think about it. Eddie probably thinks about it too much. I just . . . want everyone to be careful. I want *you* to be careful. To be safe.'

I tried a smile. 'I will be,' I said. 'And hey – superpowers, remember?'

She smiled back, but hers looked as convincing as mine felt.

Smiley Joe. The phantom child-eating monster. It sounded ridiculous. It *was* ridiculous. A terrible tragedy around which a web of stories had grown, people's imaginations filling in the blanks, nonsense . . .

Except that deep down, I knew it was true. I just knew.

And I'm going to find the bastard.

Sharon went for a bath about an hour later so I got my notebook and went to the phone. I made sure that Connor and Sharon's number was withheld before I dialled.

It rang.

It rang.

159

It rang.

Click. 'Hello?'

'Hi.'

'Stanly?' Miss Stevenson had sounded tired when she'd picked up, but now she was wide awake and agitated. 'Are you all right?'

'I'm fine. I just wanted to say I'm sorry. About the play.'

'Oh, it's . . . it's fine. Just so long as you're OK.'

'No, it's not fine. I ruined it.'

'You did no such thing.' She sounded more like a teacher now. 'You did *not* ruin the play and don't you ever tell yourself you did. Now, I don't completely understand what happened. I'm not sure I even partially understand it. But I know that you were pouring your heart and soul into your performance, and I know that if there'd been *anything* you could have done you would have done it. Things were out of your control. I don't blame you. It's a shame, but I don't blame you.'

Relief flooded my mind and my body. Connor's story about Skank had lifted a weight from inside me, and Sharon's Smiley Joe tutorial had put some of it back, but now it was at least tempered with relief. Miss Stevenson didn't hate me. That was something.

'Stanly? Are you still there?'

'Yes. Um . . . I can't talk for long. I just wanted to ask a few things.'

'Where are you?'

'I can't say. My parents know. They're all right.'

'Stanly, I don't think there's—'

'Please. I just want to know . . . how's Kloe?'

'I . . .' said Miss Stevenson, hesitantly. 'I think she's OK. She was . . . well, you can imagine, she wasn't too good when you left. I had no idea that you two were so close. I mean . . . I could see the chemistry in rehearsals, but I didn't realise . . . she came into school the next day, came to see me. Managed to smile a few times. You haven't spoken to her?'

'Not yet, I . . . I mean, I haven't got her number with me . . .'
Worst. Excuse. Ever.

'You could find it, though? You should definitely phone her! She's—'

'I can't. I just . . . it'd be too difficult. I can't explain. I'm managing to keep things together down here, and if I speak to her I'll just go to pieces. It would . . .' Words failed me, and they seemed to fail Miss Stevenson as well. 'Ben's been suspended,' she managed, after an age of silent awkwardness.

'Is that it?' I had expected expulsion at least. Not that expulsion seemed to mean much now, on a scale of trouble to trouble. *Maybe a firing squad?*

'His parents are high up locally, and they have influence with the board of governors, so I think suspension is the best we can hope for. Personally, I think it's disgraceful and, for what it's worth, I've made my feelings known.'

'Thank you.'

'Is there anything you need?'

'No. But . . . when you next see Kloe could you tell her . . . I'm sorry. And that I miss her.'

'I really don't think I can—'

'Please.'

'Stanly, you're putting me in a very difficult position. I shouldn't know where you are. There are legal things to consider, I—'

'You're the only person.' I felt bad. I knew we were on thin ice with this. But Kloe had to know, and I couldn't tell her yet. *You're a coward.*

She sighed. 'All right. I'll . . . I'll tell her. But she'll want to know where you are.'

'You don't know where I am. You can tell her that truthfully.'

'Are you *sure* you're all right?'

'I'm fine. And like I said, my parents know.'

'Well . . . I'll give Kloe your message. But I think you should come back.'

'I want to. I have to sort myself out. I don't know how long it's going to take. I will be back . . . I just don't know when.'

Miss Stevenson sighed again. 'OK. Well, take care.'

'I won't call you again unless I really have to. I don't want you to lose your job over me. That school needs you.'

She laughed tiredly. 'Thanks.'

'Thank *you*.' I hung up, feeling better and worse, and later that night I lay on my bed, wide awake, psychically re-arranging the books on the shelves, Daryl snoring at my feet. Too many thoughts whirling around. What to do next. There was cause to be optimistic, of course. I couldn't really compain about my situation. Well . . . I could. At length. But at the same time, after a few days of being here, I had a bed, and a roof over my head. I had a job. I had people looking after me, possibly the only people in the whole of London who could genuinely understand what I was going through.

Plus, I had superpowers . . . and aye, there was the rub. Because it seemed like I had to do something about it. Maybe if I was still living it up in Middle-of-Nowheresville, Mid Wales, I could afford to hang with a girl I fancied, and be in plays, and just fly around in the woods. But now, through a shitty set of circumstances, I was somewhere big and scary and new, where there was real, bona fide *bad stuff* occurring. More than I knew.

And what do *I know?*

I knew about Smiley Joe. The child-eater. I could see a shadow of him in my mind's eye, an indistinct artist's impression, and now I could see the faces of my three American cousins as well, so young and innocent and playful. Jacob was nine and obsessed with *Star Wars*. Annabel was eight and often pretended to be a cat. Little Jade was six and had been missing two of her front teeth, the last time I'd seen her. We'd got on like a house on fire. I'd felt like a big brother when I was with her, and it was the only time I had ever wanted any kind of sibling.

That had been over a year ago. Hadn't seen them or my aunt and uncle since, hadn't had any communication apart from the twenty pounds they'd sent me for my birthday. I realised that I missed them. And I realised that those three little kids would probably make an excellent dinner for Smiley Joe. Gourmet cuisine, unless he didn't like American food. If he met my cousins they wouldn't stand a chance, he wouldn't hear their sweet, laughing voices or see their eager faces, he'd just devour them.

Except he wouldn't, because I was going to kill him one day, and I was going to enjoy it.

Monsters.

Just what you wanted.

I should be out there, hunting for him. Him, and any others like him.

Great plan. And where exactly in the million or so square miles of unfamiliar city would you start looking?

Surely I needed to be doing *something*, though? Something worthwhile? Or at the very least, something to vent a bit of the frustration I could feel building up inside. I could go to some dodgy estate, *the* dodgiest, and find a gang of knife-wielding youths and batter the crap out of them with my powers before flying up to the roof of the nearest tower block and standing on the parapet, silhouetted dramatically against the night sky.

That's not really helping anyone though, is it?

Whatever. Biff, pow, ker-plunk. I enjoyed this little mental video and played it over and over again, and gradually it blurred into a dream in which I walked through a huge estate, its decaying buildings looming at odd, impressionistic angles, stepping over the bodies of bad guys I'd taken out. In the distance I could make out a man in a grey suit. I couldn't see his face, although I *could* see his smile. 'Not bad,' he was saying. 'Not bad at all.'

I turned away, and now I was standing alone on the school stage, delivering an oxymoronic speech to an audience of empty seats. 'Oh heavy lightness! Serious vanity! Misshapen chaos of well-seeming forms!' Now I was sitting on the edge of the stage, silhouetted dramatically against nothing much, my legs dangling over clear water. 'Feather of lead, bright smoke, cold fire, sick health!'

'Stanly?'

I stood up, or was already standing up, and turned on the spot.

Kloe was there, in white pyjamas with pictures of fish all over them, holding her ukulele. She put her head on one side. 'Where'd you go?'

'Away.' The glass of milk on the low table winked at me.

'Don't finish it too quickly,' warned Kloe.

I hadn't touched my milk, but I didn't say so. 'I haven't touched my milk.' Or maybe I did.

Kloe shrugged and threw the ukulele, and I watched it skim across the lake, spinning and jumping like a strange musical fish. I was sure I could see spiders running around beneath the surface, upside-down, spindly, smoky, shiny. I waited until the rippling had dissipated and the instrument had disappeared, and turned back to Kloe.

But she wasn't Kloe. She was a gigantic head, white like nothing can be white, with huge eyes and a mouth that could swallow time. It moved towards me and I stepped backwards, finding myself at the edge of the stage. I'd fall in the lake if I wasn't careful. 'Water's better than gullet,' said Daryl's voice from somewhere. I nodded and jumped backwards.

The water was shallow, only up to my knees, and it was warm and strangely thick. It felt like leek and potato soup. I stared down, wanting to see the distortion, not wanting to see the head, and for a split second I saw someone else's face staring up at me, a human face, a stranger. Then I looked up and it was on me, the mouth was opening-

I sat up in bed. It was half past nine, and dull light was leaking through the curtains, and Daryl wasn't there. I rubbed my eyes, suddenly awake, and felt no desire to go back to sleep again.

After showering, I went downstairs to find Daryl and Connor chatting over breakfast again. These two were getting quite chummy. It was nice, in a bemusing sort of way. Connor looked up. 'Morning.'

'Morning.' I poured myself some coffee.

'Sleep well?'

No. 'Yeah, thanks. Was it eleven that Skank wanted us?'

164

'Yeah.' Connor finished the glass of milk he was drinking. 'You hungry?'

I frowned slightly. 'No.' It came out in a slow, surprised tone. Daryl laughed, and Connor raised an eyebrow. 'You sure?'

I shook my head, not as a response but so I could clear it. 'Yeah, thanks. I'll get something later.'

'Stanly,' said Daryl, in a terribly serious voice. 'I'm going to ask you something, and I want you to be honest with me.'

'OK.'

'Have you been partaking of the drugs?'

Connor cracked up. I was pretty close to cracking up too, but fought to keep a straight face. 'Yes,' I said, solemnly. 'I have been partaking of the drugs. All your drug are belong to me.'

'Thought so.' Daryl shook his head. 'I'm very disappointed, but also incredibly proud.'

'Thanks.'

'I'm much more proud than I am disappointed.'

'Thank you.'

'I think you're really, really cool. For doing all those drugs.'

'Cheers.'

'Are you guys done?' asked Connor.

'Never,' said Daryl.

CHAPTER SIXTEEN

I 10TH STREET WAS located at the edge of an area filled with myriad delicatessens, bakeries, restaurants, takeaways and fishmongers. I enjoyed the walk from the Tube station, the way the market stalls and funny T-shirts and top hats gradually gave way to a bewildering array of foods, and it was particularly invigorating in the morning, when the fish was fresh and smoky goodness emanated from every window. You could smell curry, fried breakfasts, baking bread, sticky sugar, burgers, chow mein, pretty much everything you could possibly fancy, and today it made for an especially effective wake-up call, washing away the uneasiness left by yet another weird dream.

I liked the walk back to the station in the evening as well, but for different reasons. By that time, Camden people had started to emerge, strange-looking individuals in odd outfits, sometimes garish and mismatched, sometimes almost painfully co-ordinated. Some of them looked incredibly pretentious. Some of them looked cool. But they all looked simultaneously at home and completely lost, as though they inhabited an entirely different planet from the banker types, and the *Big Issue* sellers, and the coffee shop intellectuals, and the ragged shop doorway people whose dogs were always much better groomed than they were. Nobody belonged.

Maybe that was the point of this city.

Maybe that was why I'd ended up here.

Connor and I arrived at the shop to find Skank talking in-depth with another guy in his mid-twenties, with blonde hair, a goatee beard and very small ears. They were discussing some limited run of obscure German comics, and Skank didn't even seem to notice us. Connor went to the back to hang his coat up and I assumed my position behind the counter, ready for another day's work.

The blonde guy left about twenty minutes later, and Skank came and sat by me. 'Artist,' he said, by way of an explanation. He picked up an old *Preacher* trade paperback and started to read, and that was the extent of our conversation for the day. I interacted with a few customers, turned the pages of several *Batman* comics with my mind, and thought about how much I wanted to go out and fly.

Soon.

That evening Eddie came round with a big heavy bag, which he deposited proudly in front of me. I looked up at him questioningly, and he grinned. 'Well, look inside!'

I opened it with a slight flutter in my stomach that took me back to old Christmases. There was a small amplifier inside, pretty new-looking. I grinned up at Eddie. 'Wow! Wicked! Thanks!'

'Well. You've got a guitar and nothing to plug it into.'

'Where did you get this?'

'Borrowed it off a guy at work. He and a couple of his mates had started a band and they did a few gigs, but they were always arguing so they split up. He said he's got no use for it at the moment, and that I can have it until he wants it back. Which he probably won't, ever.' He looked pleased with himself, and I held out my hand and we shook.

Connor and Sharon came in. Sharon looked tired, but she perked up when she saw the amplifier. 'Ooh!' she smiled. 'Are you going to play?'

I didn't say anything. *You* can't *play*, I thought. *I can* try, I replied. *No,* I countered. *Embarrassed.*

Eddie could tell what I was thinking. 'Hey,' he said to Connor. 'Why don't you play something?'

'You play?' I asked.

167

'Yeah!' said Eddie. 'He used to be in a band and everything.'

Connor whistled and shook his head. 'Years ago.'

'Really?' I asked. 'What were you called?'

'Doggerel,' he said, grinning sheepishly. 'Terrible name. Not my choice. We really weren't up to much.'

'But you played lead guitar,' said Eddie.

'He was good, too,' said Sharon. 'Still is.'

'I wasn't,' said Connor. 'I mean, I'm not.'

'You are, you modest mouse!'

'Good one.'

'Go up and get your guitar, would you Stanly?' asked Eddie.

I ran upstairs. The instrument was in its case, leaning against the wall of my room. I hadn't touched it for days. It reminded me too much of home. *This is exactly what you need*, I thought. I took it downstairs and handed it to Connor, who unzipped the case, wearing a half-embarrassed, half-excited grin. Eddie and Sharon were sitting side-by-side on the sofa watching, and Daryl was lying on the armchair with one sleepy eye on proceedings.

Connor hooked it up and twiddled some knobs expertly. *Twiddled some knobs expertly*, I thought. *Hehehe. Oh what is this*, I admonished myself, *Carry On Stanly*? 'You look like you know what you're doing,' I said.

'He does,' smiled Sharon.

'A bit,' said Connor. He sat cross-legged, put the guitar strap around his neck and played a chord. It sounded wrong, and he quickly re-tuned the instrument then played the same chord again. This time it sounded fine.

'Play us one of your songs,' I said.

'What? A Doggerel number?' Connor shook his head. 'No, no, no. God no. Nobody needs to be subjected to my post-shoegaze neo-Britpop hangover. Um . . . this is really hard. I'm drawing a total blank.'

'Do you know any Red Hot Chili Peppers?' asked Daryl.

'Not to play,' said Connor.

'Do some Zep,' said Eddie. 'You used to smash the Zep.'

Connor frowned slightly. 'OK . . . come on, memory, don't fail me now.' He adjusted the levels on the amp and played a few practise chords, then started to play 'Dazed and Confused', which happened to be the only Led Zeppelin song I knew. *More than a bit fitting as well.* Connor played loosely but accurately, bending strings to approximate the yowl of the original, and he sang in a tuneful, slightly gravelly voice. Even stripped of percussion, bass and everything else it sounded really good, and I glanced at Sharon, who looked entranced. I got the feeling that she missed listening to him play.

He followed it with 'Not Fade Away' by The Rolling Stones, and a few more random numbers. We attempted to sing along to the ones we knew, listening and tapping our toes to the ones we didn't. And as we sat there, Connor and Sharon and Eddie and Daryl and I, singing and smiling, I had that feeling of belonging again. That feeling that seemed so odd and faraway, that I'd properly experienced for the first time only three days ago. Already, Tref-y-Celwyn and *Romeo and Juliet* seemed so distant, and only Kloe's face stood out with any real clarity. I needed to see her. To speak to her, at least. But maybe I shouldn't? Maybe it hadn't been meant to be? Maybe, if I stayed away long enough, time would do its fixing thing. For me, and for her.

I kind of doubted it. But between my job, my new friends, my superpowers and the possibility of monsters, at least I had plenty to be getting on with.

Time did its moving thing, but didn't seem too bothered about its fixing thing. I only thought about Kloe, on average, once every two or so minutes, and each time it brought that stomach pain blossoming outward and upward, spreading to my chest, tightening brutally. I was still working up the courage to give her a call, having discovered her number buried in my notebook, but an overwhelming combination of shyness, anxiety and the fear that I would have a full-on nervous breakdown if I heard her voice conspired to stop me. I picked up the phone on the third of April, but immediately put it down again. I'll try again in a week, I thought, but I didn't.

Connor and I still worked odd hours at 110th Street, Sharon carried on with her nursing and Eddie was bouncing. Or bouncering, or whatever. He was around a lot and actually appeared to be lightening up, which suited him. I enjoyed my work and I liked Skank's company, and Daryl liked having the house and the neighbourhood to roam – he was getting more adventurous the longer we stayed – and having his pick of Connor's extensive library of DVDs. There were no more kidnappings and I didn't think about home too much, although my mother had spoken to Eddie again briefly. It had gone like this:

Eddie: Yeah?

Mum: Is he OK?

Eddie: Yeah.

And that was it. She didn't even ask about the car, which was still sitting outside Eddie's house.

In between working and doing power-related exercises, Connor, Eddie and Sharon took it in turns to show me around the city. I got the general hang of it surprisingly quickly, despite its frankly mind-boggling size, and in a pretty short space of time I had a solid grasp of London's geography, as well as a good grounding in the mechanics of the underground system and the buses, and I could navigate my way around using major landmarks, with Tube stations and street names rattling around in my head and rolling off my tongue like I'd been living there for ever. I really started to feel like I belonged in this place where no-one belongs, and that I understood it in a way that I'd never understood cities before. My idea of them from films had been as simple places, easily navigated on one level. Places where superheroes and gangsters and bumbling comedy buffoons went from A to B to do their business, or where Jack Bauer could traverse any distance in as short a time as the plot required. London had hundreds of levels, thousands in fact, and some of them fitted and some of them didn't, and I loved losing myself in it, finding random streets and little parks and tangles of graffiti, and strange grimy tangents, safe in the knowledge that I was never *too* lost, and that I could always fly away if necessary. Life was actually threatening to be good.

And then came the twentieth of May.

The twentieth of May comes every year. It's inevitable. You can't stop a day from coming, and it shouldn't be a surprise when it arrives, but sometimes particular dates sneak up on you, like they're doing it on purpose. Like this one did.

I woke up and I just knew. I hadn't been in school since March, and even then I'd only really kept track of what day it was because of the play, but I *knew*. Today was the last day, the last day for my year group before they started study leave and exams. Today they'd all be getting their school shirts signed, picking up their official yearbooks, having their own personal leaving books signed with messages in multicoloured pen, taking photographs, pissing about on the field, just like we'd seen so many top-year students do since we'd started school. The top-year students had always seemed so much older, impossibly older, but now that was us. Well. Them. The ones I'd left behind. Today everyone was supposed to be friends. Everyone getting a piece of cake. I should have been there, having people sign my shirt and write in my book.

But I wasn't. I was working in a comics shop for an eccentric millionaire. I lived with two people I barely knew and a talking dog. My cousin was a bouncer. I could move things with my mind and fly. I was living the kind of fantastic story I'd always dreamed of, and I wanted to be back at school, doing normal, boring things. It was ridiculous, *stupid*, and if the Stanly of four or five months ago could travel through time and see me now, he'd probably have a few choice words to say on the subject.

The fact that I'd missed the Prom also upset me unreasonably more than it should have, considering the stance I generally took on such cheese. I wondered if Kloe had gone, and who with. I was struck by a mental image of her signing everyone's shirt and everyone signing hers, and her dancing in a beautiful dress with some faceless new boyfriend.

Well, you haven't called her in two months.

She's got every right to find someone else.

My stomach was bubbling. I clenched my fists and the bookcase in my room fell forwards, emptying its contents on the floor in an avalanche of heavy thuds. I caught the bookcase with my mind before it could hit the floor and shoved it roughly back against the wall, but I left the books where they were. Daryl jumped up, woken by the noise. 'Woah!' he cried. 'What's going on?'

'Nothing,' I said. My voice sounded strangled. I wasn't sure if I wanted to cry or scream. There was just too much going on in my brain. Different strains of anger wrapping around one another, anger at what I was missing, anger at myself for caring so much, anger for the time I was wasting, the *powers* I was wasting.

Misery at what I was missing out on. *Who* I was missing out on.

Anger at that misery.

Round and round and round.

I refused to let myself cry, though, even though it seemed like the thing to do, and got out of bed just as the door opened. Connor and Sharon came in, looking worried. 'What happened?' asked Connor, looking at the books.

I shook my head and waved my hand, and the books flew back onto their shelves in the wrong order, some backwards, some upside-down. 'Stanly?' asked Sharon. 'What's wrong? What are you—'

'Bad dream,' I muttered. 'Books fell off. Sorry. I'll clean them up properly later . . .'

Neither of them were convinced, I could tell. 'Stanly, mate,' said Connor. 'Seriously. What's the matter? 'Cos if—'

'I just want to make a call, please,' I said.

They looked at one another. 'OK,' said Sharon. 'That's fine, go ahead.' I walked past them, down the stairs to the phone, and dialled Kloe's number. I had it committed to memory now, after so much time staring at it.

The phone rang and I rose off the ground, barely aware that I was doing it, rising towards the ceiling, counting the rings and clenching and unclenching my free fist, the shoes and coats in the hall rustling, the pictures swinging from side to side like pendulums. Connor and Sharon appeared at the top of the stairs, with Daryl between them, and and I knew they wanted to say something, but they stayed quiet.

Ring.

Ring.

My coat fell off its peg on to the floor, and I immediately sent it back up again. A picture fell, but I caught it before it hit the ground and replaced it on the wall. Another ring and I bumped my head on the ceiling.

'Hello?' said Kloe's mum's voice. She did that thing where people say their phone number back to you. I've never understood that.

It took me a moment to regain the power of speech, and when I did I still didn't really sound like myself. 'Hi,' I said. 'I . . . is . . . can I speak to Kloe, please?'

'Kloe's at school. Who's speaking?'

'It's . . . I . . . sorry, I—'

'Is that Stanly?'

I dropped from the ceiling like a sack of meat, causing Connor and Sharon to take sharp intakes of breath, but I stopped myself a foot from the ground. The pictures, shoes and coats stopped rustling. 'Hello?' said Kloe's mum. 'Is that Stanly?'

'Yes,' I said.

'Please don't call for Kloe again.'

Now I hit the floor. 'What?'

'Whatever happened, whatever you think . . . it's better for Kloe if you don't speak to her. Please don't call again.'

'But . . . but I . . .' My eyes dropped to my feet. They looked weird. *Do my feet always look weird?* 'I miss her.' The last three words were a whisper.

'I'm sure you do. And she . . . well, it doesn't matter. Please don't call again.'

'But, please, can you just tell her I—'

'No. I'm sorry, Stanly. Goodbye.'

Click.

Not much happened for a few hundred years. I replaced the phone on the cradle. Slid slowly down to the floor. Closed my eyes and squeezed out a few burning tears. Heard Connor, Sharon and Daryl edge their way down the stairs towards me. I couldn't face them. Couldn't even think about opening my eyes. I just sat there and fought to control myself, to stem the tears before they could start in earnest, not wanting to break anything. My whole body was shaking, and my chest hurt with the effort. Sharon and Connor sat and put their arms around me and Connor said, 'It's OK, mate. It's OK.'

'It's all right.' Sharon's voice was soothing. It felt like it was inside my head. Maybe it was.

When I was confident that the tears had stopped, I opened my eyes. They were all sitting around me, Connor and Sharon and Daryl, all concerned, all loving, and I managed something that was almost a smile. 'Sorry.' My voice was barely there.

'For what?' said Sharon.

'This. It's . . . embarrassing.' *God, how embarrassing. Horrendously, howlingly, hideously embarrassing.*

'It's fine,' said Connor, standing up. 'It's all good.'

Some superhero.

None of us spoke again until Connor returned with a glass of water. 'There you go.' I sipped it gratefully, and it soothed my throat.

Finally I felt able to speak. 'Today was the last day of school for my year.' I told them everything, about the shirts and the books, and the Prom, and finally I told them about Kloe. I hadn't mentioned her to either of them, or to Eddie, barely even to Daryl, and it felt good to talk about her, despite the less than satisfactory conversation I'd just had with her mum.

Everything just came rushing out, including our last goodbye in the rain, and Connor and Sharon listened in silence until I'd finished.

'You poor thing,' said Sharon. She hugged me again, and Connor patted my knee, but he didn't speak. Neither of them seemed to be able to think of anything. Daryl looked helpless but he was doing what he could, just being there. I didn't think I'd ever felt more like a child. I'd thought I was on an equal footing with Connor and Sharon, like we were friends, that it wasn't just them and their friend's little cousin who they had to look after. But now I was just a walking superpowered tantrum, stomping around their house making a big psychic mess. *Ugh*.

Presently Connor looked at his watch. 'Skank wants us at the shop soon. Do you feel up to going in?'

I nodded. 'I want to . . . it'll take my mind off stuff.'

'Good.' Connor turned to Sharon. 'Do you have to work today?'

'No,' she said.

'OK,' said Connor. 'Well, how about we all go out for a meal tonight? All of us, to celebrate the end of school? How does that sound?'

It sounded really good. 'That's great,' I said, smiling. 'Thanks.'

'Can I come too?' asked Daryl.

'I meant *all six* of us,' said Connor. 'Wouldn't be right without you. I know a really good place, and more importantly I know the owner – he'll let you bring pets so long as they're on their best behaviour and stay well away from the kitchen.'

'Pets?' repeated Daryl, coldly.

'What?' said Connor. 'Do you not self-identify as a pet?'

'Have we known each other long enough for me to say "screw you", yet?'

'Hey, screw *you*, Poochie,' smiled Connor.

'Dinner sounds . . . what's your word, Stanly?' asked Sharon.

'Um . . .' *Drawing a blank*.

'Bendigedig?' offered Daryl.

'Yes!' said Sharon. 'Bendagiddig.'

The dog laughed. 'Good try.' He looked at me. 'The Welsh is strong with this one.' Now I couldn't help but laugh.

'Great.' Connor got up. 'I'll call Eddie and Skank.' He left the room.

Sharon looked at me, and the concern was still there in her deep blue eyes. 'Are you sure you're all right?'

'Yes,' I said, truthfully. 'Not hugely happy about what Kloe's mum said . . . but at least I worked up the bollocks to ring. Which is something.'

'She was probably just shocked. She'll come around.'

'Maybe.'

'I knew there was something,' said Sharon. 'I knew there was something you weren't telling us, and now I think about it, what else could it have been but a girl?' She smiled.

I had a shower and shaved with the electric razor that Eddie had insisted on buying for me after I got the job at 110th Street, and headed back downstairs for breakfast. 'I spoke to Eddie,' said Connor. 'He's free tonight. So's Skank. We'll all meet at the restaurant at eight.'

'Great.' I sat down and Sharon put some toast in front of me, and I ate quietly. Eating felt good. 'I'm sorry,' I said, again.

'Don't be,' said Connor. 'It's fine. You've been through a lot . . .'

'No,' I said. 'About . . . you know. My powers. The bookshelf. All the . . . the stuff.'

'You didn't break anything,' smiled Sharon. 'And God knows, I've made some messes with my powers in my time. Windows smashing during nightmares, broken plates after an argument . . .'

'Oh yeah,' said Connor, smiling wistfully. 'Good times.'

'It wasn't just . . .' I tried to find the words. 'Um. I've been . . . obviously all of the training and stuff I've been doing with you guys has been great. But I can't . . . I can't say I'm not frustrated, still. I've got these amazing abilities, and not much I can really do with them. We're not going out and fighting crime or anything, after all. And . . . I don't know. I kind of lost control a bit.' They both

176

looked more concerned now, and I hurriedly said that it wouldn't happen again.

'I do understand,' said Sharon. 'It *is* frustrating. You've no idea how often I've wanted to use mine at work.'

'Have you ever?' I asked.

Connor looked sharply at Sharon, but she didn't seem to notice. 'Once or twice,' she said. 'A long time ago, and as subtly as possible. So subtly that nobody could have known, but even that was dangerous. We need to keep them a secret. There's so much about them we don't understand, we don't know how people would react, what the authorities might . . .' She smiled, and it was as reassuring a smile as anyone could have asked for, but it didn't really help. 'Look,' she continued, 'we're all in the same boat with this. We're all got these bizarre gifts, but we live in the real world, where there's just not that much scope for using them, not without being noticed. So we can definitely try to do more training stuff, keep in practise . . . but you do need to try to control them too.'

'I will,' I said. 'I'm really sorry.'

'And no more apologies,' said Sharon. 'OK?'

'OK.'

'Excellent,' said Connor. 'Ready to go?'

I nodded. 'Ready to go.'

But despite our chat, as Connor and I walked down the path, a not insubstantial part of me was desperate to just kick off and see how high I could go.

Not yet, kiddo.

Not yet.

CHAPTER SEVENTEEN

I SAT AT THE counter failing to read a magazine while Skank fiddled around on the computer. Connor was fielding questions about Alan Moore's back catalogue from a persistent customer, and Jeff Wayne's *The War of the Worlds* was playing on the new sound system that Skank had installed a few weeks ago. It was an album I'd listened to a lot – for a while, when I was a child, it was the only thing that would get me off to sleep – and I loved it, but today I couldn't concentrate, just as I couldn't concentrate on the magazine, or on anything else. All I could think about was what Kloe's mum had said.

And how much I wanted to be out using my powers.

'A girl?' said Skank, suddenly.

'Sorry?'

'A girl. That's what's wrong.'

I frowned. 'Yeah. How did you—'

Skank waved his hand dismissively. 'Not hard to deduce. Are you all right?'

'Yeah. Thanks.'

He nodded. 'Well . . . if you want to speak. I'm . . . you know. Here.' He turned back to the computer.

I smiled. 'Thanks.'

Lunchtime rolled around and I said I was popping out. Connor and I usually ate lunch together, but I wasn't feeling particularly hungry or sociable and knew that I'd need to feel both of those things this evening. At least he and Skank were both aware of my girl-related issues. Good enough cover.

I left the shop and walked up the road, through Camden and down the first random, nondescript street that I saw. I knew vaguely where I was going, I was *sure* it was around here somewhere . . .

A fifteen-minute walk later, I'd found it. An old building site, fenced off with chains, padlocks and razor wire, with various red and orange signs forbidding entry. I checked that nobody was around, then quickly rose up and over the fence and walked across the dusty courtyard towards the great unfinished building, hollow and crumbling and littered with skips, stacks of boards and old bricks. I stared at a big pile of plastic cylinders and moved my hand, even though it wasn't necessary, and the cylinders jerked up and flew into a pile of bricks with a crash. Sounded good. Looked good. Felt good. I let everything come up, everything I'd forced back down into my belly this morning, all of the frustration and the rage and the sadness, and channelled it, hurling bricks against columns, shattering sheets of plastic, overturning skips and sending barrels bouncing over mounds of rubble. Some things were slightly more difficult to move than others, but none of it was hard. More importantly, it felt *really* satisfying.

Have a bit of that, *Kloe's mum.*

Eat those, *Ben King.*

Cheerio school, no-one gives a frack about ya.

I thought of everyone on the school field, signing shirts, hurling flour, dancing and running and shouting and horsing about, and blasted a stack of old wood into a wall, splintering the rotten planks. They made a great sound.

'Impressive.'

I jumped, whirling around on the spot. There was a man standing there with his hands in his pockets, smiling. My immediate reaction, stupidly, was embarrassment, deflation. I'd basically been caught having a massive strop. But then I realised something.

I knew this guy.

'Hello, Stanly,' he said. His voice was smooth, almost metallic, and it matched his appearance pretty much exactly – skinny and pale, marginally taller than me, wearing an expensive-looking grey suit with a blue tie. His face was pinched and lined and he had small eyes, a slightly hooked nose and a mouth so thin it seemed on the verge of disappearing. His black hair, greying at the temples, looked like it had been styled with a spirit level, and his smile was about the most sinister smile I'd ever seen on a real person.

'I know you,' I said. 'Don't I?'

'In a manner of speaking.'

'You were in the woods. Months ago. You came past when I was in the tree.'

'I did.'

'What were you doing there?'

'Pretty much what I'm doing now,' he smiled. 'Spying on you. Seeing what you can do. You've certainly improved since then.'

'Yep,' I said. 'So you know that I can defend myself.'

He laughed an utterly tuneless noise. 'I'm not here to hurt you.'

'Jolly good. Now . . .' I stopped, because something else had occurred to me. I'd *dreamed* about this guy. Recently.

That's strange.

Well, this whole thing's *strange.*

*But that's strange-*er.

I decided not to mention this point. 'So,' I said, conversationally, even though I was more than a bit freaked out by what was going on. 'Do you . . . live nearby?'

That laugh again. 'Aren't you going to ask who I am, Stanly?'

I shrugged.

'And aren't you going to ask how I know your name?'

I shrugged again.

'And I'm sure you're dying to know how I came to be here, spying on you.'

'OK,' I said. 'Who are you?'

'My name is Mr Freeman.'

'How do you know my name?'

'I know all about you.'

'How did you come to—'

180

'See above.'

So basically, he's not answering questions. I nodded. 'OK. So what do you want?'

'I want to help you.' Mr Freeman took his hands out of his pockets and laced his fingers together. 'You are fairly unique, Stanly.'

'Oh really?'

'Oh yes. You may in fact be one of the most unique people in the entire world, what with your . . . enhanced abilities.'

'That's nice to know.'

Freeman smiled. 'I'm sure it is.'

Might as well try another question. 'Do you know why I have these powers?'

'There are many theories,' said Mr Freeman. 'A colleague of mine is convinced that you're descended from extraterrestrials. We try not to talk about him.'

'You don't actually know, then?'

'Definitively? No. As I say, there are various hypotheses, some satisfactory, some not.'

'Are you going to tell me about them?'

'All in good time.' He lit a cigarette. 'The purpose of this meeting, Stanly, is for you to realise that there are people in the world who know about you. Who wish to help you, and to make your existence less painful.'

'My existence isn't painful,' I said. 'Pain-free, really.'

'For now,' said Mr Freeman, inhaling. 'But nothing lasts forever.' He blew out smoke. 'And pardon me for saying so, but furiously hurling rubbish around in an empty construction site is not one of the hallmarks of a pain-free existence, in my book.'

I shrugged. 'Maybe we read different books.'

'I'm sure we do.' He narrowed his eyes. 'It's getting to you, isn't it? Hiding? Not using your powers?'

I said nothing. *I don't like this conversation.*

'Understandable,' said Mr Freeman. 'I'm sure you came to

181

London thinking that everything would fall into place, that your story would truly begin, that you would find your calling.'

'That's not how things work in the real world.'

'Don't be so sure,' said Freeman, exhaling smoke.

I stared at him. I had a feeling that even Sharon wouldn't have been able to read this guy. 'How did you know about me?' I asked. 'How were you in Tref-y-Celwyn?'

'I keep tabs on special people,' said Freeman. 'It's my job.' He finished his cigarette and immediately lit another one. 'The other thing that you must realise,' he said, 'besides the fact that there are people out there who wish to help you, is that there are people out there who definitely do *not* wish to help you. This is equally – if not more – important.'

'Cheers for that. Now are you going to tell me who you actually are? Your name and the vaguest job description ever aren't really enough.'

'I'm a friend,' said Mr Freeman. 'And I think as time goes on you're going to need as many friends as you can get your hands on.'

'I have friends,' I said.

'Connor and Eddie and Sharon?' asked Mr Freeman. 'Daryl? Miss Stevenson? Tybalt himself, Mark Topp? Or perhaps fair Juliet, the lovely Kloe?' He sighed. 'They may well be your friends, but you're going to need a lot more than that when the shit starts to hit the proverbial fan.'

He is starting to damage my calm. 'How do you know all this?' My voice shook a little.

'I told you,' said Mr Freeman. 'I know all about you. I know about Benedict King. I know about Mr Dylan, your pathologically useless headmaster. I know about your parents. I know that you have a rather unique dog, and that you enjoy watching *Casablanca* together. I *know* you. And I know where you're going. Or where you might be going, at least.'

'And where might I be going?' I asked, trying to restrain myself from psychically bringing the ceiling down on this twat.

182

'Well,' said Mr Freeman, 'if you'll let me indulge in a terrible cliché: there are some things you're not yet meant to know.' He reached into his jacket, pulled out a white business card and offered it to me. 'If you need a friend, or if your resources run dry, then use this.' I stared at the card.

Don't take it.

Take it.

Don't.

I took it, and Freeman smiled. 'You could be very useful, Stanly. You could be *powerful*. You could be where the action is, finally. Part of the story.'

'Well, gosh,' I said. 'That's lovely. But I should really be getting back to work. Bye now.' I walked past him, back out into the light.

'Be seeing you,' he called after me.

I stopped, because yet another thing had occurred to me. *You need to start carrying a lightbulb around for these moments.* A memory, buried deep, old and irrelevant until this moment. Daryl and I in my bedroom, just before Christmas, standing by the phone.

'Mystery caller,' I said. 'Didn't leave a number.'

'Ooooh. I bet it was Kloe.'

'I doubt it. She hasn't got our number.'

'Could have looked it up in the phone book,' said Daryl, as if I were a dunce.

'Hmm.'

'Who else could it have been?'

'Eddie, maybe?'

'Maybe.'

'It was you,' I said, turning around. 'You called my house. Before Christmas.'

Freeman nodded. 'Yes. But something came up, and I'm glad it did. You weren't ready then.'

'And I am now?'

'Almost.'

I stood there for a moment, looking down at the card in my

hand. It was blank on one side and had a phone number written in small black letters on the other. 'My powers,' I said.

'Yes?'

'Are they . . . evil?'

He laughed. 'Evil? Don't be silly.'

'So they're good then?'

He laughed again. 'Stanly, you have so much to learn. Gifts as powerful as yours cannot be compartmentalised in such a way. Good and evil are safety nets, simplistic, prosaic categories that people have created to make sense of the senseless. Out here in the real world, on the *real* playing field, they are essentially meaningless. You will become whatever you're going to become. And I for one can't wait to see it.'

I stared at him for a moment, then shook my head. 'Jesus, you're annoying.' And I pocketed the card and walked away.

'Probably best not to tell your friends about our meeting,' he called after me. 'They might not understand.'

'Yeah,' I said, not breaking stride. 'Whatevz.'

Back at the shop, Connor looked up from the baguette he was eating. 'Nice walk?'

'Yeah,' I said. 'Head feels clearer now.'

Clearer.

Chance would be a fine thing.

CHAPTER EIGHTEEN

'OK,' SAID SKANK, on the dot of six. 'Closing time. Everybody out. Lock S-foils in leaving the shop positions.' The single customer, a short, balding middle-aged man who was scrutinising action figures, looked up hurriedly and scuttled out without saying anything. Skank shut the till and called Connor in from the back. 'Come on, ramblers,' he said. 'Let's get rambling.'

Connor and I waited on the street while Skank closed up. He had changed out of his shorts and into jeans, and replaced his *Neon Genesis Evangelion* T-shirt with a long-sleeved red silk shirt, although he hadn't changed his sandals and his beard was still a chaotic explosion.

The restaurant that Connor knew was south, and we took the Tube. I'd half expected Skank to inspire peculiar looks, but nobody batted an eyelid. Of course they didn't. If you batted an eyelid every time you saw an odd-looking individual in London, you'd end up with repetitive eyelid strain. Skank, for his part, barely seemed aware of anybody around him. Even when we got off the train and left the station, diving into the melee of people, he moved as if they weren't there. I was still enjoying the novelty of such immense crowds, such variety. Dreadlocked skaters, smartly-dressed business people, old people wrangling hyperactive children, people speaking English, people speaking Chinese, people speaking French, people speaking God-knows what, happy couples, grumpy couples, blondes, brunettes, redheads, bald men, bald women, a blue-haired girl with an electric violin doing a pretty impressive cover of 'Billie Jean' – Skank gave her a fiver – and so many others that you barely had a chance to register before they vanished forever.

As we walked, I wondered if Mr Freeman was still watching me.

The day had aged, and a ribbon of pink now curled lazily across the sky as its blueness dimmed and the clouds filed themselves away to be relieved by the stars. The air, despite the car fumes, was thick with a golden duskiness that always felt uniquely British to me. I looked at Skank and asked him if he knew where we were going. He shook his head.

Connor laughed. 'We're nearly there.' We turned down a narrow alley lined with red brick buildings, walked to the end and took another left, emerging in a small courtyard full of bright, exotic plants in terracotta pots. A green door was set into one wall, with tall windows on either side through which I could see a small restaurant with a tasteful crème and green colour scheme. There were only seven tables and only two were occupied: one by a young couple and the other by Sharon, Eddie and Daryl. Daryl actually had a seat to himself and the couple at the other table kept eyeing him with interest, but as the waiter brought a tray of drinks to the table he barely acknowledged the presence of my dog. *This city just gets stranger and stranger.*

We entered the restaurant and the waiter stopped on his way back to the kitchen, swivelled smoothly on the balls of his feet and grinned widely, exposing shark-like rows of disconcertingly white teeth. He was about twenty and looked vaguely Italian American. 'Connor!' he said, in a New York drawl. 'My man!' The two of them shook hands.

'Ray,' smiled Connor. 'Good to see you. How's Bonnie?'

Ray shrugged. 'Same old, same old. Baby this, baby that. I'm lucky I can make a badass tomato sauce otherwise she'd have no more use for me. I'd be working, sleeping *and* eating here.' I had to stop my eyes from widening. *Comin' straight outta Goodfellas, y'all better make way.*

'Ray,' said Connor. 'This is Skank, My boss.'

Skank and Ray shook hands. 'Good evening, Mr Skank,' said Ray.

Skank nodded. 'It is.'

Ray raised an eyebrow and turned to me. 'This is Stanly,' said Connor. 'New recruit.'

'Pleased to meet you, kid.' Ray held out his hand and grinned. 'How's it going?'

I grinned back and shook his hand. 'I'm good, thanks.'

'Good. It's good that you're good.' Ray handed Connor a menu and hurried off towards a steamy adjoining room, and we sat down.

'Yo,' said Daryl.

'S'up,' I said. 'How's sitting with the big people?'

Daryl looked around and sniffed. 'Well. Y'all will do, I suppose.'

'Is that waiter for real?' I asked.

'I'm never sure,' said Connor. 'Chico Marx via Scorsese, right? He's a good guy, though.'

'He called me "pal",' said Daryl. 'He can stay.'

The food came promptly, and was exceptionally tasty. I had a well-done steak in some sort of garlic butter sauce with sautéed potatoes, and it might have been the best steak I'd ever had. I'd only had about three, so the competition wasn't exactly stiff, but it was one of those meals where you can't quite believe what a great time your mouth is having.

We didn't touch on the subject of school for the first hour. In fact, it was mainly Skank who spoke, which surprised me. He was absolutely full of anecdotes and amusing stories and the best part was that I was certain they were all true. They had to be; I don't think the guy was capable of embroidering a story. There was one about a full-moon party in Finland that involved strange injections and magic mushrooms, but Skank was at pains to point out that he and his then-girlfriend hadn't been involved in anything unsavoury. 'Of course, we weren't raving,' he said, as he tucked into his chicken, 'we were just having a quiet time in the bungalow.'

School finally came up during dessert. Skank had asked whether this dinner was marking some special occasion, and Sharon had exchanged Meaningful Looks with Eddie and Connor, and a reassuring one with me. 'We don't have to talk about it.'

I shrugged and took a sip of my beer. 'It's fine.'

Eddie didn't know all the details of my little episode that morning – he had the footnotes, but that was about it – and leaned forwards. 'Go on then,' he said, 'spin the yarn.'

I rolled my eyes in a here-we-go-again – more for my benefit than theirs. 'Don't get your hopes up. It's pretty boring.'

'Boring sounds good to me,' said Daryl. 'I've overloaded on Skank's interesting stories, need something dull to take the edge off.'

I laughed and went into the explanation again, the leaving books and the signing of shirts and the Record of Achievement ceremony and the Prom and Kloe. Everything apart from Kloe sounded impossibly silly and almost meaningless by now, so I tried to get it all over with as soon as possible, and all the while, at the back of my head, I was thinking about Freeman. About all the questions I should have asked him. And about what he'd said.

Probably best not to tell anyone about our meeting.

And when has that ever been a good idea?

Rarely if ever. All the same, though, it seemed harmless to keep him to myself for a while. I could tell them about him if and when he became important. Right now he was interesting, but that was about it.

Yeah. That's it.

Finally I finished the story, along with my hot chocolate fudge cake and ice cream. I wasn't sure if it was because I'd told it all now, or because I'd really let loose that afternoon in the building site, but I was starting to feel much more sorted in my head, and made a promise to myself that this was the last time I'd do this particular monologue.

It's all me, me, me with you, isn't it?

Yeah. It's all you, you, you with me.

188

Everyone was silent for a bit. They'd all said the right things at the right moments (I had also added the story of Performance Night, as I was starting to call it, because Skank hadn't heard it and Connor and Sharon had only had a majorly abridged version), but now none of them really knew what to say to follow it up. I could sympathise. I wouldn't have known what to say, either. Luckily Eddie had the perfect silence-breaking idea, signalling Ray and ordering more drinks. When Ray returned with the tray of beers – Daryl's had a straw – Eddie raised his in a toast. 'To the end of school. Good riddance. I always hated the place.'

I laughed, and we toasted and clinked our bottles, although Daryl sort of shuffled his around with his nose rather than raising it. Everyone made sure to clink with him, though, and we drank, and I felt the stigma of the twentieth of May washing calmly away.

When the bill came, they all insisted that Daryl and I shouldn't have to pay – it was their treat for us. Skank wanted to pay for everybody, but they wouldn't let him. They wouldn't even let me see how much it cost. It was nice, but I also felt bad.

Be the kid. You'll pay them back one day.

Finally we stepped out into the street, full and a tiny bit tipsy. It was a little before ten and almost completely dark. Skank lit a cigarette and Sharon looked at Connor. 'What now?'

Connor shrugged. 'How about Blue Harvest?'

Eddie looked up from tying his shoelace. 'Blue Harvest? That's the best idea you've had since . . . well, since recommending that rather tasty Czech lager.'

'Damn right,' said Connor. 'None of your heathen English water.'

'What's Blue Harvest?' I asked.

'You'll see,' said Sharon. 'It's definitely the best idea. Come on.'

'I think I'm going to take a rain check,' said Skank. 'I've got a load of cats at home who never learned how to be self-sufficient.'

Ah yes. Schrödinger, Felix, Doraemon and Miss Kitty Fantastico. Skank had told us all about his cats.

'OK,' said Connor. 'Later, dawg.'

We exchanged goodbyes and Skank told Connor and me not to worry about coming in tomorrow. 'Shop won't be open,' he said, blowing out smoke. 'I have some things to do.'

Connor nodded. 'OK. See you.'

'Laters,' said Skank. 'And thanks. Mighty fine shindig.' He turned and walked off into the darkness.

'So,' said Daryl. 'Blue Harvest, eh?'

Blue Harvest turned out to be a jazz bar one bus ride away. It didn't look like much from outside, just a windowless front with a wooden door and Blue Harvest written on the wall in dim blue neon, but when the door opened and Connor led us inside, Daryl let out a whistle. 'Now that's what I'm talkin' about,' he said.

I'd never been to a jazz bar, but as far as I was concerned any jazz bar that didn't look like this had no business calling itself a jazz bar. The place just looked *cool*. There was a round, shiny black stage with a piano and a drum kit at the back, where a lone female saxophonist was playing something lovely and laid-back, and an even shinier bar adjacent to it, with racks and racks of bottles behind. A very pretty lady (girl?), probably approaching the end of her twenties, was standing behind the bar watching the saxophonist. The walls were lined with pictures of musicians with their instruments, and there were small black metal tables all around the floor with three chairs to each. There was only a handful of other patrons, all of whom were drinking, surprisingly enough. The lady behind the bar exchanged a wave with Eddie, and we all pulled up chairs and sat down.

'This place is awesome,' I said.

'You ain't seen nothing yet,' said Connor. He looked at Eddie. 'Game?'

Eddie inhaled sharply and shook his head. 'Ooh . . . I don't know, mate.'

'Come on!' said Connor. 'You lot got me to sit down and do Connor's Teatime Requests on Stanly's guitar! And you get *paid* for this.'

'Wrong tense. I *did* get paid for this.'

'Paid for what?' I asked, raising my hand. 'What's going on?'

'You'll see,' said Sharon. She grinned and put a hand on Eddie's shoulder. 'You probably definitely should.'

Eddie looked at me, then at Daryl, then at Sharon, then at Connor. Then he looked up at the stage, and his eyes rested on the lone saxophonist for a minute. He nodded slowly and stood up with an air of resignation that was obviously an act. I could see that he was excited. 'OK,' he said. 'I'll be back in a minute.' He walked over to the bar and had a quick word with the girl, who handed him a key, then he disappeared through a door at the back.

I looked at Connor. 'Is Eddie going to sing?'

'You'll see.'

We went up to the bar to get drinks. 'Hi, Hannah,' smiled Sharon.

'Hiya,' said the barmaid. 'What can I get you?'

Sharon order a Sea Breeze and Connor ordered a vodka on the rocks for himself and a tequila for Eddie. 'Eddie drinks tequila?' I asked. I don't know why I was surprised. Connor nodded. 'He can drink just about anyone under the table and still walk in a straight line. Ridiculous. Wish that was my superpower.'

Daryl didn't want anything to drink, and I selected a random beer, which turned out to be some sort of ale for grown-ups. It was tasty, but more potent than I was used to. 'You guys know the barmaid, then?' I asked.

'Her name's Hannah,' said Connor, sipping his vodka. 'She and Eddie went out a while back. Pretty serious. They were thinking about moving in together, getting joint ownership of this place.'

'What happened?' I asked.

Connor looked at me. 'What do you mean?'

'I think I mean . . . what happened?'

'Nothing happened, particularly,' said Connor. 'They broke up. Nothing nasty about it. They're still good friends.'

'Her brother didn't help,' said Sharon.

'Brother?' I asked. *Ooh, gossip.*

191

'It's not for us to say, really,' said Connor. 'I'm sure if you ask Eddie he'll—'

'—be incredibly awkward and evasive and not answer the question properly?' I said.

Connor laughed. 'Something like that.'

We watched the saxophonist in silence until Eddie came back. He was carrying a small black case under his arm which he set down on an empty table. He opened it and started to assemble a clarinet, and suddenly I remembered my conversation with Mum, and it made sense. I watched with interest. I don't know much about clarinets, but it looked pretty expensive and classy, and he assembled it deftly, blowing a long, low note that had a syrupy richness to it. He played in harmony with the saxophonist, who nodded at him.

'Nice,' said Daryl.

I looked at Sharon. 'Is he good?'

She smiled. 'He's not bad.'

Eddie stood at his table pressing the keys of the clarinet, warming up his fingers, watching the saxophonist. She finished with a swinging number and we all applauded, whistling loudly, and she grinned widely as she bowed, flushed and sweating. She put her instrument away, stepped down from the stage and walked over to Hannah, who had what looked like a Bloody Mary waiting for her.

'So Eddie used to play here a lot?' I asked.

'Yeah,' said Connor. 'Before he and Hannah started to think about running it together.'

I wondered what had happened between them. Connor had been a bit too quick to gloss over it. And Sharon's comment about the brother . . .

Keep yer beak out, Bird. See any of your beeswax round here? 'Cos I don't.

Oh shut up.

Eddie walked up to the stage looking nervous but confident, his shirt sleeves rolled up, hair artfully messy. He adjusted the microphone and spoke into it. 'OK. Um . . . I'm going to need a bit of a hand. Hannah? Will you do the honours?'

Hannah grinned and folded her arms. 'What's it worth?'

Eddie seemed to think for a moment. 'I'll buy you a drink.'

'I own the bar, you berk!'

Eddie nodded. 'OK. From a different bar, then.'

Hannah considered, then shrugged. 'OK.' She stepped out from behind the bar, walked up on stage and seated herself at the piano. They tuned up, and Eddie nodded and leaned in to the mic.

'OK. This one's a tune you'll all know, probably. Just to get you into the swing of things.' He turned and said something to Hannah, who nodded and played a series of chords that sounded familiar. Then Eddie came in with the melody, and I knew it instantly. 'Day Tripper' by The Beatles, albeit jazzed-up to high heaven.

The two of them sounded great together. Hannah was no slouch on the piano and Eddie was more than a bit not bad on his clarinet, and when their first number was over they received a standing ovation. They busked some old Sinatra-style standards, some random bits and pieces, a couple more Beatles numbers and 'Petite Fleur' by Sidney Bechet, which I recognised because it was a favourite of my American aunt Susan, and when they'd finished that, Hannah called Eddie over and whispered in his ear. He laughed and nodded, and they started to play a waltzed-up version of 'Zorba's Theme', which is one of those pieces that everybody knows even though nobody ever seems to have seen the film. The whole room cheered. The saxophonist went up to join them for this one, and she and Eddie improvised lots of little riffs that spun around each other, intricate little ornaments and inter-weaving harmonies, and Hannah joined in, her fingers dancing effortlessly across the ivories. They gradually upped the tempo, the audience clapping enthusiastically in time, and Eddie and the saxophonist screamed a harmonised crescendo, and as Hannah's last cascade of piano notes finally brought the thing to a halt the room erupted again. They received another standing ovation, and I clapped and whooped until my hands and throat were sore. Eddie gave Hannah a hug – you could definitely see that there were some lingering feelings there – and shook hands with the saxophonist, then cleaned and disassembled his clarinet and came back over to our table. He downed his tequila in one, wiped his mouth on his sleeve and grinned. 'I've really missed that.'

'That was *fan*tastic,' I said, holding out my hand. I might have been a bit tipsy. 'Bloody amazing. Totally . . . I mean absolutely, just totally . . . just a total beast.'

'"Beast"?' asked Sharon.

'Yeah,' I said. 'Um . . . beast.'

'Still got the magic touch,' grinned Connor.

'Well,' said Eddie. 'I try.'

'And not just with the clarinet,' said Daryl. 'I could see the way Hannah kept looking over at you, and the way she hugged you. She still fancies the pants off you, mate.'

This was greeted by a half-amused, half-awkward silence. I could see both Connor and Sharon fighting valiantly not to laugh, but I couldn't manage it and corpsed magnificently, which set everyone else off. When the laughter subsided Eddie managed an embarrassed grin and ruffled the fur on top of Daryl's head. 'Thanks, mate,' he said. 'Cheers. Always worth hearing the dog's opinion.'

CHAPTER NINETEEN

I SPENT THE NEXT day watching TV and practising with my powers. Connor had received one of Eddie's mysterious calls and disappeared, and Sharon was working, so Daryl and I were left alone. I had purchased some vintage Power Rangers action figures from the shop with my employee discount, and now I was psychically making them act out situations randomly barked at me by Daryl. 'Red fight green!' he'd yell. 'Red do a backflip! Green's drunk all of Zordon's secret hooch! Tango! Cartwheel race! Twerking nine to five! Do the dance of joy!' Admittedly my attempts looked like primitive stop-motion, as I still wasn't quite dextrous enough to move multiple limbs independently at the same time, but with every new instruction I felt like more walls were breaking down, like I was getting closer to complete mastery. By the time everyone got home I had my Red and Green Rangers doing a passable interpretation of Michael Jackson's 'Thriller' routine, and although they didn't find it quite as side-splittingly hilarious as Daryl and I did – God knows why – they were still appreciative.

Yeah, wicked skills. You're more than ready for a superpowered fight to the death with a child-devouring monster.

Skank wanted us in the shop again on Saturday, which was totally miserable because it was a horrible day. The heat was incandescent, the humidity unbearable and it was claustrophobic, even in an open space. The buildings dripped with sweat. Cars sounded unhealthy. The air was like hot wet cotton wool, and it was not fun being cooped up in 110th Street for four hours with no air-conditioning and only two small fans between us. Connor and I went home hot, tired and grumpy, our clothes sticking to us like wet newspaper. 'Would have thought Skank could afford to invest in some air conditioning,' I said.

'You wouldn't be the first one to have that thought,' said Connor.

That night I lay in bed wearing just my boxer shorts, my body sticky with sweat, the windows wide open, my head pulsating. I hadn't had a headache in months and now here one was, on the hottest night of the year, when I had a burp in a hurricane's chance of getting to sleep. I lay on my back, flipped over onto my side, then onto my front, then onto my other side, then stood on my head ('cos why not), then sat up, then put my legs against the wall, then turned my pillows over and tried to burrow into my mattress, but nothing worked. Daryl had chosen to sleep downstairs on the sofa where it was always cool. Unfortunately, there was only room for one to sleep comfortably and he'd bagsied it. I seriously considered sneaking down there and psychically levitating him on to the armchair, where he would fit just as comfortably – as I had pointed out, to no avail – and taking the sofa for myself. I could easily do it without him waking up.

He'll whinge all bloody day tomorrow, though.

I could deal with his whinging, but more importantly he had *bagsied* the sofa. And the laws of bagsy and shotgun were immutable. I'd rather boil to death than live with that dishonour, so I tried to sleep.

Eventually, though, I couldn't take it anymore. There were no painkillers in the house (which, considering a nurse lived there, was just this side of unbelievable) and the heat was so oppressive that I was having visions of my head exploding, just like I'd had so long ago, on that night when my whole life had changed. Skull and brain bursting, eyeballs popping like overripe plums, viscera spilling from empty eye sockets and ears and mouth, taking teeth and tongue with it. It was not pleasant. I was going mad. I had to get out.

I dressed very quickly, made sure the bedroom door was shut and flew out through the open window and around the side of the house, alighting on the pavement. I looked up at the building. *Eddie would kill you if he knew you were doing this*, I thought. *Screw it*, I replied. *With a cherry on top*, I added.

I walked for a very long time, passing pubs and drunks and silent shops and homeless people and stray dogs and haughty cats. Nobody paid me much attention, which was nice. It wasn't as hot as it had been inside, but it was still far from comfortable, and I tried not to think about my headache, but it didn't work. I could actually feel my exploding head. *Don't think about exploding heads. Think about something more interesting.*

Yeah. Like films.

Oh that's a good idea. Films like Scanners?

Oh piss off.

Before long I realised that I was walking parallel with the river, and reasoned that the closer I got to it the cooler it would be. *Sherlock Holmes strikes again.*

I said piss off.

I stood resting on my elbows on the wall, watching the river's sluggish progress beneath Southwark Bridge, Blackfriars Bridge and, in the distance, Waterloo Bridge. *Under the bridges.*

Under the bridge downtown . . . 'Is where I drew some blood,' I murmured. 'Under the bridge downtown . . .' I half-expected Mr Freeman to appear out of the darkness and finish off the rest of the lyrics for me. Seemed like the kind of cryptic bullshit he'd pull. But no, I was alone.

I wondered who he might be. Government? Very possible. It stood to reason that there were others out there with abilities like mine, and as useless as the government seemed to be in many respects, I doubted it was the kind of thing that would pass them by.

What had he meant, though? About my story beginning?

Did he have a job for me?

Could he see the future?

Bollocks. No-one can see the future.

Hmm. And a year ago, no-one could fly or move things with their mind. Except now people can. You can. I slowly rotated a rubbish bin three hundred and sixty degrees with my mind, demonstrating the point to no-one in particular.

He knew all about me.

He knew where I worked.

Presumably he knew where I was living.

And he knows where I'm from.

I jumped up onto the wall and sat with my legs dangling over the river, staring into the implacable water. I hadn't exactly liked Freeman. The whole 'you're not ready to know' thing grated. But I couldn't pretend not to be glad that he'd appeared on the scene. It meant that there was something going on. Something beyond. Something I could be a part of, that might well suit my new abilities. I jumped off the wall and dropped straight down, stopping myself less than a second before I plunged into the river, and kept myself there. To all intents and purposes, it looked as though I was standing on the water. I grinned and walked out a little way, positioning myself so precisely that my footsteps actually fell on the surface, causing the water to ripple outward.

Cool. Not much use, but cool.

I was half-considering going off on a hunt for Smiley Joe, and telling myself that that ranked among the stupider stupid ideas I'd had in my time, when the sky suddenly filled with a white so bright it was no longer white. It was a hole torn in reality, revealing the colour of nothingness below, and it shocked me so much that I lost control and sank up to my knees. 'Bollocks,' I said, rising back up, my shoes, socks and jeans sodden. It didn't exactly matter, though, because seconds later there was a rumble of thunder, and it started to rain. It didn't mess around. Within seconds it was pouring, wonderful cool rain that soaked into my skin and my hair and my eyes, trickling, caressing. It hit the ground like bombs, and the surface of the river became a maelstrom. I rose back up and flew home, trying not to think about lightning. *Would your powers work on lightning?*

Bows and arrows.

Then another thought came, one I'd been entertaining for a while now.

How high can I go?

I was floating outside my open window. My door was still closed. I hadn't expected Connor or Sharon to come and look in on me before, and they definitely wouldn't now that the storm was upon us. People don't want to get up if it's pissing down with rain in the middle of the night; they like to snuggle in bed and listen to the wet bullets hitting the roof.

I looked towards the sky. Another sheet of lightning, and shortly afterwards another kettle drum boom of thunder trying vainly to keep up. *You'll get struck by lightning.*

No, I won't.

I flew straight up, my clothes clinging to me like desperate children, rain pounding my face and wind stinging my bare arms as I headed for the dark blanket of clouds. Breathing was difficult but not impossible, and as I picked up speed I sneaked a look down, and almost fell. I could see the entire city, a diagram of towers and estates and neon and orange, the waves on the river bucking like wild horses, the streets awash. I could see the face of Big Ben, the dome of Saint Paul's Cathedral, the Eye, the churches, the shining, anonymous skyscrapers. I could see the river snaking its way through it all, see cars shrunk to pinpricks of light, and I could feel the storm valiantly trying to drive me from its domain. *Stay away*, I heard the rain whisper. *This is where we live.*

Not any more, I replied. This defiance of nature gave me a burst of power and speed, and now I was inside the clouds, choking on moisture, unable to breathe, my body numb from the cold and tingling with electricity, but I didn't care, I *belonged* here now. I could see lightning and feel the vibration as the thunder erupted all around, and I pulled against the current of air, summoned every last shred of energy and strength and channelled them into my body . . . and broke through the clouds.

'Scuse me while I kiss the sky . . .

Here, all was peaceful. A carpet of white hiding the world, and star-spangled black above, tinted midnight blue by the moon's ethereal ghost. For a full ten seconds I basked in it, the tranquillity, the awe-inspiring spectacle. I left Mr Freeman behind. I left London behind. I left Smiley Joe behind. I was free.

And then I tried to breathe, and I couldn't.

Panic.

Don't panic.

Oh, OK then, thanks, I won't panic.

I was drowning. I was six years old again, running around in the back garden of my grandparents' house, the country limp in winter's clenched fist, the trees and roofs brushed with powdered sugar. I was skipping, I was laughing, I was running to the frozen pond . . . and I was breaking the ice, plunging into the water, unable to breathe, unable to think, dying . . .

No.

Not again.

Dad's not here to pull you out this time.

I closed my eyes and let myself drop. I fell back through the clouds, crashing through this upside-down ocean in the sky, my lungs screaming. My body felt dead. I dropped like a rock, broke the clouds again and was back in the storm, and now it was almost as though I *had* been struck by lightning. One last burst of energy lit me up, and I forced myself to turn and face the world as it rushed back towards me, and I flew again, back down, back towards the city and safety. With every metre my will threatened to give out, my energy swearing it would burn away and leave me plummeting towards the tarmac. I could just imagine Eddie and the others reading my obituary.

Stanly Bird, Blossoming Superhero, Dead at 16

Or maybe there'd be something tasteless on the Internet.

Superpowered Slacker With Ideas Above

His Station Ends Life Looking Like a
Chicagotown Pizza

No thanks, I thought. Not going out like that. I summoned Kloe's face, letting her smile urge me on. Come on, she whispered, her voice cutting through the rage of the storm. Come on, not much further.

I was nearly there. A hundred metres. Eighty. Sixty. Forty. Twenty. Ten. Five. One.

I landed clumsily in next door's back garden and collapsed, a crumpled heap on a bed of drowning grass and liquid mud. I lay there for several minutes, breathing, shaking, watching the storm, and eventually managed to get to my feet and float up and across to the house. I hung outside for a minute, letting the rain wash the mud from my clothes, then hovered back through the window and stood in my bedroom, rain dripping from my body and hitting the floor. I shook myself like Daryl did on the rare occasions he allowed himself to get wet, peeled off my soaking wet clothes and hung them over a chair, hoping they'd be dry by the morning. *Unlikely.* Then I dried myself off and got into bed. *Let's not do that again,* I thought. *For a while.*

Agreed.

As I lay there, totally drained, my thoughts turned to Mr Freeman again. Government spook? Nazi? A member of some ancient cult? A talent scout for a superpowered football team? And how could he know all that stuff about me? It wasn't possible.

When the shit hits the proverbial fan . . .

Not if.

When.

I didn't like the sound of that.

I stuck to my decision not to tell the others about my encounter with Mr Freeman, or about my little jaunt above the clouds. What was I going to say, after all?

Me: Sorry. I sneaked out in my lunch break to smash things

201

with my brain and met a mysterious well-manicured cigarette-smoking man who knows more about me than I do and who may well understand my destiny. And also I sneaked out in the middle of the night for a wander around a city I don't know very well, kind of hoping for another chance meeting with said mysterious man or maybe with the child-eating monster that Connor swears doesn't exist, and then there was a storm and I decided to just fly straight up into it 'cos hey, what the hell, what else would I have done under the circumstances?

Eddie: (unable to speak due to his head spontaneously exploding)

So although I felt guilty for keeping it from them, I pretended that nothing had happened. I kept the business card hidden in my wallet and I went about my new life, eating, watching DVDs, playing my guitar, working, talking, exercising with my powers. I was getting good. I didn't attempt any more skydiving, but I knew I was in control. The powers were working for me. It was a good feeling, but there was always that nagging voice at the back of my mind telling me to be careful. There were things at work, things I didn't understand. Things that could hurt.

So, what else is new, I thought, and beat the other voice into submission.

A week or so after my first meeting with Mr Freeman, I was sitting at my window, watching the city. I wondered what was going on out there and why I was in here. I looked at my watch. Just after midnight. London would be awake for hours yet. Connor and Sharon had gone to bed almost an hour before and they were both sound sleepers. Daryl was on the sofa downstairs. I was in no danger of being discovered.

I put on my shoes and socks and my baggy black hoody, pulled the hood up and floated silently out of the window, across the garden and over the back fence, touching down in an alleyway lined with rusty bins and old newspaper. An imperious-looking tabby eyed me suspiciously then slunk off into the shadows. Somewhere a dog whined. I put my hands in my pockets and walked. The pavements glistened, reflecting the glow from the lampposts.

As I walked I thought about Connor, Sharon and Eddie. How come they never went out? Why were they never walking around in back-alleys in the middle of the night, looking to do some good? They'd had their powers for years. I gathered from what they'd said that Eddie and Connor were virtually indestructible, plus Connor had that neat gravity-shifting thing. Sharon's telekinesis was better than mine. And yet here I was, alone, looking for a fight in the city.

I felt the darkness absorb me, like a drop of oil vanishing into a pool, becoming one. My senses were charged and ready: I could smell the wet tarmac and the rubbish and the scents of life and death, hear cars and muffled voices and those ever-present sirens, taste dirt and water. I was an indistinct shape passing over elaborate graffiti and chewing-gum stains and empty boxes, part of the claustrophobia. London's shadow.

'Leave me *alone!*'

Jackpot.

I stopped immediately, working out where the voice had come from. I was at a crossroads where three different alleys met. One held darkness, one led to the road – and one hid two figures. A small one and a large one. I crept forward and ducked behind a yellow skip to get a better look. A girl about my age, skimpily dressed, shivering and crying, and a man standing over her, *looming*, dressed in black. He had his hands on her arms and was trying to get close to her. She kept on trying to push him away, but now he hissed: '*Don't make another sound or you'll regret it.*'

'Excuse me,' I said, stepping out from behind the skip. 'That's not very nice.'

The man turned his head, took me in. Started to walk towards me. His hand went to his pocket. 'I'ma give you five seconds to get out of here,' he said, 'else you're gonna regret ever layin' eyes on me.'

'Already there, mate.'

Now he moved, very fast. For a second I saw his face – an ugly, contorted mess with sunken eyes and a twisted mouth – and then his hand came out of his pocket with a knife and he thrust it forwards.

Only I wasn't there. I'd flown into the air, spun and landed behind him, and his lunge sent him totally off-balance and he crashed into the skip. He rapidly regained his balance, roared and ran at me. I realised that the girl had run away.

Then something occurred to me. I threw a punch in the man's direction, although there were still about four feet between us, and let a thought fly with it. My fist passed harmlessly through the air and I felt nothing, but the man's nose was crushed and blood started geysering down his face and into his mouth. *Sick.* I grinned.

The man was shouting incomprehensibly. He lunged at me and I used my mind to hurl him straight over my head. He hit the wall, slid down and landed in an undignified tangle of limbs and rubbish. A cat fought to escape from this peculiar mess of living and dead trash, hissing and spitting, and the man got to his feet, took one last frightened, impotent look at me and ran. He took a right, and I saw that he was heading for the main road.

My blood burned. *You're going down.*

I turned and ran back the way I'd come, taking a left instead of a right and ending up on the pavement. The man saw me and headed across the road. The lights were green. He was going to get away.

No, he's not.

I picked up a car and hurled it with my mind, and it slammed the man into a wall, splintering and bursting his body, suddenly frail and pathetic. The vehicle's windows shattered and it rolled onto the pavement, leaving a bloody stain on the wall, and I rose up into the air, chuckling. People were screaming, cars were honking, the sirens were coming. I could feel power and electricity, a surge of something that lit me from the inside. My veins bulged and glowed, my muscles rippled, my brain flexed. I felt like I was casting off chains, snapping them link by link, free.

I was a god now.

I picked up another car and sent it flying down the road. It landed on its roof and skidded along, scattering broken glass, and when it exploded I felt it. Fire was my gift. The street ignited, plumes of twirling colour, every possible hue of red and gold and orange blossoming as my power reduced the place to ruins.

'Stanly.'

I turned to my right. Mr Freeman was standing there, his pale face illuminated by the glow of the flames, the screaming of the burning street. He seemed worried. Our eyes met, and I didn't like what I saw in his. 'I was hoping you would go the other way,' he said.

I shrugged. 'I like this way.' I flexed my mind, deciding what to do to him, what was best, to show him. 'Phenomenal cosmic power, motherf—'

My eyes opened and I raised my head from my arms. I was sitting at my window, facing the city. It was just after midnight, and I could hear sirens.

Dream. Just a dream.

I hope so.

Sweat-drenched and dizzy from the throbbing in my head, I stripped to my boxers and lay down. The duvet would be cool for a minute, maybe a minute and a half, and then I would boil myself to sleep.

I don't want to sleep.

Agreed.

No more of those dreams.

Definitely.

Godhood is not in this season.

CHAPTER TWENTY

Skank didn't want us to work the following Saturday so I breakfasted early and headed out into London on my own. Connor seemed uncertain, but he had no real grounds for stopping me – I think he believed me when I said that I could take care of myself, and I doubted his reluctance stretched to serving as my unpaid bodyguard for the day. Sharon was working and Daryl had set himself up in the garden with a multi-pack of crisps and a stack of magazines, and I had a suspicion that Connor wanted to sit and play guitar all day without the benefit of an audience. As for me, I just needed to get out and have some time on my own, to think things over and probably not come to any conclusions.

The weather was perfect and I took a bus to Waterloo and wandered out into the city. Eyes followed me wherever I went: supermodels advertising perfume, film stars standing proud and Photoshopped in front of explosions and weddings and exploding weddings, lurid caricatures leering from rainbow forests of graffiti, bored shop window dummies sleepwalking through sterile fashion shows, cheerful and cheerless people criss-crossing and intersecting, ignoring one another, going about their business. London felt both familiar and alien today. I passed a clarinet player doing his best to squeeze out 'The Long and Winding Road', an upside-down trilby in front of him, and took pity because it held only fifty pence and a bent cigarette. I gave him a pound and he nodded, distracted by the discordant farting noise coming from his poorly-kept instrument.

'*Big Issue*,' said a tall man in brown. '*Big Issue*. Best way to start your day, with the best magazine . . .'

Snatches of conversations entered one ear and emerged a second later from the other, leaving me with *to be continued* a million times.

— *told her it was over, but will she listen* —
— *hated that album, he was never the same after* —
— *dropping by uninvited* —
— *even think* —
— *and don't come back* —
— *need flour* —

I drifted enjoyably and eventually found myself outside a little bakery that was pumping out wonderfully fresh smells. French loaves, Danish pastries, colourful frosted cakes, gingerbread, sausage rolls, Cornish pasties. I bought a sausage roll and a coffee and resumed my wandering, thoughts bouncing around my head like multicoloured balls trying to escape their pit.

My mother's voice. *Edward was always a bad apple...*

Eight years was a long time, and people change, but I still found it strange that there was so little correlation between my parents' picture of Eddie and the kind, funny, dependable guy on whom I'd dumped all my troubles two months ago. I only vaguely remembered what he'd been like before he'd moved, but even then I'd been sure he was kosher. I remembered my uncle Nathan well, a short bald man with a good sense of humour and a taste for cigars, but all I could really remember of Eddie was a quiet, brooding guy with that indefinable distractedness – and a smile. I was sure I could remember a smile.

People change.

And where were he and Connor always going? Maybe I was wrong, perhaps they *were* going out and fighting crime? Superpowered vigilantes on the prowl for wrong-doers in the big bad city. It sounded awesome, but somehow I doubted that was it. I was sure there was something else going on.

Superpowered cage fighting? Probably be good money in that.

Don't be stupid.

Crime? They were certainly powerful enough. *Power corrupts. Absolute power corrupts quite a lot.*

Godhood is not in this season.

Then there was Mr Freeman, his unsettling whiff of government conspiracy, the faintest odour of prophecy. I wouldn't trust the guy as far as I—

Powers, remember?

OK, as far as *Daryl* could throw him.

And what about the talking dog, genius?

Oh, forget that. That just . . . kind of . . . happened.

'Oi watch it!'

I jumped, shaken out of my tangle of thoughts. Whoever I'd almost walked into had already disappeared down the street. *Whatever.* I slowed down and looked around, seeing that my walk had led me to St. James Park.

What's the date?

Twenty-ninth of May, I think.

What exams would you have been having today?

Who cares? We don't need to do exams! Powers, remember? A possible calling? Of sorts.

Shiny.

The park smelled alive, bright and green and full of trees and birds and blossom. It reminded me of home; this oasis of nature in the middle of an artificial steel and concrete entity. This place was the eye of the storm, silent peace at the centre of a dark mass. All I could hear were birds, children having fun, and water. I wandered towards the lake. People sat on blankets and ate ice cream, teenagers played football, young couples lay side-by-side, kissing in the grass. Children giggled and screamed and their parents half-heartedly told them to be quiet, but everyone was enjoying themselves far too much to be cranky. This was exactly what I needed. I wandered to the edge of the water and stood, staring into it, breathing deeply, listening to the symphony of the park.

Something made me look up. Kloe was on the other side of the lake, staring at me. She was alone. She'd had her hair cut slightly, and there were blonde highlights in it. For several seconds neither of us could move, and then she smiled and the world was perfect. The smile held more happiness than I ever thought I was capable of inspiring, and she started to run around the edge of the lake. I ran as well, both of us keeping our eyes locked on each other, smiling, laughing, and finally we reached the path and kept running, and when we met we wrapped our arms around each other and hugged tightly, and I kissed her and she kissed me, and I remembered the taste of her lips from opening night, only this time we were meeting, not parting, and the beautiful bittersweetness was just sweetness, because I wasn't going anywhere. Hundreds of thoughts flashed through my brain. Had Miss Stevenson given her my message? How could she possibly be here when there were exams going on? How could she possibly be *here*, of all places? Would she stay? Was she even real?

Who cares?

We kissed for a long time that didn't feel long, and when we broke apart we were flushed and gasping. Kloe caught her breath and looked at me like I was a time capsule from centuries ago. 'You . . .' she said, breathlessly, 'you . . . you're . . .'

'Um,' I said, smiling. 'Hi.' *Well done.*

She smiled back, and the smile quickly became a grin, and then a laugh. 'Yeah, hi.'

We found a café and shared a massive chocolate and vanilla sundae. When we weren't eating we were talking, and breathing came third. Kloe was here for four days – her first exams had been on Tuesday and Thursday, and they started again next Tuesday. She had come down yesterday, ostensibly to go around some museums for exam research, and had been staying with her aunt down in Surbiton. She was supposed to be heading back on Monday. I tried not to think about that bit.

'Mum and Dad weren't too happy about me coming down right in the middle of revision,' Kloe said. 'I don't think they believed me when I said I was doing research. But I just had to get away for a bit. I told them I could revise wherever I was. And I feel on top of things, mostly.'

'What exams have you had?' I asked.

'Music, German and English. Music was a total bastard. German was pretty easy.'

'You were always really good in German,' I said.

She smiled. '*Danke schön, mein liebchen.*' Her eyes dropped to the table. 'Sorry. Yuck. Cheesy.'

'It's OK, I don't know what *liebchen* means. How was English?'

'Fine,' she said. 'You'd have found it easy, I think.'

'Really?'

'Yeah. The *Romeo and Juliet* questions were obviously easy, and the *Of Mice and Men* stuff was pretty straightforward.'

'What about the poem?' I asked. 'Isn't there a poem as well?'

Kloe nodded. 'I didn't find it hard. I'd read it already, though. What are the odds?'

'What was it?'

'Emily Dickinson,' said Kloe. '"The Mystery of Pain". Mr Grant said he was quite surprised about that because it was fairly high level.'

I couldn't think of anything to say for a minute. What did missing all my exams mean for my future? Did I have one? *Best not to think about that.* 'Did Miss Stevenson give you my message?' I asked.

Kloe nodded, and swallowed a mouthful of ice cream. '*Oooh* . . . cold . . . ow . . . OK, gone.' She exhaled sharply. 'Sorry. Um . . . yeah, she gave me your message. At the time I was pretty pissed off that you didn't call me.'

'I couldn't find your number,' I said, lamely. 'Genuinely.'

Kloe scowled, but couldn't help laughing. 'OK. Well . . . worst excuse ever. Congratulations.'

'I did find it, though,' I said. 'Really. And I did ring . . . I spoke to your mum.'

She raised her eyebrows. 'You did? When? She didn't—'

'She told me not to call again. That . . . that we shouldn't speak to each other.'

Kloe frowned. 'Hmm. Yeah. That sounds familiar. They . . . ah, whatever, it doesn't matter. I've stored up nearly seventeen years of goodwill with my parents, especially compared to my siblings. If I want to see you, I'm going to see you.'

Eight ball, corner pocket. I smiled. 'How were things at school after . . . you know?'

'Same but different.' Kloe had another spoonful of ice cream. 'Ben was suspended.'

'I heard. Miss Stevenson said that'd probably be about it.'

'So unfair. If it hadn't been for his parents . . .'

I shrugged. 'Never mind, eh?'

She nodded slowly. 'Everyone was talking about what happened.' I suddenly pretended to take an interest in the red and white checked tablecloth. Kloe leaned forwards. 'What *did* happen?'

'You were there. You saw.'

'I saw Ben try to cave your head in with a wooden pole,' said Kloe. 'And then I *think* I saw you throw him out of the room without touching him.'

'That's about what happened,' I said.

'But that's impossible,' said Kloe. 'I said at the time, it was impossible. There had to be another explanation. 'Cos it's impossible.'

'Kloe—'

'But it wasn't, was it? I mean . . . it's not. 'Cos you can do it.'

'I can do quite a lot of things,' I said. 'And I'll tell you, I'll tell you all of it, I'll show you. If you want. But I . . . I just want to be sure you're not completely freaked out. That you're not going to run away.'

'Look,' said Kloe. 'I don't understand it, but I'm not going to treat you like a freak. Sure, it was weird and . . . well, yeah, pretty bloody weird. But . . . sorry. Where was I? Um . . . yeah, sure it was weird. But I don't care. All I care about is you, and that you're OK. And that we're together. Everything's good.'

I nodded. 'Me too. That's how I feel.' I held out my hands and she took them and I squeezed hers.

'You're right, though,' she said. 'You are telling me everything. And showing me. If I'm going to have a boyfriend with magic powers, I want to know all about them.'

'I don't think they're magic,' I said.

'I think you might be, though,' said Kloe. We held each other's gazes for a long while, then Kloe looked away, giggling. 'God. The cheese just keeps on coming.'

'Yeah,' I said. 'We should probably stick a plug in it. But before we do, quick question. You remember you gave me a Christmas card at . . . Christmas?'

'I do.'

'Did I get an extra kiss?'

She affected an unimpressed face. 'Maybe.'

'I *knew it*!' I grinned. 'Knew it.'

'Don't get cocky,' she said.

'Yes, ma'am.'

'And don't call me "ma'am".'

'OK.'

Kloe sat back in her seat. 'So. What the hell have you been *doing* for two months?'

'Long story.'

'I have time. I don't have to meet my aunt until later.'

'OK.'

I told her everything. Well . . . not *everything* everything. Just enough. I told her that I'd illegally driven to London – she was impressed by that – and that I'd gone to Eddie's, and that he'd set me up with Connor and Sharon. I told her about the job at 110th Street and Blue Harvest and Eddie on his clarinet. I told her about my powers, and about how fast they'd been developing, although I glossed over the extent of my flying and omitted Mr Freeman and Smiley Joe entirely because I wasn't sure she was quite ready to handle those revelations. She accepted the power stuff fairly readily, but seemed to have trouble wrapping her head around the idea of a talking dog. That actually surprised me – I was so used to Daryl that it seemed as though everyone else should have been, too. 'I'm not sure I believe you,' she said.

'You'll meet him soon,' I said. 'Then trust me, you will believe.'

'Rightio.' She shook her head and looked into the empty sundae dish, taking it all in.

'I assume that the play didn't run Friday and Saturday nights,' I said.

She looked up, and for the first time there was anger in her eyes. 'What do you think?'

'I'm sorry,' I said. 'If I could have—'

'I know,' she said, shaking her head. 'I know. Don't worry. It's fine. It's just . . . it's just a shame we couldn't have one night.'

'That's what I said.' *Change the subject, right now.* 'So,' I said, not at all smoothly, 'what does everyone else think about my little telekinetic thing? What's the official theory?'

'Most people think you just threw him,' said Kloe. 'Selective memoryness.'

'Makes sense, I guess. So everyone doesn't think I'm a freak?'

'Well . . . a few people do. Because if you didn't have mind powers, you at least had some kind of super strength, which is freaksome in its own way. Zach said he'd known for ages, that you'd had a fight and used some sort of power on him. No-one really gave much of a shit what he had to say, though.'

'Zach?' My mind was blank. Then . . . 'Oh, *Zach*! Wow. I'd forgotten all about him.'

'He's going to some farming college in Scotland in September,' said Kloe. 'Thank God.'

'What about you?' I asked. 'What are your plans?'

'Sixth Form,' said Kloe. 'Staying on at school with Mark and everyone.'

Mark . . . 'How is Mark?' I asked.

'Fine,' said Kloe. 'He was pretty freaked out about you, but then so were most people. Charlotte swore you were on PCP or something. That you'd taken it to help your performance and gone mental.'

'Great.'

Another long silence, during which there wasn't much in the way of eye contact. We were definitely good at chatting, but there were some kinks to be ironed out. Too many awkward pauses. 'You're going back on Monday, then,' I said, finally.

'Yeah,' said Kloe. 'And . . . what about you?'

'I . . . I don't know. I can't really go back. Not yet. Things are happening. Well. They might be.'

'What things?'

I didn't answer. 'Stanly!' she said.

'Things I don't understand,' I said. 'There's stuff to work through. I have to think about what's going to happen.'

'Don't you want to come back with me?'

I couldn't say what I wanted to . . . could I?

Of course you can.

Say it.

Kloe leaned forwards and lifted my face by my chin. 'I said to myself that I shouldn't say this,' she said, 'because it's silly and rash and mental and far too early and we barely . . . but . . . seeing you now, and how I felt when I saw you in the park, and when you left, I . . . sod it. I love you.'

She beat me to it!

Don't be a fool.

Me or her?

You, you berk. Tell her.

I looked into her eyes. 'Me too.'

She raised her eyebrows. 'You . . . love you?'

I stared at her for a moment, and then we both pissed ourselves laughing. 'Yes,' I said. 'I love me. It's . . . it's taken a while for me to come to terms with it. But yeah, I really do love me.'

'That's great,' she giggled. 'I'm really happy for you.'

'Thanks.' The laughter subsided, and I looked at her. 'You know what I meant.'

'I know what you meant.' She took my hands again and we sat for a very long time without speaking. This time it was fine, though.

Congratulations. You only completely and utterly ballsed up the key moment.

Got away with it, though.

Playah playah.

Later on I walked Kloe to the station and we did some impressively awkward standing around, looking at each other and then looking away. 'So,' I said.

'So.'

'Can I . . . see you again?'

'Er . . . no. Our paths must never cross again.' She made a you-are-an-unutterable-cretin face. 'What kind of a question is that?'

'Sorry.'

'You're a slight numpty, do you know that?'

OK, marginally better than unutterable cretin. 'I do now.'

'I mean, for ages I thought you were really cool,' she said. 'Ever since we started doing the play. Your whole quiet, reserved thing. Observing from the sidelines. Never giving up more than what was necessary. Pretty sexy.'

Wow. Good to know. 'Thanks,' I said.

'But it's all just a cover, isn't it?' she said. 'A tangled web of lies to conceal the fact that you're a massive spaz.'

I laughed. 'OK. I hold up my hands. You've found out my terrible secret.'

'And I'm going to tell *everyone*. They'll run you out of town.' Her eyes widened. 'Sorry! That was really tactless.'

'It's fine. To be fair, I kind of ran myself out of Tref-y-Celwyn.'

'Fair enough.' She leaned over and kissed me. 'I'll phone you tonight. And see you tomorrow.'

'OK. Bye.'

'Bye.' We held each other's gaze for a long minute. 'It's amazing to see you,' she said.

'You too.'

She turned and ran towards the escalator, stopping at the top to blow me a kiss and stick out her tongue. Then she was gone, and I didn't feel light anymore.

'Touching.'

I didn't need to turn around. 'What do you want?' I said.

Mr Freeman walked around and stood in front of me. 'I thought perhaps another chat was in order.'

I shrugged. 'Fine. Whatever.'

'Let's walk, shall we?'

'Walking sounds good.'

The station smelled of food and hot metal. We strolled towards the exit, past shops, entrances to the underground system, signs for buses and taxis, boards showing train times and, of course, people. You tended to see the largest number of dfferent people in and around train stations and I looked around, interested as always, but also glad to be distracted from my new, mostly unwanted companion. A little girl in dungarees was jumping up and down with excitement. Her mother wore a floaty, flowery summer dress and exhaustedly brushed a sweaty lock of hair from her daughter's eyes, telling her that Uncle George would be there soon. A man in a business suit and an overcoat walked by checking his watch, and a twentysomething guy in beige shorts, sandals and a loud Hawaiian shirt open over a heavily-tattooed chest sloped past in the opposite direction, fanning himself with a newspaper and dragging a sports bag like an un-cooperative pet. We left the station and walked silently down towards the riverfront, Mr Freeman very subtly taking the lead. I looked around and pointed to a bench where two men sat, hidden behind newspapers. 'Yours?' I asked.

Mr Freeman looked impressed. 'Very good. Yes, they're mine. Highly paid. Very professional. Usually very discreet. How did you guess?'

Truthfully, I wasn't sure. 'Superhero's intuition,' I said.

'Ah.'

'So,' I said. 'You must be fairly high up in the sinister, shadowy corporate hierarchy to merit minions.'

Mr Freeman laughed. 'Minions, eh? I like that. I'll tell them.' He reached into his jacket and withdrew a packet of cigarettes. The suit was either the same one he'd been wearing the last time we'd seen each other or he had a wardrobe full of duplicates, which wouldn't have surprised me. He lit a cigarette with a match instead of a lighter. 'Sinister, shadow corporation, did you say? Lovely. Who's been filling your head with such preposterous notions?'

'Good word that. Preposterous.'

'Isn't it? A wonderful word to get your tongue around. It's like *soliloquy* or *ethereal* or *somnambulist*.'

'Yeah.' We walked alongside the river, past human statues and buskers and other novelty acts. The humidity had returned and the sky was having a half-hearted crack at rain, managing a very light drizzle that was more annoying than refreshing.

Mr Freeman blew out smoke. 'So, who *has* been filling your head with such notions?'

'Just every film and TV series I've ever seen,' I said. 'And every book I've read. And most of the stuff you've said to me.'

He laughed. 'If I were to tell you that it's a tad more complicated than that, would you believe me?'

'Why not?' I watched a large boat chug by, with people eating lunch on the top deck.

'Was there anything you particularly wanted to talk about?' asked Mr Freeman. 'While I'm here?'

'A few things,' I said. 'Dreams being one.'

'Dreams?'

'Yes.' It hadn't occurred to me until a second ago that this guy might be a good person to talk to about my messy subconscious, but I figured he was a weirdo and might well appreciate my weirdness, so I told him about the dreams, about killing and fire, feeling colder as I remembered them. He listened in silence, and nodded when I'd finished. 'You enjoyed it.'

'Parts of it, like the power,' I said, feeling an urge to be truthful.

'I enjoyed the . . . the clarity? Knowing that I was better, that I was going to win.'

'There you go again,' said Mr Freeman. 'Winning. Losing. You're going to need to think outside the box if you're going to live in this world, Stanly.'

'I already live in this world,' I said.

'I'm not talking about *this* world,' he said, gesturing at the city around us. 'Winning, losing, they're . . . troublesome. Like good and evil. Useful in the short term, perhaps, but in terms of the big picture they're unhelpful at best. There are no winners and losers in *life*. People talk about triumph over adversity, but life *is* adversity. Some things you can shrug off and then you can go about your business once more, other things may grind you down or kill you. It's all about putting yourself in the best possible position to continue your story. You can win or lose against a speeding train or a bolt of lightning, but you can't beat *existence*.' He tossed away the glowing butt of his cigarette.

What the hell is this clown babbling about, asked a portion of my brain that spoke in Daryl's voice. 'I was talking about dreams,' I said.

Freeman laughed. 'I'm sorry. I don't mean to get bogged down in philosophy or semantics . . . I just want you to understand that winning is a relative term.'

'There are no sides then?'

'Oh, there are, most definitely. And it would definitely be better for one to . . . win, to put it in easy-to-swallow terminology.'

'Don't you want to win?' I asked.

'Winning, to me, implies finality,' said Mr Freeman. 'A definite endgame. I hope to endure, and I hope that events will unfold in a certain way. I hope that you will be a part of those events.'

'What do you want from me?'

'It's more about what *you* want,' said Freeman. 'What do you wish to accomplish? What do you want to do with your powers?'

'Help people,' I said.

'Why?'

'What do you mean?'

'I mean, why? Why do you want to help people?'

'Because . . . because I'm stronger now. And stronger people should protect weaker people. There are too many bullies, too many people in pain.' It was strange having to vocalise these thoughts. I'd certainly had them, but they'd been so abstract. It was also strange how uncertain I sounded.

'Admirable,' said Freeman. '*How* do you plan to help these people, may I ask?'

'I . . . don't know.'

'By fighting? Roaming the world, seeking out evil-doers and striking them down? Laudable, but impractical.' He lit another cigarette. 'Perhaps you could wander the streets of London, using your powers to solve the homeless crisis. However that might work.'

'You're hilarious.'

'I'm not necessarily being sarcastic. I'm just trying to help you think practically. Are you going to fly to war-torn countries, seek out troubled villages to protect from mobs and militias? Descend from the sky like an avenging angel, a one-man Magnificent Seven? Could you do that? Are you prepared for what you'd see? Would it help?' *Jesus, it's like talking to the careers adviser again.*

'What do you think?' I asked.

'I think that you should follow your instincts,' said Freeman. 'Do what *you* think is right. You'll soon find out whether it's the right course.' He regarded his cigarette thoughtfully.

'Maybe I'd rather be a bad guy.'

'Meaningless concept,' said Freeman. 'But I agree, you could just as easily go the other way. Be stronger. Operate on a different level, a higher level.'

'Why would I want to?' I said, feeling oddly offended that he was seriously entertaining the idea.

'You asked me to analyse your dreams,' said Freeman. 'You said you liked the power.'

'Yes, but—'

'It's understandable. Power is . . . tasty.'

'I didn't like what came about as a result, though,' I said. 'I didn't like the killing. I didn't like the flames.' I also didn't like this conversation. 'And anyway, there's other stuff. In the dreams. I feel like they're showing me things that I shouldn't, *couldn't* be seeing. What does it mean?'

'Dreams are equal parts truth and nonsense,' said Freeman. 'Some may mean something. Some may *seem* to mean something. But you take from them what you want. And it's not beyond the realms of possibility that your powers are having an effect on them. Very little research has been done on the subject, but I would not be surprised if you and those like you are more – how can I put this – *attuned* to the world, and events, around you. It's just that you are not yet able to process all of this extra information consciously. Just my little pet theory.' Freeman smoked for a moment before continuing. 'Maybe you did enjoy the killing in the context of the dream, because it meant power and control. Someone of your age is a bubbling stew of confusion, and you have the added, highly confusing bonus of supernatural abilities. It follows that you would welcome the feeling that you are the master of your – and maybe everyone else's – destiny. It doesn't mean that you're going to become a mass-murdering supervillain. Unless you want to. Which I wouldn't advise. There are quite enough nasty people operating as it is. I can safely say that you belong on the side of the angels, so to speak.'

That was reassuring, even if it was coming from him. 'Who are these nasty people?'

'You'll find out soon, I'm sure.' Freeman looked at his cigarette again. 'Let's just say that not everyone I work for has humanity's best interests at heart.'

There was an unspoken *don't push* at the end of the sentence, so I focused on something else that surprised me. 'You're not the boss? You're just a minion too?'

He laughed. 'There's that word again. I like it. I think I'm going to use it more often.' He blew out smoke.

We sat down on a bench and Mr Freeman finished his cigarette and threw it away. He didn't light another one. 'You didn't answer my question,' I said.

He nodded. 'Yes, Stanly. I am a minion, of sorts. And I have minions of my own. Two of them will shortly be fired because they were so distracted by that trio of mime artists that they temporarily lost sight of us. As far as they know, you could have popped me like old fruit using the powers of your mind by now.'

'Are we talking losing-their-job fired or *bang* fired?' I asked, miming a gun.

Mr Freeman smiled a faintly disturbing smile. 'I'll leave that to your imagination.' He lit another cigarette. 'Your Kloe's a very pretty girl.'

My muscles tensed. 'What does she have to do with you?'

'Nothing whatsoever,' said Mr Freeman, blowing out smoke. 'I was just making an observation.'

'Well, don't,' I said. 'Kloe is one topic of conversation that is not open to you.'

Mr Freeman shrugged. 'Fair enough.' We sat in silence for a few minutes while he smoked, and then he said, 'You know you don't belong together.'

I almost hit him. Instead I focused on an empty McDonald's box and mentally crushed it into dust. 'Say what?' I said, in as casual a voice as I could manage.

'I don't mean that you don't have feelings for one another,' said Mr Freeman, 'or that those feelings are anything less than genuine. But if you are going to explore the darker side of this world and develop your own powers, how long before she gets hurt?'

Reasonable question, said a voice in my head. *You shut up*, said another one.

'I'll die before I let her get hurt,' I said.

'That's exactly the attitude that's going to totally spoil everything,' said Mr Freeman. 'Don't bother dying for her. Just cut her loose. I'm sure that she's one in several million, but she's not a luxury that you can afford. She's going home on Monday; the best thing that you could do is just let her go and make sure she doesn't look back.'

'Are you planning something?' I asked. 'Because if you hurt her—'

'For goodness' sake,' said Mr Freeman, sounding cross for the first time since I'd met him, 'I have no desire whatsoever to harm a hair on her pretty little head. But just think. She could quite easily get hurt.'

I didn't say anything. I hated the fact that he had a point. 'I suppose it comes down to what we were talking about before,' said Freeman. 'What do you want to do? Do you want to help people? Fight "bad guys"? Or have a happy home life with your girlfriend and your buddies and your job in the comics shop?'

Not talking about this any more.

Take control again.

'Think I'll have both, ta,' I said.

Freeman shrugged. 'It's up to you.'

'It is. Anyway. I have more questions.'

'Please, fire away.'

'Who are you?'

My companion laughed. 'Complicated question. And probably fairly tedious.'

'Do you have powers?' The thought had only just occurred to me, but it suddenly seemed obvious. Freeman laughed again, but it was a different laugh this time. It had an edge of . . . was it regret?

'If only,' he said. 'That would make things an awful lot easier.' He stood up, withdrew his wallet and handed me a ten pound note. 'Go and see *Casablanca*. There's a showing at the Old Elizabeth tomorrow. My treat.'

I pocketed the money. 'Thanks.'

'You're quite welcome.' Freeman looked around, as though checking the coast was clear. 'Do be careful.'

'One more thing,' I said. 'Smiley Joe.'

Something flashed across his face. It didn't last long, but it was intriguing: a weird mixture of guilt, loathing and . . . triumph?

When it passed he smiled, though it was more of a grimace. 'A monster that needs annihilating.' He fixed me with a stare that startled me with its intensity. 'If only there were people out there capable of completing such a task.'

'If only,' I said. 'What do you know about him?'

'*He* is not a *he*,' said Freeman, lighting yet another cigarette. 'And *it* is not the only abomination to stalk these streets, to lurk in the dark and prey on the weak. Its modus operandi, however, is crueller than most.'

'Children.'

'Yes.'

'Have you seen him?' I asked. 'I mean . . . it?'

'Truthfully, I don't know,' said Freeman. 'I'm not convinced that the face it shows its prey is its true face. I wonder if it chose a face that it thought would be comforting or amusing to children.'

'The big head?'

Freeman nodded. I had to stop myself from shuddering. The sounds of the world seemed muffled all of a sudden, the air was cold and dead. 'Where is it?' I asked.

'I wish I knew,' said Freeman. 'Good luck.' He turned and walked away, and I sat and absorbed what had been said.

Great, said Daryl's voice from the back of my head. *Your guardian angel, eh?*

Did he actually tell us anything useful?

I think he did.

He's still irritating.

CHAPTER TWENTY-ONE

I GOT HOME JUST after five, irritated but intrigued. Neither were helped by the heat and the headache that had sprung up. Connor was sitting on the sofa with Daryl watching a badly-dubbed kung-fu movie, and the two of them were providing a sarcastic running commentary. 'Afternoon,' said Connor.

'Hi,' I said. 'Sharon about?'

'She's not going to be back until late tonight. Why?'

'Just wondering.'

'You hungry?'

'No. Completely not. Too hot.'

'Eddie wanted you to give him a call.'

'Why?'

'Didn't say.'

'In that case, he can call me.' The elation of seeing Kloe again had been significantly tempered by what Mr Freeman had said, and I was in no mood for Eddie's neuroses. I was halfway up the stairs when Connor came out into the hall and called after me.

'You OK?'

'Five by five,' I said.

'What?'

'I'm fine.'

At about half past seven the phone rang. I was lying on my bed reading a book of Charlie Brooker's columns. I really needed to laugh, and it was helping. I heard Connor answer. 'Hello?' he said.

'Uh . . . who is this? Oh. Oh! Hi. Yeah, I'll just call him. Stanly!'

'Who is it?'

'It's Kloe!'

My heart burst out of my chest and hit the wall, leaving a bright red stain. 'OK! I'll be right there!'

'Hi,' said Kloe when I got to the phone.

'Hi,' I said. 'How are you?'

'Good. You?'

'Also . . . good.' *Cringe.*

Kloe giggled. 'Good. Um . . . do you want to go out again tomorrow?'

Screw Mr Freeman. 'Yeah! Yes. A lot.'

'OK. Where?'

Twilight?

What's that?

Eddie's club?

You're going to take her clubbing?

We don't even know if she likes clubs?

Plus I'm not sure about taking her to a club called Twilight.

Plus we're kind of underage.

What do you suggest then?

Stop manifesting your internal conflicts!

'Um,' said Kloe. 'I was wondering . . . do you think we could go to that jazz bar you were telling me about? What's it called . . . ?'

'Blue Harvest?'

'Yeah!'

'Could do, yeah. It doesn't open until late-ish, though.'

'We could do something else first. Go and see a film, maybe?'

'Yeah, great!'

'OK. Well . . . I'll meet you at Waterloo at twelve, how does that sound?'

'It sounds great . . .' *Oh shit.* 'Hold on.' I put my hand over the receiver. 'Connor?'

'What?'

'Does Skank want us to work tomorrow?'

'Uh . . . yeah.'

'Do you think he'd mind if I . . . could I take a day off?'

'Why? Oh . . . for . . . yeah, I should think so.'

I took my hand off the receiver. 'Yeah, that's great.'

'Great!'

'OK. I'll see you tomorrow.'

'See you tomorrow.'

'So,' said Daryl later on that evening while Connor cooked supper downstairs and I tried to read my book. 'Date with Juliet.'

'Yep.'

'It's strange,' he said. 'Her being here.'

'She's staying with her aunt.'

'No, I mean you meeting. What are the odds that you'd be at the exact same place at the exact same time? It's impossible.'

'Improbable,' I corrected him. 'Coincidence.'

'I stopped believing in coincidences when you got telekinesis and levitation for your sixteenth,' said Daryl. 'Everything happens for a reason.'

'Maybe it was fate, then. Destiny.'

Daryl snorted. 'Why not?' I asked. 'I can fly, for Christ's sake. I can move things with my mind.' I swapped several books around on the shelf to illustrate the point. 'You don't know what other unbelievable nonsense might be true too. Plus, Mark Topp told me that the first person his sister met when she got off the plane in Thailand was from Tref-y-Celwyn. It's a small world.'

'Fine,' said Daryl. 'Fair points, all well made. But . . .'

'But what?' I asked. 'Are you going to tell me that Kloe's part of some mega conspiracy now?'

'Is it really such a stretch?'

'I think you need to stop this now,' I said. 'It's verging on accusation.'

'Maybe it is,' said Daryl.

226

'I think I've had enough of this conversation,' I said, turning back to my book.

Connor had cooked risotto and I ate in silence while he and Daryl talked about the films of Quentin Tarantino. They were halfway through dissecting exactly what was wrong with *Kill Bill Vol. 2* when the doorbell rang. 'I'll get it,' I said.

It was Eddie. He was wearing black and blue and looked tired. 'Hi,' he said.

'Hi.'

'Did Connor give you my message?'

'Yes.'

'Why didn't you call me?'

I shrugged. 'Forgot.'

'Can I come in?'

I stood aside. 'Sure.' He walked past, hung up his jacket and headed to the kitchen. Connor stood up to greet him while I sat down and carried on eating. Eddie helped himself to a beer from the fridge.

'So,' he said. 'Get up to much today?'

'Went out,' I said.

'Where?'

'Into town. To the park.'

Eddie and Connor exchanged looks. Eddie narrowed his eyes. 'Did something happen? You seem a bit . . . off.'

'He has been all evening,' said Connor. 'Except when he talked to Kloe.'

I felt myself going red.

'Kloe?' asked Eddie. 'Your girl, Kloe?'

'Yeah,' I said. 'Met her in St. James Park. She's down until Monday.'

'Well, that's great, isn't it?'

'Uh-huh.'

'Then why the lack of joy?'

'I'm just . . . tired, I suppose.' Then I remembered Kloe's request.

'Um . . . Kloe wants to go to Blue Harvest tomorrow. Does it open on Sundays?'

'Yeah,' said Connor. 'Around six.'

'Could we go?' I asked.

Eddie shrugged. 'Of course. I have to work at eleven, but I could come for a couple of hours.'

My spirits lifted. 'Great! Will you play?'

'Well . . . are you sure you want us to be there?'

'Yeah,' said Connor. 'Don't you want to be alone with your lady?'

'I'll talk to her,' I said. 'Ask her if she minds. I don't think she will – she wants to meet you all. Will Sharon be working?'

'I can't remember,' said Connor. 'I'm sure she'll come if she isn't, though.'

'Great.'

Daryl hadn't said anything, but I knew what he was thinking. *That's ridiculous. Someone manipulated Kloe into being in London to mess with me? He has no evidence. And it's ridiculous.*

He's just looking out for me.

Screw him, said my sulky teenager voice, a voice I hadn't heard from in a while. *None of his business.*

It still doesn't make any sense.

'You all right?' asked Eddie.

'What?'

'You went a bit catatonic for a second.'

'Sorry,' I said.

'Must be love,' said Connor, winking at Eddie. 'Only a woman could infiltrate a lad's brain like that.'

Eddie laughed. 'I dimly remember the feeling.'

'Speaking of something that's a different subject from my love life,' I said, 'how about *your* love life? Are you going to ask Hannah out again?'

Eddie fidgeted uncomfortably. 'I don't . . . it's not really . . . it's complicated.'

''Cos of her brother?' said Daryl, casually.

Eddie shot Connor a look of death, and the Irishman held up his hands. 'Don't look at me. These two are like the Spanish Inquisition. They thumbscrewed it out of us.'

'I bet.' Eddie stared intently at his beer. 'Partly her brother, yeah. He made things very difficult for us. For her. He still does.'

'How come?' I asked.

'Hey,' said Eddie, 'how about we don't talk about this any more?'

'I'll stay out of your romantic entanglements if you stay out of mine,' I said, holding out my hand.

'Deal,' said Eddie, and we shook.

I lay on my back on a hard floor, my body hot and so tired I could barely move. Invisible hands wrung out a cold sponge over my forehead and the water dripped onto my face. I heard helicopters in the distance, rotors cutting air, spinning blades talking to one another. The ceiling came into focus, a primitive painting in primary colours. A grey man, a red boy, a white dog, a blue girl, yellow fire. I could hear scuttling.

Spiders . . .

In the distance forests burned and houses crumbled. A low, sexless voice was talking in my ear, scratchy like worn vinyl. 'Pain has an element of blank.

'It cannot recollect.'

'When it began, or if there were.'

'A day when it was not.'

'I love poetry.'

'Do you.'

'Yes.'

'My Emily knows, she does. Miss D's got the skills.'

What is this?

Someone was picking out a melancholy Spanish melody on a guitar. I could see the shadows of fingers dancing on strings and the air buzzed as the notes vibrated. The tune was familiar but lost. Once again I could hear scuttling.

Spiders . . .

'Stand up.' Freeman's voice. I stood up. The room was square and made of brown and rust. It smelled like . . . 'Fear?'

'Yes,' I said. 'Right.'

Freeman laughed and all his teeth fell out. His next non sequitur was simply a formless mumble, falling backwards into a great mouth on the front of a big giant head.

Spiders . . .

A small figure in red pyjamas, and then—

I opened my eyes and was immediately wide awake. It wasn't like waking from a nightmare. My heart was beating normally. It was just . . . wakefulness. I looked at my watch. Ten past three.

I won't be sleeping again.

I got out of bed and pulled on black jeans and my black hoody. Cool night tonight. London beckoned.

What else ya gonna do?

As I floated out of the window, I heard a low voice. 'Oi. What are you doing?'

I turned, hanging in mid-air outside the window. Daryl had been sleeping on the chair in the corner of the room and now he was staring accusingly at me. 'Can't sleep,' I said. 'Going out.'

'What if someone sees you? What if—'

'I'll be fine,' I said. 'Powers, remember?'

'But what if—'

'God, you sound like Eddie.'

'He won't be happy. Connor and Sharon won't be happy.'

'They won't find out unless you tell them,' I said. 'Are you going to tell them?'

'Of course not.' Daryl did a sort-of shrug. 'Fine. Just be careful.'

'I will. Don't wait up.' I turned and looked to the end of the garden, to the orange lights and the gigantic shadows beyond. Where to go?

Where to go?

I shot upwards, gaining height even faster than I'd intended, and came to halt when I was high enough to see most of the city.

Part of me wanted to go straight for the centre, for the big buildings, to dance from spire to spire, run down the faces of skyscrapers, skate the bridges, surf the Thames. But I knew it wasn't a good idea. Too many people with cameras on their phones. Too many CCTV eyes. I knew if someone captured me flying on film it would find its way back to my new guardians.

And then what? Either they'd know it was me, or they'd think there was some other kid flying around, and then—

I mentally slapped myself. Enough tangents. I had a whole city to play with. It was the middle of the night. If there was any time to be doing this, now was it.

So what to do?

I half-considered finding some grimy estate and looking for trouble, acting out my little mental short film, but I knew that if I went looking for it I might end up causing it rather than simply finding it. Whereas if I didn't go looking for it, maybe it wouldn't occur at all. Going out and helping people was one thing, but I wasn't going to go and pick a fight for no reason. That wasn't me.

That's not me.

My eyes fell on Big Ben and I grinned, took all the caution and tossed it to the winds. Making sure my hood was up, I zapped towards the great clock tower, staying high and hoping I was small and dark enough to avoid whatever radars kept the centre of the city safe. I alighted on the top-most tip of the tower, crouching perfectly still, balancing like a dancer, keeping myself hunched over and inconspicuous. The endless dark bright shatter of London lay before me, laid out like Christmas presents. The height was dizzying. Somehow being on a building felt more dodgy than being in the air. In the air, I had to fly. Here, I had something to fall from. I hopped off the spire and dropped down towards the enormous, luminous face of the clock, down to the hour hand, which was perfectly horizontal. I stood there and breathed, an ant on ol' Ben's huge metal moustache.

I'm not Peter Pan, I don't BEEP with fairies . . .

As I stood there, watching and drinking in the cold air, I felt a rush in my stomach that travelled decliciously up to my chest. At this precise moment, I *owned* this city. I could cross it in minutes. Leap its buildings in a single bound. I could take on whatever it had to throw it me. Mr Freeman's employers, Smiley Joe . . .

At this precise moment, I knew that I was going to be a superhero.

Somehow, someday, I was going to do it.

I *had* to.

Later, as I floated back through my bedroom window, I saw that Daryl had waited up for me. He asked what I'd been up to and I told him, and I could tell he was impressed, although he hid it well. 'Been done,' he said. 'Standing on the hands of the clock? Definitely been done.'

'Maybe,' I said, as I got back into bed. 'But it was still cool as *shit*.'

'Shit ain't cool, grasshopper.'

'You know what I mean.'

'And it's still a cliché.'

I closed my eyes. 'You're just jealous.'

'Bored now.'

'Whatevz.'

'Are you still talking?'

'Nooope.'

CHAPTER TWENTY-TWO

CONNOR HAD ALREADY left for work when I came down for breakfast in the morning, but Sharon had the day off, and we sat together and ate croissants and drank coffee. 'OK,' she said, after a while. 'What's wrong?' The way she looked at me, her eyes so full of affection, was how I remembered looking at my younger cousins. That sibling protectiveness. *I've only known her since March. I must be doing something right.*

Did I ever wish for an older sister?

Kinda feels like it now.

'I . . .' Words stalled. 'Um . . .'

Sharon laughed. 'All right, so there definitely *is* something wrong.'

'Yes.' I finished my coffee and glanced at the clock. Half past ten. *Just go for it.* 'Does the name Freeman mean anything to you?'

Immediately, her expression changed. The concern was still there, but there was anger too, writing itself across her brow. She nodded. 'Yes. You've met him, then.'

'Yeah.'

'When?'

'First time was the week before last. And then I saw him again yesterday, after I saw Kloe off.'

'What did he tell you?'

'That I have a destiny, sort of,' I said. 'And power.'

'Did he give you a card?'

'Yeah.'

'He gave me one too,' said Sharon. 'And to Eddie and to Connor. All of us, separately. He talked to me like I was some . . . chosen one, or something. Talked to the others that way too. Made us all feel special. And then afterwards he just discarded us.'

'After what?'

Sharon looked pained. 'He's part of something. Something big. I don't know if it's government-related or not, but it's definitely big. He used us all to get rid of . . .' She blinked very fast. *Don't cry. Tell.* 'Things.'

'Things?'

'You remember when you first came here, when we went out to the playground,' said Sharon. 'Connor and I had that . . . discussion. About Smiley Joe. The reason I was so surprised, why I'm *still* so surprised about Connor's attitude, is that there have been other monsters. Before Smiley Joe. And we've *fought* them.'

I remembered Freeman's words. *It is not the only abomination to stalk these streets.* It wasn't that I hadn't believed him, but hearing it from Sharon . . . it suddenly felt real.

Monsters.

Plural.

'When was this?' I asked.

'I was sixteen,' said Sharon. 'I'd only recently discovered my powers and I was freaking out, to put it mildly. I was living rough around London, mixing with . . . the wrong people. And one night I was wandering around in a daze and I met Freeman. He looked rich – he was wearing an expensive suit – and he gave me his card and some money and told me he'd be around. Being young and braindead I figured I had an ally.'

'A guardian angel,' I said, darkly.

'Hmm,' said Sharon. 'Not long after that he turned up again, out of the blue, telling me that I had a choice, that I was destined for great things. Then on our third meeting he told me about this creature living in the sewers. People called it the Worm. I'd heard about it, figured it was just an urban legend, something to scare kids, but Freeman told me it was real. He told me that if I could destroy it then I'd . . . I'd be saving lives. That I would prove myself. I was going through some stuff at the time and I . . . anyway. That doesn't matter. I was terrified, absolutely out of my mind, but I went down there, down to the sewers, and I fought this thing . . . and I killed it.'

'What was it like?'

'I don't . . .' The memory was obviously making her uncomfortable, and I hurriedly apologised. 'It's OK,' I said, 'don't worry.'

'It's fine,' said Sharon. 'It . . . it was huge. Disgusting . . . like a massive slug with a teeth. I can't even describe the smell. Never been so scared in my life . . . but I managed to kill it.'

Fair play. 'And Freeman?' I said.

'I never heard from him again,' said Sharon. 'I'd not long met Connor, and when I told him about it he told me a similar story, except that his was some kind of flying creature. He didn't go into much detail. Again, Mr Freeman severed all contact with him after he defeated it.'

'And Eddie?'

'We met him a couple of years later. Another variation on the same story, but he refused to tell us about his monster. He never talks about it, and none of us have heard from Mr Freeman since. And now you're his new project, by the looks of things.' She shook her head, her lip trembling with anger. 'Bastard.'

'He didn't mention a monster to me,' I said. '*I* brought up Smiley Joe and asked some questions, and he went a bit funny and left.' *The implication was there, though.*

'Hmm.'

'Did he know a lot about you?' I asked. 'Freakishly private stuff?'

'Nothing a bit of research and detective work couldn't uncover,' said Sharon. 'Why? He knew a lot about you?'

'Too much.'

'Well, don't trust him,' said Sharon. 'If you see him again, tell him you're not interested, and come back and tell us immediately. He's . . . bad news.'

I nodded. 'OK. Thanks. Sorry . . . I know I should have told you immediately.'

'It's all right,' said Sharon. 'I remember what he's like . . . the things he has to say. How it feels. It's scary, but in a way it's exactly what you want to hear.'

'Yeah.' I shifted uncomfortably in my seat. 'Um . . . so you all know about monsters, then. But . . . Connor *swore* there was no Smiley Joe. Acted as though it was completely ridiculous . . .'

'Mm.' Sharon nodded. 'Yes . . . it's just something he wants to leave behind, and he doesn't want it to affect you the way it affected us. And the only way he feels he can deal with it is to pretend it never happened, and that it couldn't happen again.'

'I imagine he wasn't happy with you, then,' I said. 'Pushing it.' Immediately I wished I hadn't said that, but Sharon just smiled.

'Neither one of us is the boss of the other,' she said. 'And anyway, it gets very boring if you agree on *everything*.'

I laughed. 'Yeah . . . s'pose so.' I looked at the clock again. It was nearly eleven. 'Oops. I'm meeting Kloe soon. Better get going.' I got up and headed for the door, and was just on my way out when something occurred to me. I turned around. 'Sharon?'

'Yes?'

'Are you going to tell Connor and Eddie about Mr Freeman?'

'I think we should,' she said. 'They'll want to know. They *should* know.'

'OK,' I said. 'Yeah . . . I guess. Um . . . can I do it? I'll . . . I'd like to pick the right moment. I imagine they might not take the news as well as you.'

'I imagine you might be right.' She nodded. 'All right. Deal.'

'Thanks.' I said. 'I'll call you later and let you know about Blue Harvest, OK?'

'Sounds good.'

Even though I left early, traffic conspired against me and I arrived at Waterloo fifteen minutes late, cursing at a billion decibels inside my head and sharing in the festival of eye-rolling and declarations of 'typical' that were the only real communication strangers seemed to have on public transport in London. Kloe was waiting by the station exit. 'Sorry,' I said. 'Gremlins, or summat.'

She nodded and rolled her eyes theatrically. 'Typical.'

'Like, *so* typical.' We giggled, and hugged, and I don't think I could have felt further away from the idea of monsters.

Kloe had never seen *Casablanca* and I hadn't watched it for over a month, and I figured I might as well put Mr Freeman's money to good use, so we decided to go and see it. Kloe was excited about Blue Harvest and eager for Sharon, Eddie and Connor to join us. 'I'd love to meet them,' she said. 'They sound really cool. Plus I need to vet them, to make sure they're looking after you properly.'

'They make me sleep in a cupboard under the stairs,' I said. 'And they feed me crusts and old rain water.'

Kloe nodded approvingly. 'Sounds about right.'

The film was at four, so we spent three and a half hours wandering around eating and talking. So much talking, it was amazing. We talked about food (A Very Good Thing), films (things by which I lived my life, and things that Kloe put on in the background while doing other things), school (or lack of same), TV (see above re: films), politics (that didn't last long), religion (Not A Very Good Thing), music (I'd never even considered Beatles vs. Stones to be a real thing, as The Beatles were so obviously, demonstrably superior, but it turned out that Kloe was a Stones girl – go figure), terrorism (Most Definitely Not A Very Good Thing), and everything in between (not literally). After what Sharon had said, I was glad that we disagreed on some things. It felt healthy. Kind of sexy, even. We also discussed Kloe's aunt (not such a sexy topic), who was aware of her parents' wishes regarding me and had not been entirely happy with our plans for today. 'I kind of guilted her into being OK with it, in the end,' said Kloe. 'She told me this story years ago, about a boyfriend she had when she was fifteen, who her parents hated, and I shamelessly used it against her.'

'Was she cross?'

'A bit,' said Kloe. 'But also kind of proud, I think.'

She ended up dragging me around H&M because she needed to buy a top and wanted me to help her, and as we drifted around the women's clothing section looking at bikini tops, T-shirts, strap tops and every other conceivable type of top, I had a thought that I didn't really want to have. 'Um . . . Kloe?'

'Mm?' she asked, distractedly, holding a white Pink Panther strap top against herself.

'Did you go to the Prom?'

She turned around very quickly. 'What?'

'Did you go to the Prom?'

She looked at the ground. 'Um . . . well . . . yes.'

'Oh.' *Great.* 'Who with?'

She looked hurt. 'Who did I go with? I didn't go with anyone, you dickhead. I wanted to go with you, but you were sort of elsewhere.'

'Sorry . . .' *Way to go, Stanly, you plank.*

She waved her hand. 'No, I'm sorry. That was unfair.' She put the top back on its hanger. 'Basically, I got dressed up and went with a couple of friends. Spent most of the time talking and drinking from various hip flasks. Nearly lost it at the last song, 'cos it was a slow number, of course, but Lynsey asked me to dance and it was fine.'

'Lynsey?' *Lynsey, Lynsey . . .* 'Blonde Lynsey?'

'Yes,' she laughed. 'Blonde Lynsey. She caught her boyfriend getting off with Tilly Sharpe halfway through the dance so we decided to dance together and take the piss out of all the slushy couples. Is that OK?'

'Fine,' I said. 'Fine. I just . . . well. You know.'

'Yeah.' She took a powder blue T-shirt off the shelf and held it up. 'What do you think?'

Nice? I think? 'Nice,' I said. 'Try it on.'

She popped to the changing rooms, and emerged a minute later wearing the T-shirt. 'What do you think?' she asked again.

'Um.' I was going crimson.

'Too tight?'

No, just tight enough. 'Um, a little, maybe? A bit. Um.'

She settled on two tops in the end, one white and one blue, and we got to the cinema in plenty of time, bought far too much confectionary and sat down, ready for the film to begin. By the time Humphrey and Ingrid said goodbye at the misty airport we were both glassy-eyed, which I took as a good sign, and I squeezed her hand and she put her head on my shoulder. We left the cinema with our arms around each other, and Kloe asked what the time was.

I looked at my watch. 'Quarter past six.'

She looked into my eyes. 'What do you want to do now?'

'It's open now, but the music doesn't start until later,' I said. 'What do *you* want to do?'

We found a park bench and amused ourselves until seven.

'So,' said Connor. 'It's certainly a pleasure to meet the original Romeo and Juliet.'

Kloe's cheeks went a bit red, but she laughed. 'Yeah. It's pretty disgusting, isn't it?' She sipped her wine and gave me a cheeky look, and I smiled back like a lovestruck goon.

Connor grinned. 'Well I think it's nice. And so long as you can avoid any misunderstandings with sleeping drugs and Friars who should know better, you should be fine.'

'Check,' said Kloe. 'No suicide confusion. We were actually going to have mobile phones in the play 'cos it was modern dress, but Miss Stevenson decided we couldn't because if everyone had phones, that would basically negate the entire plot.'

'Good point.'

'You know,' I said, 'maybe we should forget about that aspect of our courtship, for the sake of not jinxing it.'

'Our *courtship*?' said Kloe.

'Shut up, I stand by my word. And yeah, we should definitely probably forget about the play. Otherwise you get into the whole Juliet-being-fourteen-years-old thing, and Romeo being a whiny douchebag. Plus, like you said, suicide confusion.'

239

'It *is* a pretty shoddy love story.'

'I know, right? So maybe . . . I dunno, at the most we're like the best possible version of Romeo and Juliet, who were both of age, and Romeo wasn't a whiny douchebag, and there was no issue with their parents, and everything was just fine. Rubbish from a tragic drama perspective, but better in pretty much every other possible way.'

'Whatever you say,' said Kloe, and we shook.

Connor laughed and glanced in Eddie's direction. 'Yo, Edster. You here?'

Eddie nodded distractedly. 'Yeah.' He kept fiddling with his empty glass and glancing towards the bar, where Hannah was talking animatedly with a young scarlet-haired jazz violinist who had finished playing about twenty minutes ago. Now there was a hiatus. The place was fuller than last time, and I was sitting with Kloe, Connor and Eddie at what I'd now decided was 'our usual table'. Sharon had developed a headache and decided to stay at home. The other patrons were an amusingly varied mix: a pretty blonde girl in a blue dress sitting with a clean-shaven denim model-type guy; a distinguished-looking man with white hair, dressed in a suit, sitting alone; a guy and girl with matching hemp outfits and dreadlocks who had been texting pretty much the whole time they'd been there. The violinist's companions – a bald guy who played the piano and a young woman who sang – were sitting at a table near the back, drinking silently, while the violinist chatted to Hannah. I could see why Eddie was getting pissed off, although he was making it embarrassingly obvious, and I was trying to think of something not Hannah-related to say to distract him when he very abruptly stood up, excused himself and disappeared to the men's toilets.

'What's up wit yo cousin?' asked Kloe.

'He and the girl at the bar used to go out,' said Connor. 'He gets jealous.'

'Oh.' Kloe didn't look convinced. 'But he was sort of strange outside when we first met.'

'He's sort of strange generally,' said Connor. 'Don't get me wrong, he's my best mate and I love him but . . . well, Stanly, you know, don't you? He's weird.'

'Always has been,' I said.

'Look who's talking,' said Kloe, sticking her tongue out.

This public flirting thing is really kind of sexy.

You think?

You enjoyed snogging on a park bench while the world and his wife and our Mrs. Reynolds wandered by, didn't you? Face it. You like other people seeing how all over each other you are.

So what if I do?

Man, I don't care. Just so long as she keeps—

'Hey,' said Kloe in a low voice. 'Look at that lot.'

Connor and I looked in the direction she was pointing as casually as we could. There was a group I'd not noticed before sitting at the very edge of the room, right by the toilets. Four guys. Two of them were black and two were white, and their outfits were all blacks and greys. None of them seemed terribly cheerful, and one kept glancing at his watch. I definitely didn't like the look of them, and nor did Connor, by the tone of his Meaningful Expression.

'Do you know them?' asked Kloe.

Connor shook his head. 'No. But they don't look friendly.'

'We could talk to Hannah,' I said.

'And tell her what?' asked Connor. '"I'm getting a wicked bad vibe off those clowns at the back, please throw them out"? And anyway, she's too busy charming the strings off that violinist.'

He has a point.

Kloe was looking suspicious. 'Do you guys, like . . . fight dodgy people with your magic powers, or something?'

'I wish,' I said. 'And they're not magic.'

'*Sorry.*'

Connor tried to change the subject. 'So. Do you reckon Eddie's going to play?'

'I bet he will,' I said. 'He'll play solo 'cos he won't even want to make eye contact with Hannah, let alone talk to her. And he'll play the best he's *ever* played in his entire life because he wants to make the violinist look like a tone-deaf corpse plucking a toilet brush.'

Kloe laughed. 'You're funny.'

'He is,' said Connor. 'I like him.'

'I like him too.'

'Yeah,' I said. 'I like me too.'

Just then the door to the club opened and a guy entered. He could have been anything between nineteen and thirty-something, and something about him immediately felt *off*. Skinny and pale and dressed in what I can only describe as charity-shop detritus, he had a shaved head and many piercings and was incredibly twitchy, fiddling with his hands as he made his way hurriedly across the room, and constantly glancing behind him as though he was being followed. Hannah clocked him and her face shifted instantly to worry . . . and anger.

I wonder . . .

I turned to Connor, who looked almost as pleased to see the guy as Hannah did. 'Is that . . .'

'Hannah's brother, yeah,' said Connor. 'Billy. Bad news.'

Kloe shot me a questioning look, and I tried to communicate the phrase *I'll explain later* with just my eyes.

Hannah came out from behind the bar to intercept Billy and they spoke in low voices, Billy gesturing randomly and moving nervously from foot to foot. It looked like she was telling him to get lost, but he wasn't having any of it. Now Eddie emerged from the toilets and *he* clocked Billy, and I actually felt a jolt in my chest, because if someone had ever looked at me the way Eddie looked at Hannah's brother, I think I would have literally pissed myself with fear. He stalked over to them and didn't bother to moderate his tone. 'What the hell are you doing here, Billy?'

The other patrons were taking notice now, looking nervously at one another and muttering. 'Connor,' I said. 'Should we . . .'

'Maybe.' Connor stood up slowly, keeping his eye on what was happening.

'Get out of my *face*, asshole!' yelled Billy in a high, nasal voice, pushing past Eddie and heading for the toilets. Touching him felt like an impressively ballsy move, considering how close Eddie seemed to be to throwing a punch. My cousin moved to follow, but Hannah grabbed him by the arm and shook her head. The door to the men's toilet slammed behind Billy, and immediately the four bad-vibe guys sitting nearby stood up and moved towards it, and I was sure I could see the butt of a weapon inside one of their jackets. *Oh shitting hell.* 'Connor,' I said again. 'Those guys . . .'

He'd seen them too, and started towards Eddie and Hannah, but then the door to the club burst open and three more men entered. One was big and wore an expensive-looking black coat, while his two companions were short and shorter, respectively. Short Guy wore a black leather jacket and carried a silver handgun, while Shorter Guy wore a brown leather jacket and was wielding some sort of machine gun. Big Guy had a sawn-off shotgun, and he was . . . was he *grinning*?

Yeah. He's grinning.

The four guys by the toilets saw the new arrivals and immediately whipped out weapons of their own. Somebody screamed. 'Where is he?' said Big Guy.

'He got off the train at Go Fuck Yourself Park!' yelled one of the other group, a ratty blonde guy who also had a machine gun of some kind.

Oh God. It's—

'*Everybody get down!*' bellowed Eddie. '*Now!*'

Then violent things started to happen.

CHAPTER TWENTY-THREE

I CAN'T REMEMBER WHO said that being shot at is the most exhilarating thing in the world – I'm pretty sure someone did – but whoever they were, they were wrong. During the next few frenzied minutes I came to the inescapable conclusion that there is nothing remotely exhilarating about having bullets fired at you.

The first thing was the noise. The gunshots were loud, so loud, so much *more* than loud. Each one was like being punched in the eardrum. The next thing was terror. Terror like I'd never felt outside of a nightmare, terror that drove any thought of super-heroics from my head, so that all that was left was *the noise* and *don't get shot, oh God, don't get shot.*

Eddie dived forwards, grabbing Hannah and pulling her around to the side of the stage to safety. Connor, who had moved so fast I was barely aware of it happening, was already dragging Kloe and me down, bringing our table with us to create an impromptu shield. I pulled Kloe to me, one eye on the chaos reflected in the mirrored glass wall above the bar. The violinist who had been talking to Hannah had scrambled over the counter, and now the blonde guy who had shouted before ran across the room and leapt after him. The rest of the gunmen had scattered, diving for cover and firing off rounds, and someone had been caught in the middle, a random guy, multiple blasts tearing shreds out of his chest. He went down immediately, floppy like a ragdoll. I fought the urge to throw up.

This isn't happening.

All around us, people were screaming. The old man had fallen off his chair and was lying on his back, clutching his chest and moaning inarticulately. The violinist's companions had thrown themselves to the floor, and now the singer was screeching and crying, trying to crawl towards the bar to reach him, but the piano player was being sensible and holding her down. Kloe was screaming too, and I held on to her as Connor hooked another table with his leg and pulled it over to provide more cover. The beautiful couple sitting near us had run towards the door and the man had made it out, but the girl had not been so lucky. A stray shot caught her in the arm and the force of it spun her right around and she collapsed against the wall, howling in pain, blood spurting.

In the arm, though?

That's OK, isn't it?

No-one dies from being shot in the arm?

Do they?

I was disorientated but I could still see everything clearly. Does that make sense? No it doesn't, but then again, this situation didn't make sense, whichever way you put it. My only experience of gun battles was in films, all balletic grace and unlimited ammunition and doves flapping in slow motion, and generally innocent people didn't get caught in the crossfire. This was different. This was the most horrible thing I'd ever seen in my life.

Big, Short and Shorter had all taken up positions behind tables, and they and their four opponents were firing blindly. The shotgun went off with a thunderous *ker-boom*, tearing chunks of plaster from the ceiling. Pictures shattered and fell to the floor. A stray bullet hit the piano with a discordant *plunk* sound. I could hear Hannah yelling and crying, and now Blondie popped up from behind the bar and squeezed off a few rounds. He quickly disappeared again, though, because the answering clatter of fire came from the machine gun, a horrendous motorcycle rattlesnake sound. Bottles exploded in showers of multicoloured liquid and tinkling glass, spirits flowing along the countertop in rivers, and

Blondie's hand emerged from behind it waving his gun and laying down more shots.

I was suddenly aware that Connor was speaking and I turned my head to hear what he was saying. Bullets whizzed over the top of the table, impacting against chairs and tables and, by the sounds of it, another person. 'Don't even think about doing anything!' he yelled. 'Let them shoot it out!' At any rate, I think that's what he said. Every word was punctuated by gunshots or more explosions, or hysterical and obscene screaming. The gunmen were yelling insults at each other. *Insults. A slagging match*! *For God's sake, this is a battle to the death*! I managed to offer a nod, and hugged Kloe to me and stroked her hair. She was shaking, and I whispered that it was all right, which might have been the biggest lie I'd ever told anyone. Somehow I felt like the only reason I wasn't having a nervous breakdown was because of her. Because I had to keep it together.

At least, that was what I told myself to avoid hyperventilating.

I chanced another look at the rest of the bar. The air stank of blood and alcohol and hot metal, and one of the first lot of guys, Billy's allies, or whoever the hell they were, was lying on the ground with holes in him, blood spreading from underneath. Now Blondie and Big jumped up at the same time and Blondie emptied into Big's face and I gagged, feeling vomit at the base of my throat. *No. Not what this situation needs*. I forced it down. Hannah screamed her brother's name, and Eddie yelled something indistinct to her, and Connor yelled, 'Eddie, don't be a dickhead, just stay where you are man!'

Eddie? Stay where? What's he going to—

Then I heard Blondie cry out as his gun clicked on empty, and there was a thud as he dropped back down to hide, and Short took that opportunity to jump up and fire over the table. One of the other guys went down, choking on blood bubbles, and the other came up and fired straight into Short's chest, pulling the trigger again and again until there was nothing left in the weapon. The force of the attack sent Short stumbling backwards against the wall, and the pictures behind him were splattered with dark red. He coughed, gurgled and slumped to the floor, and I saw one of Billy's guys cast away his empty weapon and reach into his jacket to draw another one, but Shorter had waited for his turn and wasn't going to waste it. He jumped up and fired one bullet, although the trigger kept on clicking uselessly as he tried to make more come from nowhere. His target keeled over backwards, knocking a table over, and lay still on his back, smoke rising from the centre of his skull.

Immediately Blondie jumped up again, having reloaded, and fired. He took Shorter down, then slid clumsily over the wet bar and hit the floor on his knees. 'Ah, bollocks,' he said, wincing. The gunfire had stopped but people were still crying and moaning, and Blondie stood up and barked in the direction of the toilets. 'Billy! Get out here!'

Billy didn't appear, and Blondie raised his gun and fired into the air. 'Billy!' he yelled. 'Get out here! Everybody else stay down, or you're getting a *fucking* bullet! *Billy*! Get your worthless arse out here *now*!'

I heard the toilet door, and Billy emerged looking even paler than before, if that was possible. Blondie nodded at him. 'Come on,' he said, and ran towards the door. He left the club without looking back and Billy stumbled after him, but he was too slow, because now Eddie was on his feet. He tripped Billy and the guy went over hard, slamming face first into one of the few tables that was still upright. He cried out in pain and Eddie yanked him to his feet, turned him over and slammed him down on the edge of the stage. 'What have you *done*?' he yelled. 'You little piece of shit!' Connor got up and hurried over to them, talking to Eddie in a low voice, something about calming down, about leaving it for the police, whatever, I didn't even care, I didn't care how it had happened or what was going to happen. I stood up, ears ringing, and Kloe came shakily with me, and I hugged her to me and said what you were supposed to say. I told the girl I loved that everything was all right, even though it wasn't. Not by a long shot, no pun intended. I could hear those ever-present sirens in the distance, and now they were finally on their way somewhere, and supposedly they would take care of everything. They were the police. The law. They represented stability and consequences, and they would make things right.

But they wouldn't, would they? They couldn't.

Because they have no real power.

And who does?

The confusion evaporated. The cotton wool that had built up in my ear drums fell away, and my head was no longer thick. All I could see was that I had to go after Blondie, and I had to take him down.

I gently pulled away from Kloe. She looked into my eyes with her glassy red ones and I was taken back to opening night, when she looked at me in the rain, just as she was doing now. The end of the world comes in all shapes and sizes. She swallowed several times and managed to whisper, 'What are you doing?'

'I have to get him,' I said. 'I have to go after that guy.'

Her eyes widened. 'What? What do you mean? Why?'

'We just *lay here*,' I said, keeping my voice low and one eye on Connor and Eddie. They had their hands full with Billy, securing him to a chair with someone's sweatshirt, and I had a feeling they wouldn't sign off on this idea. 'Me and Connor and Eddie. We're the ones with the superpowers, we're the ones who are supposed to *change* things. To help.'

'But you couldn't have done anything,' said Kloe. 'It was all just . . . it happened so fast.'

'*I* could have,' I said. 'I could have.'

Kloe stared at me . . . and then she did something strange. She nodded. 'Go,' she said. 'Go and do it.'

'Are you sure?'

'Yes,' she said, her voice trembling but still strong. She kissed me. 'Go.'

'Go where?' said Connor. Somehow he'd managed to appear right next to us again, and I jumped. Eddie was kneeling down next to Hannah, talking softly.

'I'm going after that other gunman,' I said. 'The blonde guy.'

'You are *not*.'

'I am. I have to. I have to do something. We let this happen.'

'We didn't let anything—'

'*We let this happen!*' I said, finally losing my temper. I pointed at the bodies, at the blood, at the terrified people hugging one another on the floor, still cowering behind tables even though the danger had passed, and at the well-dressed old man, who had managed to crawl over to the shot girl and was now putting pressure on the wound, talking calmly to her, making sure she stayed conscious. 'We're meant to *stop* this sort of thing!' I said. 'Surely this is why we *have* these bloody powers in the first place? *This is why we're here!*'

'Stanly, we couldn't have—'

'Yes we *could*! We could have done something! I could have deflected all their bullets without even moving. Taken their guns away. Beaten them to the ground. But I didn't, because I was too *scared*. Well, bollocks to that. That's *not good enough*.'

Connor was angry, but I could tell that at least part of him agreed with me. I could see it in his eyes. He glanced towards Eddie. Any second he would call him over, and Eddie would try to stop me. He was strong. He'd probably be able to. Connor probably could as well. Definitely, in fact. *I don't want to fight them.*

So don't.

'Stanly—' began Connor.

'I have to,' I said, and ran.

It was dark outside now, and the air had cooled. It cleared my head, wiping away the confusion and pushing my supper back down to my digestive system where it belonged. The urge to retch wasn't entirely gone, but I fought it. *No. Calm down. No time for this.* I could hear Connor and Eddie shouting my name, and people in the street were speaking to me urgently, asking what had happened. *No time.* 'Did you see a blonde guy run out of here?' I asked. 'Ratty-looking, holding a gun?'

Someone nodded, and pointed across the road towards an alley.

'Thanks.' I dashed across the road, ignoring the barrage of follow-up questions, and headed down the alley into the beckoning darkness.

Let's hope he did go this way, eh?

I ran, picked up speed, left the ground and flew, head first, arms by my sides, down the alley, past bins overflowing with rustling rubbish and newspapers, past empty drinks cartons and cigarette butts and metal doors that led nowhere, and red bricks and boarded up windows, the wind dampening my fear and fury, a slipstream forming in my wake. Within a minute I was bearing down on Blondie, his boots crashing against the tarmac, his breath coming in frantic gasps. I flexed my mind *don't want to kill him yet want to hurt him first don't lose control* and pulled his feet out from under him. He flipped over and hit the ground chin first with a yelp of pain. I landed and waited for him to stand up. I wanted him to look me in the eye.

He turned around, took me in, frowned. 'Who are you?'

'I was in the bar.'

A sneering smile. 'Citizen's arrest, is it?'

I shook my head.

'Thought not.' He reached into his coat and drew his gun. I'd been wondering about bullets. Was I fast enough? *We'll find out now.* I flexed my brain and felt that invisible bubble press out in the direction I wanted, just as Blondie pulled the trigger. The bullet changed direction totally and hit the wall, shedding sparks. Half a second later and it would have been too late.

Reflexes are definitely improving.

But maybe pre-empt it next time, eh?

Blondie was momentarily frozen and that was my moment. I whipped his gun away with an invisible mental tentacle and punched him with my brain, right in the face, as hard as I could. His head snapped back and he cried out, and I lifted him off the ground, holding him in the air. I floated the gun up off the floor and pointed it at him, and he quivered. 'Please,' he said. 'Don't, I've got, I've got money—'

I didn't speak, just moved the gun closer to his face, brushing his cheek with the hot barrel. He was pleading, sneering, threatening, trying anything, but I barely heard him. *Don't shoot him.*

Wasn't gonna.

Instead I turned the gun around and whipped him hard upside the head, vicious enough to drew blood. Then I dropped the gun and hurled him against a wall, letting him sprawl to the ground, and before he could try to get back up I grabbed him again and hurled him against the opposite wall. Down he went again, and I let loose with more psychic punches, a thunderous avalanche of blows, so much harder than I could ever have managed with my fists, and pretty soon his nose was broken and his lip was split and I knew his eyes would blacken and he was screaming for me to stop. For mercy. My mercy! He'd just killed people and he wanted mercy. I carried on hitting him and now he was practically unconscious and —

I was barely aware of it before it took me out. There was *something*, the suggestion of a heavy mass at the very edge of my peripheral vision, and a white blur, and then I was being grabbed from behind by powerful arms, far too powerful, utterly unyielding, and there was a hand over my mouth, and wow, sleepy, really sleepy, like, suddenly, properly, hey, where's Blondie gun, gone, I'm . . . seriously . . .

CHAPTER TWENTY-FOUR

THE FIRST THING I became aware of, as consciousness dribbled slowly back, was my arm. No . . . both my arms. They felt like they do when you fall asleep on top of them, like unresponsive implements, long bags full of sand that won't do what you tell them to do. Then I remembered my eyes, and forced them open. I was lying face down and my mind was spinning around and around, my vision a haze of dots and stars, and as I started to regain feeling in my flesh I became aware of hard, cold ground beneath me, and bits of grit biting into my face, and dust in my nose and mouth. I coughed and my body jerked harshly. It wasn't nice, but it helped to shake me more fully into wakefulness. Motor control started to return, sluggish but definitely present, and I pulled myself up into a sitting position and immediately slumped backwards. Luckily there was a wall behind me, but I hit it a bit too hard and my head swam with fresh pain. Everything shifted blearily for several more seconds before coming abruptly and harshly into focus. A cheap cinematic trick.

I was in a small square room lit by a single buzzing bulb, with a low ceiling and rusty brown walls. The concrete floor was dusty and the only really noticeable feature besides the light was the door – heavy-looking, metal, no knob.

Let me guess: it can only be opened from the outside. Let's stop and marvel at that.

OK. Kidnapped. That's . . . really very bad.

But by—

Um, have we not noticed the little girl in the red pyjamas?

She was sitting against the opposite wall, staring interestedly at me. Her trainers were dirty, as was her face, but her eyes were bright. There was a black scarf on the floor next to her. 'Hi,' I said.

'Hello.'

I rubbed my head. 'Did you happen to get the serial number of the elephant that trampled me?'

That got a laugh. It was a lame joke, but every little helps in desperate situations. 'It was Smiley Joe,' she said.

Smiley Joe . . .

Oh no.

'Are you sure?' I said, trying to ignore the chilly heat prickling up and down my spine. 'How do you . . .'

'I saw him bring you in here. You were asleep.'

'He took you as well?' She nodded. 'How long ago?' A shrug. I looked at my watch. Just before midnight. What time had I left Blue Harvest? It seemed so long ago. Half past eight? Nine o'clock? It hadn't taken me long to catch up with Blondie . . .

You were about ready to kill him.

This is possibly not the time for that thought process.

Twenty past nine? So about two and a half hours? If it was even the same day. I looked back at the little girl. 'How long have I been unconscious?'

'A few hours, I think.'

'OK . . . what's your name?'

'Tara. What's yours?'

'Stanly.' I held out my hand and she shook it solemnly. 'Pleased to meet you.' I got unsteadily to my feet.

'You don't look very good,' said Tara.

'I feel worse.' *Is this what being chloroformed feels like? Is that what he used? Or does the bastard have magic hands that make you unconscious?*

Oh who cares, let's get out of here. I staggered over to the door and put my eye up against the crack at the edge. All I could see was black. I closed my eyes and flexed my brain, thinking *unlock,*

unlock, unlock, but nothing happened. *I suppose it doesn't work like that.* I scanned the room again and started feeling my way along the walls, trying to be calm and methodical when what I was actually feeling was tentacles of panic reaching up from a black lake of dread in the pit of my stomach. *Stay calm. Breathe.* I felt around the entire room and tried a few psychic punches, but it was entirely solid and nothing yielded. Where the hell were we? I could hear a muffled rattling somewhere . . . *Tube train?* I tried hitting the ceiling. Still nothing. 'Bollocks!'

'You shouldn't swear,' said Tara.

'Sorry,' I said. The incongruity of the order, and the serious little voice that delivered it, actually beat back some of the panic. Some.

'Well,' said Tara, 'that's what Jacqueline says, but she actually swears quite a lot of the time. The other week she dropped a tray and all the stuff on it broke and she said the S-word.'

'Who's Jacqueline?'

'My foster mum,' said Tara. 'Jacqueline. Mrs Rogers.'

'Oh,' I said. 'So you're . . .'

'Not an orphan,' said Tara. 'I don't think I'm an orphan, anyway. I think my parents were in trouble and they left me on Jacqueline's doorstep when I was a baby. I don't remember them, though.' She hugged her knees, and I looked around helplessly, trying to breathe normally. *Come on. Organised thoughts. You've been kidnapped by a horrific monstrosity of some kind. That's extremely bad, and probably well worth freaking out over. But there's also a small child here. So you owe it to her to not be scared.*

I forced a smile, hoping it looked friendly and reassuring rather than fake and desperate. 'Are you . . . hungry?'

Tara nodded. I put my hand in my pocket, remembering a Twix that I'd bought at the cinema and forgotten to eat. It was melted and squashed but she took it with a smile. 'Thank you.' She started to eat it slowly, delicately licking the melted chocolate off her fingers, and I stopped trying to escape and sat and watched her eat. It's amazing how old you feel when you're nine, but when a sixteen-year-old looks at a nine-ish-year-old they seem so tiny, so young. When she finished the Twix she scrunched the wrapper up and put it in the pocket of her pyjamas. *She's been brought up well. She won't even litter a horrible room where she's been trapped by a monster.* 'Thank you,' she said.

'No problem. So . . . do you know what happened? How did Smiley Joe . . . where did he . . .'

'Mr and Mrs Rogers had an argument earlier on,' said Tara. 'It was the first time I ever heard them argue. Really, *ever* in my life. And they were shouting and I didn't like it so I went out for a walk, and I got lost . . . and I'm not sure, I think I fell asleep, and I woke up here.' She pointed at the black scarf on the floor. 'I was blindfolded.'

Jesus. That's horrendous. 'You don't remember him bringing you here, at all?'

She shook her head. 'No.' To her credit, she seemed fairly together about the whole thing. I could only imagine the kind of state I'd have been in if something like that had happened to me, even at my age. I tried my smile again. 'Well, don't worry, OK? I'm not going to let anything happen to you. We'll find a way out, and I'll take you home.'

Tara nodded. It looked as though she actually believed me. 'I've got special powers, you know,' I said.

She didn't look impressed, which I supposed was fair enough. 'Really?'

'Yeah. Check it out.' I jumped to my feet, lifted up off the ground and hung in the air, enjoying the way her nonplussed expression erupted into an awestruck supernova of joy.

'Oh my God,' she said. 'You can *fly*, that is *amazing*!'

'Can do this as well.' I thought at her, and she floated up into the air to join me, shrieking with delight.

'Oh my God!' she said, again. 'Oh my God, how are you doing that? How are you making me do that?'

'Told you,' I said. 'Special powers.' Tara was grinning widely, and it made me grin too. I actually felt a good deal less scared now.

Let's hope she does too.

I brought us back down to the ground. 'How come he managed to get you?' she asked. 'If you've got those powers?'

Ouch. Awkward. 'I kind of . . . I was distracted,' I said.

'Who by?'

'I was chasing a bad guy,' I said. 'He'd . . . done some really bad things. He killed some people.' *Why the* hell *are you telling her this, you dickhead?* 'Anyway. So . . . yeah, I chased him, and I'd caught up with him, and Smiley Joe must have sneaked up on me.'

'Did you kill the man?' asked Tara.

'No!' I said. 'No. I hurt him, and I probably shouldn't have . . .' *Probably? Probably shouldn't have? Well done. Anyone would think you'd never spoken to an impressionable child before.* 'But no, I didn't kill him.'

She nodded. 'That's good. Even if someone's killed someone, then you shouldn't kill them. Killing's always bad. Oliver . . . Mr Rogers . . . he fought in a war. I don't know which one. And I heard him say once that the first time he killed someone it was the worst thing in his life he ever did. I wasn't supposed to hear, though.'

'Oh. Um . . . well, thanks.' *Interesting kid.*

She smiled. 'That's OK.' *Really interesting.*

I took another brief, futile look around, thinking hard at the stupid door and the stupid walls, trying not to let 'mildly peturbed' blossom into 'oh Jesus we're completely screwed'. 'Right,' I said. 'Well . . . not to alarm you or anything, but I'm having trouble with the door. And the walls. I think . . . I think we might have to wait until he comes back.' *Oh God, really?*

'Really?' said Tara. *My thoughts exactly, mate.*

'Yeah,' I said. 'But it's OK.' *It is? In what possible way?* 'It's OK,' I said again, probably for Tara's benefit, 'because I'll be ready for him. And I'll fight him. And I'll get us out of here.'

'All right.' Tara shifted uncomfortably. 'It's cold.' She took the scarf and wrapped it around her neck, shivering, and I crawled over and hesitantly put my arm around her. She seemed grateful. 'What do you know about Smiley Joe?' she asked.

'Not a lot, really. Just stories I've heard.'

256

'Me too,' said Tara. 'I know he's a monster and that he eats children. I was at a sleepover and one of the girls told us a story about him, and they said he could turn into a giant spider.' *Christ alive, I hope not.* 'But I don't think that's true. Other kids at school said he was something from Hell, or just a mad man with a big head.'

'You saw him, though,' I said. 'When he brought me?'

'Sort of,' said Tara. 'When I heard him coming back I put the blindfold back on . . . but I peeked a little bit, over the top. I still couldn't see very well, though . . . his head didn't seem that big.'

Well, that's a relief, I guess. Or possibly not at all. I tried to smile comfortingly. *Maybe we shouldn't talk about him any more?*

'Do *you* know what he is?' Tara said.

'I don't much care,' I said. 'All I know is that he's been killing innocent people for too long and he needs to be stopped.'

'Can you stop him?'

'I can have a damn good crack at it.'

Tara nodded seriously. 'I think it's probably OK to kill monsters. Isn't it?'

There was something disturbing about this little girl talking so casually about killing things. In fact her entire manner was pretty strange, but all the same I felt an instant affection for her. You know how with some people you know instantly whether you like them or not? This was like that. It was strange, something in me knew, just *knew* that it was my duty to protect her, and it wasn't just that she was young and I was older. There was something else. Something bigger, although I had no idea what it could be. 'Maybe,' I said. And I hugged her, and we waited for the monster to return.

CHAPTER TWENTY-FIVE

'It doesn't make sense,' said Tara, after a while.

'What doesn't?'

'Why would Smiley Joe leave us here. Where would he go?'

'Haven't heard many more stories about him,' I said. 'Or seen anything on the news . . . he must be hungry. Maybe he's gone to get more food.' *Wow. That's such a great thing to have realised. I'm so glad I thought of that. What a lovely thought.*

Shut up.

'Children,' corrected Tara. 'Not food.'

'Sorry.'

'How old are you?'

'Sixteen.'

'You're not a child.'

I laughed. 'That's what I thought. I imagine I'm at the upper end of his . . . menu spectrum.' *She's like nine years old, remember? Maybe try and moderate the bad taste gallows humour.* 'How old are you?'

'Nine.' *Good guess.* 'Nearly ten, though.'

'Aha. And you've lived with Mr and Mrs Rogers all your life?'

She nodded, and her hair bounced. 'Yes. They don't know who my real parents were. I didn't even have a birth certificate or anything. I'm a complete mystery.' She said the last four words proudly. It made me laugh. 'So,' she asked. 'What's your story?'

'Not much to tell,' I said.

'Everyone's got a story,' said Tara. 'You seem like you must have a long one, with your powers and stuff.'

I laughed again. 'Long-ish . . .'

Tell her. Tell her everything.

Really? Everything?

Yes. I think she can handle it. She seems weirdly strong. Something about being a child, maybe.

OK. Deep breath.

And I told her my whole story, starting from levitating above my bed for the first time on Friday, September the twenty-third, all the way up to the catastrophic gun battle at Blue Harvest. She didn't say anything for the duration of the tale, which took a long time to tell. By now it was approaching half past one, but I wasn't tiring. Nor was Tara, by the looks of things. She still cuddled up against me and I still had my arm around her, but neither of our voices betrayed tiredness; there was no yawning, no sleepy blinking. I felt strangely proud of her.

You barely know her.

I feel like a big brother.

The last time I felt like that was with the lil' cousins. They'd come visiting from America, and I'd been in charge of them while the grown-ups had talked about boring stuff. Big cousin Stanly in charge of the little ones. I'd liked the feeling. The only time I minded being an only child was when I met young children with whom I got on well. Those were always the moments when I thought *why can't I have someone to look after?*

Now I do.

'So you can properly fly,' said Tara. 'Wow. That's am*azing*. What's it like?'

'It's kind of difficult to describe.' *Bollocks. It's easy to describe.* 'It's . . . it's like total freedom. Escaping from everything. When I'm in the air it feels like I can do anything I want. Nothing's a challenge anymore. And you'd think that would make things boring, if everything felt easy, but it doesn't, it's just . . . one of the few times I feel properly at peace.'

'Even when you nearly got struck by lightning?'

'*Especially* when I nearly got struck by lightning.' That was bollocks too, but it sounded good.

Tara laughed. 'That's *so* cool.'

I looked down at her. 'OK then. I've told you my life story, which I seem to be telling to everyone all the time lately, so how about you? What's your epic mythological saga?'

'Nothing,' said Tara. 'Tonight is the first time I ever did anything bad. Sneaking out of the house. I've always been the best possible daughter.'

'Good for you,' I said. 'Gotta start somewhere. What about your . . . interests and stuff? What kind of music do you like?'

'Beyoncé,' said Tara, immediately. 'I think she's great. I saw her in New York.'

'Really?' I was genuinely impressed.

'Yes! Jacqueline and Oliver's niece lives there, she's called Monica and I really like her. We visited them and she and her boyfriend took me to the concert.'

'And was she good?'

'She was *amazing*! She's just so cool! She's got so much attitude and she's *so* gorgeous and such an amazing singer. Some of the sexy sort of stuff she does is a bit yuck, but oh my God, the show was so, so, *so* good.'

'So you enjoyed it, then?'

Tara laughed. 'I get babbly.'

'Well it could be worse,' I said. 'You could be into McFly or something.' *Is that what young girls like these days?*

'McWho?' she asked.

Obviously not.

I laughed. 'Never mind.' Tara laughed too, and the laugh became a sneeze. 'Bless you,' I said.

'Thank you,' she said. 'So what were you like before you got your powers?'

'What?'

'I mean, what sort of person were you?'

260

The question took me totally by surprise. 'I . . . um . . . well . . .'

'You said you didn't have many friends.'

'I was pretty antisocial,' I said.

'Why?'

'I liked my own company. Plus I was kind of grumpy. I dunno . . . to be honest, I never really felt like I had much in common with anyone. Getting involved seemed to involve so much effort, and like I would have had to explain myself. My thought processes, and stuff.' I shrugged. 'Seemed easier to just be a loner. Plus I did kind of like being enigmatic. The weird one.'

Tara laughed. 'That's strange. You don't seem like that at all.'

'I think that I've grown as a person.' My backside was getting numb and I shifted position. My mouth was dry from all this talking and the lack of anything to drink, but I wanted to say as much as possible in case we didn't get out alive. *Nice. Maybe don't mention that particular morbid gem.* 'Before I got my powers I was kind of suffering from this . . . like a sort of insomnia. Nothing seemed really real or important and it all just drifted meaninglessly by. Apathy, I suppose. Very 21st century.'

'What's apathy? Like . . . boredom?'

'Kind of. Not caring. Disaffected, disillusioned, detached. Like, what's the point.' I could see her repeating these new words to herself and committing them to memory. 'I just didn't have anything to focus on. I briefly considered pursuing a career as a hitman.'

'What's a hitman?' asked Tara.

'Someone who kills people for money,' I said. It sounded a lot worse put like that, and Tara's eyes widened. 'I was always watching films about them,' I explained. 'They kind of glamourised the job . . . to be honest, the lifestyle appealed to me more than the killing. The loner thing. Wearing cool clothes and being cool.'

'But not the killing?'

'I never really thought about that side of it,' I said. 'I never understood what killing meant until tonight.' I tried to moisten my mouth. 'When I got the powers something in me changed. I just

261

. . . I felt this . . . cathartic thing. I was free suddenly. And I started making friends. Or at least, I started talking to some people. And I got involved with *Romeo and Juliet*, and . . . and I got together with Kloe.'

Kloe's face in the rain.

And in Blue Harvest, telling me to go.

'Are you worried about her?' asked Tara. I must have been silent for a while.

'Mm? Oh. No . . . Eddie and Connor'll look after her. And her aunt.' *She leaves today.* 'She's going home today. I . . . I hope I get to see her.'

'You will,' said Tara. 'You'll see her again.' *Unless her parents doubleplus forbid her from seeing me again 'cos I nearly got her shot.*

Or maybe she won't want to see me again 'cos it'll remind her . . .

I shouldn't have left her . . .

But then Tara would have been alone . . .

'She told me to go,' I said. 'She told me to go after the guy. And if she hadn't . . . I don't think I would have gone. I'd have stayed and let him get away.'

'And I'd be in trouble,' said Tara. 'Funny how things turn out, isn't it?'

Not for the first time I wondered if she was really that young. I laughed. 'Yeah. Funny.'

She didn't say anything, just shifted slightly. 'Do you know what Mr and Mrs Rogers were arguing about?' I asked, out of nowhere. *None of your business, Stanly, is what they were arguing about.*

Tara shrugged. 'I didn't really listen. I just heard.'

'I know what you mean.' I really did, and she knew I did. Now she yawned, and I stroked her hair a little, hoping it was comforting.

'I'm scared,' she whispered.

'Don't worry,' I said. 'As long as I'm here nothing's going to happen to you.'

'What if—'

'Stop that right now,' I said, mock sternly. 'We'll have no more of that talk, soldier.'

'OK,' she said, giggling slightly. 'No more.' She sat up and rested her head against my shoulder. 'Do you like Beyoncé?'

'Yeah,' I said. 'Although I liked her Destiny's Child tunes better.' *One other unexpected thing I have in common with Daryl.*

'I haven't really heard much of them,' said Tara. 'But Beyoncé really speaks to me.'

'I wouldn't say I find her stuff particularly meaningful,' I said, 'but she knows how to put a decent song together. And helluva voice, definitely.'

'What kind of music do you like?'

'All sorts. Chili Peppers, Coldplay, Beatles, Sinatra.' *My dad likes Sinatra.*

'Oliver likes this guy called Paul Robeson,' said Tara. 'Jacqueline doesn't, she's all into classical music. It's funny, sometimes I'll be at home and Mr Rogers will be doing his writing and humming along to 'Old Man River', and then some other time Mrs Rogers'll be cleaning the sink or cooking and listening to *La Bohème*.'

'*La Bohème*?'

'Opera,' said Tara.

'Oh. I don't know much about opera.'

Tara yawned widely. 'I'm tired. But I don't think I can sleep.'

I hugged her a little tighter and after a minute or so of silence I started to sing. It was a song that my dad used to sing to me when I was very young. He'd had a good voice then. 'There must be some kinda way out of here, said the joker to the thief. There's too much confusion, I can't get no release . . .' Tara's eyes closed and she smiled. I continued, softly, gently. By the time I had finished the song the little girl was breathing regularly, drifting in peace, and a torrent of forgotten images were pouring into my head. I had learned about sense memory – you smell a pine tree and a whole lifetime's worth of happy Christmases flood your head, even if in reality they were all miserable. The song made me long for home so much that my chest burned. I had never felt so far away. I wanted to see my parents again, walk in the wood, sleep in my own bed.

Stop that. You have to be strong now.

Yeah, ya pansy. Be strong.

Be strong for Tara and Kloe.

OK?

OK.

Good.

I must have nodded off because suddenly Tara was shaking me. 'Stanly!' she whispered. 'Wake up! Stanly! Please, wake up!'

I was groggy for a few seconds before everything came back to me. The room, the kidnap, the door, my young charge. I snapped awake and leapt to my feet. 'What's wrong?'

'I can *hear* him,' she whispered. 'I think he's coming back.'

'OK,' I said, trying to keep my voice level. 'Stay behind me. As far away from the door as possible.' She did as she was told and I stood, facing the door. *Mustn't tremble.* I'd thought that being shot at was the scariest thing ever, but this . . . this was on another level. This was true nightmare fear. No, worse than that . . . but I had to be strong. I was the grown-up. I couldn't lose face. Couldn't freeze like I had at Blue Harvest. If I was going to be a superhero, I had to *be* a bloody superhero.

Strength, strength, strength.

I tried to psyche myself up the way I had backstage months ago, thinking of Bogart and Jack Bauer and the rest of that hard-as-nails crowd. I was just another addition to their ranks. I was—

But, oh God, I can hear him too. Unhurried footsteps closing in. Footsteps on metal and concrete, getting closer.

Tara was shaking behind me. 'Don't worry,' I said. 'It's fine. It'll all be fine. Just stay behind me.'

He was nearly here. The monster was nearly here.

'Stanly—'

A rusty-sounding click. The damn thing had a lock after all. *Shit. Nice one.*

'Stanly, you're gonna win. You're gonna get him.'
'Shiny,' I said.
'What?'
'I mean . . . yeah.'
The door opened.

CHAPTER TWENTY-SIX

Something was standing there. Was it Smiley Joe? Was it looking at us? I couldn't come to a definite conclusion, partly because of the silent scream of *ohnononononononono* that was filling my brain, and partly because the thing had no face. It was human-shaped, definitely, with a heavily-built body in a brown suit and faded yellow tie, hands hidden within white surgical gloves, but the head was just . . . blank. A white orb, as white as the lightning on the night I touched the sky, utterly featureless, and no bigger than a normal head, although oddly enough this last fact didn't really comfort me. He – *it?* – stood there, motionless, taking us in – *is he? Is it?* – his – *its? Oh God* – intimidating bulk filling the doorway. He didn't seem to be breathing, there was no movement whatsoever . . .

And then there was. Three slits appeared in the face, two where eyes should have been and one where the mouth should have been, as though someone were cutting shapes with an invisible knife, and as I watched, my skin crawling so intensely I felt as though I was going to shed it like a cartoon, they expanded slowly, making a weird soft *sluicing* sound.

Oh God.

It is *him.*

Smiley Joe stared at us with his brand new eyes, enormous dead scarlet plates, pupiless and perfectly round, the lower half of his face now dominated by a dark crescent moon mouth locked in a hideous grin. No lips, no teeth or tongue, just the smile, huge, twitching disgustingly at the corners, a smile that could swallow joy. A black hole of a smile. I wondered if the bastard had smiled when Louise burned him. My mind warped back to my brief conversation with Mr Freeman, his idea that this thing had chosen a shape it thought would appeal to children.

Well, Jesus. I wouldn't want to meet the kid who'd want this fucker for a friend.

Tara whimpered behind me. I stood firm, trying to be galvanised and steadfast while my body did its best to collapse into a twitching puddle of ruined nerves, and still Smiley Joe didn't move or speak, he just stood, blocking our escape route, grinning a grin of sleepless, haunted nights. Did his heart beat? Did he *have* one?

'Stanly—' whispered Tara, her voice shaking with terror.

'Don't worry, kiddo,' I said. Being tough was the only way to to avoid pissing myself and dying. 'I'm going to put this son of a bitch in the *ground*.' I flexed my brain and threw a psychic punch, channelling all of the energy that had begun to bubble like a spicy stew when the door had opened. It would have dented a human's face.

It had no effect on Smiley Joe. He just stood there, taking us in with his infinite eyes. I flexed again. Still nothing. I tried again, and again, and again, each time harder than the last. Absolutely nothing. The monster just stared at me. 'D'oh,' I said.

Then he lunged. The movement was fast and jerky and *wrong*, like a spider, like he was suddenly occupying a space he shouldn't have been able to reach in such a short time, and ripples spread out across his face as though things were moving around beneath the skin. He reached for my neck, his arms seeming to extend, or maybe it was just my perception, except no, now he moved his head and it *expanded*, becoming twice, three times, four times as big as it had been – *oh shit oh God he can* grow – and I cried out and flew to one side of the room, psychically yanking Tara out of the way of his charge, keeping her behind me. The monster stopped and turned in our direction and his head briefly shrank again, contracting with a movement that reminded me of breathing, and then he was coming at us again, still terrifyingly silent, head growing, mouth widening, big enough to swallow a child in one bite, moving with that awful speed, like stop motion that had been completed in a hurry. Tara was screaming and I used my brain to push her towards the doorway, dodging in the other direction, hoping to confuse him. 'Run!' I yelled. 'Get *out*!'

She was out, away, safe – *well safer than you anyway* – and I grinned triumphantly and spat in Smiley Joe's face as he turned towards me. 'How d'you like that? Guess you should have gone to Chicken Cottage, saved yourself some time!' *Oh yeah. Lame quips. That's the OH NO—*

Smiley Joe threw his face forward, his impossibly wide mouth stretching even further – *oh Christ oh shit he's going to eat my head* – and I ducked, brought my head up into his stomach and charged forwards, carrying him with me, using my brain and my flight to power my charge, too close for him to reach me with that horrendous mouth. I stopped in the middle of the room and he flew against the opposite wall, hitting it hard, his weight working to my advantage. He fell like an inanimate object, barely seeming to register the impact as he calmly, robotically righted himself. He lunged again and I punched him in the eye. It felt wet and malleable, like hitting jelly, and my punch had no discernible effect. His counter attack, a punch to my face, looked almost lazy, but it landed like a sledgehammer and I staggered, my vision blurring; I was pretty sure I could feel my brain bouncing between the walls of my skull. Smiley Joe thrust his head forwards and bit down, but instinct kicked in and I left the ground, rising straight up over his head, and flattened myself against the ceiling, just high enough to be safe. I lay there and tried to think straight, which was tricky while Smiley Joe was jumping up and down beneath me, biting manically. He didn't bite like a person or an animal, though, he didn't even seem to have jaws; it was more like a film of white skin grew over his mouth then retracted at lightning speed, making a wet, slippery noise that made me feel sick. *Ig-bloody-nore it! Attack!* This time I tried to throw him, wrapping invisible tentacles around his body and *hurling*, but he didn't move. Somehow, he was negating my powers. Perhaps he was immune in some way?

Or he's just one tough bastard.

Whatever. He's not getting us.

I dropped down hard, using my mind to augment gravity's effects, and managed to knock the beast to the ground, and before he could grab me I was up and out of the room, sure that at any second I was going to feel a hand around my ankle. Our prison cell opened onto a basement area, with steps leading up to a closed door on which Tara was banging frantically. I turned and pulled the heavy prison door shut less than a second before Smiley Joe reached it. He slammed into the other side, the force of the impact causing the whole door to vibrate, and I yelped as I fumbled with the lock. *Lock it lock it lock it LOCK IT!*

It's locked.

I did it.

I saved us.

I fought the child-eater!

Well done. Let's save the seventy-six trombones for later though, yeah?

I stood and took in our new surroundings, breathing regularly, trying to bring my heart rate down. One dusty bulb cast less than twenty watts of glow over a dank, grimy cellar, cobwebs lining the vertices where walls met ceiling. 'The door's locked!' said Tara.

'Let me try,' I said. I flexed my brain. Nothing. 'Goddamnit.' I looked around again. 'There must be something . . . come on . . . think, thinkthinkthinkthink . . .' My eyes darted from here to there and back again . . . and then they fell on a grate in the floor at the back of the basement. *Lightbulb.* 'Tara! Get down here!' I ran over to the grate, trying to ignore the sound of Smiley Joe's fists thumping on the other side of the door, and knelt down, concentrating on the grate. *Must work fast.* I wrapped tentacles of brainpower around it, every one that I could spare, and pulled. It didn't move . . . but I could definitely feel some give. This was going to work. The monster may have been able to shrug my powers off, but this was a grate, a floor, regular materials, concrete and metal. Real world stuff. I pulled again, yanking as hard as I could think, visualising the tentacles, great huge muscled implements, wrapped around with chains. The grate actually shifted a little this time.

'OK,' I said, taking a deep breath. 'Come on, you sonofabitch. Let's *go*.' I gritted my teeth, closed my eyes and siphoned every ounce of strength that I had in my fairly slight body, channelling into a single thought, focusing. *More, more. More strength. Forget your body. Brain strength. It's infinite, you idiot.* I groaned with the strain, pulling, pulling, *pulling,* feeling like I was ripping myself apart. *COME ON, BRAIN! THIS IS BENEATH YOU! LITERALLY AND FIGURATIVELY!*

'It's coming!' said Tara, clapping. 'Come on, Stanly! You're doing it! Come on!'

With a final heave and a strangled yell, I ripped the grate clean out of the floor, bringing bits of broken stonework with it. Tara whooped triumphantly and hugged me. 'Yes!'

'Thanks,' I panted. 'Come on. Get down there.' That had taken a lot out of me, but there was still much to do. Miles to go before I slept. I wrapped a tentacle around Tara's middle and lowered her through the hole I had created in the floor. After the grate, she seemed to weigh almost nothing. I felt her feet touch the floor below and dropped down after her, into a long, narrow white tunnel with moisture and dim lights on the walls. It curved away around a bend, disappearing into gloom, and I grabbed Tara's hand. 'Come on.' We ran along the tunnel, passing endless identical lamps and electrical boxes and bricked-over doorways, and finally we reached the end, where three white steps led up to a door marked NO ENTRY. I didn't need my powers for this, one good kick was enough to break it open.

The door led straight into one of the main underground tunnels, pitch black and hot smelling. I listened out for trains, but heard none. They must have finished by now. I scooped Tara up and asked her if she was ready to fly, and she wrapped her arms around my neck and whispered, 'Yes.'

Right. Here we go. I jumped out into the tunnel and flew to the right, grateful to leave the ground, to feel weightless again. It was darker than dark, and I only just managed to avoid the walls, feeling that strange underground wind, hyper-aware of the tracks crackling with electrical malevolence below. *Come here my pretties*, they seemed to say, *let us burn you.*

Man, I really need some sleep.

Tara held on to me tightly and didn't say a word, and eventually we reached the platform. The trip had been years long. I looked at my watch. Quarter to three. Definitely too late for trains. *Bendigedig. Would have been rubbish to escape the clutches of an evil monster and then get shmooshed.*

'That was cool,' said Tara.

'Thanks,' I said. 'Now hopefully we'll be able to get a bus from somewhere nearby. I don't recognise the station, but there'll be night buses. There's always night buses. Let's head up and have a gander around.'

'OK,' said Tara. 'But . . . won't it be locked up there?' *Practical kid.*

'I don't think that'll be a problem.'

We walked up the still, silent escalators and through the underground station, vending machine sentries and peeling poster faces watching us suspiciously as I levitated us up and over the barriers. The entrance to the top was indeed blocked by a heavy metal gate, but after ripping chunks of concrete out of the floor, getting through it was child's play. It was almost a comfort to know that if everything went catastrophically wrong, I had the option of a pretty lucrative career as a burglar.

The city was cooler now, and much quieter. Tara was hugging herself and shivering, and I took off the blue long-sleeved shirt I was wearing over my T-shirt and gave it to her. It wasn't much, but it was better than a poke in the eye with a blunt stick, as my mother used to say. 'Thanks,' said Tara.

We found the nearest bus stop, and I worked out that it would take at least two night buses to get us back to Connor and Sharon's. That wouldn't do. Tara was far too tired. So was I, for that matter, so we walked until we found a cash point and I withdrew a physically painful amount of money and hailed a cab. The driver gave us a strange look but didn't comment, and I gave him the address and off he drove. The taxi smelled faintly of sick, but compared to Smiley Joe's nightmare dungeon it was a luxury limo.

We arrived outside the house. The lights were on, and for the first time it occurred to me that I might be in trouble. *Oh dear. Best go back to the child-eater's dungeon, then.* 'Are you OK?' I asked.

Tara nodded sleepily. 'Don't worry,' I said. 'We're here now.' I paid the taxi driver significantly less than I'd been expecting – although to be fair I'd been expecting a fortune – and we walked up the path. I rang the bell, and somebody rushed down the hall and opened the door, and I looked into Sharon's face. She was wearing her fish pyjamas and a dressing gown, and there were huge bags under her eyes, and she immediately grabbed me and pulled me into a hard hug. 'Oh, thank *God*,' she said, over and over again.

Tara was caught between us, but she was quiet and kept her arms wrapped around me for the duration of the embrace. I felt safe in Sharon's arms, but if I let myself become too comfortable I felt like I might lose my composure and start freaking out, so I broke the hug and tried to sound casual. 'It's all right. We're fine.' We went through to the living room and Sharon looked down at the little girl. 'Who's this?'

'Hi,' Tara yawned. 'My name's Tara.'

'Long story,' I said. I knelt down and said, 'We'll take you back to Mr and Mrs Rogers tomorrow, OK? Just for tonight you'll sleep here. All right?'

At that moment Daryl galloped in. He was about to speak, but then he saw Tara and simply barked a greeting. I wasn't used to hearing him bark. It wasn't hugely convincing. 'Daryl,' I said. 'Take Tara upstairs to my room. I'll sleep down here tonight.'

Daryl barked and started to walk up the stairs. Tara followed him. 'I'll be up in a little while,' I said. 'OK?'

'Yes,' said Tara, staggering upstairs after my dog.

Sharon watched them until they were out of sight, then turned to me and spoke in a low voice. 'What the hell is going on? Who is that?'

'Connor and Eddie told you what happened?' I asked.

'Yes, but—'

I don't generally like to interrupt, but I had to. 'After I left Blue Harvest I caught up with the gunman. I pummelled him, and then I . . . I was knocked out. Or chloroformed, or something. When I woke up the two of us were locked in some sort of bunker.'

'Chloroformed? Bunker? By who?'

'Smiley Joe.'

Sharon went pale. 'Are you—'

'Fine,' I said. 'We were there for a long time, but when he finally came in I managed to fight him off and lock him in there. As far as I know he's still there. Then we came back here.'

She nodded. 'OK.' Her voice was barely there.

'Where are the other two?' I asked.

Now her voice – and the colour in her cheeks – returned remarkably quickly. 'Looking for you!' she said. 'Where do you *think* they are?'

'I'm sorry I worried you,' I said, 'but we don't have a lot of time. Smiley Joe is locked up. He's contained. We have to call Eddie and Connor, and we have to go and kill him once and for all.'

'Stanly!' protested Sharon. 'This is not the time for—'

'There's literally never been a *better* time.' I pointed up the stairs. 'He was going to *eat* her! Her. That tiny thing. He's killed so many. *Too* many. It's way past his time.'

Sharon seemed ready to protest again, but thought better of it. 'You're right.'

'Good,' I said. 'Right. Um.' *OK then. Thunderbirds are go.* 'Does Connor have his phone on him?'

'Yes.'

'Call him,' I said. 'Tell the two of them to meet me on the street outside White City.'

She nodded.

'Is Kloe OK?' I asked.

'She's fine,' said Sharon. 'She's back at her aunt's. Her aunt was fairly hysterical.'

Relief and remorse flooded my body, bursting bubbles and flavouring my blood, and I almost collapsed from it. *No time for that. No time.*

'Call them,' I said. 'I'm going upstairs.'

Sharon picked up the phone and I ran up to my room. Daryl was standing guard at the door, a beagle trying to be a wolf. 'Is she all right?' I whispered.

'Didn't say much. I think she's asleep already.'

'Will you watch over her?'

'Of course. Something's going down, isn't it?'

'It is,' I said. 'We're going to kill him. Smiley Joe.'

He wanted to come, I could tell, but I'd given him a job, and he was going to do it. 'I don't suppose I need to tell you—'

'I'll be fine,' I said 'Just . . . look after her.' I stepped past him and pushed the door open slightly. Tara looked very, very small underneath the duvet. She was definitely asleep. *Snug as a bug in a rug, whatever that means.* Her expression was peaceful, her breathing light. I hoped she was having happy dreams. Her serenity had a calming effect on me, and I took a few seconds to rein in my adrenaline and even attempt a smile before leaving the room. 'You can sleep on the bed,' I said. *As though he needs my permission.* 'I expect she'll like the company.'

Daryl nodded. 'Stanly?'

'Daryl?'

'Come back in one piece, yeah?'

That made me laugh. 'I'll try my best.'

Sharon had made the call. 'They'll meet you,' she said. 'Be prepared – they're a wee bit pissed off with you.'

'Fair dos,' I said. 'Thanks for that.' I pocketed a London A-Z and pulled on my trenchcoat, which made me feel at least fifty per cent more like a monster killer. *Plus, warm.* 'We'll keep in touch.'

'Be careful,' said Sharon.

'I will.' We hugged tightly, and Sharon whispered, 'You are infuriating.'

'Thanks. Make sure Tara's all right, please?'

Sharon nodded. I opened the door and went back out into a night full of demons.

CHAPTER TWENTY-SEVEN

THE MOON WAS full, which seemed appropriate somehow,
and as I touched down in the shadows a little way from White
City and replaced the A-Z in my pocket, I suddenly thought that
it might have made sense for me to fly Tara straight home earlier,
rather than faffing around with taxis. Well done. Could have saved
time and money.

Needed to recharge, though.

Important.

Big boss battle this way comes.

I headed for the station, coat blowing in the wind, trying to feel
like a badass, and wondered whether we'd come out of this alive,
which was a fairly un-badass thought.

*Of course we will. Three of us this time, remember? One of you
the first time, and you survived.*

*We weren't on the offensive then. And he's indestructible, or
something.*

Nothing's indestructible.

Unless he is.

Shut up, brain.

But—

Shut up, brain.

Now Eddie and Connor came into view and my stomach tensed.
Connor was facing away from me, a column of smoke rising from
his hidden face, but Eddie immediately saw me. 'Stanly!' He ran
over and hugged me, and I let him, but when he pulled away he

looked furious. 'Don't you *ever* do anything like that again.' *What am I, seven years old?* 'For God's sake, you could have been killed!'

'Wasn't,' I said. 'I'm fine. Bollock me later, OK? This is more important.'

Eddie breathed deeply and clenched his fists, but he nodded. 'Yeah.'

Connor threw away his cigarette. 'You OK?' His voice was oddly level, as though he was angry but knew it was pointless expressing it.

'Fine,' I said. 'Are you two game for this?'

They both nodded. 'You got a plan?' asked Connor, which was surprising but gratifying.

'As far as I know, he's locked in a bunker underground,' I said. 'Near an entrance to the Tube. The actual tunnel the train goes through. Pretty sure it's under a warehouse, so I figured that if we find the warehouse, we find the monster. And then kill the shit out of him.'

'Sounds plan-like.'

You've changed your tune. 'I thought you didn't believe in him,' I said. 'You said so yourself.'

A grim smile. 'I say a lot of things.'

'Fair enough,' I said. 'Ready?'

Eddie nodded. 'Let's get rambling.'

There were many, many warehouses, and they all looked infuriatingly similar. Some were in use, but most of them were dusty and boarded up and full of empty crates. We searched among frozen conveyor belts and cobwebs and cardboard and junk for over an hour, combing basements and breaking open doors, and at no point did anyone say more than was absolutely necessary. There were things I was dying to know – how had Kloe seemed, did the police want to speak to me, were there any more survivors, was Hannah OK, what had happened to Billy – but finding and annihilating Smiley Joe took precedence. We were on a mission. We were the hunters, finally. This was what I knew we were made for, why some random act of nature had cursed or blessed us with these powers. Doing good. Protecting things that needed protecting. This was why I'd come to the city in the first place.

I thought it was because you ran away because Ben King arsed up your play.

You can't even let me have a few seconds of righteousness? There are *things that need protecting. People. Like Kloe and Tara. Plus, if I've learned anything from comics, it's that I should be free to retcon my own plan at any time.*

That string of thoughts made another occur. 'This is a bit sexist really, isn't it?'

'What?' asked Eddie, tossing aside a couple of boxes, looking for gratings.

'The three guys out hunting monsters,' I said, 'the women at home. Kloe at her aunt's, Sharon looking after Tara.'

'Who is this Tara?' asked Connor. 'Sharon mentioned her briefly on the phone but I—'

'I'll explain later,' I said. 'But do you get what I mean?'

'Yeah,' said Eddie, 'I suppose. Kloe doesn't have any powers, though. Otherwise I'm sure she'd be here. Our power isn't "being men". It's, like, super strength and stuff.'

'Anyway, Sharon swore she wouldn't do any more killing after the Worm,' said Connor. 'And she hasn't.'

'What about you two?' I asked. 'Have you killed anything since your little challenges?' *Do they know I know?* It didn't matter now. We were just leaving our umpteenth warehouse, and as Eddie pulled the door shut he exchanged a Meaningful Look with Connor. 'What does that mean?' I asked. 'Are you finally going to tell me why you've been sneaking off for the past two months?'

'We've been hunting Smiley Joe,' said Connor.

Of course they have.

All bow before Stanly, Derp King of the United Derps of Derp.

'When you first arrived, the three of us had a long talk about Mr Freeman and how he used us to kill monsters and then discarded us,' said Connor, 'and how we didn't want the same thing to happen to you. We thought it was pretty likely that he'd find you – he always does – and that you'd probably want to go out monster-hunting.'

'And that even if we told you not to, you'd probably sneak out on your own and do it anyway,' said Eddie.

Wow. It's like they know me.

'So we figured we'd take Smiley Joe out and save you the trouble,' said Connor.

'And also save London's children,' said Eddie. 'Obviously.'

'Why didn't you go after him before?' I asked. 'Before I came on the scene?'

'The same reason we don't go out every night fighting crime in dark alleys,' said Eddie.

'Apart from the fact that a lot less crime happens in dark alleys than you'd expect,' interjected Connor.

'*Because* we still don't understand our powers,' said Eddie. 'Why we have them, what we can do.'

'Who cares *why*?' I asked. 'Honestly? I literally couldn't give a shit where they came from. The point is that we *have* them and we can use them to do good.'

'Well, maybe after this little exercise we can start,' said Connor.

'Hmm,' said Eddie. He didn't sound convinced, which made sense, because Connor hadn't sounded convincing. 'How about this one?' He broke open another door.

The place was immense, with a high ceiling and shiny hooks hanging down, and the usual assortment of empty boxes and broken crap, the windows so caked with dust and cobwebs that no moonlight could possibly find its way in. Eddie took out a torch and shone it around, and I led us over to a door at the back. 'This looks like it,' I said, starting to feel buzzed. I was getting my opening-night cocktail again, albeit a remixed version – one part trepidation to one part excitement to several more parts *oh Jesus what am I doing* and *oh yeah* and *no seriously, what the friggin' goddamn hell am I doing?* This was it. I *knew* it.

Connor tried the door, and it clicked stubbornly. 'Locked,' I said, usefully. 'We might have to—'

Connor wasn't waiting. He raised his foot and slammed it against the door, shattering the lock, and it swung open. Pathetic fingers of dim light crept out of the basement, illuminating the bunker . . . and its broken door.

Oh . . .

'Balls,' I said. 'He's out.' The door was hanging off its hinges, twisted totally out of shape. He was even stronger than I thought.

'He must be around here somewhere,' said Eddie. 'He—'

'— is most definitely around here somewhere,' said Connor. His voice sounded green, if such a thing were possible, and he was looking back the way we'd come. I followed his gaze, and so did Eddie.

'Oh,' said my cousin.

Smiley Joe was standing a little way away, silently taking us in. He had his face on, that ghastly face, and as I stared at him I felt madness prickling at the back of my brain, and silently congratulated myself that I hadn't lost my mind yet. *There's still time, though.*

'Jesus Christ,' said Eddie.

'I second that blasphemy,' said Connor. Neither of them seemed willing, or able, to make the first move, and still Joe stood, watching. *He's doing a threat assessment. Which one of us is going to cause the most trouble, which one he can take out first.* It suddenly occurred to me that I'd never seen Eddie in action before.

'He can make his head go bigger and smaller,' I said. 'Watch out for that. Also his arms, I think, maybe. Plus he's incredibly strong. And he might be able to do other stAHHSHIT—'

Smiley Joe had reached out and pulled a lever, rattlesnake-quick, flooding the entire warehouse with light. We were used to moonlight and Eddie's crappy torch and were momentarily blinded, and that was the demon's moment. He went straight for Eddie, traversing too much space in too little time, like a computer game dropping frames, and gripped my cousin's shoulders and shoved him backwards. The two of them stumbled across the room and crashed into a pile of crates at the back, splintering wood and sending a cloud of choking dust into the air. Smiley Joe was on top of Eddie, trying to bite his face, but Eddie had his hands around the beast's neck, just managing to restrain him, his face totally obscured by Joe's massive head.

I looked over at Connor. 'What do we —'

Connor didn't look at me. He was reaching inside his coat, and when his hands emerged they both held guns. I know nothing about guns so I couldn't tell you what make they were, but they were big and black and silver and looked seriously dangerous and I didn't like them. After everything we'd seen at Blue Harvest, and he was using these death-dealing monstrosities.

No time for that, you nit.

Connor fired once at Smiley Joe and the bullet hit him straight in his back. It left a hole in his suit, but there was no blood. The monster swivelled his head, climbed off Eddie and moved towards this new attacker with his lopsided, skittering gait. Connor was calmly discharging bullets, poker-faced, his arms totally steady, the reports of his guns so loud that my head hurt, and I was just standing there uselessly while he unloaded bullet after bullet into the rampaging demon, tearing gashes in the brown fabric of his suit. The body hits might have slowed him down slightly, but the bullets bounced off his head like drunken fireflies, completely ineffectual; in fact, his head was *growing* as they hit him, that nightmare grin getting wider, as though he were mocking Connor's efforts. *Is he absorbing them?*

Let's hope it's a coincidence . . .

Smiley Joe threw a punch. It knocked Connor to the floor, but he was still firing as he fell, and the guns clicked on empty as he hit the ground. He immediately discarded them, swung his leg to knock Joe off balance and sprang to his feet, and at the same time he shifted his centre of gravity and planted his feet on the wall so that he was standing on the vertical surface, jutting out like a human decoration. *Weird.* Joe ran at him and Connor threw a whomper of a punch and the demon actually went down, but he still didn't make a sound. He never did.

Where did Connor get those guns?

And how hard must that punch have been?

Not now!

Eddie was running back towards them. Connor was back on his normal axis, and Smiley Joe had got back on his feet quickly. The monster was deceptively spry, considering how big his head was, and now he delivered a roundhouse kick to Connor's stomach that would have broken me in two. The Irishman went down really hard, choking and winded, and Eddie dived in and started hammering Smiley Joe with a meteor storm of blows, his fists pumping like flesh pistons, the same way you'd hit a punchbag if you were really, *really* hacked off and had superpowers.

And still I stood there, doing nothing.

How about doing something, *then?*

I looked around for something to throw, settled on a large plastic crate and levitated it towards Smiley Joe with as much force as I could muster. It broke over his swollen head, distracting him long enough for Eddie to kick him in the face – *plenty of face to kick, eh* – and knock the monster backwards onto the broken conveyor belt. I started to pelt Joe with as much crap as I could find, whipping crates and tubes and junk from all corners of the room.

This is my thing. I throw stuff!

Yay.

Eddie had pinned Joe down and was delivering vicious volleys to his face, and I had to make an effort not to hit him with any of my makeshift projectiles. Joe's head kept expanding and contracting, as though he were trying to find the optimum size, and his arms and legs were spasming frantically like an insect trying to right itself, but amazingly Eddie was too strong. I had never seen him this way: he moved with an alien fluidity, a vessel of liquid power. Connor was up now, and he reached into his long coat as he strode over to Eddie and Joe. *Jesus, what else does he have in there?*

282

Wow. Shotgun.

Connor jumped onto the conveyor belt, face set grimly, and lev-
elled the gun at Smiley Joe's head, point blank range. 'Move!' he
yelled. Eddie threw himself backwards and Connor fired, the recoil
shaking his body. The blast was thunderous and echoed around the
huge room like a cluster bomb, and my ribcage juddered. Smiley
Joe wasn't wounded, but he seemed weakened, at least. There was
a loud, solid *ker-chack* as Connor cocked the weapon, and he fired
again. I had given up throwing things. Eddie moved back in, peril-
ously close to the shotgun, and kept Smiley Joe pinned down with
punches, hitting his body with enough ferocity to shatter concrete,
and Connor was emptying shells into his face, but still the sonofabitch wasn't visibly taking any damage.

He is *indestructible.*

Nothing is indestructible! How many times!

I started to half-run and half-fly around the room, my eyes
zipping everywhere like hyperactive marbles, desperately trying
to find something remotely useful. There had to be *something*. I
heard two shouts and two crashes and chanced a look back, and
saw that Connor and Eddie were both on the ground with Smiley
Joe advancing on them, his head expanding further than I'd seen it
go yet . . . no . . . not just his head. He was getting taller, his shoulders broader, his limbs longer and thicker. *Holy bloody shit.*

Why didn't he do this before?

It did seem to be taking a lot of out of him, so maybe that was
the reason. His pace was slowing, his movements becoming more
sluggish. Still, he was *massive* now, a good few feet taller and wider
than he had been, and his arms were so long that he was using them
like extra legs, like a praying mantis designed by a howling psychopath. Connor's shotgun was empty and he was struggling to reload
one of his discarded pistols. Eddie was getting up, fists clenched
determinedly, even as his face betrayed real fear at the monstrosity
bearing down on him, and I thought *no.* I filled my lungs and *flew,*
barrelling through the air like a missile. I slammed into Smiley Joe
as hard as I could, wrapped my arms as far around his chest as I

283

could, and carried him across the room, thinking myself strong-er, *making* myself stronger – *I don't care how big you are you bastard I have superpowers all right and goddamn you they will work otherwise what's the point of having them* – and just before we reached the other side I let him go with a final psychic *fuck off* and the beast crashed into a pile of plastic crates. They broke beneath his weight, snapping and spitting bits of orange plastic everywhere, and I banked sharply to the right because my eyes had finally fallen on something useful. A fire axe in a case. *Dumb luck.* I flew towards it and, without thinking, punched the glass. The axe fell into my bloodied hand and I immediately dropped it, yelping. Trying to ignore the pain and thinking *you absolute twat*, I quickly attended to the shard of glass embedded between my knuckles. It stung like a bastard, to put it mildly, and I gritted my teeth and pulled. The shard slid out of my hand with a fleshy slurp, bringing blood with it, and the pain was sharp and hot, but I put psychic pressure on the wound, picked up the axe again and returned to the fray. Eddie was attacking Smiley Joe with everything he had, and although the lumbering beast was a good deal slower now, when his punches hit they *hit*: one sent Eddie flying, and he stag-gered drunkenly before diving back in. By this time Connor had reloaded and was firing non-stop. Each time he emptied a gun he quickly reloaded and started again, and by now Smiley Joe's suit was torn to ribbons, but I could see no skin beneath, and it sud-denly occurred to me that his suit had grown when he had grown. It wasn't even a suit, it was *part* of him somehow.

What the hell is this thing?

Time to find out.

Smiley Joe batted Eddie on the head like a cat would, knock-ing him brutally to the floor, then spun gracelessly and swung at Connor. The Irishman ducked and rolled beneath the sweeping arm, letting the monser punch himself off-balance, and Connor wasted no time in helping Eddie up. He started to walk backwards, dragging Eddie with him, putting ground between them and the beast and firing one-handed, bellowing obscenities, his voice almost entirely drowned out by the clatter of shots. Smiley Joe kept coming, hideous and misshapen, and for a slow-motion second I took it all in: Eddie and Connor, dirty and bruised and bleeding, visibly tiring, and their opponent who simply refused to die.

Not anymore.

He won't refuse this.

I flew towards them with the axe raised above my head, yelling 'Say hello to my little friend!', 'cos why not. Smiley Joe turned awkwardly, and as I brought the axe down I remembered chopping wood for the Rayburn with my dad, him teaching me the exact angles and how much force to use, and I applied all that now and it was a *perfect* chop. It split Smiley Joe's huge head right down the middle, to his neck, and the two white halves fell away on either side.

There was no brain inside. No bones, no blood. Instead, my impromptu incision revealed an ebony-black shape, like something had been scrunched up to fit inside the head – I could definitely detect what might have been legs, and the whole thing looked moist, slimy. *Glistening like wet leather,* said Richard Burton's voice in my head, and I wished I was back in the shop with Skank, listening to *War of the Worlds.* Anywhere but here, hanging speechless and paralysed in the air. *Anywhere but here with that thing what is it oh Christ it's twitching.* Connor and Eddie were staring, the three of us dumbfoundedly watching this headless body swaying on the spot, and the twitching black blob where the brain should be. Numbly I wondered if things like this often happened in London.

And then it moved, unfurling with a slippery noise, and I jerked back as it sprang free of the head, uncoiling further, hitting the ground on six, no, ten, no, a *dozen* legs, a long black twelve-legged body – *Jesus why so many why does it need so many WHY* – and no discernible front or back end. It stood where it had landed, possibly looking at us, possibly not, and now the great body from which it had come toppled backwards. It hit the ground with a dead thump and immediately began to shrink, losing definition, the suit colours blending away as the whole thing degenerated into a shapeless, oozing grey mass. It smelled kind of acidic.

The black thing ignored the death of its vessel, or whatever the body had been. As we watched it suddenly jerked, and then *split* at the middle with a wet ripping sound, becoming two six-legged blobs, and now mouths – oh yes, *mouths* – multiple mouths opening all over the shiny black bodies like eyes and, oh God, what mouths; ringed with teeth, lamprey mouths with blood-red tongues lolling. These two new abominations – *monsters, things, how do I even describe them* – moved into what I felt I could safely assume were fighting positions, hissing like broken steam valves, and for a moment they stood there, all mouths agape, too many legs, too many teeth, just too goddamn much of everything.

'Um . . . Connor?' I squeaked. 'Guns might be nice now?'

The first thing leapt at me, all of its mouths wide open, its breath and flying saliva smelling of decay and death, and at that moment I realised where the children went. I jumped into the air and it missed, but only just, and I turned around, still airborne, levitated the creature and threw it. Happily, whatever strength or mojo this thing – *things?* – had had before was gone, because it left the ground easily, crashing through several boxes and rolling away. It righted itself messily, hissed and scrambled back towards me, all its legs pumping. The other was busy with Eddie and Connor, who were doing a lot of dodging and not much attacking. With every movement they made the creatures seemed to get bigger. *Not that shit again.* I flew higher and the beast stood its ground below me, jumping up and down, spit flying from its multiple mouths, and I looked around, spotted the axe and psychically swung it. The blade severed one of the creature's legs and it let loose a nails-down-a-blackboard scream and caught the weapon in one of its mouths, razoring it to shreds, hissing and shrieking with a rage so horrifying and primal that I couldn't hope to understand it.

Something about the intensity of the creature's roars, and the sheer unutterable fucked-upness of the whole thing, caused me to momentarily lose control of my flight, and for one second, maybe less, I dropped towards the creature, giving it the opportunity to leap up and latch on to my left arm, one mouth extending, jaws seeming to unfold from nowhere. I felt its teeth sink into my flesh and I screamed in agony and rose again involuntarily, thinking *no no no no,* and the thought manifested as a command, stopping the creature from chomping any further. It kept trying, though, and there was already plenty of blood, but I kept thinking at it, thinking *no,* keeping the bite at bay, and as I focused my energy, trying to drown out the pain, it was as though some sort of connection had been established, I could *feel* the thing's strength, its power, its nightmarish anger, and I dropped back down to the ground, brain bellowing almost as loudly as my mouth, and whipped up a cloud of debris with my thoughts, taking anything I could grasp and battering the beast with it; a vortex of sharp plastic fragments and wood and broken glass from the case I'd smashed tore into the thing, this filthy foul alien *thing,* I didn't care what it was, I didn't care where it had come from, I didn't care if it had a self or if it could think, if it even knew what it had done, I just wanted it to *hurt* and to *die,* and I was on my feet now, standing my ground, eyes fixed on the thrashing, gnashing bastard, no more flight, just lots and lots of *pain,* and still it tried to chomp down and I thought *no* and *NO* and *NONONONO* and I felt something give, something at the other end – *yes yes yes* – and the teeth came free of my arm, my thoughts forcing the jaws back, *back* where they weren't supposed to go, and there was an awful, brilliant crack as something in there snapped, and I dropped the plastic and the glass and picked the creature up with my mind and started *slamming* it against the floor, again and again, harder, harder, *harder,* yelling, not words, just noise, and I could feel it losing, feel it weakening, feel it *dying – yes yes yes come on die die die DIE I swore I'd kill you one day I promised I would –* and I could see all of the children that it had taken, ghostly faces at the edges of my vision, phantom hands clapping, voices chanting my name, cheering me on as I pulverised it, black goop flying from its limp corpse in viscous, stinking ropes – *eat me, would you? Eat Tara, would you? CHEW ON*

THIS – and it was dead now, I knew it was dead, but I wanted it *ruined,* I wanted it in bits, I wanted it humiliated and pathetic, and I kept smashing it against the floor, and still they were cheering, I could hear my name – *Stanly*! *Stanly*! *STANLY*! *Stop it, it's dead* – and yeah, God, I knew it was dead, that was the point, *wait, stop, what*—

A hand grabbed me and pulled me around, and I came within an inch of blasting Connor with my brain. 'Stanly,' he said, strong hands on my shoulders, eyes locked on mine. 'It's dead, mate. OK? It's dead.'

The red cloud of hate and fury evaporated so suddenly that I felt lightheaded. I glanced towards the creature's splattered remains, utterly still, mouths slack, and as I watched it began to shift shape as its first body had, turning grey and sludgy, a spreading pool of some unearthly, wrong-smelling substance. Dead.

God it had better *be dead.*

'Sorry,' I said. 'Got carried away.' *Where did I go?*

'Yeah.' Connor let go, although his eyes lingered on me. I didn't need Sharon's empathy to see that he was freaked out.

After that fight, he's freaked out by me?

That's a good sign.

His look was making me feel uncomfortable, and I suddenly remembered that there had been a second creature and turned towards Eddie. He was lying on the ground with the thing prone on top of him, his arms still fastened around it. Seemed that he'd managed to snap something essential. There were also a number of bullet holes all the way along the creature's shiny bulk. *Took both of them to kill it.*

Who's the badass now?

Eddie had also been looking at me with an uncertain expression, but now he seemed to realise what was about to happen and hurriedly pushed the body away, just as it started to melt. My cousin shuddered and wrinkled his nose distastefully. *Yeah. Wouldn't want that crap all over you.*

The three of us stayed still for a long, silent moment before

Connor and I simultaneously lost our legs and collapsed in the middle of the carnage we had created. Somewhere, I was sure that Mr Freeman was ticking a box on a score sheet.

Connor and I simultaneously lost our legs and collapsed in the middle of the tarmac, we had created somewhere. I was sure that Mr Fessleman was holding a box on a little shelf.

CHAPTER TWENTY-EIGHT

It WAS A while before anybody spoke. Eddie had torn off the sleeves of his shirt so I could improvise some bandages for my arm and hand, and Connor had smoked two cigarettes. I was the first to break the silence. 'Can I have one of those?'

'No.'

'Thanks.'

Finally Eddie got to his feet. 'Just to be clear . . . does anyone know what just happened?'

I wondered what he meant by that. The monster? Or what I'd done? It wasn't a conversation I was particularly in the mood for, so I just shook my head, as did Connor. Eddie pursed his lips and nodded slowly. 'OK. So . . . let's go now, shall we.' It wasn't a suggestion.

We left the warehouse, walking slowly. Moving was pretty painful – even the dudes with super strength seemed stiff. 'The car's parked around the corner from the station,' said Eddie.

'Whose car?' I asked.

'Yours.'

It was just after five and dawn was breaking on the edge of the world, flavouring the sky with blue, pink and lazy gold, the horizon beginning its slow burn as the embers of the sun re-lit themselves. *It's gonna be a bright, bright sunshiny day.* The light, in its fearless infancy, made me feel better. Today the world would wake up with one less monster in it. London's children would be safer. I'd done a good thing.

And sometimes people lose their tempers.

Eddie unlocked the car and we piled in and he started to drive. Still nobody seemed particularly keen on speaking. 'So what happened after I left Blue Harvest?' I asked.

'Police came,' said Connor. 'Took witness statements. Ambulances came for the wounded and . . . the dead.'

The dead.

Jesus.

'Did they ask about me?'

'No,' said Eddie. 'It was strange. I'm sure I heard that old guy say something about you, but the police didn't ask any questions.'

'I must have friends in high places,' I said. 'Is Hannah all right?'

'No,' said Eddie. 'She wasn't injured, but she was really shaken up.'

'How about Kloe?'

'She was worried about you,' said Connor. 'Worried that she'd told you to go. That you might get hurt.'

'What did you say?'

'That you were stupid,' said Eddie, 'but that you could handle yourself. I just hoped it was true.'

'It was,' I said.

'Seems that way.'

I didn't like his tone, but I was still dead set on not having that particular conversation, so I ignored it. 'Any idea why it all kicked off?'

'Billy.' It sounded as though Eddie were dead set on avoiding *this* conversation, but I felt entitled to a few answers. 'Yeah?' I prompted.

'Some drug deal-related mix up or other, I imagine,' said Eddie, after exchanging an exasperated look with Connor that I was pretty sure he wanted me to see. 'He wasn't talking, but it's just the kind of shit he's always getting tangled up in. Usually people don't die, though. Little bastard.' I opted not to push further, and there were no more words for the duration of the drive.

We pulled up outside Connor and Sharon's place and got out, Connor first, then me, then Eddie, walking in single file along the untidy path. The downstairs lights were off. I was looking forward to crashing into my bed.

What, with Tara in it?

Balls. The sofa, then.

Connor took out his keys and moved to unlock the door, but it swung open by itself, and suddenly everything was bad again. 'Oh no,' he said, running in.

Sharon was lying in the hall at the bottom of the stairs, dried blood under her nose and at the corners of her mouth. Connor dropped to his knees beside her and pulled her into his arms. 'Oh my God,' he said, again. 'Sharon? Can you hear me? I'm so sorry, I'm so sorry . . .'

'Is she alive?' asked Eddie, pretty tactlessly.

'She's breathing.'

A power chord of fear and a trickle of insidious realisation that crept through my veins like an oilslick. I ran, mounted the stairs, sprinted up to the landing and kicked my bedroom door open. No Daryl, no Tara. The duvet was in a heap on the floor. I ran to the bathroom. No dog and no little girl, but there was a man in there, lying in the shattered remains of the shower cubicle. He was out cold, his face and hands a mess of blood, one of his arms very obviously broken. *Did* Sharon *do that?*

Who cares, keep looking. I ran into her and Connor's room, where I'd never been. Bed, shelves, books, small television, lamps, a very tasteful dressing screen with Chinese letters, candles. No Tara. No Daryl. I ran back to the top of the stairs and tried to yell, but my voice caught in my throat and only a panicked burble emerged. I tried again, and managed to choke out, 'They took them! They took Tara and Daryl!'

I ran downstairs. They had moved Sharon into the living room and laid her down on the sofa, and Connor was wiping her forehead tenderly with a moist cloth. Eddie was standing at the window, his fingers moving restlessly. *He wants to hit something.*

Might he hit me?

I'd like to see him try.

Bad thought. Bad thought.

'Did you hear me?' I said.

Eddie turned around. 'No. Sorry.'

'They took Tara. And Daryl's gone too.'

'Shit!' Eddie punched the wall and made a dent. Plaster broke and dust rose.

'There's a guy up there,' I said. 'In the bathroom. He's unconscious, too. Looks pretty battered, I'm guessing Sharon took him out.'

'Good,' said Eddie, cracking his knuckles. 'Let's wake him up. Do some battering of our own . . .'

'Wait a minute,' said Connor, 'she's coming round! She's coming round!'

Sharon's eyes were flickering and she coughed. 'Connor?'

Connor bent and kissed her forehead. 'Jesus Christ, babe. You shaved about twenty years off my life.'

She dragged herself up into a sitting position, wincing. 'Well, I'm sure they would have been . . .' She coughed. ' . . . Rubbish anyway.' She looked to me, then to Eddie. 'You . . . what happened?'

'Smiley Joe's history,' said Eddie, gently. 'But that's not important. What happened here?'

'It . . .' Sharon looked at the clock. 'About an hour ago.' She was slurring slightly. 'I was upstairs, I heard the door. They just kicked it open, burst in, three guys. Big. They came straight upstairs. Wanted to know where Tara was. I think one of them must have had powers, mine felt . . . it was like they were being dampened, somehow. I tried to fight them off anyway, managed to get one. Daryl was helping, but . . . they pushed me. Down the stairs. That's all . . . oh God, is she—'

'She's gone,' I said. 'They took her. And Daryl.'

Sharon closed her eyes. 'No . . .'

'We have to go and get them,' I said. 'Right now.'

'Use your head,' said Eddie. 'We don't even know where to look.'

'I know where to start,' I said.

'Where?' asked Connor. 'The guy upstairs? It's not that I'm not tempted to cause him some pain, but if he's some kind of trained professional it could be hours before we get anything out of him . . .'

Wow, they leapt to torture pretty quickly. And I get in trouble for going postal on a child-devouring hellbeast. 'No,' I said. 'Not him. The one person I've met who seems to have half a clue about what's going on. Freeman.'

'*No*,' said Eddie. 'We're not going anywhere near that arsehole.'

'We may not have a choice,' said Sharon.

'We *don't* have a choice!' I said, my voice getting louder of its own accord. 'He's the only person!'

'You might be right,' said Connor, 'but we all threw our cards away years ago.'

'I still have mine,' I said.

'You *met* him?' said Eddie. Considering what was occurring, it seemed like the wrong thing to get angry about, and I stood my ground.

'Of course I met him!' I said. 'We were talking about him earlier! I assumed you knew!'

'Sharon told us she'd warned you about him,' said Connor. 'She didn't say you'd seen him.'

'Well, I have seen him,' I said. 'Twice. And he knows everything, I'm sure of it. He knew all about me, about Daryl. He was *in* Tref-y-Celwyn one day, in the woods. He saw me flying.' *So he's either an Oracle, extremely intuitive or a very anal-retentive spy. Whatever.* 'I'm going to call him.' Mine and Eddie's eyes met directly. 'Are you going to stop me?'

My cousin didn't say anything. He just lowered his head and shook it very slightly. I went to the phone, reaching into my wallet for the white card, and for the first time I noticed that the number had too many digits to be a regular phone number.

Seems legit.

He picked up after four rings. 'Hello?'

'You know where they've taken them,' I said. 'Tara and Daryl.'

'Stanly. I hear you eliminated Smiley Joe. Nice work.'

'Where are they, Freeman?'

'I can tell you. But it means trouble.'

'Tonight's been a good night for trouble,' I said. 'A little more won't hurt. Plus, if they don't give them back . . . we'll kill their guy.' *Oh, will you now?*

'The one they left behind? I think that demonstrates pretty categorically how bothered they are about him. You can mount his severed head on a post and use it as a letterbox for all they care.'

D'oh. 'Fine,' I said. 'But we'd like to give him back all the same. Apart from anything, I'm pretty keen to use the shower at some point. Got some dead monster to wash out of my hair.'

Freeman chuckled. 'Oh, Stanly. You're much more fun than your cousin.'

'Keep giggling, asshole, and you'll see how much fun I can be.'

'Fair enough, fair enough, not the time. All right. Meet me at six thirty. The Jonathan Kulich Gallery.'

I looked at my watch. It was five to six. 'Where's that?'

'I'll text the address to Eddie,' said Freeman. 'All right?'

'Fine,' I said. 'No tricks.'

'I wouldn't dream of it,' said Mr Freeman. 'You can just stuff the . . . "minion" in the boot of your car, if you like.'

'Will do,' I said. 'One more thing.'

'Yes?'

'Are you anything to do with this?'

'Apparently so, now. See you at six thirty.' He hung up, and I put the phone down and returned to the living room. Sharon was on her feet. She looked better already.

'Well?' said Connor.

'He wants us to meet him,' I said. 'He's going to text Eddie the address.' As I said it, Eddie's phone bleeped. He took it out, looking surprised and irritated and interested all at the same time.

'How does he have my number?'

'Not the biggest surprise of the night, is it?' said Connor. 'So where are we going?'

'Not too far . . . but I'll have to drive pretty fast to make it there by six thirty. We should leave now.'

Sharon looked panicked. 'Wait a second! I'm in my pyjamas!'

'You're not—' began Connor.

'Don't you *dare* tell me I'm not coming,' said Sharon. 'They broke into my home, attacked me, kidnapped our friends. Give me one minute.' She dashed off upstairs. *I'm glad she's coming.*

We waited. Connor quietly loaded his weapons, Eddie stared broodingly out of the window and I kept moving my left arm, which by now stung rather than burned. 'Where did you get those guns, by the way?' I said.

'Skank,' said Connor.

'Oh.' *Figures, I suppose.* I turned to Eddie. 'You were pretty sharp at the warehouse,' I said. He just nodded. *OK, let's not chat then.*

Sharon came down, fully dressed. 'All right. Let's go, shall we?'

'Oh, hold on,' I said. 'We should get the guy from upstairs . . .'

Sharon twitched her head to one side and a large mass of suited man came tumbling down the stairs, coming to rest in a heap at the bottom. He let out a deep groan and Sharon smiled. 'Got him.'

Wow. I'm really *glad she's coming.*

Eddie drove very fast, probably over the speed limit, not that I was really worried about that. Nobody said a word. The tension crackled like static. Sharon and Connor sat in the back with their heads on each other's shoulders, holding hands, and I was in the front with Eddie, watching the rapidly lightening city slowly come to life. We passed very few cars, but people were already beginning to move, to yawn on the pavement and light their first cigarettes. Normality.

And here we are, speeding to a clandestine meeting with a guy in the boot.

I glanced at Eddie, his jaw set, eyes burning. How was this going to go down? Who were we about to meet? I wondered if more fighting was on the cards.

If there is, it'll be different.

I know.

It won't be like fighting monsters.

I know.

Do you think you can kill real live people?

If it's them or Tara, or Daryl . . .

You have to be completely sure about this. One hundred per cent resolved. You need to disconnect everything. No passion, no anger, no misery, no quips. No losing control. Just you and your power and the people on the receiving end.

I know this.

Let's hope so.

The weather was playing the fool, the cinematographer's award-winning dawn already giving way to grey clouds, the sun dimming as quickly as it had risen. *So much for a bright, bright sunshiny day.*

'Nearly there,' said Eddie. 'Two minutes. Everyone ready?'

A general chorus of 'yes'.

'Don't trust a word Freeman says,' said Eddie. 'Even if he's truthful about finding the girl and Daryl he'll have an ulterior motive. He always does.'

'You really don't like him, do you?' I asked.

Eddie looked at me, but said nothing.

Ouch.

We turned a corner and parked down a side street. *Hopefully we won't get ticketed or clamped or something.*

Yes. That's definitely the most worrisome thing that could happen.

But the car's stolen, technically, don't want Mum finding out . . . Seriously?

Leave me alone, I'm really tired, OK?

We walked down the street and round another corner, where Mr

Freeman was sitting on a bench, smoking a cigarette. Beyond him was a very large square white building with barely any windows, overlooking the river. *The Jonathan Kulich Gallery,* I read. Why did he want to meet us here?

I ain't lookin' at no paintings, suckah.

We walked guardedly towards Freeman, whose face betrayed nothing. Eddie and I were at the front, with Connor and Sharon flanking us. No sign of any goons. Freeman stood up and smiled. *Inappropriate.* 'Edward,' he said. 'Sharon. Connor. Good to see you. And you too of course, Stanly.'

'You haven't aged a day,' said Sharon.

'Too kind,' said Freeman.

'But you looked pretty old then, too,' said Connor.

Oh, SNAP. Freeman chuckled. 'Make this short, Freeman,' said Eddie. 'We want to find Tara and the dog.'

'Dog?' said Freeman. 'I'm afraid I know nothing about Stanly's . . . rather unique pet. All I know is that several rather powerful people are holding the little girl – don't ask me why for I have no idea – and that you four don't have a businessman in *Deliverance*'s chance of taking her away from them without my help. So I would appreciate it if you'd either stay civil or be quiet.'

Eddie made to move forward but I grabbed his arm. 'Eddie,' I said, warningly. 'We need him.' Mr Freeman smiled slightly. He was obviously enjoying this. Something told me that the two of them hadn't got on very well when they'd first met, either. Eddie nodded reluctantly. 'OK,' I said. 'Who exactly are these people?'

'Two of my employers and some of their . . . *minions.*' Mr Freeman crushed his cigarette butt under his shiny black shoe. 'As I said, I don't know why they need the girl, but if they've gone to these lengths they're unlikely to give her up unless I can appeal to their better natures.'

'And what do we do?' asked Connor.

'You stay quiet while I work,' said Mr Freeman. 'Taking the child by force should be a last resort, if it's a resort at all.'

I glanced at Sharon. She didn't look like she was reading him but I knew she had, and she caught my look and nodded. *He's telling the truth.*

As far as we know.

'OK,' I said. 'Take us to your leader.'

'Step this way,' said Mr Freeman. He turned and started to walk away, but then I remembered something.

'Oh,' I said. 'Um, what about the guy in the boot?'

'Just leave him there,' said Freeman, dismissively. 'If they want him back, they can get him afterwards.'

'And if they don't want him back?' asked Eddie.

'Then you can release him into the wild,' said Freeman. 'Come along.' We exchanged shrugs and followed him towards the front door of the gallery. The building didn't exactly tower above us but it was fairly imposing all the same, and there was definitely *something* wrong. Something beyond the KEEP OUT and TRES-PASSERS WILL BE PROSECUTED and ESSENTIAL MAINTE-NANCE signs. I could smell it somehow, an unquantifiable threat, an oddness. It didn't help that the gallery really stuck out amongst the anonymous industrial buildings that surrounded it. It was like someone had just plonked it down with no thought for architec-tural consistency.

Like the rest of London, then.

Mr Freeman opened the door, revealing a vast white lobby with crème furniture and a mahogany reception desk. There was a lift at the very back into which we all squeezed, and Freeman pressed the button for the second floor. The doors closed, hydraulics thumped and whirred and we began to move upwards. The mirrored lift looked high-tech, but it sounded old and cranky. A bland, synthe-sised version of 'The Girl from Ipanema' began to play wonkily over the lift's rusty groans.

This lift moves very slowly.

'So, why are we here again?' I said.

'To rescue your little friend,' said Mr Freeman, checking his watch. 'And, as a bonus, to meet two of the many faces of the Angel Group.'

'The Angel Group?' said Sharon. 'And they are . . .'

'You'll find out,' said Mr Freeman. 'Good things to those who wait, and all that.'

The lift thunked to a halt and the doors opened onto a long corridor with many doorless openings on either side. Mr Freeman started to walk, and as we followed him I looked nervously to the left and right. Each room was basically the same: white walls, a polished wooden floor, over-stylised, uncomfortable-looking chairs, and lots of paintings. Those were the only real variables. Some were random splashes of colour, some were Picasso-style messed-up faces, some were charcoal, some were watercolours. Neither me nor my friends said anything, but our ageless guide couldn't seem to contain himself. 'This *is* exciting, isn't it?' he said.

'I'm thrilled,' said Connor. 'This definitely beats a lie-in, a fry-up and not having had my house broken into and my girlfriend assaulted.'

'Oh come, come,' said Mr Freeman. 'I agree there has been some unpleasantness, but this is a very important step for young Stanly.'

'Less of the "young", if you don't mind,' I said. What he'd said hadn't actually bothered me, but I hoped that being belligerent would obscure how apprehensive I felt.

'Sorry,' said Mr Freeman. 'What I mean is, you are about to reach a significant rung on the ladder you started climbing last September. I would have thought you'd be excited.'

'What the hell are you talking about, you fucking weirdo?' said Eddie. Sharon actually sniggered, and a smile twitched at the edges of Connor's lips.

Freeman was entirely unphased. 'Stanly understands,' he said.

Do I?

Sod it, just maintain an unimpressed expression and walk like you're ready to cook some fools.

'Nearly there,' said Freeman. He opened another white door and we stepped through into . . . yet another corridor. *Too many corridors*. I decided to voice my opinion. 'Too many corridors.'

'I know,' said Mr Freeman. 'It's like being trapped in an old episode of *Doctor Who*. C'est la vie, eh?'

This one was identical to the last one, visually at least, but in terms of how I was feeling, there was something different about it. Something really, unsettlingly wrong, even more so than before. It positively stank of foreboding. *I never liked that smell.*

'Here we are,' said Mr Freeman. We were standing in front of yet another door, but this one was stainless steel and had two potted plants on either side. Even those were weirdly imposing. Mr Freeman knocked and it echoed dully, and we heard an answering female voice from the other side. 'Come in.' Freeman winked at me, and opened the door.

And here – we – go.

CHAPTER TWENTY-NINE

This room was different from the others. It was a lot bigger for a start, and the walls were off-white and covered in blown-up black and white photographs of various places in London. The Houses of Parliament. Big Ben. One of the parks. Some Tube station I didn't recognise. They were all slightly disquieting. I couldn't put my finger on it, but they creeped me out.

There's a lot of that going around.

The ceiling was transparent and I could clearly see that my bright sunshiney day had been incapacitated, dragged away and replaced with pouring rain. The elevator and the corridor were like worlds to themselves, and no sound from outside penetrated those ominous walls, but now I could see the pencil-lead sky, and hear the chaotic tapping of raindrops hammering against glass. In the very centre of the room was a shiny square table, behind which sat a man and a woman in transparent seats, flanked by three other men who looked less important but more physically threatening. The seated man was in his forties, I estimated, and slightly built, and wore a dark suit. His black hair was severely neat and his dark blue eyes were riveting and cold. The woman might have been younger than him, possibly closer to Sharon's age, although possibly much older too, with pale skin and long, shiny mahogany hair. Green eyes, mauve lipstick, scarlet trouser suit. The three statues behind them all had their arms crossed and regarded the five of us impassively. Two of them were regular bodyguard types: big guys with crewcuts, muscles bulging under their suits. One was blonde and one was slightly greying, but that was the only real difference between them.

The third guy was the one I didn't like. He was as tall as the others, but skinny and lithe, with chalk-white skin, spiky black hair and hard dark eyes, and wore a black suit with a white tie. He was like an anime character come to life, and I could sense power in him. The other two were Rent-A-Fists, your common or garden security lumps, but Number Three was very, very different. *Keep an eye.*

Mr Freeman stepped forward and bowed his head slightly. 'Pandora. Lucius.'

Dark-haired, cold-eyed Lucius nodded. 'Freeman.' His gesture and speech were as curt as his expression. Pandora smiled impenetrably.

'Well, here they are,' said Mr Freeman. 'As promised.'

I knew it. I knew it!

No you didn't.

'You son of a bitch!' yelled Eddie. 'I knew we shouldn't have trusted you!'

'Edward,' said Pandora. Her voice was reasonable but hinted at fire. 'I'm afraid I must ask you not to harm Mr Freeman.' She then fixed our very own Judas with a smouldering stare. 'He hasn't sold you down the river.'

'What has he done, then?' said Eddie.

'Up until very recently we didn't even know you existed,' said Pandora. 'Freeman kept you all from us. A . . . pet project of sorts. But we uncovered his deception and said that if he brought you before us – just to talk, you understand, nothing more – we would . . . feel more kindly disposed towards him than we might otherwise have.'

'That sounds an awful lot like selling us down the river,' I said.

'You say tom*a*to, I say tell your cousin to calm down if he wants to get through this alive,' said Pandora.

'No-one's telling me to—' began Eddie, but Sharon put a hand on his shoulder and he fell silent.

303

'I delivered them,' said Mr Freeman. 'You have what you wanted.'

'Yes, we do,' said Pandora, moistening her lips. *Does she have a forked tongue? No. Damn.*

'Well?' said Freeman.

'Well, what?'

'You promised me clemency,' said Mr Freeman. There was a note of panic in his voice and I could see sweat on the back of his neck. Outside, the rain fell like peas on corrugated iron. Pandora glanced at Lucius, who simply stared at Freeman, the edge of his mouth twitching with . . . was it disgust? *He's scary.*

Not as scary as she is.

Freeman was shaking, and now Pandora turned back to him and smiled dangerously. Freeman obviously knew what the look meant. 'No,' he said. 'You promised me! *You swore to me!*'

Pandora shrugged. 'I lied. I thought you'd be more familiar with the signs. You're *so* good at it, after all.' Lucius inclined his head and the two bodyguards drew their weapons and fired. One bullet from each gun, that was all it took. Mr Freeman jerked, groaned and dropped to his knees, clutching his chest. His pale hands came away stained red, and with a final gurgle he fell forwards and hit the floor. Pandora's face wrinkled with distaste.

I stared at Freeman. My hands were numb. A dark pool began to spread from underneath his body, glassy crimson on the light wood floor.

They shot him.

Why?

I felt sick. I'd seen death already tonight . . . but it's different when it's someone you know. Even someone you don't necessarily like all that much.

It also felt like we'd just lost any bargaining power we might have had.

'Lucius,' said Pandora, as though he'd bought the wrong type of wine to a dinner party. 'Was it really necessary to do it in here? What a mess. And we can't exactly leave it for the cleaners.'

'We needed to show them,' said Lucius.

'I thought he worked for you,' said Connor. I couldn't see his or Sharon's reactions because I was now staring fixedly at Pandora and Lucius. *Keep eye contact. Keep 'em in your sights.*

And don't look at the horrible murdered corpse.

'He did,' said Lucius. 'But his extracurricular activities have been something of an embarrassment. Manipulating empowered teenagers into doing his dirty work for him ... secret projects ...'

Empowered. Hmm. Good word.

'Too dirty for you?' I said.

'Not at all,' said Pandora. 'The key word is "extracurricular". We can't abide such behaviour. Insubordination of any kind will not be tolerated.' Her eyes fell upon Eddie. 'The Shadow Man.' They moved to Connor. 'The Gargoyle.' They moved to Sharon. 'The Worm.' Finally they came back to me. 'Smiley Joe. "Monsters".'

'What are they?' asked Connor. 'Where did they come from?'

'Somewhere unpleasant,' said Lucius, in a voice uncannily reminiscent of my talking-to-morons one.

'A place that would likely drive you mad if you attempted a visit,' said Pandora, 'and about which we know frustratingly little. Which was all the more reason for the creatures to be delivered to us alive so we could study them and, if possible, use them to our advantage.'

'Mr Freeman obviously thinks ... thought differently,' I said.

'Mr Freeman was a complex man,' said Pandora. 'Brilliant at his job. Uncompromising. Fiercely intelligent. Extremely charismatic, as you all know. But haunted by past mistakes, and rather too concerned with a battle between good and evil that he'd never admit to believing in. We have slightly higher ambitions than the simple extermination of beasts.'

'Beasts that terrorise the city?' I said. 'That kill children?'

'Shame, that,' said Pandora, although she didn't sound at all sorry. 'And a shame about Freeman, too. But he crossed some lines, so ...'

'So you killed him,' said Eddie.

'You're obviously blessed with enhanced powers of observation,' said Lucius.

'Don't start with me, arsehole.'

'Are you going to kill us, then?' I said.

'Why would we want to do that?' asked Pandora. 'Why would we want to hurt any of you?'

'You broke into my house,' said Sharon. 'You attacked me and you stole from us.' She pointed at the scary bodyguard with the spiky hair. '*He* attacked me.'

'Oh yes,' said Pandora. 'That. Sorry. My plan. Lucius wanted to negotiate for the little girl. I had a feeling that you wouldn't give her up.'

'You're damn right,' I said. 'Where is she?'

'She's safe,' said Pandora. 'Don't worry, we didn't bring her here to hurt her. We brought her because she is important. We need her.'

'I thought you wanted to see us,' said Sharon.

'We can multi-task,' said Pandora.

'She's just a little girl!' I said. 'She couldn't hurt anyone! What possible use could an evil organisation have with her?'

'Evil?' asked Pandora. 'You think we're evil?'

I frowned. 'You're not?'

She rolled her eyes. 'Didn't the name give you a clue?'

'I thought it was ironic.'

Pandora laughed. 'Charming. No, it's true. We're . . . how can I put this? I wouldn't say we're "good" because . . .'

'Not this again,' I groaned, pointing at Mr Freeman. 'I heard this "relative concepts" guff from him.'

'So what *is* your purpose?' asked Sharon. 'What *is* the Angel Group?'

'The Angel Group,' said Pandora, 'in the simplest possible terms, is a special corporate interest working to ensure that things run as smoothly as possible on this troubled little planet.'

I heard Connor stifle a laugh. 'Would you care to share the joke?' asked Lucius.

'Have you watched the news at all, lately?' said Connor. ''Cos if that's your idea of things running smoothly . . .'

'We tackle those problems that we think can, and more importantly, *should* be solved,' said Lucius. 'Society's ills, political whims, ideological conflicts and the like are not necessarily our foremost concern.'

'So what exactly *do* you do?' I said. 'I'm still not clear. *How* do you make things run more smoothly? Or do you just take lots of really long lunches?'

'You think you four are the only people on this planet with supernatural abilities?' said Pandora, pityingly. 'Are you really that naïve?'

'No,' said Eddie. 'But we never found out how many there are, or where they are.'

Number Three still hasn't moved.

I have a feeling we'll know about it when he does.

'Well, they are everywhere,' said Pandora, 'and not all of them are as decent as you. Just the other week a young activist with abilities quite similar to young Stanly's attempted to kill the Prime Minister.'

'Don't think I would have lost much sleep over that,' said Eddie.

'I'm no great fan of the Etonian buffoon either,' said Pandora, 'but his death would have caused a fair amount of chaos, don't you agree? And that's the operative word here – chaos. We don't want chaos taking over. We're trying to prevent humanity from unravelling like a ball of thread.' She glanced up at the ceiling, at the pissing wet day. 'I know the world is far from perfect. People are dying every day. Things . . . aren't great. Makes for some serious neuroses. I'm probably one of the colder hearted people you're likely to meet, but sometimes even I need to relax with a glass of wine and several diazepam.'

'Your point being?' said Sharon.

'My point *being*,' said Pandora, 'that life goes on. People go to work. They talk. They laugh. They shop. They make love. They go to the cinema. They see their friends. Chaos has not yet taken a foothold.'

'Not round here, anyway,' said Eddie.

'You think you know what chaos entails?' said Pandora. 'Trust me. You have no idea.'

'And that's why we're here,' said Lucius. 'We're doing God's work.'

I noticed that Pandora looked uncomfortable at that. Eddie snorted. 'You must be joking . . .'

'Does the phrase "mysterious ways" mean anything to you?' said Lucius, sharply.

'Does the phrase "join us in the twenty-first century, you Dark Age muppet" mean anything to *you*?' shot back Eddie.

I couldn't help smirking at that. *Good one.*

'I assure you,' said Lucius, 'that the twenty-first century, and the potential centuries beyond, are of the utmost concern to us, and to the Lord. He despairs of what has become of His creation.'

'But, according to Lucius, he likes to maintain a policy of non-interference,' said Pandora. *Ouch. Careful with that sarcasm, you'll have someone's eye out.* 'So we interfere on his behalf, because apparently that's fine.' Lucius didn't look happy with that remark, but didn't speak.

'You don't sound like you believe it,' said Sharon.

'Lucius is a man of faith,' said Pandora. 'I take a different approach. Our group is diverse, and you might say . . . divided . . . in terms of the small print. But on the big issues we are united.'

'World domination, is it?' I said.

'It's not on the agenda,' said Pandora. 'Although I won't lie – it would probably solve a few things.'

That's not a yes.

Not a no either.

'You still haven't told us what you want with Tara,' said Eddie.

Pandora turned to Lucius. 'I can handle things from here if you wish, Lucius. I know you have some important business, and you've met the new empowered, as you wished.'

Lucius looked unsure. 'I can stay if you—'

'I'm fine.' It seemed that despite their ages Pandora ranked slightly higher than Lucius, and she wasn't afraid of showing it. Lucius nodded, stood up, got his coat and briefcase and headed towards the door we'd come through. The spiky-haired guard radiating danger went to follow him, but Pandora said, 'Leave Leon if you please, Lucius? Just in case.'

Lucius didn't look happy but nodded and left. Pandora waited until the door had closed then shook her head. 'I do find it terribly embarrassing when he starts on the religious angle. I assure you, for the most part we're *extremely* progressive.'

'Tara,' I said. 'Why did you take her?'

'All I'm prepared to say is that she is important and needs protecting.'

'I can protect her.'

'Really?' asked Pandora.

I nodded, suddenly realising that my knuckles were completely white. *I didn't even know I was clenching my fists.* 'I can. And even with all your talk of looking after the world, I trust you to the sum of diddly squat to the power of bugger all, with a piss off on top. I'm not leaving her with you.'

'Well,' said Pandora. 'We'll see.'

'No, we—'

'Shut up,' said Pandora, shaking her head. 'You need to do a bit more listening and a bit less of this.' She mimed a flapping mouth with her hand. 'Now,' she continued, 'I was intrigued when Mr Freeman told me he'd been keeping tabs on some new empowered. I thought we were aware of them all. Obviously not. So it's been both delightful and fascinating to meet you.'

'What do you want with us?' said Sharon.

'Ideally, we'd like you to join us. The arrangement could be mutually beneficial. You four would no longer have to operate outside the law. You would be employed. Paid. Comfortable.'

'And in return?' said Eddie.

'We do their dirty work,' said Connor. 'No deal.'

'No deal,' said Sharon.

'Damn right, no deal,' said Eddie.

I didn't say anything. 'Stanly?' said Sharon. 'Say "no deal". It's a whole united-against-them sort of thing.'

That's a very bad decision you just made, Stan.

Shut up.

Sorry. Just making an observation.

I know. I just don't like to be called Stan.

I shook my head and walked forwards, stepping over Mr Freeman's body – *oh Christ he's really properly extremely very dead* – maintaining eye contact with Pandora. I stopped by the table, close enough that I could have reached out and grabbed her, and leaned in. 'Give Tara back.'

'In exchange for what?' asked Pandora.

'Me,' I said.

'Stanly, no!' said Sharon.

'Be quiet,' snapped Pandora. She raised one interested eyebrow. 'You.'

'That's the deal,' I said. 'I'll do your bidding. You can use my powers to implement your will, whatever. But give Tara back.'

Pandora actually looked contrite. 'I'm sorry, Stanly,' she said. 'I'm really not sure that it can work like that.'

I shrugged. 'Fine. Then we'll take her.'

'Stanly. Don't.'

I knew that voice. I turned around. The door had opened without anybody hearing, and someone was standing in the doorway.

It was Daryl.

CHAPTER THIRTY

Daryl walked past us, ignoring Mr Freeman's cooling body.

'Daryl?' said Connor. 'Where the hell have you been? What happened, did they kidnap . . . dognap you too?'

'Hardly,' said Pandora. 'Why don't you tell them, Daryl? There's been a bucketload of exposition already, I'm sure a bit more won't hurt.'

'Tell us what?' I said. 'How does she know your name?'

Daryl jumped up onto the table, turned around and looked straight at me. 'I'm sorry,' he said.

No.

It's not possible.

No.

NO!

'You,' I said. 'You . . . were working with them? Spying on me? This whole time?'

Daryl shook his head. 'Not exactly . . .'

'What do you mean, *exactly*? What *exactly*?'

He didn't seem to be able to answer. His big eyes looked sorry, but I couldn't trust them. 'You . . .' My voice broke slightly. I could feel tears behind my eyes. *Not now. No time for that. Can't be weak.* 'You didn't just . . . we didn't meet by chance?'

'We *did* meet by chance,' said Daryl, 'I swear. I . . . I used to work with the Angel Group. Years ago. I knew about people with powers, about monsters, everything. But I left it all behind, it all got too much, and I ended up living in the middle of nowhere with a boring old man. I wanted nothing to do with any of it. And then I met you, and suddenly you developed powers . . . and I didn't know what to do. I didn't want to tell you everything.'

'Why?'

'Because . . . I didn't want you to think I'd lied to you.'

'Oh,' I said. 'Cool. That's nice. How exactly the hell do you think I'm feeling now?'

'I—'

'I *trusted you*. I shared everything with you. You were my most . . . my *only* friend. You . . .' I didn't want to say *you betrayed me,* because if I said it then that meant it was true. *But it is true.*

Shut up. Seriously.

'I'm sorry,' said Daryl. 'I really am. So . . . I didn't know how close—'

'Stop talking,' I said.

'*Please* listen,' said the dog. 'I didn't betray you. I decided to tell Freeman about you. He used to be my . . . my partner, I suppose. We worked together. I told him about you and I asked his advice on the condition that he *didn't* tell the Angel Group. He owed me. He said to get you to London and at first I considered it, but then I realised it was a bad, bad idea. Hence me trying to get you to stay in Tref-y-Celwyn. When that didn't work and we ended up in London, I figured I might as well keep in contact with Freeman, just in case.'

'You trusted him?' said Eddie, incredulously.

'More than I trust the rest of them,' said Daryl. He glanced at Pandora. 'More than I trust this bitch.'

'Daryl,' said Pandora, mockingly. 'I'm hurt. Although actually . . . is "bitch" really an insult, coming from a dog?'

'Eat it,' said Daryl. 'So anyway . . . I told Freeman what else I knew and he said he wouldn't tell the Group. And then he told me he'd met you, and not to contact him again, that he'd get in touch with me if he needed to. I had time to think about things and realised I'd made a terrible mistake, but it was too late, and I didn't want to warn you because . . . well, you can imagine.'

'Not really,' I said, even though I could.

'When you told me to guard Tara I really did,' said Daryl. 'I swear. I fought those guys who came and took her. One of them is now minus a hand.' He nodded towards the human animé character, Leon. 'If it wasn't for this one . . .'

'That reminds me,' said Pandora, 'Lucius wasn't particularly happy about you mutilating one of his men. He's expecting an apology.'

'We've got another one in the car as well,' said Connor, 'if you're interested . . .'

'To be honest, Pandora, I don't particularly give a rat's ringpiece what Lucius expects,' said Daryl. 'Bible-thumping bollock-ache.'

'So where have you been since they took Tara?' I said. 'What, you figured you'd just leave Sharon at the bottom of the stairs and go and get some breakfast?'

'I've been looking for Tara, of course,' said Daryl. 'I didn't want to leave Sharon, but I could see she would recover, so I had to make a choice. I didn't want the trail to run cold . . . I tracked them here.' He looked at Pandora. 'You're going to kill me, I suppose?'

'Don't worry Daryl,' said Pandora. 'I have no intention of harming a defenceless creature like you. At the moment.'

'I'm not exactly defenceless,' Daryl growled. 'I believe Lucius got the one-handed memo.'

'Touché,' said Pandora. 'Stanly, in the beagle's defence, before today I'd heard nothing from him for a number of years. Honestly, I thought that he was no longer with us. So he didn't sell you out to us. Just to Freeman.'

I was barely hearing this. 'You should have told me,' I said. 'As soon as I got the powers, you should have *told me*.'

'I wanted to,' said Daryl. 'You think I'm just some Lando now. I'm not. I might have gone about things the wrong way, but that's what you learn working for these people. You get . . . really good at rationalising deceit. But my purpose was true, everything I ever *said* to you was true. My feelings, my opinions, my thoughts. They were all me, one hundred per cent. A regular dog's love is unconditional. I chose mine.'

I shook my head. *What the hell do I say to that?*

'How touching,' said Pandora. 'I may be sick.'

'Shut the *fuck* up, Pandora,' said Daryl, 'or I swear to Lucius' non-existent god . . .'

'Don't come back,' I said.

Daryl looked at me. 'Don't . . .'

'Don't come back to me.' I stared at my . . . at the dog. My dog? The dog? I didn't know what he was. I didn't know anything any more.

'He is sorry,' said Sharon, gently.

'I am,' said Daryl. 'I swear, I . . .'

'Don't come back to me,' I said again. 'If you're going to go anywhere, go back to Tref-y-Celwyn.'

'Go back and live with your parents?' asked Daryl. 'I know I did bad, but that's a fate worse than death . . .'

'I think you should probably leave now, Daryl,' said Pandora.

And at that moment, something changed. I didn't know what it was. I didn't know what Daryl sensed in her voice that he didn't like, because I certainly hadn't heard anything. But the beagle turned slowly around and looked straight at Pandora, who looked straight back at him, and now I could see something. A twitch. A flash of something in her eyes. Daryl started to laugh. 'What?' asked Pandora.

'What's going on?' said Eddie. 'What the hell is he laughing at?'

Daryl shook his big head. 'I should have smelled it when I first came in. I must have been distracted by the waves of affection coming at me from every direction.'

Pandora didn't move, but she definitely looked nervous. 'What are you talking about?'

'What did she offer you all?' said Daryl. 'Power? A post with the Group? Something like that? She is composed of pure lies. And she's planning something. I'd grab Tara and get the hell out of here if I were you.'

'Shut up,' said Pandora. 'I have no idea what you're talking about.'

'I think you do,' said Daryl. 'This is all very nice. Clever. The whole top-floor end-of-the-line final-act room-of-revelations thing. Meeting the big bosses. It's very cinematic. Right up Stanly's street. Exactly what you needed to get him and the others here.'

'I'm offering peace—'

'You cannot trust a word this woman says, Stanly,' said Daryl. 'Get Tara and get out.'

Now Pandora moved, jumping out of her seat and running behind the three guards. 'Don't let them leave,' she said. The three started to move towards us, while Pandora ran towards one of the massive framed photographs on the wall. I blinked. Something had changed in the pictures. They suddenly seemed so much more . . . alive. *What the hell is going on? I'm so confused!*

No time to be confused. Got to find Tara.

'Pandora!' I roared. 'Where is she? Where's Tara?'

Pandora didn't answer. She ran towards the wall, jumped . . . and went straight through one of the photographs, disappearing entirely, leaving nothing but a few ripples. Gone.

'NO!' I said.

Everything went mental. Two of the guards drew guns, Leon lunged towards us and I ducked, sending out a spray of psychic hits that knocked the weapons away. Connor, Eddie and Sharon jumped in to engage the guards and Daryl leapt towards Leon. 'Go after her Stanly!' he yelled. 'We'll handle these wankers!'

Through a photograph?

Bugger it.

I ran, and jumped, and was somewhere else.

CHAPTER THIRTY-ONE

THE TRANSITION BETWEEN the gallery and wherever the hell I'd ended up was subtle, at least in terms of how it felt, like entering a slightly colder room. Visually, though, it was like being whacked with a mallet made of pure vertigo; there was no colour here, just greys and blacks and whites. I took a look around. I was in Hyde Park . . . sort of. The trees were skeletal, the sky a dead haze. No sun. No sound. Glancing down at my hands and clothes, I saw that they were entirely monochrome.

Well, this is peculiar.

'Hello?' I tried. No response. I tried again, but louder, and this time I was sure I could hear mocking laughter coming from somewhere . . .

Then she was on me. She knocked me into the charcoal grass face-first and I rolled over and kicked out clumsily. It was a lucky hit and Pandora went down, and I was immediately back on my feet, ready. I flexed my mind and picked her up by her neck, and she clutched at her throat and gurgled as I held her there. 'Where is she?' I said. I loosened my hold enough for her to answer but she just spat. 'OK then,' I said. 'We'll come back to that. Question two. What the bloody hell is going on?'

'The Angel Group has . . . other uses for your kind.' Pandora's voice was an ugly choke. 'You need to be out of the way.'

'Why?'

She spat again. I tightened my hold and her face went whiter. 'Weren't expecting this, were you?' I asked. 'Didn't think we could take you, did you? Newsflash, Little Miss . . . Massive Bitch. We're a lot more powerful than you think.' *Is this an OK thing to be doing? She is a person, after all.*

Some people are bad, though.

Pandora managed a twisted smile. 'You talk too much.'

'Really?'

'Yes.'

Something touched my back, a crackling force surrounded by power, and we were somewhere else again. The colours shifted, white and black to red and blue to green and orange and yellow, and through the kaleidoscopic palette I could see that we were in an office with a floor-to-ceiling window, high above London's infinite, intimidating sprawl. The city was engulfed in a storm, a storm too enormous to be real, curtains of rain lashing at the buildings, the wind causing the skyscrapers themselves to ripple, and across the gulf was a building I didn't recognise. It might not even have existed. *This is definitely the weirdest thing to happen today. Which is kind of impressive.*

Don't panic.

Just go with it.

Haven't really got a choice there, have I?

I looked at Pandora and smiled the scariest smile I could muster. 'No—' she began.

'Yes,' I said, and flew forwards, grabbing her around her waist. I thought *SMASH* and the window splintered apart, and wickedly sharp fragments fanned out into the air as we entered the maelstrom, ploughing into howling eddies of wind and whips of rain, big fat drops that exploded as they hit. I held onto Pandora and we flew across the abyss towards the skyscraper opposite, colours flashing, shifting in time with the lightning. It was as though I'd flown into someone's particularly messed-up acid trip. The woman was writhing and struggling in my grip, and I tightened it. 'I wouldn't struggle!' I yelled, trying to make myself heard above the savage roar of wind and water. 'I might have to drop you!'

'*You little shit!*' screamed Pandora. She managed to wriggle out of my grasp but held onto my left arm, her fingers digging into my monster bites, and I bellowed with the pain, sounding like what I'd imagine an enraged moose would sound like. Seizing the advantage, Pandora swung herself up and sat on my back with her arms around my neck. Half-blinded by the coruscating rainbow of water, my body numb, the wind tearing at my soaking clothes, my flight started to falter. We were only about fifteen feet from the other building, and Pandora was screeching. '*PULL US UP! NOW! Or I'll break your neck!*'

She meant it. I pulled us up. It was amazing that my reflexes worked so well because this impossible storm was killing me inch-by-inch. I saw the two of us in the glass as we flew up the side of the building, the mad reflection of a snarling woman on the back of a flying boy, and when we reached the roof I fell gratefully to the floor, exhaustion filling me up like wet cement poured into a body bag. Everything that had happened today broke free of the mental cage I had created to contain it, and now my body wouldn't respond. My bones were weak with fatigue, my throat choked by the rain, my lungs full of water, my arm bleeding. I tried to crawl towards the door at the centre of the roof but a foot caught me in the ribs and I spun over. The impact knocked the wind out of me and I retched violently. I looked up to see Pandora standing over me, her hair tangled and sodden, water running down her face. 'Enjoy *that*?' She kicked me again. My ribs felt like they were about to shatter. I had never felt pain like this. 'How about *that*?'

Another kick. I rolled and my flesh screamed.

FLASH! We were somewhere else. I felt cold stone under my face. The Tube station. Black and white, but lines of green kept sizzling and the walls drifted in and out of colour, red to black, black to blue, blue to—

THUD!

Something did break this time. I felt it, and heard it, two ribs cracking, and I retched again, vomiting water laced with copper-tasting blood. The blood stuck around my lips and bubbled in my throat. My head was starting to cloud with pain. I wanted it to be over. My vision kept threatening to give out.

No . . .

Blue . . .

Must . . .

Red . . .

Get . . .

Green . . .

Tara . . .

Purple . . .

Back . . .

The rain was still falling, even inside this imaginary Tube station. Photographic physics. Was my pain even real? Maybe . . .

Pandora had stopped kicking me. She knelt down in front of me and lifted my head by my chin, like Kloe would, although not quite as tenderly. Blinking to maintain focus, I looked up into a face of pure malevolence, my neck straining. 'I was going to leave you to Leon,' she said. 'But I'm starting to enjoy this. I don't get to do much fighting, I usually send other people to do it. Although it *is* a shame, really. I genuinely thought you could be useful.'

I tried to answer but only blood came out. Pandora waited patiently. I think she wanted to hear what I had to say. *And I want to say it.*

Finally the words came. Every syllable was agony. '*You . . . can't . . .*'

'Can't what, Stanly? What can't we do?'

'*Can't . . . can't win . . .*'

'I think we can,' said Pandora. 'I think we *have*.'

My body was shutting down on me. I was going to fall asleep and Pandora would kill me and I wouldn't wake up.

Screw this, in a big way.

We were somewhere else again, back in the park. I could dimly see green grass and black and white trees, and still the rain fell.

I'm not going out like this. The hell . . .

An empty street with blue buildings . . .

With . . .

319

The Thames, its waves red, *orangeyellowpurplegreen*—
THIS.

'AAAAAAAAAAARGH!'

The scream I wrenched from my throat was inhuman, the feelings behind it were primal and the blood that came with it was mine. I dragged myself up, using my mind to yank my anguished body from the floor, puppet master barely able to drive the puppet. Body might have been on the way out, but my brain was intact, and my brain was my fists, my feet, my everything. Pain was just signals, white noise above the raging storm. We were back on top of the building and I had my power back.

Pandora took a few steps backwards. I staggered towards her, spitting blood and wheezing, my left side threatening to collapse with less than the recommended number of ribs to hold it up, but I could do it. I had strength. More than I knew. *Except I do know.* I flexed my mind, lifted Pandora up and stumbled towards the parapet, levitating her out and holding her, squirming, above a drop of thousands of feet. Imaginary feet, maybe, and an imaginary drop . . . but I had a hunch that it wouldn't matter. 'Now,' I slurred, trying not to either faint or drop her, 'you're going to tell me . . . where Tara is.'

'*Please let me down!* I'm sorry! I'm sorry, I'll—'

'*Where is she?*'

'I'll show you! I'll show you! I promise! Just . . . please don't kill me! *Please!*'

'Let's . . . go then.' I rose from the ground and began the long and agonising flight back towards the other building, still holding Pandora in mid-air like a ragdoll.

Back and forth, back and forth.

See-saw, Marjorie Dor, Johnny shall have a new master.

He shall have but a penny a day.

Because he can't work any faster.

I pretended I wasn't carrying myself. I wasn't the puppet master, he or she or it was elsewhere, connected to us by invisible strings, guiding us across the gulf. In the distance I saw a sheet of lightning erupt like a volcano beneath the surface of this false reality, shaking everything, casting its killing light over the city, and seconds later the thunder came, an epic drum roll from above the clouds, a heavy metal sky concert. The puppet master drew us back across, through the vertical ocean.

See-saw, Marjorie Dor, Johnny shall have a new master.

Twenty feet.

He shall have but a penny a day.

Ten feet.

Because he can't work any faster.

Another flash. For a second we were back in the park, then we were flying again, then we were in the Tube station, then we were by the sea, then there was sky, and the colours were too much . . . back in the sky . . . I was going to drop her and die . . . *no* . . .

We were back, through the broken window, in the office. I dropped Pandora unceremoniously on the ground but kept myself floating. The moment my feet touched the floor again I knew my legs would give way, my body would fall apart like loose timber and I would die in a puddle. Pandora picked herself up, eyeing me with real fear. *You'd better believe I'm scary.* 'OK,' I said. 'Where . . . is she?' The words still hurt, my oesophagus burning with sulphur.

'This way.' Pandora crossed the room and walked through a hole in the air, and I followed her, wobbly, through another photograph. We were in a room . . . a proper room . . . real physics . . . real colour . . . it was done.

And there she was.

The sight gave me strength. Tara was lying on her back in a cosily-lit room with her eyes closed, listening to Beyoncé on a posh-looking hi-fi system. Realising that somebody was there, the little girl opened her eyes and jumped to her feet. 'Stanly! You came!' She stopped, eyes widening at the sorry state I was in. 'What *happened*?'

'I happened,' said Pandora. She turned to face me, and she had a gun in her hand.

Oh shit.

'Nobody threatens me,' she said. '*Nobody.*'

Doubleplus sh—

She pulled the trigger. Tara squealed. I looked down at myself. There was a hole in the left of my chest, where my heart was. I was no longer flying. I was standing, swaying. Dull pain started to spread, blood trickled. I felt more of it coming up in my throat, a geyser of red. It came up and caught in my teeth, and I watched it dribble down my chin and hit the floor. *I'm staining Tara's nice white carpet.*

Now I was really going.

Big red stain . . . .

I was dying, very fast. Shortly everything about me would cease to be. I would just be a shape on the floor, a pile, dead flesh.

Tiny little person.

A hole in my heart.

So fragile.

So much blood . . . such a tiny hole.

Fire again.

What?

She's going.

What?

To.

My instinct told me what to do. My reflex powered it. My brain flexed for the last time, and there was a scream and a crash, and I looked up from the stain I was making to see Pandora lying in the corner. Her gun had fallen away. Her eyes were closed.

Like mine.

My eyes closed.

I'm dying.

Dying.

Dead.

This'll be the day that I—

CHAPTER THIRTY-TWO

NOTHING MUCH HAPPENED, maybe for a very long time, maybe for no time at all. There were no celestial trumpets, no glowing escalator. I didn't get a sepia-toned slideshow of Stanly's Greatest Hits. I just ceased to exist. Like sleeping.

And then there was the most subtle spark, the barest flicker of awareness. It was dark. I *knew* it was dark. Dark was what was happening. But also . . . I could see something flashing, almost subliminal, a single frame in the blackness, irregularly appearing and disappearing. It was . . . me. Smiling at myself. A knowing smile. An *I told you so* smile, even though I'd not told myself anything.

Nobody ever tells me nothin'.

Hahaha.

Then light.

White light.

Bright.

Too bright!

Too bright white light!

Hehehe.

Rhymes.

Eyes opening.

Opening?

Is this the escalator? Or is it an elevator?

Also, why is it playing 'Irreplaceable'?

I sat up. A room. White carpet, red stain. Teddies. Pandora in the corner. Speakers belting out 'you must not know 'bout me' in

Beyoncé's voice. No pain. I looked down at my chest. No holes. I looked at my arm. No teeth marks. I looked at my left side. All ribs accounted for.

Tara's mouth was open. 'You're . . . you're OK?'

'I . . .' I nodded slowly. 'Seems so.'

'How?'

My mouth opened and closed, at a loss, and then I looked at her, *really* looked at her, and something occurred to me.

No way.

It can't have been . . .

They did *say they needed her for a reason.*

Power?

'You,' I said. 'Was it . . . you?'

The little girl looked bemused. 'I . . . I don't know. I didn't think I had powers.'

'Maybe you don't even know you do.'

She shrugged. 'It doesn't matter for now,' I said. 'I'm just . . . glad.' I grabbed her and pulled her in for a hug, and she hugged me as well, and I felt her tears on my neck. 'I'm sorry,' I said. 'Sorry I let them take you.'

'It's OK.'

It's OK, she says. Kid gets kidnapped by a monster, then kidnapped again, all in the same night, and it's OK.

I couldn't tell you how long the hug lasted. Moments like that are impossible to measure anyway, even without the benefit of death and resurrection. All I knew is that when we broke apart I had made a decision.

Anyone ever lays a hand on her again, I will kill *them.*

I stood up and glanced at Pandora. Her eyes were flickering, and now I could hear a familiar pawing at the door. I opened it with my mind, revealing Daryl, one ear torn, blood around his muzzle. 'You found her,' he said.

'Yes,' I said. 'The others OK?'

'Some bruises going around, but they're all right.'

'Good. Take Tara to them and get everybody out of here.'

'But—'

'Do it,' I said. 'Tara? Go with Daryl and get out of this building, please. Be safe.'

Tara's eyes were wet and she looked concerned. 'Don't kill her.' *Goddamn mind reader.*

'I won't,' I said. 'Go on, sugar plum. Wait outside.'

Sugar plum?

I used to call my little cousin Jade that.

So long ago.

Tara nodded and left the room, closing the door very carefully behind her. I walked over to Pandora and watched her come to. When she saw me the colour drained from her face as though we were back inside the black and white photograph. 'I killed you!'

'Came back,' I said.

'How?'

'Are you seriously telling me that you were so desperate to get hold of that girl that you didn't bother to check what her power is?'

Pandora looked befuddled. 'I . . . *she* did it? She . . . my God . . . it can't be. It can't be! She's . . . powers shouldn't manifest until at least early puberty! And she's so . . . small.'

'She is.'

'What will you do with her?' said Pandora.

'I'm taking her back to her foster parents.'

'She doesn't belong with them.'

I narrowed my eyes. 'Do you know anything about her real parents? You seem to know everything else. What happened nine years ago?'

'Why don't you ask her foster parents?'

'I'm asking you.'

Pandora laughed. 'How have you made it this far with such an incredible lack of brain cells?'

'What are you talking about?'

Pandora shook her head. 'She's yours.'

I frowned. What had she just said? *What did Pandora say?*

What? Huh? 'What do you mean, "mine"?'

'I mean what I said,' said Pandora. 'Tara is your daughter.'

Red alert.

We have just lost cabin pressure.

What the fnunck?

'What are you talking about?' I said. 'That's impossible.'

'Nothing's impossible,' said Pandora. 'Everything's—'

'Spare me,' I said. I was having trouble keeping my voice steady. 'She's nine years old. How can I possibly be her father?' *Plus the fact that I haven't actually ever . . .*

'Ask Mr and Mrs Rogers,' said Pandora. 'They'll tell you.'

'They know?'

Pandora nodded. 'They know.'

I was having understandable trouble processing this new information. I could barely stop myself from screaming. My head felt like it was going to explode, yet again. I was going to shower Pandora with viscera and I doubted that Tara could save me a second time.

Tara.

My daughter.

I have a daughter?

'What if I don't believe you?' I said.

'Then don't,' said Pandora. 'But as I said, reserve judgement until you've spoken to the *foster* parents.'

Fine. Fine. Mind completely blown, world turned upside-down. Just . . . deal with this. As it comes.

First, we need to have words.

'Are you going to come after us again?' I said.

She didn't say anything. I looked around, found her gun, levitated it into my hand and pointed it at her head. She flinched. '*Are you?*' I said.

Pandora gulped. 'I . . . I don't know. We wanted to recruit you, but . . . after all this . . .'

'OK. I was sort of hoping you'd say something like that.' I started to walk slowly back and forth. *Soliloquy time.* 'It's nice that I finally know what to do,' I said. 'Who to fight. If there's a fight to be had, that is. It's nice to know that a monster with more monsters inside its head isn't the weirdest thing in this city. I mean, what was that whole acid trip photograph thing about?'

'You know nothing of this world,' said Pandora. 'Or any other.'

'Whatevz,' I said. 'Anyway. It's nice to finally know what's what. And it's nice to know that my little girl is going to grow up to be a big powerful girl. And it's also nice to know that coming back from the dead yields positive results.'

Pandora frowned. 'What?'

I crouched down beside her. 'I can feel it. The power I had before, the power I could always feel but not quite access. It's all there now. That little trip beyond the beyondness of things really put it into perspective.'

'You—'

'Shh,' I said. 'Like I said, if there's a fight to be had, I know who to fight. But it's not something I want. You say you have the world's best interests at heart and until I see something that contradicts that I'm willing to let bygones be bygones. You leave us alone, let us go about our business, stay away from Tara, and there won't be a problem.'

This was helping. Making threats and being overly dramatic was a good distraction from the revelation that was still screeching around my head, blending my brains and threatening to disintegrate my skull. 'That's the deal,' I said. 'Take it or leave it.'

Pandora nodded slowly. 'I suppose we'll take it. For now.'

'That'll do,' I said, getting back to my feet. I headed for the door, put my hand on the handle and turned my head slightly. 'Pandora,' I said. *Scary voice. Come on, scariest voice you can manage.*

'What?'

'When I say stay away from Tara,' I said, 'I can't emphasise enough how much I mean *stay the goddamn hell away from Tara.* If anything happens to her, *anything*, then I'm going to be really, really, *really* angry. And I'll find you. And I'll find Lucius. And anybody else. *Everybody* else. OK?'

327

As I walked I thought about it. Leaving Pandora alive felt like a bad decision, one I could well end up regretting . . . but I couldn't kill her. I wasn't there yet. I hadn't reached the point where I could knowingly cut off her oxygen supply or set her on fire or put a bullet in her head. I had my power but I couldn't use it for that.

Yet.

The rain had stopped but it was still gloomy, and the pavements shone. They had brought the car around to the front of the gallery, and Connor was sitting on the bonnet smoking a cigarette, his face ablaze with cuts. Sharon had her arm around him. She looked pretty good considering what had gone on. Eddie, who had a ripped jacket and plenty of wounds of his own, was leaning against the car with his own arm around Tara. There was no sign of Daryl.

They all saw me, and Sharon jumped off the car. 'Stanly!' She ran over and hugged me tightly. 'We thought we'd lost you.'

'Likewise,' I said. When we broke apart Eddie was there, and then Connor. 'Leon's history, I presume?' I said.

Eddie nodded towards one of the many smashed windows, then towards the river. 'You'll believe a man can't fly.'

It was fairly lame but we all laughed. It felt good to be able to laugh. 'What about Pandora?' asked Sharon. 'Did you . . .'

'She's still in one piece,' I said, 'but I think I put the fear of us in her.'

'Did she tell you anything?'

'Yes. Tara's my daughter and we're all heading for a massive apocalyptic war with a mysterious evil organisation.' I didn't really say that. I just shrugged. 'Not really.'

'She tried to kill him,' said Tara.

'Not hard enough, by the looks of things,' said Connor, eyeing my bruiseless form.

'Well,' I said. 'She's better at admin and stuff.' I looked around. 'Daryl?'

'He brought Tara then went,' said Eddie. 'Just said he'd be around.'

I nodded, my stomach knotting. *Don't cry, kid. It'll really spoil the whole nonchalantly heroic leader thing you've got going on right now.* 'Good.'

'What are we going to do now, then?' said Sharon. 'It's not over, is it?'

'Nope,' I said. 'But at least now we know who the bad guys are.'

'Do we?' said Connor.

Did we? I couldn't tell. Does anyone really know? 'We'll be all right,' I said. I hoped that I sounded convincing.

'Come on,' said Eddie. 'Let's get the fu . . . dge out of here.'

'Good plan,' I said, taking Tara – my daughter's hand. 'How are you feeling, kiddo?'

'I'm fine,' said Tara. *'Cos of course she's fine. 'Cos she's the toughest kid ever invented.* 'But I'd like to go home soon.'

'Don't worry,' I said. 'After a bit of sleep and some food that's our very next stop. I'd like a chat with them anyway.'

Understatement of the . . . well, there isn't a big enough time span.

You didn't tell Tara?

How could I?

I suppose . . .

You didn't tell the others, either.

No.

Are you going to?

We'll see.

'Hey,' said Connor, as we pulled off. 'Isn't that dude still in the boot?'

'Bollocks,' said Eddie. 'Remind me to let him out at the first Tube station.'

CHAPTER THIRTY-THREE

OLIVER AND JACQUELINE Rogers lived on an estate, not far from the alley where I'd met Tara. It was a good-looking place with rows of houses that approached the same tidy, respectable theme in different (but still tidy and respectable) ways, and the Rogers lived at Number 43, a pretty white house with an immaculate front lawn, perfect beds of soft soil and straight, multicoloured flowers. It was just after two o'clock and the storms had passed. The city was still wet, but the sky was a brilliant blue and the sun was blazing with real enthusiasm, its ego stroked by hordes of plump, admiring clouds.

We'd gone back to Sharon and Connors' place after the assorted chaos at the gallery and discussed what had happened over a substantial breakfast. Then we'd all had a nap, and then we'd all had indigestion, and then I'd volunteered to take Tara home. I was trying not to think about saying goodbye to her.

I was also trying not to think about Kloe. Had she already left? Would she call? I hoped she would. I needed her.

Luckily for me, I had a whole other set of thoughts jostling for space in my mind. Thoughts like WHAT THE HELL and NO, SERIOUSLY, *WHAT THE HELL*. Thoughts like *what am I going to say*, and *what are they going to tell me*, and *probably shouldn't be sick*, and *what if Pandora was lying*, and *what if I get arrested for kidnapping a minor*, and *oh God I'm going to be sick*, and—

'Are you all right?' asked Tara. She was still in her red pyjamas,

but she also wore a white coat of Sharon's that was much too big
for her.

'Me?' I blustered. 'Fine. Why wouldn't I be?'

'You look like you're going to be sick.'

'Too much fry-up.' *And the revelation that you're my daughter.* I grinned too widely and knocked on the door too loudly.
We immediately heard somebody running, and a short, stocky
woman in her late fifties opened the door with such urgency that
it banged against the inside wall. She had short ginger hair and
wore a flowery skirt and a black cardigan over a white blouse, and
when she saw Tara she squealed. 'Oh, Tara! Oh thank *goodness*!'
She scooped the girl into her arms and hugged her like a mother
would, planting kisses all over her. 'Oliver!' she cried. 'She's come
back! She's here!'

Mr Rogers appeared behind her. He was slightly older than his
wife and taller, bald and distinguished-looking, and wore a blue
shirt and smart black trousers. His face shone with relief and he
took his turn to envelop Tara in a bear hug. It was only after the
heartfelt greetings were over that either of them seemed to notice
me. 'Oh,' said Jacqueline, clutching her chest, eyes widening
behind her glasses. 'It's—'

'This is Stanly,' said Tara. 'He saved me from Smiley Joe! He
was—'

'Tara,' said Oliver Rogers. 'You're all dirty. How about I take
you upstairs and run you a bath and then Jacqueline and I can
have a talk with this young man?'

They know me.

They remember me.

How?

Tara nodded. 'OK!' She went upstairs with her foster father.
'And we should phone the Family Liaison Officer,' Oliver called
down the stairs. 'Just to let him know that she's all right.' Jacqueline nodded and invited me into the house. It had brown carpets
and an abundance of nick-nacks – photographs in tasteless frames,
little statues and boxes and flowers in vases and crystal ashtrays

that I'm sure were never used. I liked it. It felt like a home. Jacqueline showed me into the living room, which was very green, and I sat in a flowered armchair and looked around awkwardly. The place was like London – nothing matched, yet everything kind of did.

'Would you like a drink?' asked Jacqueline. She looked as awkward as I felt, which was oddly comforting.

I shook my head. 'No, thank you.' She nodded and hovered, waiting for her husband, who thankfully appeared within a minute. They sat down on the sofa opposite me and Oliver took his wife's hand in his. 'We know who you are,' he said.

How? HOW? 'I was told that might happen,' I said. 'But . . . we've never met.'

'We have,' said Oliver. His voice was calm but his eyes were not. 'Nine years ago you turned up on our doorstep with a beautiful young woman with dark hair. You were carrying a little blonde baby girl in a basket, fast asleep. You asked us to take her in. Told us that she was in danger as long as she was with you, that you knew she would be safe here. You . . . we didn't understand at first, you knew so much about us. You see . . .'

'We can't have children of our own,' said Jacqueline.

'So we agreed to take her in,' said Oliver.

I don't understand. 'Did I name her?' I asked. My voice cracked like plaster.

'You told us her name was Tara,' said Oliver. 'Tara Sharon Davies-Bird.'

Davies. Kloe's surname.

She's Kloe's and mine.

I can't . . . I don't. . . . what is *this* . . . Tears were streaming silently from my eyes, I was so tired, so floored by what I was being told. I forced myself to speak and my voice caught in my throat, emerging low and guttural. 'That wasn't me,' I said.

'It was,' said Oliver. He looked sad, but strong. I must have looked like such a child. 'Maybe not *you*, but it was . . . you. You were older. Maybe twenty-five, twenty-six.'

'I don't understand,' I said. 'This doesn't make any sense to me, I can't . . . I brought her back in time, somehow?'

'I assume that's what must have happened,' said Oliver. He was shaking his head, trying to process it. 'It's the only thing that . . . that makes sense, insofar as any of this makes sense . . .'

'I didn't tell you at the time? Kloe and I . . . we didn't explain?'

'There was nothing about time travel, if that's what you mean,' said Oliver. 'Although you did mention something about a . . . an organisation, or a company perhaps?'

'The Angel Group?'

'Yes,' said Oliver. 'That's it. You said that if they were ever to come looking for her then we had to take her away. Thankfully they never have.'

'It doesn't make sense,' I said. 'They operate in this city, they knew about Tara . . . why would we try to keep her from them by hiding her so close?'

'People often miss what's right under their noses,' said Oliver.

I nodded. 'You're right. I . . .' Without warning, I started to sob. I broke down in front of these people who had first met me nine years ago as an adult, who had sheltered a daughter that I'd only just met. My mind hurt. I couldn't comprehend it, how it worked, how everything fitted together, Kloe, Tara, the Angel Group. It would have been too much even if I hadn't just had the night I'd just had. Jacqueline stood up, came over and put her arm around me and whispered soothingly in my ear.

Time.

We travelled in time.

We brought our child . . .

'Are you here to take her back?' said Oliver.

'No,' I said, trying to regain my composure, tears running into my mouth. 'I was only told this morning that she was my daughter. I didn't think it was possible, I wanted to know if it was true . . . it didn't seem . . . and now you two . . .'

'I always wondered what it would be like when you returned,' said Oliver. 'I must admit, I never expected anything like this.'

'Because it's not possible,' I said. *Like flying? Like talking dogs, and monsters, and photographs that take you to another world?*

'Impossible things are funny,' said Jacqueline. 'Sometimes they happen.' *Tara obviously learned mind-reading from her foster mum.*

I made a superhuman effort to rein in the confusion, stem the flow of tears. To be strong. 'The Angel Group aren't going to come looking for her,' I said.

'Who *are* these people?' said Jacqueline. 'The government?'

'No,' I said. 'At least . . . I don't think they are.'

'Are they evil?'

'I don't think so,' I said. 'Maybe they're worse. They think they're doing good.'

'The worst atrocities are always committed under the guise of righteousness,' said Oliver.

I nodded. *Depressing, but probably true.* I noticed a copy of yesterday's paper on the coffee table, open on the crossword page with a pen next to it, and I wrote down Sharon and Connor's phone number. 'Call this number if anything happens,' I said. '*Anything.*'

'So you're planning to stay in London?' asked Jacqueline. She had been so nice to me, but there was that motherly protectiveness too, slightly defensive. I wondered what she thought, whether she was worried I would swoop in and take Tara away.

Not unless I have to.

'I want to know *why* I ran off before,' I said. 'The only way I'm going to find out is if I stay where the action is.' I took a deep breath. 'This is insane.'

Oliver stood up and held out his hand. 'Welcome to the world.' We shook. 'It's good to see you again,' he said. 'The first time we met I told Jacqueline I had a feeling about you. I could just tell that you were a genuinely good person, someone who wants to do right. I stand by that.'

I smiled. 'Thank you. That . . . that means a lot.'

Jacqueline hugged me. It was awkward but sort of nice. 'Are you going to say goodbye to her?'

I could barely comprehend the idea. Saying goodbye to my daughter when she didn't know I was her father? When we'd only just met? It wasn't possible. I shook my head. 'No,' I said. 'Tell her . . . tell her that I'll be in touch. Is that all right? If I come by every now and then? Maybe take her out?'

Oliver nodded. 'Yes. That's fine. I know you'd never let her get hurt.'

'I'd die first,' I said, offering what I hoped was a nonchalant smile. 'It's not as final as it sounds.'

Neither of them understood but they smiled, thinking I was joking. Maybe I *was* joking. *Haha, it's funny 'cos it's true!*

God, I need to go back to bed forever.

Jacqueline opened the door and I stepped outside. The air smelled fresh and new but there was a tangible bittersweet tinge to it, and I turned and shook hands with Oliver again. 'I can't thank you enough,' I said. 'There's nothing I can say. You've . . . we couldn't have picked a better home for her.'

They both smiled, happy but sad, just as I felt. 'Thank you for giving her to us,' said Jacqueline. 'I can't imagine how hard it must have been.'

I shrugged. 'I guess I'll find out. See you soon.'

And I turned and walked away.

CHAPTER THIRTY-FOUR

Connor was waiting for me when I got back to their house. 'Kloe called about five minutes ago,' he said. 'She's leaving in an hour.'

'Thanks.' I'd barely been aware of the journey home, I was so exhausted, so overwhelmed with new information, new thoughts, new feelings.

'By the way,' said Connor, holding out a folder. 'I wanted to show you this.'

'What is it?'

'Just look inside.'

It was very thick. I opened it and was faced with a crude but fairly accurate drawing of Smiley Joe. 'What is this?' I said.

'Our research,' said Connor. He seemed to want me to look at it so I obliged, even though I didn't see much of a point. It was certainly pretty comprehensive. Newspaper cuttings, magazine articles, a few sketchy witness statements, forensic reports that read like riddles, artists' impressions, photographs that were blurry and obviously faked, even a comic strip from *Private Eye* suggesting that Smiley Joe was part of a Conservative plot to eat as many poor people as possible.

But the thing that caught my eye was a black and white photograph of a boy and a girl, younger and older respectively, standing side-by-side with her arm around his. The girl was very pretty, her brother handsome in a young way. Their names were Carl and Louise Harris. 'The only survivors,' I said.

Connor nodded. 'Until now.'

I looked at him questioningly. 'There's an address on the back,' he said. 'You do what you think is right.' He smiled enigmatically and walked away, leaving me both confused and enlightened.

I put the folder down, picked up the phone and dialled.

'Hello?'

'Hi . . . is that Mrs Markovsky?' Kloe had told me that her aunt was married to a Russian dude.

'Yes. Is that Stanly?'

'Um . . . yeah.'

'Personally, I don't think Kloe should see you ever again.'

'I understand that. I didn't mean to—'

'Don't tell me. That's not what I want to say. What I mean is . . . it's not my decision. And Kloe says she loves you, so I suppose you can't be all bad.'

I smiled. 'Thanks.'

'But if you *ever* put her in danger like that again . . .'

'I won't. I promise.'

There was a shuffle and a click, then Kloe's voice, breathless. 'Stanly?'

'Yeah, I'm here.'

'Oh my God! You're all right! I thought you were dead or something! Even though Connor said you were fine . . . I didn't know . . . Oh my God, what *happened*?'

'I got the guy,' I said. 'Didn't kill him, don't worry. And then I . . . I had a bit of an adventure. There was a girl in trouble. I helped her out.'

'A girl?'

'Don't worry, she's nine.' I realised that that sounded dangerously weird. 'It'll be better if I tell you the story face to face.'

'Okaaay. Well . . . did Connor tell you I'm leaving in an hour?'

'He did.'

'Will you come and see me off? I'm getting a train from Paddington.'

Shit. That's quite far. 'I'll come,' I said. 'Of course. I'll see you there.'

How am I going to get there in time?

Can't fly in broad daylight . . .

. . . can I?

No.

Cab.

Goodbyes. Kisses and hugs and tears. A sky too blue to be perfect. Hot bodies against one another. New burning, aching pains.

'I don't want you to come with me,' whispered Kloe, her head buried in my shoulder. 'Even though I do.'

'I know.'

'You have things to do.'

'I do.' *If only you knew.*

'I'll come back. When the exams are over I'll be back. My aunt said I can spend the whole holiday here. My parents might take some convincing, but . . .'

'That's . . .' I couldn't think of a word. Maybe because there wasn't one.

'I'll call you every night,' she said. 'I love you.'

'I love you.' I kissed her gently. Our lips moved slowly, tenderly, and there was a passion that you couldn't bottle, a passion that would one day create a beautiful little girl. *I should tell her.*

No you shouldn't.

The kiss stopped, a guard whistled. Kloe's eyes bled salty grief and I kissed her forehead. I had helped her with her bags. Now all the train needed was her, this girl, my girl. She turned and made for the open door, then ran back and leapt into my arms and I held her off the ground and we kissed one another's hot lips again, as if trying to draw out souls, trying to take the essence of one another so we could hold it like a photograph during long nights alone. The guard whistled again. *Give us a minute, yeah?*

Our last kiss broke and I set her down. She was wearing one of the tops that we had bought yesterday. *Yesterday? Was that it?* I felt as though I'd lived an entire life since then, a whole new existence. Become a new person. Kloe's lips moved and no sound came but they spelled out 'I love you' and I copied her, and she got on the train and the doors closed and she ran to the window and pressed her hands and nose against it, steaming it up with her tears and wiping it with her sleeves, and the train groaned and started to pull away and I chased it along the platform, waving and smiling.

She'll come back.

I know.

Time to go home and mope, yes? Then sleep?

Almost.

The street was everything that the Rogers' estate wasn't – grimy, dull and faded, stinking of homeless dogs, unfulfilled potential and sadness hidden behind ugly curtains. I walked up a path through a mouldy garden towards a small house coated in grubby whitewash, took a deep breath and knocked. There was a long silence, for a change, and the door opened a crack, revealing a wrinkled, suspicious eye. 'Yes?'

'Do Carl and Louise live here?'

'Who are you?'

'I'm . . . I'm a friend.'

'You look like a student. Are you a journalist? If you're even thinking about trying to interview them I'll call the police!'

'I just wanted to tell them something,' I said. 'I think it might . . . it might help.'

Silence. The door opened a bit more and an old lady looked me up and down. She was like a squat baby who had been left in the bath too long, and she smelled faintly of marzipan. 'What do you mean, help?'

'I have some news,' I said. 'About . . . you know.'

Her eyes widened and for a moment I thought she wasn't going to let me in, but I saw something in her relent and she suddenly seemed much smaller. 'They're in the living room,' she said. 'Please don't be long.'

The hallway was dark and I could smell baking and cold tea. The old lady opened a door to her right and poked her head round. 'Carl? Louise? There's someone here who wants to speak to you.'

A woman's voice, so soft I couldn't hear the words. 'Don't worry,' said the lady. 'It's just a boy.'

Just a boy. How long since that was true?

'I'll be right out here,' said the lady. 'Don't you worry, loves.' She turned back to me. 'In you go. A few minutes, that's all.'

I entered a room with yellow walls, a brown and orange carpet and mustard furniture. An old TV set stood in the corner, silently playing some daytime soap opera or other, with the subtitles on. Louise and Carl were sitting side-by-side on a sofa. They were recognisable, but it was as though a short-sighted artist had made statues of them out of ash based on a very rough drawing. Louise's youthful beauty had faded, her face was lined, her hair was lank and had no colour to it, and she was very thin. Carl was even worse. At least Louise's eyes had some semblance of life behind them; his were dead in their sockets, focused on nothing. His face was drawn and haunted and he hunched as though his skeletal body had never been used. He looked so old, much older than his older sister.

'Who are you?' said Louise. Her voice was a whisper, a drowning lily pad in a frozen pond.

'My name is Stanly,' I said. 'I came to tell you . . . I thought you should know . . .' I took a deep breath. Louise looked almost interested. Carl's eyes hadn't moved. 'I thought you should know that he's dead,' I said. 'Smiley Joe is dead.'

It took a long time to sink in. Finally Louise's eyes glassed over and she began to weep silently, and at the same time she smiled, probably for the first time in years, and some of her old beauty returned to her face, colour blossoming triumphantly on her cheeks. Carl looked up at me and the haunted expression broke slightly, revealing the promise of something better behind it, something optimistic. He didn't smile but he opened his mouth, and Sharon's voice echoed in my head. *Carl didn't speak and he hasn't since.*

340

Excitement flared in my stomach as he moistened his lips and then, for the first time in so many years, words emerged.

'Thank you,' he said.

CHAPTER THIRTY-FIVE

THE NEXT MORNING. Just after four. Wide shot of the Heron
Tower. Zoom, focus. Me, sitting on the parapet, coat wrapped
around me, legs dangling over vast, full emptiness. It was quiet, or
as quiet as London could be, and the barest sliver of gold and pink
was beginning to glow on the horizon.

Daryl rested his chin on the ledge next to me. 'So you're here to
stay?'

I nodded.

'They'll still be around. The Angel Group. They'll stay on you.'

'You'll make sure of that, I suppose.' It was unkind, and I felt
bad for saying it, but I wanted him to know that things were not
OK between us. Almost as much as I wanted to say that I forgave
him.

'No. I know where my loyalties lie.' He looked up at me. 'Do
you?'

I didn't say anything. There were plenty of things I could have
said, plenty that I *wanted* to say, but it felt more natural to let yet
another of Stanly's legendary awkward silences spool out. Daryl
seemed to take the hint and nodded. 'So, where do we stand?'

'Me and you?' I said. *Together. That's where we should be
standing.* 'For now, unless you get some new information that I
might need, we stand a long way apart.'

'Fair enough.' More silence. I felt Daryl building up to say
something else and cut him off.

'You'll be all right on your own?' I asked. *Just say it's fine. Say*

it's all OK, and that we can talk it through and cry and share our
feelings and it'll all be fixed. Say he's your best friend, and that all
is forgiven. Tell him to come back to Connor and Sharon's.

'I'm sure I can find some chatty stoner to give me a ball and biscuit to call my own,' said the dog. 'I'll be all right. I'm more concerned about you, to be honest.'

'I can handle whatever they throw at me.'

'And if they go near Tara?' I still hadn't told the others that she was my daughter. I hadn't told anyone. To all intents and purposes she was just my sort-of-adopted little sister.

'Then I'll fight them,' I said. 'And I'll win.' It sounded almost as badass out loud as it sounded in my head, while also sounding twice as ridiculous, somehow. It was Daryl, though, so it didn't matter. The sun started to rise, painting the slumbering sky with flashing strokes of brilliant red, and I stood up, balancing on the parapet. The height was dizzying, but I wasn't worried. I was sure I'd been scared of heights at one point.

Not any more.

Plenty of new stuff to be scared of now.

Daryl laughed. 'What are you sniggering at?' I said.

'You're actually going to jump off the building and fly away, aren't you?'

Now I couldn't help smiling. 'I'm a superhero now,' I said, pulling my hood up. 'That's what we do.'

And I jumped off the building, fell into flight and began the first dawn patrol of the city.

My city.

THE END

ACKNOWLEDGEMENTS

I CLAIM SOLE RESPONSIBILITY for this book and its publication. Any and all successes can be attributed to me and me only. I had no help from anyone. This book is a triumph of individualism.

Not really.

First, my indomitable (and possibly superpowered) agent, Ben Illis, without whom I would only be writing these acknowledgements in my mind while pouring cheap whisky over myself in some gutter somewhere. His endless support and encouragement have kept me going through rejections, sulks and crises of confidence, and his astute feedback and constructive criticism have been invaluable in moulding this book from a piece of coal with potential to the much more awesome piece of coal you now hold in your hands.

To Jen and Chris at Salt, I write THANK YOU on the sky in huge red letters for, y'know, agreeing to publish the thing, and for being so supportive throughout a pretty daunting process. The feeling of finding a publisher who gets what you're trying to do – and who isn't going to say 'yeah we like it but could Stanly be a twelve-year-old football player to appeal to that demographic, and could he have an older sister who's a vampire, and maybe Daryl could be a labrador, or a cat, and also could he not talk' – is hard to describe.

To Peter Stead, Cerys Matthews and everyone else involved with the Dylan Thomas Prize and the Sony Reader Award – without that amazing boost to the book's profile (and my own confidence) these last few years would have unfolded very differently.

To the friends who read the very first scrappy draft and said that they liked it – Martin and Kate *et al*, I'm looking at y'all – and to my friends in general for being massively supportive and encouraging while simultaneously keeping me grounded with endless piss-taking.

To Mrs Smith and Mr Evans, for nurturing and educating and encouraging. The world needs more teachers like you.

To my family, for all the love and support. And for not telling the authorities about my telekinesis.

To my parents, for everything. I could write a whole other book on this subject.

To Catherine, because without you none of this would be anywhere near as much fun. Also see above re: pouring cheap whisky over myself in some gutter somewhere.

And finally to anyone who does me the honour of reading this book. 'Cos that's what books are for.